I0675478

Follow
The Southern
Cross

J JAY ROSS

AUTHOR'S EDITION

J Jay Ross

For
Shannon, the little blond-haired girl who spent her summers
across the street, a lifetime of memories...

"...little threads that hold life's patches of meaning together."

Mark Twain

J Jay Ross

J Jay Ross

Follow the Southern Cross

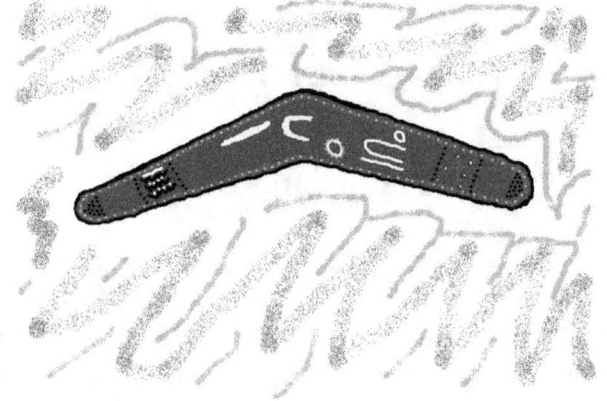

J Jay Ross

FIRST CHAPTER

THE FLIGHT

The light came on automatically when the door shut and the switch was pulled to the right; the flickering fluorescent bulbs startled Mike as he fumbled with his kit he took a moment to settle his heart rate back down before continuing. He looked in the mirror directly in front of him; once again he was alarmed at the image he was looking at. Older-the stubble was streaking grey on both sides of his cheeks; it almost made him look distinguishable, almost. His hair was receding, he could see that, and knew that it would climb back even more from where it was waiting right now. Maybe in another ten or so years…

Mike was a fairly good looking man, obviously a few years on his face from stress and the tell-tale crow's feet after working out in the sun often could be seen at the corner of the outside of each eye. His hair was brown, but also greying in places. His eyes were blue, but more of a darker variety than the sky colored ones that movie studios were so fond of. His angry or frustrated stare could be deadly, knife sharp, if he wanted it to. But right now he was concentrating on his hair…

He wondered if he should shave it off, his hair had begun growing backwards maybe less than a quarter of an inch, but the start of his hairline was clearly visible to him and he was troubled by the pace backwards it was taking, he was after all only thirty-eight years old. Mike hated the fact he was going bald at this age, but also thankful he wasn't like his father, who was nearly bald at twenty-one.

He had time, plenty of it; it would be more than three hours still to Hawaii. *As long no one had any emergencies with their bowels or something…* He smiled at the sad image in the small mirror. Mike took the razor from his shaving kit and the foamy shaving cream; he hated the smell, kind of minty-menthol-it reminded him of his grandfather at the rest home before he passed, but it left his head feeling cool after the blades scraped across his skin.

"Face first…" He told the man in the mirror, and then he proceeded to shave his stubble. After coming down with the razor from where he wanted his side burns to end and down to the bottom of the cheek he stopped and turned his head sideways to get a profile view.

"Hmmm." He repeated the action for the other side of his face. "Yeah…"

He drew the sharp double bladed disposable razor along his chin line from ear to ear and brought it up each side along the sides of each moustache end and formed the patch around his mouth for a goatee. He stood back and surveyed his work from as far as the chemical/suction toilet allowed. Smiling, he dipped the razor in the tiny sink and swished it around while admiring his handy-work.

"Yes, that's got it." There was a slight rumbling sound and the room dipped. "Damn turbulence."

He had dropped the razor.

Mike retrieved the old Gillette Safety from the sink and shook the excess water off, turning his head to examine the starting point for shaving it. He decided to let his hair grow out on top; maybe it would make him look more distinguished, with the goatee and all. He liked the old thing, it was antique looking and the blades were harder and harder to find-the double edged kind-but he was used to it, taking the style of shaving up from his father so many years ago.

There was a knock at the door, startling him. "*Is everything all right then?*"

"Fine, I'm okay just shaving and freshening up a little."

"*Very well, you should come out for a bit, the pilot says the aircraft may be a tad unstable.*"

"All right, I'm almost done."

"*Excellent, thanks.*" Mike heard footfalls moving away from the door.

No worries… Mike whispered to himself as he finished up his work and cleaned the razor off. He patted a little shaving lotion to his face to ease the sting and put all of the items back into his kit. He looked one more time in the mirror to make sure everything was straight, placed the shaving kit under his arm and slid the door latch to UNOCCUPIED.

The stale air hit him as he walked the aisle to his seat; he had three seats actually, since the flight was under-booked. People in the rear of the aircraft were allowed to smoke since the flight was five and a half hours long to Honolulu and he grimaced as he walked by them.

I need a smoke… He said to himself, fighting the urge since he quit the day he got out, and had daily urges that would change his mood, frequently.

Mike navigated the narrow passage on the right side of the Boeing 747 Jumbo Jet towards the third row back just aft of the First Class section, where his *seats* were. He liked the fact he didn't have to share the other two spaces on the aircraft with anyone alongside. Someone always wanted to talk about something uninteresting or about their kids or their families or their recent divorce or something even less annoying, like the weather.

Moving down the aisle with a touch of grace added to his *air-legs* (the flyers equivalent of sea-legs) he counted heads, it was force of habit-the job-and he always liked to know the odds against him. Not that were any terrorist activities, it was nineteen ninety-two after all and the skies had somewhat been very safe over the last few years. Mostly.

Once in a while a whack-job from some crappy bass-ackward country wanted to hijack a jet to Cuba, and Mike was sure that the dumbass was unhappy when he learned the sad way of life the Cubans lived under communism. He cracked a smile when he pictured the idiot hijacker later jumping on an ironing board or something trying to float to Florida, to get a taste of freedom and some shark would come along and eat him.

Karma, it was good thing, and Michael believed in it more than ever now. His life had changed because of things that made only sense to him, and the way he was changing his style of living.

"*Beer mate?*"

"Huh? Oh no thank you, I'll just have a Coke if you would, please." Mike said to the flight attendant, a male and a handsome one at that.

"Coke then."

The attendant whirled and walked up the aisle to the beverage cart and retrieved a can of the cola, a cup of ice. The attendant returned with the familiar red can and stopped at Mike's side. Handing him the cup full of ice, the attendant opened the Coke and set it on the tray in front of Mike. The man was about twenty eight; he wore the standard for Sydney Airlines, a white suit shirt with gold epaulets and white pressed shorts-the things that always reminded Mike of Captain Stubing from *The Love Boat*- Nah, more like Gofer…

His fair hair was combed neatly with straight edged part down the right side (facing him) with a curl just above his blue eyes and thick blond eyebrows. He walked with a jubilant step; like he was enjoying his job, hell he might as well, he gets to fly everywhere and see exciting things.

"Enjoy mate…" Then the little man spun on his heels and walked to the next occupied seat.

Good-day then… Mike smiled as he watched the attendant perform the same maneuver for the rest of the aisle.

Service-another reason he was happy to be flying Sydney Airlines, other than its impeccable record of flight safety, and no hijackings, it was the best service for overseas flight anywhere. So far Mike was impressed, and he was only three hours into his flight from Los Angeles.

Years from now, Mike would hear the voice of Rod Serling in his head: *"If the man called Michael Greene had any idea of the weeks ahead of him he might have stayed home, he was nervous enough about traveling overseas but the unseen that lie ahead would change his world, forever. When a person turns right at a corner or jumps from a dock into water, he knows the future probably won't change much by doing these simple things. Just a holiday trip would change the course of Mike's life from the day he boarded the flight, till the day he would pass away. A right turn could run you smack into a bus, jumping off a pier you could land on a rusty piece of metal under the water and you could end up with a fatal infection.*

Any inclination would have made life easier for him, he could have stayed home and lived life out the way it was heading, or the way he saw fit. But Mike had already set the changes in motion, he had already turned right at that proverbial corner-and fate was waiting for him-a destiny full of sadness-maybe joy, if he tried not to change his direction. Mike had turned right; in front of a bus."

Tired a little, he sipped his Coke and tried to figure out the small headphones. The in-flight movie had technical troubles, so the attendant put on a series of *Mr. Bean*, a British comedy show featuring Rowan Atkinson. The show was mostly slapstick and the main character never spoke, he just made grunts and noises. It was harmless fun and better than the in-flight movie anyway, a burned out love story that featured more F words than a 70s porno. Mike became attached to the shows, it was hilarious at moments, and he had not really laughed very hard in the last year and a half. Mike started to doze, with his Coke can in his hand.

"Ladies and gentlemen, g'day from the flight deck, this is your Captain and we are on approach to Honolulu International, about sixty miles out. It is eleven-twenty in Hawaii now and the temperature is thirty-one Celsius, or eighty-eight degrees for you Americans. If you are flying on to Sydney, please remain in the security area of the terminal, so you won't be checked again and it will make things smoother for you when you reach Kingsford-Smith International Airport. Thanks and g'day. For those of you departing here in Honolulu; g'day and thanks for flying Sydney Airlines. Attendants, prepare for landing, thanks."

The beginning of the announcement woke Mike up, he realized he had not replaced his cola back on the tray, but someone had done it for him. He smiled and shook his head, *didn't even wake me to do it either.*

"Mr. Greene?" The attendant was back.

"Yes?"

"You may remain on the aircraft if you like mate. They won't be but a few minutes for petrol and an inspection of the plane. The flights staff will be changing now and thanks for flying Sydney Air..."

"Thank you... that's very nice of you."

"G'day then, I hope you enjoy the rest of your flight." The attendant offered a hand, Mike shook it and the man whirled off towards the front of the Boeing.

Jeez, I wonder what first class is like.

As Mike watched the debarkation of passengers and cleaning around the cabin by ground workers, he wondered what he was in for. He knew the hospitality was legend in Australia, the food was better than in England-which he had never been-and the sights to see were the most recommended of any country, other than Africa. As a youngster he had remembered

13

seeing the Sydney Opera House on TV and of course the last few years the U.S. had been treated to *Crocodile Dundee*, a big theatrical hit and it made him want to visit, to see the last great frontier. The advice to travel came twofold; one from his boss and his best friend, the last was prescribed-sort of-by his group counselor.

"Get out Mike. Get away from here and where you live, just go. Pick a spot on the map and go. If it was me, and I wish it were, I'd go to the other side of the world..."

And that made it official, Australia it was. After he nearly closed out his saving account of three thousand dollars and some change, knowing that his son would never see the money anyway; he walked into a small travel agency in Reno, Nevada some miles outside his home. He ordered a 'Flights of Fancy' vacation and packed to go away for a month in Australia.

First, two weeks in Sydney at the Bay Point Hotel-Rushcutters Bay. Then he would be whisked off north east to the *Outback*; aka: Alice Springs, to the place he had heard so much about in the movies. Then it was south to Victoria, Mike especially wanted to see the places where one of his favorite movies was filmed; *The Man from Snowy River*, a cowboy love-story tale that he took his son to see; Mike loved the scenery, the actors were pretty good, and Mikie-his son-adored cowboy movies.

Mike hadn't realized that spending three hours at LAX would be such a hassle, he had nothing to buy for anyone really, he wasn't much of a reader, and he recently quit drinking-so the bar was out-even though the hockey playoffs were starting, he just couldn't pull himself close enough to the lounge to watch the game so near the proximity of alcohol; his mortal enemy. The smell was enticing, the laughs and cheers of the patrons recognizable from Mike's past. A past clouded by EtOH. Booze. His mouth watered and he moved on rapidly towards the gate and an empty seat on a bench row by the windows featuring a great view of the tarmac.

So he sat, bored out of his mind in the Tom Bradley Terminal (named after the first black and longest serving mayor of Los Angeles) by gate eight and watched the planes take off and land; although he did take a little enjoyment of the people around him. Mike liked to watch others go about their day sometimes; it was part of his job in a way, to watch them. He would study their mannerisms and movements, their little idiosyncrasies of life, unsuspecting that they were being watched made it more exciting to him, trying not to be noticed following them with his eyes, noting things for future reference, and more than once this practice saved his life.

A Japanese man in a drab blue business suit and finely polished shoes was slowly walking towards the next gate with his wife who was wearing a thin flower dress and very uncomfortable shoes and had two children in tow; it was odd to Mike that the man allowed his smaller wife to handle the bags. The man seemed able enough to handle the three carry-ons, but he was apparently preoccupied with the gate numbers and his young son, who walked along beside. The man's young daughter was pattering her feet rapidly to keep pace with her mother, who in turn was doing the same to stay in time with the husband. *Foreign traditions…*

A young couple seated three chairs down from Mike were engaged in heavy kissing and giggling; a honeymoon vacation obviously well deserved. The young woman was in her late twenties, the older man-maybe in his late thirties or early forties-had the glow of a twenty year old while he was in her arms. They were unmindful for the time being, of the small man with the vacuum that was trying to get the carpet clean around their feet.

Then he saw them: *airport police.*

He noticed how casual they walked, glancing left and right at the flyers, looking at bags and smiling while they chatted. As they passed Mike heard the taller one talk about his recent affair with a very buxom girl he had met at a bar a few nights ago, the other nodding in jealousy. The two lightly armed men-side arms only-passed within a few feet of Michael and the shorter envious one looked dead into Mike's eyes, and he returned the gaze with a slight smile. The officer returned his stare forward and to his conversation. They both soon had turned out of sight down the long corridor. Mike shook his head, look 'em right into the eyes and they back down...

Things are the same for all of them-and always more worried about their lives than security...

A small crowd of elderly men and one woman passed and sat down on the row of seats directly behind Mike, the men chattering endlessly about their soon to be exciting vacation to the *Land Down Under*. They talked of visiting zoos, some old military bases and of course, the Opera House: the most famous of all images Mike could remember about Australia.

An hour later the announcement was made to board the Jumbo Jet headed to the land of Aus, with one stop in Honolulu for fuel and passengers. Mike pulled his boarding pass out of the side pocket of his carryon bag and checked it again for errors, one of his little compulsions, probably brought on by his job.

After twenty minutes on the ground in Hawaii, the new passengers and some of the ones that boarded on in LA began filing in and took their seats. Once again the flight seemed to be under-booked, there were about sixty unoccupied places to sit, and again Mike felt comfortable about stretching out across the three seats in his row. The chatter grew in the small compartment as the people boarded, finding places in the overheads to set heavy plastic bags with what appeared to be trinkets and souvenirs from the island. Mike could discern the dialects of the newer passengers; they were definitely Australian, probably returning home from an adventure off *their* island continent.

The 747 lifted off twenty minutes later and Mike was on his way to his sabbatical, his relief from the world that was enclosing him every day. It had been a long two months leading up to this trip, one month spent in incarceration of sorts, another month trying to figure where his life was going to go.

About two months before Mike was placed in the *Center*, he had the last run in with his ex, who Mike believed it was her lifelong ambition to make the world around him and his family miserable. She wanted a large advance on their son's monthly child support; he was turning sixteen soon and *needed* a car. Then she insisted that Mike pay half of the monthly insurance, which was astronomical for boys under the age of twenty-five. Another thing Mike rarely understood, why was insurance so high for boys when young girls received more citations than them, and in most cases were way more distracted while driving? He balked at the insurance co-payments and offered a second hand car that a friend of his was selling, for half the price of what the hag was asking him for.

"How can you let your son drive an old used vehicle?" She tersely asked. Her vinegary voice reminded him of the Wicked Witch of the East, in a more sour form.

"Simple, when he wrecks it the loss will be much less and the insurance will be cheaper..."

"Yeah, that's you all right. You're a cheap bastard, cheating your own flesh and blood of a rite of passage." She was hissing into the phone; "And of course you always expect the worse."

She was right to a point, Mike felt he was a little on the cheap side; he remembered when he was a young boy he wanted a skate board. His friends all had the fancy kind with rubber wheels and large fiberglass decks, but his father came home one day from work with a big smile on his face holding a small planked wooden board with steel wheels like sixties era roller skates. Mike rarely took it out, for fear of the embarrassment from his peers but in the same thought, he didn't want to hurt his father's feelings either, he had to be cautious when and where he used it and guilt washed over him to this very day. He swore he would never deny his own kids better things, but in this case,

Mike was making the decision based on his sour relationship with his former wife of eight years.

It was towards the end of those eight years that his drinking had become over the top, his work was thinning his disposition and his life seemed an endless string of turmoil and disappointment. His wife left him, moved in with her mother and took seven year old Mikie, citing the degraded condition of Mike's wellbeing. The child knew nothing of parental dispute and would eventually-with the help of his mother's coaching-also believe his father was a loser. And to a point, they were right; although in this case, losing was a team effort.

After their bitter departure, Mike began focusing on his work feverishly and drinking as much to offset the depression caused by his circumstances. He was a functional alcoholic, as many of his colleagues were at the time, so few problems arose with his work and he never drank at his job. But eventually, two months before his flight to the *Land of Oz,* the world piled on him as much weight as he could stand and his will broke; he collapsed under the heavy strain of work, ex-wife and his distant son and lowered expectations of life. The toll forced him into world of new beginnings, but at the time things fell apart, Mike was unaware of his future, uncertain of his path-if any-beyond the bottle.

"Wine, Mr. Green?" Mike was shaken from his thoughts by a stewardess… flight attendant.

"Oh, no thank you. I don't drink."

"Of course. You might want to get some sleep though sir, it is a long flight and the time change may upset your balance." Her voice was soft and caring, and of course fluid Australian.

The young girl attendant was striking in beauty; even though the uniform made her look older but Mike guessed she was about twenty-five. She wore the same livery as the male attendants, but in a better-proper way of fitting in the right places. Her hair was reddish-blonde and pulled into a neat little bun behind her small head. She was fair in complexion, indicating she spent more time indoors than out, and maybe an added lineage of Irish decent. Her green eyes emboldened this suggestion.

"Thank you I will."

He doubted it, but he didn't want to disappoint the young woman, she seemed so sweet. Mike flipped up the arm rests for the two seats next to him and found the tiny blanket-it resembled a beach towel more than anything-and placed the pillow, which was the size of a folded robe, under his head as he stretched out across the seats. His six foot-three two hundred thirty frame fit tight, with his feet dangling off the last seat into the aisle and the passing flight attendants or passengers would occasionally bump them as they walked by, then apologize to him quietly as they made their way forward or aft.

Mike closed his eyes and started to drift, he was tired, and soon he was at the first stage of sleep when the vision hit him.

Her blood, dripping off his hands and face. The girl lying on the floor, her face covered in blood. Her eyes wide open, lifeless, staring at him-accusing him...

His hands and face were sweaty, from the energy he needed for this task. He felt feverish and his gut was tight as a drum skin. His breath was shallow and rapid, another sign of him tiring, but he must finish the job at hand, or else...

The Boeing hit some turbulence, dropped a few feet and Mike jumped, striking his head on the seat ahead of him. The man in it turned to face the onslaught, not with a look of irritation, but of concern. Mike apologized with a sad smile. He was soaked in sweat and shaking coldly, he sat straight up and began looking around the cabin to see if anyone noticed his jerky movement. After surveying everyone, mostly the backs of their heads, he relaxed a little. The man seated two rows ahead of him stood and started heading towards the back of the aircraft, striking the butt of a cigarette on a Zippo lighter as he walked.

19

"Excuse me."

"Yes mate?"

"May I bum a cigarette off of you; I left mine in the luggage." Mike smiled sheepishly as if to convey his embarrassment of being so thoughtless to leave his vice in an unobtainable spot.

The man paused briefly, looking down at the sweat soaked man and trying to understand Mike's question. He smiled and offered the pack over. "Of course, you American blokes might not like these; they are much stronger than your brands. *Bum*? Hmm, in my country a bum is not a thing to say to gentleman."

Mike could care less, the more powerful the better, but his didn't understand his faux pas. "Thank you. And *sorry…*"

"You have to puff back here, behind the last loo."

He motioned with his head and Mike looked dejected a bit by the supposed rude thing he said to the man.

"Don't get your bustle in a twist mate. I'm no gentleman!" He laughed and winked at Mike who nodded his acceptance of a joke.

Mike rose and thanked the man, then followed along behind him, his mouth watering at the anticipation of a nicotine surge.

Sitting near the final row, the man quietly, there were several passengers in the back with them smoking, but it was very late in the evening and some were sleeping nearby. He was dressed in a comfortable suit, tailored that was somewhat shiny in places it came in contact with other surfaces like the elbows and backside. Mike noticed the suit when he watched the gait of the older gentleman balance his way towards the rear seating area of the Jumbo-Jet.

After they sat down Mike paid close attention to the man's face. He was in his sixties or late fifties, pink chubby cheeks that showed a few years of living well. A second chin was starting to appear, with lines of age and rich food showing around his eyes and mouth. Eating good in later years made people a little rounder, Mike mused to himself. His nose was a tad bulbous with arterial veins snaking around, making the color a little red and blue. He had a very charming smile and twinkly green eyes that were mirthful and relaxed.

"Where ya headed mate?" The man asked with smoke trailing from his nostril, the blue lines fanning out and curling up towards the white plastic paneling.

"Australia…"

The man's cheery smile widened across his face in response.

Mike caught his mistake of over simplifying his destination and offered a better answer, "Sydney. Sorry, I guess I'm just not used to flying this long."

"You're on a holiday then?" The man took a long puff as he watched Mike light up the smoke, with the Zippo he motioned to borrow.

"Uh, yes. Vacation. Had to get away for a while, things at home were wrecking my brain."

"Understood. I went to Hawaii for the same reason, get away from the drear. My wife and I…" The man motioned with his cigarette forward to a seat ahead of them, where a woman was slumped over sleeping, "…had to get away from the pace, you know. Just a bit, a couple of days to restore the passion for livin'."

Mike offered his hand, "Mike Greene."

The man returned a hand, "Steven Darling. Glad to meet you mate, it is going to be a long flight, an' few ever speak to each other on these planes, like we all have leprosy or something. Of course you could meet a bloke with a tale of woe, like a man who peddles insurance and is just one portfolio short of his commission…"

Mike smiled at the brilliant observation and inhaled deeply, his lips curled around the filtered cancer-stick. He sat back and felt the rush of the nicotine in his blood, the warmness of the smoke hit his lungs and the sudden urge to cough, which he did.

"Easy mate, try smoking one at a time, not the whole pack…"

Mike just grinned and then let a worry rush over him. *What if this guy asks what I do for a living?* He knew that few understood his job, that many were appalled by it. He would have to answer stupid questions; he would have to be told that what he did was archaic, Neanderthal even. Mike just wanted to feel the nicotine buzz and relax, maybe even try to get a little sleep. He was in no mood for getting into a discussion over his chosen profession-especially in this day and age-with what was going on in the United States right now.

"Well mate, good talk." Steven rose from the seat and shook Mike's hand. "I hope you get a bit of relaxation in Sydney, it's a beautiful place. And the folks are wonderful; you'll see it's all *fair dinkum*, about us Aussies…"

Mike smiled and thanked Steven again for the smoke, then spent the next few minutes trying to figure out what the man had said. The numbness from accelerated nicotine levels in his blood made Mike feel drowsy and he would chance taking a nap. He returned to his seats and again jammed his body into the crevice between the rows in front and back.

"G'day ladies and gents. This is your Captain, thank you for flying Sydney Airlines and welcome to Australia. We are about fifteen minutes out from Kingsford-Smith International Airport and see no delays. If you will look to the seat pocket in front of you, you will see a pamphlet that has to be filled out before you go through customs. Please fill it out and be sure to ask your wonderful flight attendants if you have any questions…The temperature in Sydney right now is fifteen Celsius and the skies are a bit cast over. It is five thirty local time. Thanks again for flying Sydney Airlines and enjoy your holiday in Australia, and Sydney."

Mike struggled awake this time and found the paper. It was a customs form for any food materials, plants, animals or any other organic substances which might be dangerous to

Australia's environment. It was marked at the bottom by the traditional: "Any unlawful items may subject passenger to delays through customs and could lead to legal charges and criminal prosecution." Another sentence directed passenger to: "Use the *tins* provided at the end of the platform to dispose of any suspected violations." *What the Hell is a tin?* Mike frowned.

The crowd jammed the cabin as the passengers grabbed their carry-ons and gathered anything else that belonged to them. Mike followed along the line towards the door, his bag bumping once and a while on his knee, sometimes on the person's bag ahead of him.

"G'day Mr. Greene thanks. G'day Mr. and Mrs. Thomas, thanks. G'day Mr. Tamorobo thanks…" The pretty flight attendant rattled the names off as the weary passengers left, some nodding at her as they passed, others just ignoring her. Mike smiled and wondered if they read the manifest in the jump seat to memorize the names of the passengers or maybe there was a secret list hidden above the head of the people on the bulkhead. One hundred and ten names were a lot to remember…

Mike stepped from the plane to the ramp and immediately the air hit him; the slight smell of kerosene-jet fuel- and *fresh air*. Moments later he could feel the humidity of the southern part of Australia, anything above fifteen percent was higher than the average at home, and small beads of sweat formed on his brow as he made his way up the gangway towards the terminal. He followed the instructions on the custom's paper and tossed his orange juice he bought in L.A into the *garbage can* at the end of the ramp. Mike smiled to himself, '*Tin…*'

He walked the path laid out from the boarding area to the customs level, and stood in line to have his passport stamped. The interior of Sydney's Kingsford Smith was in a word, light. Tall buttressed ceilings with a large oval opening in the center let in the morning light from the rising sun and shone bright white off of white painted walls and large tile flooring made the terminal look futuristic. Of course the lines, or *queues* as they were called here, were long as many inbound flights brought tourists from around the globe. The customs area was almost the same as any other, large box shaped cubicle surrounded in glass and holding a single officer on a small stool.

In America Mike noticed that the customs agents were usually tired looking, bored with their jobs and the monotony of asking the same basic questions for hours on end. Here the men and women behind the glass counters were smiling, friendly and asked the same questions each time with a familiarity. Their smart blue polo-shirt uniforms were casual looking, relaxing. The badge was a shield that could best be described as a leafless pineapple with a royal crown fixed atop and a blue banded field on both top and bottom identifying the officers as Australian Customs.

The brown haired and hazel eyed agent of about thirty behind the desk in the cubicle also wore a black vest, with the badge affixed over the left breast. Mike smiled at the woman as he handed his papers over, who then looked very carefully at the passport and visa stamp, then at his itinerary, then his declaration paperwork he filled out on the last fifteen minutes of his flight.

"G'day sir, anything to declare Mr. Greene?"

"Nothing."

"Outstanding Mr. Greene, have a wonderful stay in Australia, and welcome!"

Mike picked up his luggage and was headed towards the final area of customs which was more or less the final chance for agents to identify someone with a particular character flaw or suspicious look. Many times it was just a random thing and an agent picked out someone who seemed to be confused a little and could use a smile and proper directions. Mike proceeded towards the doors marked EXIT TERMINAL when an agent caught his eye. He saw the same smile on the face of the man as the security at LAX, but when Mike made eye contact, the agent's demeanor changed and he took a step in Mike's direction with a look of concern.

The new agent was wearing the polo type shirt but no vest, but he was wearing a captain's kind of hat. He seemed to Mike to be in his forties or early fifties, red cheeks and thin, masterly looking and as usual, he had eyes that twinkled with joy.

The agent nodded at him and smiled, "G'day sir."

"Hello." Mike was slightly nervous, the security cops in LA hardly batted an eye at him, but here they seemed to sense something.

"Would you mind following me with your luggage bag please?"

"Sure..." Mike's mind raced. *What could they be looking for?* He tried going over the contents of his bag in his head, *but if I...Oh crap! ...*

His pulse raced as he approached a room with six long tables, at each table there was a man in similar uniform and each with a passenger from Mike's flight. The man nodded to a vacant table and smiled, "If you please sir, place you bag here." A lump formed in his throat as Mike complied.

I'm done for now, they'll probably put me on a flight right back... He feared. The man examined the outside of the case and then looked up at Mike.

"First time in Australia?"

"Yes."

The agent snapped the suitcase open. "You have nothing to declare?"

"Nothing of importance..." Mike held his breath.

"What's this then?"

The agent reached into the bag and came out with a small black leather wallet with a basket weave pattern and opened it. He looked at Mike and then at the wallet, and showed it another customs agent close by. The gold and blue brass glittered in the face of the man; each of the seven points of the star was a reminder of the old west badges that told people who you were. He looked at Mike and smiled.

"*Howdy Sheriff*!" The agent exclaimed in the worn out cliché, an American western accent. A few guffaws emanated from the crowd around him, mostly the other agents.

"I'm a cop." Mike overly defended.

The customs agent looked over his sharp nose at Mike and said, "I should hope so…"

Another agent walked over, glared at the photo ID and then back to Mike and said, "So you're a policeman?"

"Yes."

The agent nodded and walked away with a smile flashed at his colleague.

"You may carry your wallet with you sir, it is okay." Then a small frown appeared of the custom agent's face. "Just don't go flashing this around, we use shields here mainly, you would confuse a bloke."

"No, of course." Mike felt a little better, accpepted.

The agent grinned wide as the Cheshire cat and asked in twangy American again, "You ain't packin' any heat, are ya?"

"No guns, they're all at home, in America. " Mike smiled blushingly.

"Very good then." The agent rummaged through the bag and took out some clothes, then replaced them. "I guess we can trust a fellow policeman…" He repacked the bag, snapped it shut and handed it back to Mike.

"Whew, didn't know what to expect, sir." Mike offered.

"We'll just keep that to ourselves shall we mate? Enjoy Australia." He nodded at Mike and pointed the way to the front doors of the airport. "By the by, if you would have had more than one bag you wouldn't look suspicious. There is a carrier air group in the Harbour from America, an aircraft carrier, and some crazy bloke swam the bay then climbed up a drainpipe on the ship a couple of days ago. The Yanks weren't happy about that, so we are on extra watch. You look like a protestor, not a policeman with you fancy goatee…"

Mike's face turned red, then he smiled at the revelation and the fact a guy climbed a drain pipe of a military ship so blatantly.

The morning sun was warming the ground and air, producing a heavy humidity that sunk into Mike's skin as soon as he cleared the doors from the airport. He felt musky, muggy, like he needed a shower, something he hadn't been able to do for the last seventeen hours since leaving Reno. He let his eyes adjust to the brighter light then looked left and right for a taxi, he would have liked to rent a car but wasn't sure about driving in a foreign country.

There were several cabs at the curb, but no drivers. Mike cleared his throat with enthusiasm and a squat man appeared from behind a taxi and tossed a cigarette butt to the ground. "Taxicab, mate?" He was wearing khaki shorts and a brush shirt, with an oiled leather hat, not one with the corks on strings like Mike had seen years ago in a *Monty Python* skit.

"Yes, thanks."

He pushed his bag forward and the cabbie passed it by, still holding out his hand. Mike thought he was looking for a tip for the moment, then realized his mistake, took the man's hand and shook it. The cabbie had a crocodile tooth bracelet that clacked as Mike shook his hand; the little man shook Mike's hand roughly, firmly, with much enthusiasm and then reached down to pick up Mike's suitcase. The man had on way too much aftershave, there were small sweat stains on his pocketed khaki shirt under the arm and he seemed jittery, like he'd had too much coffee so early in the morning.

As usual so far, the man was pink faced and a little scruffy, maybe a two or three day beard coming in, but it fit the image of Crocodile Dundee, the visage that the Australian tourist authority was no doubt trying to cash in on. His eyes glittered like everyone else's and Mike began to wonder if there wasn't something they put in the water to make everyone so gleeful.

"Travelin' light today eh?" The man beamed as he hefted the case to a shoulder. "This box'll set off the fly cops... Did they shake you down mate?"

"Hmmm?"

"The agents, customs. A bloke who displays only a carry on and one piece of luggage usually set them off."

"Oh, yes as a matter of fact."

"No worries... mate. They look gruff and mighty, but get them pissed and they are as tame as a goanna in the sun..."

"Pissed, why now would I want..."

"Drunk. Sorry mate. They call it pissed, Ireland, Scotland, England, ya know. We call it pissed. Never reckoned why."

"Oh."

"Oh."

Mike let the cabbie walk towards the back of the cab to place the suitcase and carryon in the *boot*, or trunk. Mike walked to the nearest door, fumbled with the handle. Then he looked down inside, he realized he'd made another critical error. The jolly cabbie looked up above the lid and smiled at him.

"I'll *drive* mate..."

Mike was standing at the *right* side of the car, the driver's side.

"Sorry, I am just..."

"Say nothing more mate, it happens every day with you Americans here. And a few other foreign types, it just happens."

His smile stayed locked on his face as he thumped the bags into the small compartment. Mike lowered his head in shame and walked to the left side of the car, opened the door and slid into the passenger seat. The cabbie did the same for the driver side, he turned the key and the car buzzed to life.

The cab was pleasant enough, small-an older Mazda sedan jobbie that had great gas mileage and poor comfort, the ashtray was full of butts, the radio was playing solid gold eighties music from America and the cabbie was chatty. He was very friendly, seemingly enough, and most of his banter took a few minutes to sink into Mike, he was almost like an interpreter trying to figure out what language his client was using. After a few moments, Mike was able to discern the rudimentary basics.

Five minutes of maneuvering the roads of the airport on the left side of the road, Mike was happy he decided not rent a car; he would probably have caused a terrible accident. The cabbie made it look easy and he swished back and forth across lanes and onto the main highway. The first road sign Mike recognized said '*Botany Bay*' and he chuckled to himself.

"*Star Trek?*" The cabbie beamed.

"Pardon?"

"*Star Trek: The Space Seed.* Ya know-the Botany Bay-the spaceship that *Kahn* was aboard when Captain Kirk found him."

Mike felt a rush of familiarity over him. "Oh yeah..."

"Me? I'm a big *Trek* fan too. Grew up watching it, one of my favorites, as you can see why..." He gestured at the sign as they flew under it in the cab. "First time in Australia?"

"Yes, anywhere really."

"You'll love this place mate. Everyone is friendly, not fake friendly like the bloody French. Ya know, 'Hi I'm Monsieur Big Nose and I'll be happy to *geeve* you a *rrrooom* for a large *teeep*'" The cabbie smiled doing his best French imitation and Mike laughed; he was feeling more comfortable by the second. "Australians strive hard to make everyone happy, this place is our home and we are happy to have you visit and would like you to go back then tell all your friends what a great time you've had so they will visit too...right then?"

"I will."

"Okay, clear of the airport mate. Where to?"

"Bay Point Hotel."

"Ahhhhh, Rushcutters Bay. Lovely place, lots of big rooms and a fancy pub with a casino then."

"I guess... I'm not much of a gambler or a drinker. I heard it was the best place to stay."

The airport itself was on a man-made peninsula that stretched out into the bay, almost like SFO San Francisco, but in a larger scale. They passed the final buildings closing in the area and a view was arriving for Mike to enjoy, his first scenes of Australia from the ground. The cabbie circled the airport Marsh Street that extended out from Qantas Drive via Airport Drive and the road doubled back *under* the airport on the M 5 Motorway towards the coast and crossing the runways in a very large tunnel as Jumbo-Jets landed and taxied overhead. On the other side of the landing strip the M 5 became the M 1 Motorway and then it turned into Southern Cross Drive heading northeast.

The cabbie chatted on about the sights to see, but Mike was beginning to feel tired and just wanted to rest. As they entered the southern parts of the city, it reminded him of the larger ones in the U.S., mainly San Francisco although it wasn't as hilly; Sydney still had small hillsides with homes and businesses. He felt a little disappointed that the city he had heard so much about seemed much like any other big city he had visited. Large cranes were working high in the air building skyscrapers and large office buildings; they resembled the few dozen cranes constantly working in Las Vegas-always building-never stopping. Mike felt a drain upon his psyche, he was afraid the two weeks here would be wasted on very few sights and the same old big city attractions he could have gotten thousands of miles from here in Vegas.

The sky was overcast, maybe from an early morning fog off of the coast a few miles away; the air was wet with humidity. Mike assumed it was near sixty-five or seventy percent-maybe more. At home in the desert it hovered usually around ten or five percent. It was warm for so early in the morning, but the breeze that wafted in from the open windows felt good on Mike's aching body.

Mike began to wonder how much longer the ride would last, the driver was an outgoing kind of guy and he noticed this about every Australian he has met so far; a pleasant disposition-very friendly and always smiling. He talked a million miles a minute, but enough words got through for an understanding. Mike was getting anxious about his trip though, a lot of money spent and so far, not the magical stuff he'd expected.

The cabbie continued on his lne of thought, "Bay Point. Not the best hotel, but a good one. If you don't mind being so close to *Kings Cross*."

"Kings Cross..." It was a question.

"Yeah, we'll pass that in a bit, you'll see why. Do you fancy golfing, mate?"

"Not really, never tried."

"How about zoos? Got a real fancy one here in Sydney, one of the best in the world, they've even got one of the largest crocs ever in captivity. And the regular paddocks of koalas, roos, emus and Tasmanian devils."

Several more minutes of guide and ride and the cabbie made a sharp left on a street called Kings Cross Road. Traffic was building and the drive was getting slower, the cooler air being replaced by warmer stale air with a slight taste of sea on it. Mike was staring out the window when he noticed someone out of place: it was a woman, dressed *very* casually, with a few thin garments and a bright smile. She stared at Mike as the cab passed and nodded at him as he came into her view.

A *prostitute*. Mike has seen this kind before; he's even arrested a few. Even though Nevada still has legal prostitution and the famous "*Ranches*" just a few miles inside his patrol beat.

"Lady of the evening?" He said out loud to no one really, but the cabbie picked up on it.

"Hooker. Yeah sure, careful if you walk by this area, ya know how they got the name right? As you pass they hook their arm around yours and then bargain for a while."

The driver made a few quick turns towards a long highway that rolled over a few hills towards a large building in the center.

"This is Kings Cross." He pointed out the window to the several women, a few gathered at each corner. "It's legal here.

But the patrols have been stepped up a bit for the next few weeks."

"Why now?"

"You Yanks have an aircraft carrier here, names *Blue Ridge* I believe-yeah, *Blue Ridge*. Came in last week, you see this is the fiftieth anniversary of the Battle of Coral Sea. Your Vice President was here for that, stayed just back there a ways. That's the reason for all the security cops and *militree*."

"So the police stay away to beef up security at the port?"

"Harbour mate. No, the Yank sailors love *the* hospitality. Ya know what I mean? These girls will make more in a few weeks with the American ships in town, than I can muster in all of six months."

"Now I know what you mean." Mike did, he had always heard the rumors of how much the girls at *The Mustang Ranch* made, but never saw any proof of it. But every weekend the lot was full of cars, limos, and taxis.

A few more minutes and the cab swung into driveway of the hotel. It was older looking, sort of like the Hotel De Anza in San Jose, California-Mike loved that place. This place was much taller and had a larger girth around the ground level; concrete that was sandblasted white with exposed rhyolite finished the outer walls that went at least ten stories or more and each level had a small balcony separating each room with a wooden partition. The main doors were glass with brass frames, gold leaf brushed lettering said BAY POINT HOTEL AUSTRALIA, then off to the right facing towards the building was a small cubicle made from seamless glass and it had one comfortable looking seat in the center of it, a radio on a small bench. A fancily dressed Eastern Indian man in a red bellman cap came out of this booth and quickly opened the passenger door as the cab stopped.

"G'day and welcome to the Bay Point Hotel. You *are* Mr. Greene?"

The cabbie was still jabbering in the background, the doorman spoke with a broken Indian/Australian accent and it sounded rather unique. He had an acetate nameplate that read TOMMY engraved in red on gold.

"Yes…" Mike nodded as he rose from the seat to the sidewalk.

"Very well, then. You are one of four guests we expect today sir…" The man gave him a wink, "that's how I knew you who you were…" He let out a big smile, like he just told a huge joke.

Mike stood off to the side of the cab and the doorman leaned in to the door of the taxi and stared at the cabbie until his attention was turned. The cabbie broke off in mid-sentence and smiled back at the Indian doorman. "Oh, hey mate!"

"Bags?" The doorman named Tommy asked, slightly impatient.

The cabbie motioned to the rear of the car with a smile.

"That'll be twenty-three dollars seventy-five thanks." The cab driver shouted out to Mike.

Mike took out a nice new fifty dollar note, one of the unique Australian currency notes he had picked up at the airport in LA.

"Here ya go." Mike leaned in and handed the man the note.

"Look here mate," The cabby said as he revealed a coin changer he wore around his belt, just like the ice cream man had in Mike's neighborhood when he was a kid.

The cabbie used his thumb to send a few coins in change to his hand, and then he pulled a few notes from a hidden wallet in his jacket. "Here's a little secret." The driver displayed the coins in an open hand to Mike. "This big one, it's a fifty cent piece. This tiny one is the ten cent piece; this one is the twenty-five cent piece. But the crème of the crop is this little bugger here." He hefted a small coin almost the size of an American dime, but nearly three times thicker and gold colored. "This heavy little sort is the two dollar coin, be mindful when counting out your change. You think you're giving ten cents, but with his little darling, you're giving two dollars."

Mike picked the golden coin from the man's hand and examined it closely, "I'll be damned. A two dollar coin? That makes more sense than a silver dollar or a paper dollar."

"Right. Mathematically mate, you'll use that coin more than you would any other form of note here, everything works out novel that way."

"Thank you very much…" Mike returned the two dollar coin to the cabby's hand along with three dollar notes he was just given.

"Thanks mate!" He smiled as he whirled around to his place behind the wheel and pulled out into traffic, leaving Mike alone with the doorman Tommy and his bags on the curb.

"You shouldn't tip Mr. Greene."

"Pardon?"

"Tipping, it is neither compulsory nor expected here in Australia. Our wages are sufficient enough-by reason of itself tipping is not a common thing. Just so you know…"

The doorman smiled as he hefted the bags through the tall glass doors towards the marble counter where the front desk was. Inside, the exterior's detail was expanded. More cut concrete with right angles and peppered with aggregate wash, larger than life windows with thick brass or no framing at all, depending on the area. The marble was expensive Italian white, the floor was matching with a pattern Mike once thought he heard called Tuscan, with muslin edgings done in smaller slates.

"Sorry, where I come from its how some of our workers earn a living."

Mike explained as he followed the man to the counter, where a tall woman in a semi-tux was waiting and smiling in the usual Australian fashion. Her hair was auburn and eyes shone green. She was about twenty-five or six and of course the glimmer was in her smile and face. Her cheeks were pinkish with a darker rouge applied higher up and her lips were outlined thinly with dark lipstick then feathered into a bright red to fill in the fleshy parts.

Mike paused at the great desk in the reception area and took in the immense lobby. Glass walls and a double set of glass in brass doors revealed a small pub behind him, small and cozy, like a little corner bar back home. It seemed to be closed now, the room was dark, no one was at the bar and the TV wasn't on. He would be sure to avoid this area at any cost.

A small restaurant of about twenty seats sat to the left of the pub, and a little behind it, Mike figured a Dutch door or passage would link the two, just as many restaurants and bars do in America. The restaurant faced directly out onto the street that Mike had come in on. He wished he'd looked at the name of some of the streets, but it all passed by so quickly, and he was tired. Large bay windows gave spectacular views of the street, there was a small park across the way and then other rows of hotels behind it.

"G'day. May I help you?"

The soft heavy accented Australian voice belonged to the clerk behind the desk.

"Yes. You have a reservation for…"

"Mister Greene eh?" She jumped on his answer, "See you right here on my screen…" She made a clucking sound with her tongue and then said, "Well, I'm very sorry Mr. Greene but your accommodations won't be ready for at least another hour. May I suggest you grab a bit of tucker or perhaps the pub could whip you up a brilliant bloody Mary?"

Mike sighed. "Can I go in and sit down? I don't drink, but a Coke would be nice."

"Of course Mr. Greene. Right up, you may leave your bags here and I'll tend to them until your room is ready, shouldn't be more than a few ticks or two…"

Mike nodded with a forced smile of frustration and headed for the lounge area of the pub. The desk clerk summoned Tommy the doorman to fetch Mike a glass of fountain cola and he did. Mike sat in a comfortable chair that was like a combination seat with a stool, mostly like a chaise lounge on a patio, but upholstered and very comfortable.

The pub had a casino combination, not that the two were combined, it was as if they were two entities, one half bar with TV and tables scattered around an area about forty feet by fifty; then the casino area had banks of slots-poker machines mostly-along the walls directly to the right and behind the pub itself, almost another room, there were tables in here too, but smaller and only three seats to each table. Maybe six or seven at the most, many were obscured by the dark. It was too early for the pub to be open Mike assumed, hence the lack of light.

The bar area was simple enough, a large mirror behind it that gave a view nearly of the whole pub except the casino, but it also gave a person sitting there a look at the lobby and reception area though the large glass panes that separated the two. Chimneys, rocks, shot glasses and large beer mugs sat upturned on a white linen runner in front of the mirror. A TV was off to the corner of the bar facing the greatest concentration of the seats in the room, but the small size of the cabinet limited the viewing. Get here early or miss the game.

Mike was right about the Dutch door access to the kitchen/restaurant area, one was located to the left facing the bar, it was closed now but he was sure it opened as soon as the pub did to allow customers to have drinks poured for lunch or dinner. He saw a dark haired woman of nearly forty watching him move to the chaise lounge thing. Her eyes were sparkling, but there was more to it. *Was she ogling him?*

He took a sip of his drink, made a face at the surprising amount of sugar in the soda then leaned back and closed his eyes to rest.

A man's heavy breathing. Sirens and tires screeching all around him. Blood all over his hands; on his face, on her face, on everything…

Mike kicked his feet out in reaction to his dream and knocked an ashtray off the table in front of him. He sat up quickly and looked around the room, frightened by the dream and the few moments of not knowing where he was. He was sweaty and shaking when his eyes met a beautiful young woman's behind the bar. Her hands were on her hips, fists balled. In one hand was a dishrag, her face was cold-emotionless. She stared at him as he stared at her, then his eyes dropped to the fallen ashtray on the dark carpeting.

"Sorry." He said quietly, his voice cracking with sleep.

The barmaid's expression didn't change. She sighed irascibly and pursed her lips tightly; she was gorgeous, even mad. "Too pissed to find your room eh?"

Mike tried to sit up as best he could, but the length of the chair kept him from getting into a proud pose, he looked like a kid stuck on an oversize beanbag chair.

"Uh... No, no. My room wasn't..."

The receptionist interrupted his defense as she walked into the pub and nodded at the blond haired barmaid. "Your room is now ready, Mr. Greene."

He struggled for a moment getting to his feet, pulled his shirt tail down and let his expression change from embarrassed to pristine, as if he was never in the compromising position in the first place. He nodded at the barmaid and winked, "Ma'am."

She nodded slightly, then began shaking her head in disdain as his attention was turned towards the lobby. Mike followed the clerk to the marble counter, glancing once over his shoulder at the pretty young woman in the bar, her eyes were to her task of cleaning and she didn't even seemed fazed by him at all. Just back to work. He looked back to the clerk and finished his check-in.

"*Baggage.*"

"Bellman's got it."

The barmaid was slowly drying a glass from behind the darkened bar as another woman approached from the restaurant. Natalie McMaster was your average waitress, her middle age figure was the envy of many a beach goer when she bared it during the warmer days at Gold Point or Surfers Paradise and her face was pleasant enough to turn the heads of younger men. Her brown eyes were sad and droopy; she was looking as if she was feeling randy about the newcomer. She tapped the barmaid on the shoulder as she approached and offered her opinion of the man that just entered the lobby area.

"No dopey." The barmaid said, "The man's got issue-farm written all over him."

Natalie looked at her companion and smiled slyly, "Yeah, and a nice bum."

The barmaid looked down to the glass she was drying and added quietly, but with a sad smile sighing, "*Yeah...*"

Mike received his room key-room 2114-second floor by the pool terrace the clerk said with a confident smile. An aboriginal bellman appeared from the office area behind the clerk and with a charming smile. He hefted Mike's bag up and offered his hand for the carry on Mike was still clutching from the pub. Mike smiled back and gave the bag to the short and somewhat round man. His face was dark, darker than anyone Mike had ever seen before; his eyes were brown with an intense look of softness, like there was nothing that could bother him. His nose was plump; the nostrils nearly went from one side of his mouth to the other.

Mike followed the man to a hallway partially concealed by an immense concrete wall that had holes in it at even spaces and about three inches round. Apparently these were supposed to suggest the cement wall was actually a slab of granite or something harvested from a quarry somewhere.

In the hallway was one elevator. *Lift*, as the bellman said in a heavy accent. "This way to the lift then mate!"

The lift was a black iron gated enclosed structure about five foot by five foot. It was an antique for sure and the small operator at the handle on the left side facing in was dressed the part in a small red coat and round page's cap. Old fashioned. The teenage looking boy smiled and nodded when the bellman said, "Two mate, round the *gahdan*, up the *shoft* and settle 'er on silk then." He spun and winked at Mike. "Fancy gents and their rides eh?"

Mike smiled like he knew what the hell was going on or what the bellman had said. He hoped it was the right thing to do, smile. He nodded and made a sound that could've been mistaken for an affirmative. "*Ahemyup*."

On the second floor Mike went out first and the bellman followed. Mike stopped at a large glass enclosure that led to the pool area. It had been a long time since Mike had seen and indoor pool this large. Sure, a few of the casinos around Reno had them because of the year around use, catering to skiers in the winter. But not like this. There were glass partitions that rose about six foot high around the kidney shaped Olympic sized pool, the water was an inviting deep blue at the far end which had tiles made to read 3 M. Meters obviously, Mike did the math and concluded it was nine feet deep there. He looked to the end closer to where the doors opened up in front of and of course the tiles read 1 M. The water at this end was much lighter blue, like the shallow beaches at Lake Tahoe. Crystal clear.

" 'Oughta see it at night mate." The bellman said quietly, "Room's this way…"

Mike turned and followed the man to the end of the hall. Door 2114. The bellman used the key he asked for from Mike and opened the room up, he pressed the door inwards and waved Mike in first. As Mike passed he finally got a glimpse at the acetate nameplate on the little guy's breast. Jimmy.

Mike said, "Thanks, Jimmy."

There was the bed, white on white covers and comforter, the nightstand that bore a phone and a remote control for the television-which was cleverly disguised in an armoire. The room was spacious in a false sense, it was made with lots of angles and low ceilings around the commonly used areas like the bathroom and the bed, lower in the small hallway. The view from the balcony was beautiful, Mike's room sat just a little higher than the building opposite and he could see the *Sydney Tower* a ways from where he was, the building the cab driver described as the second tallest structure in Australia. And the second tallest standing observation tower in the southern hemisphere. The Tower was really a thick building atop a spire, not saucer shaped like the Space Needle in Seattle, Washington. More of a large peach basket with windows all the way around and then above it a thinner drum of more windows and an observation deck on a place the cabbie called "The Eye".

Jimmy the bellman gave a tour of the room and the amenities; the bath, the bidet and instructions on how to use it. The proper use of the house phone to call for midnight *tucker*-room service-and how to use the valet for laundry.

"The Bay Point demonstrates the finest service anywhere…" the man proudly spouted his well-written and rehearsed line. He strode back to Mike and handed him the room key and asked if there was anything he needed.

"No thanks, I just want to get a nap." His eyes were burning from the lack of sleep.

"Very good sir, dinner buffet is served at six-downstairs next to the hotel pub and casino. It's recommended for the price and is closer than anywhere you can walk on foot here in Rushcutters Bay."

"Thank you." The man backed out of the door and Mike felt compelled to give him a tip but as his hand moved forward to the bellman, the man's dark hand went up.

"No tips thanks… some take it as an insult. G'day and enjoy your rest…"

"G'day."

Mike gave the room a once over again; the carpet was a light blue mixed with little pink sparkles here and there. The wood work on the armoire and table by the window were different colors, the table and chairs were light oak, the armoire cherry-wood. Above the bed was a large painting of what Mike guessed to be Sydney Harbour, with ancient sailing ships coming in. They were rather adventurous cheapie oils-the kind you'd find at an airport hotel with a huge sign above them that read STARVING ARTIST SALE, but rather dusty along the frames.

The bed was inviting and he needed rest, but Mike was afraid of the dreams that came with sleep. Not every time-but enough to make a person weary of sleeping-if that were possible-to be too tired to be too tired of falling asleep and waking with a nightmare hinging on your mind. Vividness was the problem, the clarity of the dreams made Mike wonder when he could tell the difference between reality and the nightmare-it made him worry that some night he would wake and not know the difference any longer. He worried that he would wake, and for the rest of his life live in the dream, instead of being able to push it away-he worried the dreams might drive him back to the bottle.

He kicked off his shoes and sat on the bed, under the oil painting, he laid back with his head under the largest ship. He tried to dream of a life that would be normal, he thought of how he could rebuild his life once he returned home, to go back to work, to find some woman to date.

A relationship, that scared him more than anything at this point.

The world faded as Mike's eyes tightened and reality bid farewell and he sailed away on a wavy sea with that big ship under his feet, drifting and rocking…

He didn't know how this would all turn out, but there was a pang of fear about this trip, something that…

CHAPTER TWO
SHANNON

The room closed in on him, he could feel the breath of the other men in the circle. One man had the foulest odor coming from his lungs, another was huffing and puffing, just in from smoker's corner. Everyone is dressed casually, sweats and tees or slacks and polo shirts, some even are wearing just jean shorts and sandals with wife beater tops. In the center of the circle sits a medium sized man; white shirt, black leather vest and Roper lace up cowboy boots. This man's name is Jack G. His eyes are soft, caring; a kind of brown that a puppy has. His hair is long and ponytailed, grey stripes are found here and there in his mane. He's the center of attention now.

"Mike, would you like to tell us a story now?"

"No sir. I'm just here for the coffee and doughnuts." A small chuckle echoed in the room.

"Very funny... how about it. You have been here two weeks and have yet to fully open up to us. Just a little snippet. Sharing will help you to relieve the pressure."

"Not today, Jack."

"Very well. Larry, how about your story."

"Sure, it goes like this... Mike killed this girl you know and he wasn't even sad about it..."

Michael knocked the lamp off the fancy night stand next to the bed when he was violently awakened by *the* dream. Sweat poured from his forehead and shoulders, the sheets were soaked through. Mike felt he was almost swimming.

"Jesus...That one was getting just as bad as the rest..." His voice crackled in the empty room. He sat up and reached down to pick the lamp and shade off the floor then arranged them back on the table, further from the bed this time. After examining the lamp for damage-which he found none-he looked at his watch. The digital dial read 5:45 pm but Mike didn't feel all that rested for ten hours sleep, and then he realized he hadn't set his watch to Australian time yet.

Okay, Australia is sixteen or seventeen hours behind Nevada? It's uh, eleven forty-five... oh crap. Three hours sleep, no wonder you are so tired Mike... He surveyed the room for a clock and found one on the opposite table; indeed-it was eleven forty-five a.m.

He stretched for a few minutes and found his shoes he kicked off and he had one foot in before he realized he hadn't showered in two days and was badly in need of one, so he removed the shoe, his socks and casually undressed on his way to the bathroom. He stood ten minutes under the pounding hot water then finally switched it to cold to wake him up a little more when remembered he had forgotten his shaving kit in the room. He bowed his head and shook it. *It's going to be a long month...*

Mike primped himself in the mirror by the little hallway next to the bathroom; he was not very pleased with the stranger staring back at him again, this time in full length view. *I need a drink...* He smiled as he gave his final semi-approval of his attire and cleanliness; he wasn't venturing far today, just down to the lobby and then a bite in the restaurant. He could spend the rest of the day in his room planning his sightseeing trips from the selection of pamphlets he would grab by the check-in desk. He frowned on a city tour, from what he had seen on his way to the hotel, he wasn't very impressed. The construction and closeness of a large city didn't excite him very much, he had seen pretty much the same thing in Vegas and wasn't particularly fond of walking around in a strange place alone, with no clue how to get anywhere and no one to talk to about what he saw. It wasn't that he was scared of running into trouble, god help anything that crossed his path when he was this way.

He walked from the elevator onto the fine marble tile in the hallway that leads out of a thin vestibule towards the lobby; in the background he could hear the clatter of dishes and idle chatter of patrons in the restaurant. He thought for a moment about heading for the bar, a place he should not be found if he was to remain sober for any period of time, so he decided to have a bite to eat at the little restaurant.

To access the restaurant he had to pass by the lounge, so Mike steadied himself for a trip across dangerous land as he kept his eyes focused on the entrance of the little café ahead of him. *A meal then maybe a walk…*

For an instant he thought he could make it straight through but something-no-*someone* caught his eye. She was beautiful, a little over five-nine, five-ten maybe; light blond hair pulled back into a ponytail with a bang on each side drifting down to her soft cheeks. She was clearing a small table in the little casino area, a room adjacent to the bar that had about twenty-five poker machines.

It was the angry young bartender from earlier.

The young girl was smiling as she did her work; her mind was in a distant place, or was dwelling on a recent happy occasion, whatever it was her smile made the tanned face seem so much brighter, so alive, so young… Mike pulled his lips tight to the side, noting she was probably about twenty-three or four, at least a dozen or more years behind him and way more full of life.

He didn't know why he did it or what if anything he hoped to accomplish by it, but he sashayed towards the half circle bar that sat opposite the poker room and pulled himself onto a bar stool. She was the most remarkable thing he'd seen in years, or at least one that had spoken to him. And it wasn't as if her words were encouraging or engaging, he thought she had made a comment about him being drunk as he napped in the pub. She didn't seemed too happy about him being there, but then again she didn't frown or yell or anything that might indicate that she was extremely displeased with him.

He waited with a little excitement, but the young woman circled the tables and collected the ashtrays and empty chimney glasses, Mike thought ashtrays were the absolute epitome of man's vice. He hated the fact he smoked-but he disliked stubbing out a butt in a tray filled with a half dozen or more. It was just a little unsettling to him that he had to touch other people's ashes.

The young girl was dressed in the appropriate clothing of the hotel, a black vest over a white blouse with the sleeves fluffed a little at the shoulder, black pants and leathery black shoes, modern at least-Mike hated the look of old fashioned polished shoes. She filled the slacks out quite well; her behind was the perfect fit. Mike wondered if she had the pants tailored, her lean torso left everything to the imagination, she somehow seemed the part of a bartender in every aspect, and she looked to be in her element here. The young girl whirled unexpectedly towards the bar, catching Mike's downward gaze at her behind and she bent her knees to level her eyes at his.

"I'll be just a flash..." She said with little emotion. Mike's eyes immediately darted to hers, but it was too late he realized, she had seen his ungentlemanly stare.

She cleared the last table placing small rock glasses on her almost over full tray and danced her way back to the bar, at least it looked like a dance to him, and he seemed stricken with her lighthearted movements. He gave the room another once over, observing the empty poker machines and shook his head in disapproval, then slowly reconnoitered the rest of the area as he turned his stool to the forward position. Mike was wondering to himself, was she moving a bit more spry like since he entered, she didn't seem so chipper as he walked by. Not until she noticed him, well-it as more than likely his imagination.

"May I serve you something sir?" Her voice was angelic, she had the slightest accent, not overbearing like the rest of the Australians he had met prior; hers was subdued. There was a tingle in her speech, like a singer whispering a soft soprano note; it made the little hairs on the back of Mike's head stand. It wasn't the short curt tone from this morning. Matter of fact, it was if she didn't recognize him at all.

"Do you have a Coke?"

"Flat or high?"

"Pardon?"

"Rum or …"

"No booze. I… don't drink."

The bartender whipped a can out of the ice bin in front of her and slid a fingernail under the pop-top opening the can with a fizzy relief. She produced a chimney glass from under the bar, and began to pour the Coke into it, set the glass and the can onto the counter, then lifting the glass so she could put a Foster's Beer coaster under it.

"Two dollars fifty thanks…"

Mike dropped two, two dollar coins onto the counter and pushed them towards her; she smiled, retrieved them and spun on a heel to open the register. She turned to Mike and set a one dollar note and a huge fifty cent piece next to his can. Instinctively he pushed the fifty cent piece into the glass trough-the lip that falls below the edge of the bar for filling drink glasses-in America that signals a tip. He knew he made a mistake the very instant the coin hit the lower tray as the bartender picked the coin up and set it back in front of him.

"No need to tip here in Australia, especially New South Wales, mate."

"Sorry, I forgot. The cabbie took my tip earlier and the bellman warned me, I just have a habit of doing it for exceptional service." Even though Mike's face was discolored a little red, he smiled confidently, to convey his satisfaction of her service. "Where I come from tipping is considered part of a person's income, as a matter of fact most casino workers and bartenders rely on tips."

"The wages here are satisfactory enough." She smiled softly.

"If you don't mind me asking, how much do you make?" The bar was empty and Mike wanted her full attention, for as long as possible.

"Not at all mate, roughly seventeen dollars fifty per hour."

"Wow! Where I come from a bartender makes about five bucks an hour, *plus* tips..." Mike was shocked; *I wonder what a cop makes here?*

"Where is it you come from, if *you* don't mind me asking?" Her eyes focused on him intensely for a moment.

Mike heard a tiny bit of mocking in her voice, it was a teasing, playful, sound.

"America."

"Yes, I have that part figured out, the accent and all." Her face was emotionless now, as if she were enjoying a dry joke on Mike's behalf.

She smiled slowly as her brow wrinkled and the corners of her mouth formed little half crescent dimples, Mike noticed a slight cleft in her chin. Her face was thin; she had the cutest little nose under sparse, well-manicured eyebrows and two little moles-one on her cheek and another just below her lip on the right side broke the perfect symmetry, but it was her eyes that caught Mike's attention. They shone lightning blue, a brighter blue than sapphire; when she smiled, they smiled. They looked at Mike and seemed absorbed and full of laughter, her attitude revealed mischief, she transmitted a soft easy air about her though. She was a maverick in every sense of the word. Mike felt an instant attraction.

She was gorgeous... and very young.

"Oh, sorry. Nevada, a little town called Lockwood, it's just east of Reno."

"Sounds very... Cozy, no... intimate." She let her voice draw to a whisper, a seductive tone.

"What's your name?" Mike asked innocently enough, he'd seen her nametag, but he wasn't using his brain right now.

"You'll stare at my bum and not my knockers, eh?"

Mike flushed. "I was…"

"Why it's Shannon, Shannon Hunter." She said plainly as she used to her eyes to indicate she was wearing a name tag. "Don't tell me you haven't checked out me chest? I'd say you'd spent the better part of ten minutes gazing at me bum a bit ago!" She laughed out loud and Mike thought he heard some of the glasses on the bar jingle along. "Named after me aunt on me father's side. " 'Cept the middles, mine's Christine."

"What?"

Mike's face turned crimson, he knew what she meant, and her eyes gave it away. They were playful. Mike had never seen such intensity in someone's eyes before, he could swear he saw his reflection in them, he didn't break his gaze from them, he was fixed, falling. He was searching his memory of thirty years to try and remember when he'd last been mesmerized by someone's eyes. Sure, he'd looked into the eyes of many people, hundreds if not thousands of them mostly in the process of doing his job; but none compared with the essence of pure sky-blue he was locked onto now.

"Never mind mate, are you all right then? You seem distracted." She moved her face an inch closer to his and her eyes glistened even more.

Mike swallowed a bit and then tried to sit back, his space was being violated. Not that he minded the violator, but a squinch in his stomach and a shiver of cold air down his spine told him that he was treading on dangerous ground here.

"Sorry, I was just…" He dropped his eyes from hers, his thoughts were betrayed; "I don't know."

"Are you sure you wouldn't like something a bit more tantalizing? Perhaps a brilliant bloody Mary?" She nodded to Mike's glass, it was empty. He had unconsciously drunk it all while he was engaged with Shannon.

"No thanks, I don't drink, uh booze."

"You mentioned that."

"I, well uh…"

"Funny to hang out in a pub, if you don't wish to imbibe, you'd stand out a bit in my world of male friends as a Dag in a Boozer." She laughed at her joke, Mike didn't. He needed subtitles…

"Drinking, well it goes bad with this *recovering alcoholic* thing I have."

"Oh, a rehabber! My fault sorry. Never mind. Would you care to watch the television? I have to get ready to accept me customers and Footy fans, games always on here. Do you like football mate?"

"Hmm? Oh yes, that would be okay."

"I should have American news on now, game's on in a few after…" Shannon said as she turned towards the nineteen inch television and flicked it on. The screen brightened the bar area a little more and Mike felt uncomfortably flushed in the light; it was the six o'clock news from America. She turned and began doing behind the bar chores as Mike sat mesmerized by her movements, slow and intentional at times, then rapid and precise at others. Soon the news from the TV would draw his attention away;

"The beating case of the young black man from L A by police has entered its second week Dan…" a reporter was saying, the video of the policemen was being shown, a man was lying on the ground kicking and swinging at them and the policemen were using their batons on him. Mike grimaced.

Everyone at home knew about the case, it was going to be a landmark ruling no matter which way the jury found, either for the cops who were accused of excessive force. The accusation was intensified by the national media's portrayal of the police as racially motivated; or for the poor black man, who was under the influence of drugs but most seem to agree the beating was not warranted as the video showed. Mike had not made his mind up at all about the case, he saw both sides of the argument and was leaning towards the policemen, but he knew that his department wouldn't allow that type of behavior at all from its employed cops; the man was down and there was no need for more than one or two officers to try to subdue him, not four-unless the man was on PCP-and that hadn't been confirmed yet.

Phenylcyclohexilpiperidine or Angel Dust-originally was made as a tranquilizer for elephants and can completely block the nerve and pain centers in a human being when used; police rely on pain and nervous systems to control obnoxious and combative people.

When someone can feel no pain, they become superhuman, their bodies go beyond the natural restraints-even to the point of severe damage to their own muscles, tissues, ligaments and tendons-Mike has seen the drug in action once; a young fifteen year old girl picked up a two hundred thirty pound policeman and threw him over the hood of his patrol car. It took five officers to control her; she dislocated both her arms and one hip trying to escape the dog pile. The problem is there are no warning signs, the subject can go out of control at any time, they won't remember anything, and they can hurt quite a few others. The only telltale sign of a person under Angel Dust's influence is a minty smell as they sweat.

Shannon the bartender was watching the news from the corner of the bar where she was cleaning the glasses she picked up earlier. She rubbed a chimney glass as she watched with her head cocked to one side and her mouth drawn into a frown.

"Bloody abusive, those policemen, eh?"

"Huh?" Mike turned; he heard the question, but needed time to think. "I guess, I don't think that man deserved that much of a beating…"

Shannon's beautiful blue eyes locked with Mike's, they'd darkened a little and lost their twinkle. "Yeah, but look at those coppers, they have giant handguns on their side, then they have those sticks, not only are they bullies, the just look intimidating to any bloke…" She placed the last clean glass on the counter behind the bar, then stepped back to check her handiwork. "Americans are brutal enough sometimes, they don't need to advertise it."

"*Well…*" Mike wanted to have a rebuttal, but this wasn't his territory, let alone his country so he let it go. He sighed. "Do you have a bathroom?"

"Need a loo or a dunny?"

"Huh?"

"Gotta pee or sit?" Shannon didn't even blink.

Mike's foot slid off of the barstool rung.

"Uh, pee." Mike felt his ears turn red hot. *How can a beautiful thing like her ask a question in that way?*

"The *loo...* is to your left as you walk in that opening. The arches, then to your left, right mate?"

"Thank you."

Not only was Mike startled by the way Shannon answered his request, but as he rounded the corner past the little archway door he had another surprise; the *loo* was a trench along the back wall, a tiled step ran from one end of the room to the other, then in front of that was a metal grate that crossed from where the tile ended and went to the wall, a span of about two feet. Water ran through one end and flushed out the other, it sounded like a small creek. There were no stalls for privacy and the loo could accommodate at least fifteen peeing men at the same time, if need be, thank God there was no need for it this afternoon.

Mike finished his business alone and decided he needed to check out the dunny. He'd heard in some foreign countries that most toilets were nothing more than a hole in the floor with running water to act as a flusher. You had to hover over the hole, do your business and wipe. He felt a rush of relief when he opened a stall and saw a good old fashioned toilet complete with the tank on the wall mounted high up with a chain to flush.

"Like a child lost in a zoo eh?"

Natalie had come in from waiting tables and was looking at her friend Shannon with the interest of a man studying an

51

insect under a microscope. She was wiping her hands on her apron, both of them staring at the archway where Mike disappeared a few minutes ago.

"He's so…"

"Look at his muscles; he's no bludger, that for certain…"

"I hadn't noticed." Shannon said matter of factly.

"*You fancy him*!" Natalie announced with a tone of revelation and pure accusation.

"I do not!"

"Yeah, explain why you've been drying that same chimney glass since he walked in here!"

With that, Natalie gave Shannon a bump on the hip with her own as she went back through the passage into the restaurant. Shannon smiled to herself, Natalie was right. The man was a bit of a sight, he was strong looking. She liked his big size; she figured six-three, two hundred plus pounds and very much in shape. His biceps protruded from his sleeves in a very formidable way, not that he intended them to be, but it was hard not to notice his build. And his demeanor was curious-he acted lost-but Shannon knew in a muggy situation he wouldn't have to follow anyone, he would lead naturally; she felt it in him, in *his* presence.

His hazel eyes revealed pain, something was troubling this bloke and she couldn't help but feel a little sorry for him. He was an older than her, probably thirty-five, but he made her tingle inside; there was something about this fella. Plus he was a little out of sorts-coming to Australia and not even wanting to drink any of the wonderful beers.

And she felt bad about her accusation this morning when she came in. When she saw him lying there as she began to clean, then he kicked the ashtray off of the table and she thought that maybe he was drunk, now that she knows he doesn't drink, she felt a little twinge guilt. Daydreaming, Shannon continued cleaning the same glass for the entire five minutes Mike was in the loo.

Mike was washing his hands in the sink when he noticed his goatee had darkened more. He checked his face for any blemishes and tested his breath for freshness by cupping his hand over his mouth and exhaling. He nodded at the mirror and headed back towards the bar area, his stomach rumbling for food, finally.

The bartender Shannon had finally returned the *very* clean and *very* dry glass to the shelf just as Mike walked back into the casino/bar area. She sized him up to Mathew Wright, her lover of four years, also from America. Mathew, as he liked to be called at all times, was about a half foot shorter; he was at least sixty pounds lighter, but the stranger from Nevada had brown hair and hazel eyes, no match for Matt's brilliant blue eyes and blond locks. Mathew, what a mule's clacker he turned out to be.

Shannon felt the urge within her to forget about Mathew, the sheet trawler. She was in love with him, for sure, but on his last trip here he became so… so… abusive. And possessive. Mathew made it clear that no man-friend or lover-would ever touch his precious Shannon, ever.

An argument ensued, they fought for an hour and the great record producer from Los Angeles puffed out his chest, struck Shannon on the cheek and she stormed out. It was over for them, Shannon decided then and there. But Mathew was a powerful young man with many contacts, spies and ears about Australia everywhere and he still harassed her. Weeks later even. She was in a precarious place, up a gum tree no doubt if she were to develop feelings for this bloke.

She spied on Mike as he made his way back to the stool; his attention was diverted to the eatery, so she was able to follow him all the way to the bar. He sat down and then Shannon turned away quickly as she saw his head look for her face in the mirror in front of her.

"So, how rude of me… My country and I forget to ask your name, after telling you mine; so sir you have me at a bit of a disadvantage." She said as she turned towards him.

"Oh…yes. Michael Greene. With three E-s" He smiled, "From America…"

"Hello to you Michael Greene with three E-s, and yes I know you are from America, I can tell by your accent…" She let off a little chuckle.

"Hello? Aren't you supposed to say *g'day*?" He started to relax a little more, she was a little impish, but he liked her.

"Do I look like Crocodile Dundee?"

"Oh… I…"

"I don't. Tourists come here thinking Australians all talk like *Crocodile Dundee*, but that isn't the case. He uses slang and inappropriate words at inappropriate times."

"How so?"

"Well, it one segment he calls his young reporter girlfriend a *Sheila*. That's slang, much like calling the wife of an American Indian man a *Squaw*. It's very rude to women here. How would you like it if I called you a *Bruce*?"

Mike thought of Monty Python again, but stifled the smile that was begging to come out.

"Oh, I guess I don't have a problem with that, but then again I'm not Australian. Anything else?"

"Well, he drinks a lot of the wrong draught. Most Australians drink whatever beer is brewed in the *territree* they live in… say for instance here *Toohey's* or *Castlemaine Four Ex* would be the drink of Brisbane native…"

"Uh huh." Mike had no clue what she was talking about, but it was so nice to hear her voice just leaving her pert little mouth.

"Now *'ol Mick*, he would be having a *Victoria Bitter*."

"I see." Mike's mouth was starting to water with all the talk of beer, his mind was racing, he needed to change the subject, but the young bartender kept on.

"Would you like to try any of these I mentioned?" Her smile was warm now; she was inviting him into her space as she leaned over the bar and pointed to the tap masts.

"No...Thank you, I don't drink."

"Oh yes sorry. You said that, but I'm still in a quandary why you're in a pub?" Shannon paused for moment, and then her face lit up a little. "How long?"

"Two and a half months." He swallowed; the thought of having a beer was still haunting him even more now. "I guess I should be having lunch about now."

"Of course Michael Greene. Just wait right here..." Shannon walked off to her right-Mike's left and went around the bar to where it opened up into the restaurant. She leaned over the counter and talked to Natalie for a moment and came back. "I have you a seat right now, but they are still serving breakfast buffet until one-thirty."

"That's okay, anything will do...I'm a little hungry."

"Just around the corner Michael Greene and Miss Natalie will escort you to your table... *g'day*." She smiled and watched him walk off around the patron side of the bar to the restaurant and Natalie led him off with a nod. Shannon smiled to herself as he vanished from her sight, *interesting and a nice bloke*.

Mike ordered another Coke from Natalie as she handed him his plate, he thanked her and walked to the buffet line to gather breakfast. The buffet was aligned with what he was used to; ham, eggs-both scrambled and fried-the largest slices of bacon he had ever seen, and *pork & beans*. Mike wrinkled his brow as he thought about having beans for breakfast, he never thought of it before, but it seemed reasonable, so he spooned a modest helping to his plate, adding four slices of the giant bacon, one slice of ham, and a ladle full of scrambled eggs.

He had been sitting at his table for fifteen minutes now, twirling his fork in his pork and beans staring out the window towards the street. For a while he marveled at the traffic, passing on the wrong side, people sitting in the wrong side of the car. He was thinking about how he'd come to this place and why. But now he felt a little easier inside, he was making a friend, and she was talking to him. A good sign.

Eventually the one thing that occupied his mind for the rest of the uneaten meal was Shannon. She was captivating with her smooth accent, quick wit and somewhat nefarious vocabulary. She was young and full of eager freelance energy, she had a smile that warmed him from the toes up and a friendly sort of a way about how she moved her petite and-from what Mike could tell from her arms-muscular body. He had been smitten slightly by her, a hard thing to do since his last chance encounter ended so badly.

Mike ate more than half of the meal he placed on his plate and felt guilty about wasting the rest, but he felt sick to his stomach-he knew it wasn't the meal-it was the thought of Rika shadowing his mind; *how do I think I even have a chance?*

He shook off the vision of the young lady he barely knew months ago, stood from the table and headed for the little gift shop at the corner of the lobby. He didn't really need anything, but it was also a bypass to the bar/casino and his mood had turned sour enough not to want to spoil any time with Shannon; he would get something for his stomach and then head to his room for the rest of the day-maybe there was a good TV show on…

Shannon watched Mike fill his plate, and then as she made successive passes to the end of the bar and back, watched him sit there in silence and deep thought. She wondered what was going through his mind; he was a troubled man obviously and had recently quit drinking. A hard step for some blokes, she knew from experience barmaiding for the last seven years. She watched as Michael Greene left his half eaten breakfast on the table and headed out through the sally-way and into the trinket and toiletries shop. His expression revealed a sad man, troubled about something that burned his heart as he walked; the look of a desperate pain on his cute face. She felt moved.

Mike reached for the bromo-seltzer and walked back towards the cashier when he saw the kind of cigarettes that Steven Darling had shared with him on the flight in. They had a punch of nicotine and maybe that would help him sleep, so he asked for a pack from the small blond clerk who as dressed in the hotel attire. As he was fidgeting with his wallet and the Australian notes, the door behind him opened.

"G'day Shannon!" The clerk beamed as she made change for Mike.

"G'day." The recognizable voice made Mike's chest thump.

"Hello Michael Greene; funny seeing you here, your tummy in a bit of disrepair?"

Mike looked up from the counter as his heart pounded and slowly turned towards the voice.

"Hum? Oh yes, it's not the food though, I just have had some stomach problems lately, this'll do."

"Very good then."

"You come here often?" He said with a smile.

"Just in for a pack of chewing gum…" She held up a pack of cinnamon gum.

"Oh."

"And you've taken up smoking…" Shannon smiled and sighed at the same time as she spoke, saddened as she stared at the pack of smokes in Mike's hand.

"Well, they help me sleep sometimes, and I don't smoke all the time." Once again he was on defense.

"They are bad for you still…" She lectured.

Mike looked at the pack in his hand and put it in his pocket, then thanked the young clerk. "I guess I'll be going to my room now, got to lay down a little while."

"You… uh… coming through tomorrow? I mean to the lounge?" Her faced blushed a little.

"Will you be working?" Mike made it sound flirty, intentionally.

"Of course, eleven to nine."

"Weird hours…"

"Yeah, but it's not my hotel."

"Of course. Sure, I'll be happy to see you again tomorrow." Mike's face was warm from blood rushing up to it. He didn't want to sound lonely, but his tone gave him away.

Shannon watched Mike walk back towards the lift hall and disappear around the corner. She heard the stale *ding* of the call button and the lift operator bringing the cage down.

"He's a mighty *chipper* bloke…" The clerk offered sarcastically.

"Yes, he is that, isn't he…?" And Shannon returned to work, leaving the gum on the counter.

CHAPTER THREE

DREAMS

At times during the last few months the dreams were hard to tell from reality, all the right people were in the right places, the faces matched the situations and the horrors were gut wrenching. Usually for the first ten or fifteen minutes Mike just tossed and turned and sweated a little. Then his face would contort, and his body would writhe, shake, he would finally wake-soaked through to the sheets-even the pillow would not escape unscathed by the torment. Tonight was no different, the dreams came, the troubled images began, and he woke by falling out of bed-not common-but it happened once in a while also.

This one was a bad one. It was *her*. She was dying, he was trying to help. But, then he… he killed her.

"What's all this then?" Shannon demanded as she entered the pub to start her shift.

Tommy the doorman and Natalie were standing in the dark room, their glare to a couch in the farthest corner. On the couch was Mike, in a bathrobe from the hotel and sleeping as if her were dead, his legs on the table in front of him. A bottle of scotch sat next to his feet.

"Don't know Shannon. Found him this way when we saw the door was forced, a bit ago."

"Is he alright?" Natalie demanded as Shannon knelt down beside Mike and felt his forehead.

Shannon found a determined look and shook Mike slowly. "Michael, wake up!"

Mike stirred slowly, then he jolted when he realized where he was and what he was doing.

Shannon took a stern voice, "Did you expect to lose your sobriety on my watch, in my pub!"

"No! I had a bad dream, sometimes I sleepwalk when I dream."

"I'll be happy to watch over you in your slumber Mr. Greene, if you wish!" Natalie Cheerfully offered from a few feet behind Shannon.

Shannon turned and glowered in her direction, "Okay Missy, I should think the *woman in drought act* should be saved for another time!" She turned back to Mike, "Sorry, she's not usually to crack onto someone so fast..." She turned to Tommy and Natalie, "Alright, curtains down, everyone to work please!"

Tommy nodded and walked out the door towards his little glass cubicle out front, Natalie gave Mike a motherly look-motherly with a tinge of lust-and padded off towards the cantina.

"What is it? What can bother you so much?" Shannon asked quietly.

"My dreams, they're like nothing I've ever experienced before. They're getting worse, day by day-or night I should say. It's this being sober thing, it's like... like being in a graveyard at night. You wander amongst the headstones, you can feel the cold grip of death on your arms, trying to drag you down to the earth."

Shannon brushed a bead of sweat from Mike's brow, he cringed in anticipation of the feeling he knew would come-anxiousness, a tad bit of lust for Shannon's warm touch, her fingers were soft and gentle as she swiped the drop away.

"I'm sorry Michael."

"Sometimes I wonder if I'll wake up at all, wake up to reality or face my dreams like they are the last thing I'll ever see. It's like loneliness and claustrophobia all in one, one day, I'm afraid I won't wake up from the nightmare. I'll be lost, forever."

"Very dramatic..." Shannon used every ounce of compassion she could in her tone, she didn't' want to sound condescending.

"I feel cheated, like everything keeps happening to me and I don't deserve it…"

"Now, that sounds very selfish. I've gotten to know a bit of you, you don't seem so selfish."

Mike raised his eyes to hers, the intensity of his sorrowful look burned hotly at Shannon's insides; she was falling into this man's trance.

"Come, let's get you back to your room before someone sees you and thinks we have a new dress code…" Shannon said with frustration as she helped Mike to his feet.

As they got off the lift, Shannon shot a glance of heat towards the operator, who was smirking at Mike's condition. He quickly focused his attention to the roof of the car, did his job and got them to the second floor. The operator opened the gates and Shannon helped Mike to his door. A moment passed, she was spinning inside, her abdomen felt like a washer on the extract setting, her feet were forced forward by sheer will. He was weakened by his fear of sleep; she was the same by her need to have someone love her for no reason other than love. Not the heated passion of sex that seemed to drive Mathew, the little man that never took her out anymore. Not to the picture shows or a stage play. Not to a day on the beach, to laugh and play on the sand. Mathew wanted to hit the soft covers of her bed and stay till he had to return to America. Shannon wanted someone who'd take her to the gardens or the opera or even... share her dream.

A dream that she'd never shared with anyone before, not even Mathew, and she would probably never share with anyone ever anyways. It was pure fantasy.

It was ten thirty in the morning Australian time and a full day later when Mike emerged from the lift. He headed for the restaurant and was led to a table by the window and given his plate.

Natalie smiled at him even friendlier than she did yesterday, he noticed. She brought him a Coke without even asking him and poured it into a chimney glass, just as Shannon did.

"G'day Michael Greene." She said softly.

"Mike, please. Call me Mike."

"Mike, then."

Mike rose and filled his plate-promising himself that he would eat the whole meal today-the menu hadn't changed for breakfast, so he didn't change his selections either. He ate and thought of Shannon, her little body floating around the bar cleaning glasses and dumping ashtrays. He looked out the window trying to catch a glimpse of her-perhaps on her way in; maybe he would get to see what kind of car she drove.

He never saw her come in, but at eleven o'clock he could hear her familiar voice in the bar, talking to a customer Mike hadn't seen coming in, either. He finished off his plate and sat for a few minutes, making sure his meal would not object to its new surroundings; it didn't. In fact, Mike felt a whole world better today; he thought it was because he got a chance to talk to Shannon again...

"G'day Michael Greene!" Shannon's voice boomed over the loud seventies music playing from an antique Wurlitzer Jukebox in the corner.

"Good morning young lady." His smile almost hurt his face, grinning from just the excitement of being in her presence.

"The usual, mate?"

"Please, if you will." Mike set two, two dollar coins on the bar and watched the enchanting lady prepare his Coke with flair.

"Michael, this is Joey... How do you say your last name again, mate?" She began after the chimney glass was filled to the rim; she never took her eyes off the glass as she was talking.

"Bottano." Mike noticed a heavy New York accent.

"Bottano..."Shannon repeated for Mike. "He's from your America. Brooklyn, right Mr. Bottano?"

"Ya betcha. How are you *mate*?" It sounded American-like, not like '*might*' when an Australian pronounced it. He offered a huge hand over.

"Quite well..." Mike answered.

"Yeah, I and my little bride are here for our sorta honeymoon ya know. Her father's a businessman and he brought us here for the week. I love dis place."

Mike looked at Shannon who was trying to hide a smirk on her face, then looked at Joey. "Really, Honeymoon? Where's the lucky woman?" Mike was fighting back a giggle himself.

"Upstairs, ya know female things..."

"Oh. Of course." Shannon tipped her head.

Joey then turned his attention back to her; Shannon was wiping the bar off in front of Mike. "So, you know the area pretty good huh?"

"A bit."

"Where can we have a good old fashioned blow out?"

"Pardon?"

"Party, ya know. Were lookin' for a place to burn some calories to music and drop a couple dozen drinks..."

"I have no knowledge of a place like that..." She wanted to say: *disreputable place like that*, but she held her tongue.

"Yeah..." Joey sounded disappointed.

He turned a quick eye to Mike, "Hey Mikie, how 'bout a boilermaker?"

"No thank you..." Mike was tempted, but he would be strong.

"C'mon. For a fellow American? Honey, set us a up a couple of boilermakers..." Joey winked at Shannon, which made Mike a little uncomfortable with jealousy.

"A what?"

"Boilermaker, a shot of whiskey and a beer." Mike replied, looking at Shannon with sympathetic eyes.

"Right up." She spoke to Joey.

"You havin' one too *Mikie*?"

"Mr. Greene had too much last night, besides he's not much of a drinker." Shannon informed Joey; who looked at Mike, who smiled shrewdly.

Mike began to warm up on her tone, it upset him a little she was defending him from this brute. Joey was a big man, an obvious workout freak; Mike could feel it in his grip. His dark hair gave away his lineage, the typical Italian New Yorker, he had dark brown eyes, a broken nose-the tip sat just a hair off to the right-and a chiseled chin, which at one time or another taken a severe blow, Mike was sure. He was a half foot shorter than Mike but what he lacked in height he made up for in girth around the shoulders, Joey could probably lift a Volkswagen by himself.

Shannon placed the pint glass on the bar and the shot glass next to it. "Four dollars fifty, thanks." Joey paid and slipped a dollar note across the bar to the tip position. Shannon picked it up and stuffed it in her apron, "Thanks, mate." Mike rolled his eyes at her, and she just smiled.

She then leaned over the counter at him. She spoke in a soft whisper-like voice, but made it loud enough for Joey to overhear; Mike could smell her breath, it warm and he detected a hint of cinnamon, it made his sides tingle and he was getting aroused-slightly-by it.

"So, about last night, ready for another one?" Shannon gave him a little wink, in plain view of Joey, who was looking straight ahead, drinking out of the side of his mouth and leering sideways, hoping to get it all in.

It took a second for Mike to follow along, but he joined the ruse, using his best acting skills.

"Of course. I had a wonderful time, what's up for tonight?"

He was going to wink back but instead Shannon leaned forward and kissed him on the ear.

Michael nearly fainted as the blood rushed to head, his face reddened, his pulse raced, he felt light headed. He was *not* expecting that! He could smell her faint perfume, very sweet and tantalizing; this was going to be hard to overcome…

"Maybe we'll just let the day lead us, eh?" Shannon teased back.

Joey poured the shot of whiskey down his throat, not saying a word, but never taking his eyes off the couple. His jovial face had fallen a few inches since the conversation between Mike and Shannon began, he looked a little jealous.

"Yeah, well I wish you would spend more time with me though. I could get us a tour of the Harbour or something-you know-one of those little cozy blanket and tea rides…" Joey's eyes went from Mike to Shannon and back again.

"Of course I will lover. Let's make plans for that outing in the 'morrow though, okay?" Shannon's eyes shot Mike a look warning; Mike just smiled back at her.

"Your right honey. I'm sorry, it was me neglecting you, I promise to spend every waking hour with you next week."

"You so thoughtful lover…" She leaned over and kissed him on the cheek this time, eliciting a different physical response in Mike, but it was still pleasurable to feel her soft lips on him. *What the Hell? You're killing me!* Mike's heart pled. She directed her next smooch to his top lip, just under his nose. The skin above her top lip was moist with a hint of sweat and there was a redolence of the salty musk. Mike felt as if his knees were giving out, he was going to faint. He felt Shannon in both heat from her body and the air around her.

The acting was horrible, but it was having an effect on Joey.

At the word '*lover*' Joey got up from the bar and walked to the casino area, pretending to check out the poker machines. He kept shooting glances at Mike And Shannon from time to time, and a few minutes later a dark skinned, brown haired, brown eyed woman walked from the lift hallway into the bar area.

"Joey! Hey! '*Dare* you are!" The woman beamed with a heavy Brooklyn accent. She was taller than Joey almost, maybe just by a few inches, dark flowing hair with a wave and feather look. Her face was done bright with lipstick and rouge. Her brown eyes weren't mean but they had an intensity of being suspicious and cold. Joey turned, smiled and grabbed the young woman by the arm and walked outside with her, looking back one more time towards Shannon and Mike, who both were red from holding back laughter. After Joey walked out with his bride, they broke loose.

"Thank you so much Michael. I was in dire need of a bit of rescue from him. For a recently married man he sure was a bit randy with me."

"So I see." Mike could still feel the warmth around the place Shannon kissed him on the ear. He rubbed it softly with a shaky finger. He tried hard in his mind to recreate the essence of the kiss to his top lip.

"I'm sorry if I put you on the spot, but I needed an out and he seemed intimidated by you."

"I didn't think so; he could have eaten me for lunch."

"Huh?" Shannon's eyes narrowed.

"Never mind." Mike thought for a second about saying *Thanks for the kiss, you made my week…* but the moment wasn't right. Shannon was acting, as was he, so the point was mute. They chatted for another hour, and then Mike retired to his room, needing a nap, since he still wasn't sleeping very well.

Shannon watched him walk to the lift just like and wanted badly to walk him up like yesterday, but she really liked Michael, he seemed so gracious about everything. Any other bloke would have gushed at her little peck on his ear, he took it stride; maybe he didn't like her as much as she did him. If things got out of hand, she'd have another Mathew on her mind. Only this one she wanted so very badly…

Mike tried to fall asleep to a British TV show, he didn't know what it was called but he was a little shocked that prime time British television allowed nudity. He shook his head and leaned back on his pillow, a few hours later the dreams started, again.

Another nightmare left Mike feeling insecure, he had awakened the next morning with red puffy eyes and swollen cheeks-he had been crying all night-so he didn't venture out of his room till well after noon.

He finally made his way down to the restaurant after a long hot shower, Shannon was nowhere to be seen, but he spied Natalie in the front and she waved him frantically. She had a smile and a seat for him. Not long after he was seated she came over with a pot of coffee and kept staring towards the pub side of the place. Mike finally asked.

"What's wrong?"

"It's just that… that… there's a young bloke in the pub and he's a bit pissed, he's been making passes at Shannon and I think she's flustered."

Mike looked over her shoulder and stood up. He patted Natalie on the shoulder as he passed her and entered into the bar area through the Dutch doors. He saw only one customer, a young scrawny kid who was propped up against the bar nursing a beer, swaying a little to the left and right. He was wearing dungarees, a polo shirt that was too small and new tennis shoes. His arms were tattooed, but only just below the sleeve of his shirt. He was not very tall, nor very short; about five nine or ten, the height as Shannon the bartender. He had a very short haircut and it was black, his eyes were the same color. Like chunks of coal lodged into the center of a headlight.

Mike walked by, not taking his eyes off of him.

"Hey, how are ya?" The kid nattered to him, obviously very drunk, very young and Mike pegged him for a Navy sailor.

"How are *you*?" Mike asked back.

He had nothing against the Navy boys going out and getting blasted, plus doing the other things Mike knew the kid was in the vicinity of Kings Cross for. He felt the kids deserved it-they were the tip of the sword-always on the edge of war, ready to fight as they spent several lonely weeks at sea. That worked hard at a young man-this kid was no more than twenty-if that.

"Buy you a drink?" The boy was very drunk, but managed to get the words out. "You sound American…"

"I am. From Nevada, name's Mike Greene."

"Fred *Haa*…Hawkins." The boy looked ready to fall off his stool. "I got me a room here in this place and I'm gonna crash in a while, soon as I get this hot bartender to go with me…"

Mike felt his face flush, he looked around the casino area for Shannon, and then he looked around the corner towards the restaurant, no sign of her. He was jealous, he knew this kid was younger and probably had a better shot at Shannon, if he were sober, but the kid was off the deep end.

"She almost was ready for… She went that way…" The kid tried to point behind them, but he slipped off the stool and Mike grabbed him by the shoulder with one hand to steady him.

"Easy, stud."

Just as the words left Mike's mouth he caught site of Shannon leaving the women's restroom-he had no idea what they called that here-her eyes were a little red, anger flared inside Mike's stomach. She walked furiously past Mike and patted him on the shoulder as she went by.

"What's wrong?" He asked as he looked at the sailor.

Shannon nodded at the kid, then softy whispered; "Nothing, he was a bit forward… and *touchy*."

The kid's head was swaying back and forth and he smiled at her accusation.

Mike hadn't been in Sydney very long, but he knew *touchy* meant the kid was free with his hands. Mike fought off the urge to belt the kid out of the chair into the casino area, but held back, knowing he had at least eighteen years on the kid. He looked at Shannon and then returned his gaze to the drunken sailor.

"You say you got a room here my friend?" Mike put on his policeman voice.

"Sure do, ready willing and able…" The kid was trying to wink at Shannon.

"Why don't' you go up and have a nap, you're a little drunk."

"*NO* goddamned way man!"

Mike leaned closer to the kid. "Please don't use that kind of language in front of the lady, my friend."

"Sorry, but I'm gonna get *laid* tonight and she already said she would take me to my room, I saw her first…"

Mike glanced up at Shannon, she shook her head no, Mike wasn't looking for her response, and he knew she would have nothing to do with this drunken punk. He was checking to see how much Shannon could see of his hand on the kid's shoulder. Her view was blocked, mostly. Mike used his training and squeezed the proper place-he used this hold on hundreds of drunks at the casinos-and he knew it would work here too. The kid moved a little, shuffling his butt on the stool. Mike tightened his grip more, this time adding his index finger to the mylohoid muscle under the kid's jaw and added more pressure. This worked on drunken Indians, and no one was harder to control when drunk than a three hundred pound Indian…

The kid sat upright as the pain shot through his neck and head. Mike leaned close to him, "I think you should go upstairs, get a little rest and we can chat about the little lady later…" Mike lowered his voice so Shannon couldn't hear him, "I'm not asking now; I can escort you-if need be partner…"

The kids shook his head no and rose-cautiously as Mike released his grip on the kid's neck and shoulder. The young sailor turned and glared at Mike and then his shoulders slumped, he looked at Shannon and nodded an apology and went for the lift hall.

"*Saw… sorry… maha… ma'am.*"

Shannon let out a deep breath, turned and resumed her duties behind the bar; not saying a word to Mike-not just yet-she was trying to compose herself. Her insides were at a major conflict now, she tried to imagine Mathew trying to subdue the young man, defending Shannon's honor as it were, she couldn't see him doing it-but Michael Greene managed it without bloodshed or the authorities having to be called. Shannon didn't even know why she felt so put off by the little sailor, he was only a child, a pissed young man who had been out to sea for a long time-he just wanted companionship-she had seen this type of behavior before, she had endured the sailor's type of Neanderthal advances, *what was different this time? Why did she react so poorly to the young man's advances? She had been accosted in worse ways when a Navy ship was in the Harbour. Curious…did Michael Greene have something to do with it?*

Michael had said nothing more about the incident, and Shannon tried to put it out of her mind also. He smiled at her and she smiled back, her lips approved of his interference and she winked as he headed back into the eatery. He sat back down at the same seat and Natalie rushed over to serve him. Shannon felt a pang of jealousy as she watched Michael and Natalie joking and chatting each other up.

After an hour Mike stood and thanked Natalie for her service, she gave him a small hug and he dropped some notes on the table and winked at her as he strolled between the restaurant and the pub. Mike sat down in his usual seat; Shannon popped the top on a Coke and poured it over ice in a chimney glass. She began her usual dance of chores around him and they talked, Mike using the spinning bar seat to his advantage. As Shannon moved about the bar, he followed her by pushing the ring on the stool with his foot, turning his body like a camera on a gimbal.

Shannon kept the conversation light, Mike continued the same path. He found out that she was a student at the university here and was on break, that she was from another place called Cairns and she worked five days a week.

Shannon learned that Mike had a father in Idaho and he was an ex-machinist who was hurt on the job and had to retire. When Shannon asked Mike what he did for a living Mike dodged the question by getting up from the bar and walking to the loo, his voice trailing a false answer as he went. Shannon shook her head; she'd ask him again sometime.

They were both obviously trying to avoid the inevitable after the small talk. Small talk could lead to questions about one another, intimate questions, then the conversation would turn to love lives, then to each other's availability. They sat and chatted about nearly nothing, Shannon giving him a vocal tour of Australia for the next five hours, Mike took one break for dinner-which he ate most of-and then returned to find the bar had filled with patrons, and with it being so crowded Natalie had come from the restaurant to assist Shannon.

The onslaught of merrymakers had come suddenly, but some nights like this were expected, Shannon thought. After all the football game was on-Australian rules of course-and the hotel lounge had one of the few large screen televisions in the area, so the place was flocked on occasion with roughian footballer fans. Shannon made sure her male drinkers were happy-they would always separate themselves from the women-a tradition Shannon hated the most about drinking with the blokes; they would keep to themselves and the women were to do likewise away from the men, during public outings. The men would sit and tell tales of their mastery of their world between whistles during the game, then *shout*-an Australian term for buying another round-at breaks in the action. Every man at the table had a shout, and everyone was sure to comply.

After calming the herd with another shout of fresh beer and whiskey, Shannon noticed Michael wasn't sitting in his usual place any longer. She turned and found Michael sitting at a table in the waiting area-the room between the casino and the pub near the doors to the lobby-he had a focused look of sadness about him as he peeled the bar napkin to pieces, when he looked up towards Shannon he smiled, but it was an empty smile. She called out to Natalie, who looked at her and then at Mike and then nodded back to Shannon, who mouthed the words '*Thank You*' and she left the bar to sit down next to him.

She sighed and he sighed back, sort of a contest. He smiled at her again and started to push the seat back to get up.

"Why are you here Michael Greene?" She asked softly. He paused and remained sitting.

"I wanted to make room for your paying guests, besides my butt is hurting from that stupid stool…"

"*No*. Why are you in Sydney? Why are you in Australia in the first place?"

Her look turned sad, caring and investigative. She was studying his face noting there was something wrong with him right now. She was feeling something for this fella, he was strong and he had a quality of a man missing here in this place; friendly, chivalrous, and no drongo pickup lines…

"I'm on vacation." He said matter of factly.

"Holiday is it? Do you enjoy sitting in a hotel lobby all day or at least for three or four hours, then retire to your room for a few hours sleep? You could have done that anywhere in America for much less money. Why are you here?" She repeated the question, hoping this time Michael would think his answer out more, and enlighten her.

"I don't know. I thought things would be different here, I expected…"

"What? *Crocodile Dundee* again?" She gave him a comforting smile.

"No, but it would be nice to see him." Mike's smile faded and he looked down. "I've just had a real bad time back home, a bad experience and a friend of mine-my boss-suggested this place, he's been here before with his wife, he loved it and said I would too."

"Why don't you *love* it?"

"I guess things just don't jump out at you, tours bore me and tour guides the same. I was hoping everything was within walking distance or even a bus ride away, but then again, all the construction and the streets, they seem the same as in America, it's like nothing stands out too much."

"Well, you have to leave the hotel once in a while. I think I did see you yesterday wandering out front, but did you leave the block?"

"I walked to the little market on the corner."

"You must have traveled about three hundred yards…How adventurous of you." She let a sarcastic smile off in his direction.

"Well, I did almost get hit by a car. Look *right* first not left…" He smiled sheepishly back.

"*Very* insightful."

"Yeah, a cop explained it to me."

"You met a policeman?"

"Well, he's the one who grabbed my arm just before I stepped off the curb and in front of a bus. Boy, those bus drivers don't slow much, I thought I was at a bus stop, the bench and sign indicated so."

"You were, then." She gave him a look of sympathy, culture shock can be a dangerous flow sometimes, and he was in up to his elbows. "There's a secret to stopping a bus here…"

Shannon regarded Michael for a moment, he looked so lonely right now, not alive and confident, like just after she pecked him on the cheek yesterday when he was full of life. "What kind of bad experience?"

"What?" Mike was watching the crowd.

"You said you had a bad experience back home…"

"Oh, someone I liked, well…" The hesitation revealed his pain over it, "She died."

"Oh how dreadful, my apologies for bringing it up."

"No, that's okay. It was a couple of months ago."

Shannon put her hand on his shoulder and gave him a firm squeeze, "Would you mind talking about it?"

"Not today, really." He sank deeper into a depressed looking state. "I think I should go lay down for a while, I'm not getting much sleep lately. Bad dreams…"

Shannon waited for the perfect time; she had been contemplating the plan for a day now, seeing how much Michael hardly left the building, let alone his room. He was lonely and she knew she could brighten both their days with her idea. Now was a good time as any, as Michael rose to his feet and began to turn away.

"Michael Greene?" She raised her voice above the football fans.

He turned and looked back at her; Mike had realized he overplayed his depression a little so he smiled best he could to alleviate her concern as much as possible. "Shannon Hunter?"

"Sit down Michael; I have a proposition for you." He complied, Shannon went on; "I know this wonderful tour guide, knows the whole area of Sydney and more. The guide could take you from here tomorrow morning, say eleven a.m., out front just where Tommy stands…" She pointed to the doorman outside, "You could get a tour of The Rocks, The Gardens, Bondi Beach, even the Opera House and Harbour Bridge. Would you like that?"

"I… can't afford a large tour package right…"

"Be quiet and listen. It could be arranged to be done for free, although there are some rules you would have to recognize and follow without question."

"I don't know, is this guy reliable? I mean I'm not going to get left somewhere and expected to meet up with him somewhere else?"

"What kind of horrible excursions have you had before?"

"Well there was this one time, in San Francisco…" His smile belied interest.

"Never mind that, just be down here in front at eleven. Fresh, clean, fed, and bring a pack. You do have a pack don't you?"

"A backpack?"

"That will do, bring a canteen of water and wear good hiking shoes. Shorts are recommended, as is a light smart shirt.

You will also need a jacket and a hat." She rose to her feet, having to return to work behind the bar. "Any questions?"

"I… what does this guy look like, will he know me?"

"You do stand away from the crowd, the guide will know you. Please be prompt."

"Okay. I'll see you afterwards okay?" He turned and headed away. "Tell him I think tours are boring okay?" He disappeared into the lift hall.

Shannon watched him go. She was pushing her luck this time for sure, Mathew would not tolerate her talking to man alone in the pub, let alone arrange for a tour for the American. But that was over, if she had a way, she'd have Michael Greene explain it to her former lover. She sighed. *No, that'd end very badly for Mathew*.

There would be no bad dreams; Mike wondered why-maybe it was the fear of what lay ahead of him tomorrow. He hated trying to be nice to new people and most tour guides he knew were real stuck ups. His experience in The Bay Area left him feeling apprehensive about any tours, the end result of that last one was a fairly good one and he proposed to his future wife/ex-wife there. He was happy when they met, she was beautiful that night and the city had a charming romantic feeling about it.

He dozed in and out; from time to time he'd switch on the TV and watch a few minutes of programming and then fall asleep again. At four a.m. he woke to a British version of '*Where are they now?*', a show dedicated in finding celebrities that were popular in the eighties and seemed to have disappeared from the planet. He was dozing in and out of the program when a familiar tune caught his ears. His eyes flashed open to the screen; the music was from the movie '*The Man from Snowy River*'. He loved that movie; he'd taken his son to see it at the buck theater. They were profiling the lead actors, Tom Burlinson and Sigrid Thornton. He thought about his ex again. He thought about his son.

It was a shame they couldn't make things work out better.

Mike drifted off to sleep with the image of the City by the Bay blurring in and out. Although it wasn't a nightmare, he did dream of his ex favorably, they were laughing and running along the beach at Lover's Cove. The warm fall sands, the sky lightly misted with the breaking fog, the sounds of the waves crashing along the beach. These were the good dreams, Mike had few and far between anymore-since Rika had died, since the other girl died too…

CHAPTER FOUR
TOURING

Mike Greene awoke just after nine in the morning, he was finally getting used to the sixteen hour time change. He felt better this morning too, better than he had been feeling the last several weeks-he thought. He showered and dressed himself as instructed by the lovely Shannon, he didn't want the guide friend of hers to tell her he didn't comply-hiking shorts, a nice polo shirt, hiking boots, a jacket into his back pack and a…

Mike realized he didn't have a canteen. *Why would she think I have a canteen in my luggage?* His mind began to race, *where can I get a canteen in less than an hour and a half, I have no clue where…* Mike resigned himself to having Shannon receive a failure notice on behalf of the water bottle. *Water bottle? I saw bottled water in the gift shop…* He smiled; he would pick a couple up on the way out, after breakfast.

Mike ate and checked his watch; it was ten fifty-five; five minutes to go. If he timed it just right, he could probably say good morning to Shannon as he was on his way out-he'd really like to-he was feeling so much more comfortable here because of her.

Mike walked into the little trinket shop and found the water bottles, he also bought a pack of smokes and some chewing gum; cinnamon flavored. He went back towards the bar to look for Shannon, but she hadn't appeared yet; he saw the young sailor coming out of the lift hall and nodded in the boy's direction with a smile. The kid stopped and furled his brow like he didn't know who Mike was.

He waited for a few minutes more and Tommy came in to pour himself a cup of coffee. He smiled at Mike as he poured and even poured a go-cup for Mike.

"Have you seen Shannon, Tommy?" Mike asked.

"No mate, not yet. But you're gonna be late for your tour then…"

He pointed with his coffee cup towards the front of the hotel. Mike looked at his watch. 11:05. Mike's eyes went wide and he stumbled to his feet grabbed his pack and headed out the glass doors, Tommy rushing behind him holding them open for him. Mike reached the sidewalk and the sun hit him square in the eyes. He closed them and inhaled a beautiful new day in the air. A day of adventure, maybe. He heard a shuffling on the street in front of the sidewalk and a familiar voice called out to him, sternly.

"Are you impunctual for every event Michael Greene?" The woman's voice called from the street. Mike looked down from his relaxing breath and his heart paused.

Leaning against an old yellow and beat up Mazda pickup was a ravishing beauty; she was wearing cut-off jeans, with the little white cotton strings dangling to mid-thigh. Underneath she wore a bikini bottom, evident by the strings that protruded from each side; a bikini top, pink and light blue underneath a white tank top, and of course hiking boots. Her hair was pulled to a ponytail and fed out the back hole of a ball cap. She had an impatient look on her face, like she was late for a wedding, and did not even smile at Mike at all.

"You're the guide, Shannon Hunter?" He was excited and a little over-stimulated at her feminine casual dress, he had never seen her out of her black and white work clothes. He especially like how her pony-tail flickered in the sunlight; the gold flashing white and honey as it shivered in the slight breeze, there was an air of seriousness about her, she didn't have her relaxing smile, and her eyes were darker today than he had seen them before.

"Maybe-in about two minutes I was going to be just Shannon Hunter, the barmaid again. You cut it very close." Her expression didn't change.

Mike smiled widely at her, never taking his eyes of her as he walked past and placed his pack in the back of the truck.

The bed was fairly clean, a few leaves and an empty Fosters box. A small coil of rope and a spare tire.

"This is our tour bus?" He asked with an obvious air of excitement.

"It is *my truck*, please mind the paint." She flashed a quick sarcastic smile, then returned to her annoyed look.

"Have a splendid afternoon you two…" The doorman called, with a sly smile on his face. He returned to his booth, shaking his head.

Mike turned to thank him and added, "Are all your tour guides this cranky so early in the morning?"

Tommy, saluted him, smiled and took his seat in his glass cubicle. Mike slipped into the left side of the truck and waited for Shannon, who was just a second behind, climbing into the right hand driver seat of the mini-pickup.

"Where to?" Mike chimed with delight.

Shannon turned her head towards him, cautiously and her stare slowed Mike's pacing heart a little. There was a moment of static in the air Mike smiled sheepishly in anticipation. He knew that there was a ruse going on, he could no more see this young lovely woman being a curmudgeon as he could see himself being a cheerleader.

"First the rules, Mr. Greene. One; I am a tour guide, not a recreational area. Keep your hands to yourself. Two; I am spoken for, so no quips about our date… this is a tour for your pleasure, I have better things to do on my day off." Her voice never changed tone, "Third; and most important; I am not a trinket shop or a souvenir booth. You don't get to take me home, ask me out, touch the merchandise or buy me. Are we in clear air here?"

"Absolutely. One question…"

"Yes, Michael Greene?"

"Why didn't you tell me it was going to be you giving me the tour today?"

"Two reasons, first off I didn't want you to be over-eager about today and secondly, I couldn't find anyone else to take my place, I tried."

Her calm face turned towards the mirror on Mike's side of the truck and Shannon pulled into traffic, rapidly. She managed to dodge a half dozen cars on the way out to the freeway, Mike was not amused at her driving skills, he would have made the City of Lockwood a fortune in citations off her, just to the expressway. Even though her driving resembled the movements of an alcoholic during a sneezing fit, Shannon was able to maneuver cleverly through the traffic and Mike started to become impressed, he also became aware he was *very* smart in not renting a car.

Studying traffic signs as they went, Mike tried to establish their position constantly, just in case he wished to venture around this way again on his own. First they passed through Kings Cross and Shannon gave a brief narrative:

"Kings Cross is infamous throughout the Navies of the world and even a few tourists for its scrubby atmosphere. Be very wary of the *spuikers*- s p u i k e r s..." Mike smiled as she spelled out the word for him, "They can be treacherous and lift your pockets easily. Next are the young ladies that seem to like the company of men-at any age-as long as they are short on queries and long on dollar notes." She nodded out the window of a couple of women walking from a small crib to another, they weren't very dangerous looking. "You wouldn't want to end up a gum tree here. Any questions?"

"Yes... what *is* a spuiker?" He smiled at her, she ignored his gaze.

"A spuiker is a very dastardly sort of person, they play mesmerizing card games in front of you, lure you to play the same game for a bet, then you lose."

"Like a three card Monty."

"Yes, whatever." Shannon pretended not to know the name.

She navigated the truck off Roslyn Street towards the New South Head Road/Eastbound 76 and followed it to Woolloomooloo. Mike was trying the name in his head several times before he tried to pronounce it. He knew he'd make a fool of himself in Hawai'i, but at least here they used more vowels.

"*Woolomoo*?" Mike tried, reading the sign.

"Please don't try to speak Aboriginal." She rolled her eyes at him and whispered just loud enough for Mike to hear her, "*American tourists…*"

"Where are we headed Mrs. Hunter?" Mike acted the part of tourist now, if was a game she wanted, he would be able to play along.

"*Miss*, if you please Mr. Greene. We are headed to The Rocks."

"I've seen *rocks…*"

"These Rocks are the foundation for Sydney. It was the first settlement here in 1788. It seems the penal colony the British established prior to then, had a bit of a row with the Crown-the bullies started a revolution-so mother England started another penal colony here."

"When was this rebellion'?" Mike had heard this one, he thought.

"1776."

"Ah yes, those devilish little trifles." Mike tried his best English.

"Mocking the Queen's English is forbidden sir." She lowered her voice and turned to him, "I like your rough American slang much better." It was the first smile Shannon cracked on the trip that seemed friendly.

Mike felt a little braver now, now that he *knew* it was a game. "Miss Shannon, what kind of language is the Australian? It sounds so unusual?"

"It is, sir, the proud collection of Irish and Cockney. Unlike the bland and meaningless brogue of the Americans it has a distinct sound and its own very powerful meaning in tones and inflections, unlike the simple nasally twangs that southern American men and women use, *ya'll*..."

Shannon smiled at herself, she had Mike roused a bit. She continued with the tour.

"The Rocks was the first major establishment in Australia and the primary center for histories."

She spoke of the poor living conditions here in the 1800's, the sandstone homes that were more of slums and how, in 1900 when the bubonic plague ravaged the area, most of the historic buildings were razed-3,800 or more-to keep the infection rate low. Today she went on, the Rocks were gentrified, and still there were areas of blight. Buildings that were falling apart were sold to private buyers in hopes of renovation, but many kept them as low rent housing. As she passed them, Shannon pointed out the oldest claimed pubs in Sydney, a true bartender would. The Fortune of War and The Lord Nelson.

Mike listened thoroughly, not just to pick up a little lore and facts, but because he liked hearing Shannon speak her faded Australian accent, he loved the way she rolled her _r_ in some words, as though she had some higher learning skills, *as well she might*, he thought.

After turning onto Crown Street, which merged into the Cahill Expressway, most of which was under construction; Mike noticed a roadside sign that read: *NO TIPPING!* He looked at Shannon and dared a joke.

"So they are very strict about tipping here huh?" He gestured at the sign.

"That means no *tin* tipping. No dumping."

She tingled with his humor, though she didn't let it show. She liked this man very much, he was scared a bit, she saw that in him, but she also saw he was having a good time, his face never was clear of a smirk or smile. She'd made a difference in his life in just an hour.

After a tour by Mazda truck of The Rocks; Shannon managed a route through side streets and alleys. Mike did collect a few names in his head, Bridge Street and George Street, but the rest blurred by. They passed Circular Quay and Mike saw a road sign that read **Royal Botanical Gardens**. He hoped they would avoid the place, he had heard of the English gardens, how well and neat they are kept, but he wasn't a flower man.

A few more side streets as Shannon mastered her pickup around the left side of the road through O'Connell Street-and the large skyscrapers that occupied Sydney. Then she reversed her course towards the east and semi-circled the south end of the Botanical Gardens by means of the Cahill Expressway and once again returning to Woolloomooloo. Shannon made a couple of rights into the suburbs off Cowper Wharf Road and then a right on Bourke and another right on Wilson. After a very slow process of passing a few more houses and demonstrating the cozier side of the city, she parked. Mike made mental notes all the way, but he was sure he couldn't navigate back out on to the expressway and home to the hotel.

The homes they passed were familiar to him; he'd seen this type of architecture before. But in this setting they'd seemed more aptly used. The whole look was almost completely colonial and Victorian. The homes were well aged, obviously as old as the ones he'd walked amongst previously, but there was a sense of better use. More like an old Italian villa in the green vine covered hills.

Shannon turned her head slowly at him and smiled.
"What?"
"Time to walk…" She almost sang it.
They both exited the truck and Mike stretched by bending at the waist to touch his toes. The Mazda had very little leg room for his frame, and his knees were a little shaky from sitting. Shannon grabbed her pack out of the back of the truck and Mike did the same, throwing his backpack over his shoulder.
"Okay mate, Mr. Greene. Take a look-see around you, what do you find interesting about the flats here?" She walked as she talked, Mike followed.

Mike took his time looking from one to the other, trying to find the anomaly that made them so special, the little thing that caught the interest of Shannon. He took a moment then turned to her. "They kind of look like the homes on the Embarcadero in San Francisco."

Shannon nodded *yes* and looked at Mike. "No. Try again…"

Mike just shrugged, "I don't know, I just see some tall houses built right next to each other."

Shannon sighed loudly. It was right in front of his face. She'd tried a little subterfuge to see how excited he would get and he passed it up. Maybe he was on overload, sensory overload. Maybe later she'd spring it on him.

"Do you see the lovely ornamental iron along the front of many of these flats?"

"Oh. Yes."

Mike made it sound as if he seen it the whole time, but to him it was just part of the landscape, he would have never guessed. There were steel grates everywhere. Doors, fences, gates, windows-and it seemed they were there for more than protection.

"In the early days of Sydney, the cargo ships that would sail back to England full of livestock from here would drop off large iron bars before they left, they used it as ballast for their light human cargo for the journey here. The iron piled up at a place called Ballast Point, a ways over there." She pointed across Mike's nose. "One day this blacksmithee bloke decided to put all the scrap to use and started making these beautiful fences, gates and railings. The tale goes, that after a while nearly every flat, tenant and mansion in Sydney had some type of the iron work. Just about every smithee was a master at working the wrought metals. It even has a name: it's called *Sydney Lace.*"

Mike looked at the lovely work, it was truly a sight. If you weren't paying attention you would have never known, but he looked, and indeed every house was decorated with the *Lace.*

"Oh. I just thought it was a rough neighborhood."

She rolled her eyes at him. He smiled and added, "I like it."

Shannon heard the honesty in his voice and nodded with approval. "Now, let's walk."

"Again? Where to now?"

"The Gardens."

"Oh."

He didn't mean for it to sound so dejecting, but he was hoping for more of the open areas, maybe a nice spot to eat and look out over the bay. He loved looking out over the ocean in San Francisco.

"Don't sound so displaced. It is very lovely in there, besides the company is very brilliant."

"*Oh...*"

Mike saw a smirk on her face as she turned to walk, this was promising.

After the enormous entrance into the park, they followed a path that lead to a large round fountain and the path rounded it on both sides and merged into a single track towards the center of the park. They walked for one and a half hours, along cement paths and little dirt cuts. The grass was fresh smelling and the trees were tall, very tall. Sydney and Forest Red Gums, swamp oaks and southern mahoganies were just a sample of the four thousand seven hundred plus trees that surrounded and filled the Gardens. Mike estimated some of the trees to be forty or fifty feet high, full of branches and life. The architecture of some of the common areas were breathtaking, Mike would have never seen this through his eyes before; seen the beauty, but Shannon would stop every now and again to point out a flower or plant and explain its origin and how the Aboriginals used it for medicine or something ceremonial. It was how she described it with such care and passion, she was very knowledgeable and Mike liked that trait in her, confident of what she knew and very pleasing when she describe it for him, for someone who has seen it for the first time.

She rattled the names off of the plants so fast; Mike had a hard time keeping up. Names like; *Abelia schumannii, Acacia acinacea* and *Calandrinia remota. Calathea majestic, Chaetachme aristata* and *Polystichum setiferum.*

Shannon had recited the biological names of about thirty or so plants as they passed them, Mike had to take a breather, he said, "Don't these plants have real people names like Mary's Buttercup or Yellow Thingy Fluted Top?"

Shannon had to hide a smile, Michael had found a sense of humor in many things, and this made her tingle inside. She liked the way he could charm her. And he was doing his best.

She said, sarcastically, "I suppose they would. Like this one here…" She pointed to a small blue flowered plant that had red stamens. "This would be a Mauve Spreckled Man Flower."

"Man flower?"

"Yes, you'll see the stamen, the male part of the flower, is very showy and very prominent. It divulges itself with a brighter color than the rest of the plant because it feels so overwhelmed by the surrounding sepal, petals and of course the heart of the plant, the ovary; which is of course the…"

Mike interrupted, "Feminine part."

Shannon nodded with a sly smile. "Yes. Parts, the beauty in the flower resides in the attraction to the stamen by voluptuous petals. So it requires the beauty of the feminine parts to make the male part more attractive. The stamen resents this so it tries to be showy."

The spry banter was starting to have physical effects on Mike. Shannon had a few tingles of her own, so she changed the subject. Things could get out of hand very rapidly.

"Michael, we should press on. I'll show you something that'll make you happy."

And they walked on. Mike glanced back over his shoulder at the plant Shannon had indicated earlier, he smiled at it and gave it a wink. *Us men've got to stick together, mate*, he muttered under his breath.

After another twenty minutes of walking, Mike had to rest. He had very little exercise with this kind of intensity in the last few months and his legs were feeling gelatinous, he saw Shannon had stopped ahead at a little fountain and was admiring another garden of blue and orange flowers atop sharp looking leaves.

"Here Michael, *Strelitzia reginae…*"

"How about a little breather? My legs are giving out."

"We can rest when we arrive at *Mrs. Macquarie's Chair*."

"Whose chair? Will she mind us sitting there?"

"I doubt it; she's been dead for a century…"

Shannon smiled to herself about the small surprise ahead and began following a path towards the top of a little hill.

The hill sloped downward toward a swath that ran along the shoreline at the end of the trail on the peninsula and on the point overlooking Sydney Harbor, fashioned out of the natural rock was a large bench. Mike walked up and ran his hand across it, feeling the rough surfaces along the back and the soft smooth surface where obviously tens of thousands of tourist's behinds had sat at one time or another. A carving into the back of the rock bench described what he was seeing, but Shannon began the tour charade again.

"It's made of sandstone, carved out of the rock by convicts here in 1810. Mrs. Macquarie was wife of Major General Lachlan Macquarie, last autocratic Governor of New South Wales. This whole of land around you is called Macquarie Point." Shannon sat down and patted her hand beside her thigh, inviting Mike to do the same. "Now is your chance to rest, Michael Greene." He complied and slowly sat down, as if he were resting on a shrine of some type; he didn't want to offend anyone, though he and Shannon were the only two here now.

"Wow, this looks right out into the sea…" Mike said matter of factly.

"Quite. The story goes that Governor Macquarie had the prisoners cut this lovely seat for his Ladyship, who was very lonely. Like most spouses of Lords, she was torn from her homeland and moved to a place like this so her husband could govern. Mrs. or *Lady* Macquarie was so homesick she would sit here for hours at a time and watch the ships from England sailing into the Harbor."

Mike stared off into the distance, thinking. *What would it be like? Back here in the eighteen hundreds; thousands of miles from home, wanting to be home, wanting to see your old friends, but knowing there was no chance of it and when you could leave it would take months to make the journey. She would have been a very lonely woman...*

Then Mike's mind drifted to Rika, *she was lonely, very lonely. I wish I could have made her a place like this; she might be alive today...*

Mike's open expression turned sour, even though he should be at ease here. Shannon became seriously hurt inside. *Was she doing something wrong?*

"What're you thinking Michael Green?" Shannon broke his concentration.

"Just how lonely it must have been, so far from your home and friends. So far from your family and loved ones that you could barely stand it, then to have your husband-so caring-and thoughtful as to have this constructed so you may gaze out upon the sea and wish for your return home. He must have loved her very much. I can relate to her..."

"It is rumored that she was this way. Very sad to be away from one's family and friends for so long?"

Shannon added, looking right at the side of Mike's head, for some reason he refused to engage her eyes right now, she thought he might have a tear or two in his.

Shannon softened her voice and lowered it; "I'm not putting you off with this tour guide thing am I? I was just having a little amusement." She inched closer to him and put her hand and his thigh, Mike's leg temperature rose five degrees where her soft palm landed, little sparks of electric and desirous synergy shot through his blood. He could smell ginger and lemon grass, probably her shampoo on the slight breeze. Every so often a gust would blow a little harder than the stable air and Shannon would have to move that sill strand of hair from her face and tuck it behind her ear. This was driving him crazy inside.

"No, not at all. As a matter of fact, I thought it was fun. I'm having a wonderful time really."

He looked at Shannon and his eyes were moist, but honest.

"Then why the sadness all of a sudden?"

"I was just thinking about someone."

He looked back over the sea.

"Back home?"

She had a flash of empathy; perhaps she was pushing her luck with the humorous approach of tour guide and dry wit.

"Yes. There was this girl I knew, we were…" He paused and looked directly into Shannon's never ending blue eyes. "In a *place* together. She left one day and didn't come back, she had grown so lonely away from her friends-her family had abandoned her so one day she…" Mike looked towards the ocean and sighed; "She put a gun to her temple and pulled the trigger."

"Good Lord! What sort of place Michael?"

"Rehab." Mike sighed and looked at Shannon; he had to tell someone…

CHAPTER FIVE

RIKA

The place was called Freedom Frontiers, Mike hated the name; it sounded like a fat farm or a camp for exploring pioneers, not alcoholics and addicts.

He awoke after a long three day drinking binge in which he could remember nothing at first, then small details came to him, but his present location was a mystery and he had to figure out where he was first, somewhere in a room like a little motel room; he could see a shower stall and toilet to his right, in a small room with no door-just an opening. To his left was another double bed, unoccupied, and in front of that was a writing table with nothing on it except an old soup can painted silver with sparkly glitter on it and full of pens. The writing table came with a chair on wheels. A window was above the empty bed across from him and there was light coming from outside, and from the intensity Mike surmised that it was the sun behind the closed curtains.

A single door to the room was about ten feet in front of the foot of the bed. A door with no little slips of paper behind a plastic cover to tell him what time checkout was, so he began to realize this was no motel or hotel. He looked to his left where there was a night table, a lamp-and no phone. This puzzled Mike as he attempted a sitting position, but was beaten back down to his laying posture by a migraine. He slowly moved his to an angle where he could scan the room again.

No TV. No fancy or gawdy oil paintings on the walls. A cubicle closet with one of his suitcases on top of it. *His suitcase*! He didn't remember packing anything, of course. There was noise emanating from behind the only door to the room. He rose to his hips and elbows and closed his eyes to beat back the pounding between his ears, and then focused on the sounds.

It was the sounds of an office; a typewriter, phones ringing, four or maybe five people talking in various genders and ages. An infrequent buzzing sound way off to the left and a ways behind his door. Mike recognized this sound he thought, an electric magnet. A security device where a button had to be pushed to allow someone to pull or push a door open. Mike was able to sit up fully now, but with some difficulty as his head began swimming.

The door was locked from the outside, but next to the light switch was an intercom. After several attempts to get his feet stabilized, Mike managed to get to the door by holding onto the chair and dragging it with him. He was happy that the chair had wheels. Mike pressed the button on the panel.

"Yes Michael?" *How informal* Mike thought. It was a sharp voice of a woman.

"I want out…" His voice was crackly and breath smelled of vomit.

"Just a moment, let me talk to your counselor."

"My what?"

But the intercom clicked off, the voice had done what she said she was going to do obviously. Two or three minutes passed and Mike found himself thinking of *Nurse Ratched* on the other side of the door. He heard a click at the lock panel-he pushed the door open and found himself in a very strange place.

He knew he was going to end up in a place like this, the way he had been carrying on since… well, since *that* night. He was pounding booze like it was water for days on end and he knew he had even missed out on his job for two days in a row. It came to his mind now, he could see Kelly, his boss hovering over him saying something like, "*what the hell is wrong with you?*" and "*this is it, your outta here…*" or something like that, details were still foggy. He knew he would be in a rehab hospital detoxing, like the many drunks he had taken to the Galletti Medical Center-a place for mental patients-there was a little wing where the cops could drop off extremely drunk people, the ones that the police didn't even want responsibility for. This didn't look like that place at all.

Nor did it resemble a hospital; the receiving area was large-about sixty feet by forty-there was a outsized square counter in the center of the room, inside the large kiosk was apparently the registration staff, the billing staff and two or three secretaries. They were all busy on the phone or talking to other folks who were leaning around the counter. There were five rooms behind him-including the one Mike just walked out of-all of the doors looked alike. In front of the detox rooms was a sectional couch shaped in a U, which faced the administration counter and on the end of the work surface facing Mike was a nineteen inch television which could be viewed from the couch. There was an odor of sterility-not the kind of bleachy medicine smell of a hospital-but an aroma of cleanliness and order. The bustle continued about the place, especially around the front doors; he could see a sally port of some kind to keep the inside patients in and the outside world out.

"Mr. Greene, how do you feel?" A large man behind the counter who was dressed in a pair of tan slacks, a white golf shirt with a logo on the front stood up and walked towards the end of the counter closest to Mike. "Are you a little woozy?"

Mike made a quick inventory of his body mentally and shook his head no. He was a little shocked that he hadn't seen anyone wearing smocks or scrubs; he always imagined the counselors dressed this way.

"Very good, the effects of lightheadedness are from *Librium*, a drug we use to calm the effects of detoxing."

"Where am I?" Mike's voice still crackled with sleep and lack of use.

"Freedom Frontiers, we are in the northern portion of Oregon, near Portland. My name is Darren Talbot; I'm a CADC One here. You don't remember your flight in?"

Mike thought hard for a moment vaguely remembered a plane, Kelly was at his side, and they were having a few beers... Kelly. That rat of a boss... "A little."

"Good, could you please come over here and sit for a few minutes, I need some information from you; you were a little too drunk a few days ago to give it to me."

A few days? How long have I been out? Mike complied and moved, slowly to the chair indicated by the man on a lower part of the kiosk designed just for two to face each other this way in chairs, semi-private. Darren sat and pulled a file out of a drawer.

"How long have I been here?"

"Three days. Let's see... Michael Greene: you live on Old Bridge Road Lockwood, Nevada and your contact phone number is 775-555-2032?"

"Excuse me? That's not my number-that's my boss's home phone."

"Then that's your contact. He left it here for you in case of an emergency; it wouldn't do any good to call your house, since you will be here with us for a while."

"Did I agree to this?"

"Don't have to really, although you are considered a volunteer admission for alcoholism treatment, you are bound to the property until you pass the medical examination and are free from the side effects of the Librium. Once you're brought here, if you are highly intoxicated, you can't leave until the doc says it is okay."

"When do I see him?"

"In an hour or so, if you wish."

"I wish."

Mike was angry, not at the man at the counter, but at the whole situation, *who the hell had the authority to bring him here?*

"Michael..." Another man, about fortyish came out of one of the four hallways Mike could see from the receiving area. *How the hell does everyone know my name?* The man walked right up to him and took his hand; Mike was startled, but gave it easily. "My name is Jackson G. You can call me Jack; I'm your assigned counselor here."

"Good, I have some questions. How do I get out of here?"

"Follow me will ya? I have an office right around the corner," He turned to the big man behind the counter, "We'll finish his paperwork later Darren." And Jack walked off, Mike trailing behind, looking like a puppy that had just wet the carpet.

"So you see, Michael; Your boss talked you into coming here when you were very drunk, it is part of the rules that we keep you until you are sober enough not to be a danger to yourself or others." Jack was very thorough; he explained the plane ride, why Kelly was instructed to keep him liquored up in case he became belligerent while drying out on the plane, how it was his choice to leave as soon as the doctor saw him and cleared him, but once he left the doors to the center, he was on his own.

Kelly, his boss had not paid for a return flight, he could call a loved one if he wished for assistance, and since he lived so far away *Frontiers* could not give him a ride to the airport in Portland without a ticket. Kelly had also instructed the clinic to inform Mike that if he did quit the center before his twenty eight days were up, he no longer had a job at Lockwood P.D. In fact, they would call it a termination for extreme circumstances and he would not be able to get a cop job anywhere close, if he was able to find one anyway. The fact that Mike had disappeared for a week and never called in sick, nor called anyone for the time he was missing, went on his unofficial record as "no call, no show". If Mike left the center prematurely, the record would be made official and he would be fired.

"You see Michael, your choices are there, limited I must say, but they are there. If you stay the term, pass the course and walk away sober; you can get your job back."

"How much is this going to cost me?"

Mike was teetering on staying, only because he knew deep inside he needed the help, he hated the drunk he had become and the reason he started to binge this last go around. It was the first step to recovery, he'd hoped. But money was another roadblock for him, he had little. Just a few thousand in the bank, the muster of his whole adult life, what his ex hadn't taken he'd scrounged and saved and put away, a college fund for his son. But he had doubts that would ever come to fruition either. Then there was child support, that cost him eight hundred a month; at least the woman didn't ask for alimony.

He began to survey the small office-once a cop, always a cop-and found the room to be rather small, about eight feet by eight feet. There was no window and Jack's Wal-Mart particle board desk ran the entire length of the wall on one side. On it were pictures of Jack fishing, another with him and a bull elk, another with a young girl; most likely his daughter, they closely resembled each other. The walls around the room were adorned with more photo collages, more hunting and fishing pictures, more of the same young girl in various stages of age-but none with a wife.

Decorating the wall in front of Jack's desk and next to the patient chair were a half dozen framed licenses and certificates. Mike noticed that "Jackson Gregory" was a "Certified CADC II-CCJP-CCS", *whatever the hell all they were...* Mike thought to himself. He turned back to Jack to see he was following Mike's gaze.

"Certified Alcohol and Drug Counselor level two; Certified Criminal Justice Addiction Professional; and Certified Clinical Supervisor." Jack said, looking up over his desk at the documents on the wall. He then returned his eyes to Mike; "I guess you could say I'm pretty *certifiable...*"

Mike just grunted. He did find Jack's joke a little humorous, but was in no mood now.

"Your boss Kelly gave us the deposit, eleven thousand dollars..." Mike's eyes hit the roof of his head, "...and your insurance will kick in for the rest of the eight thousand, we even anticipate a full refund to your friend Kelly. He sounds like one of the best friends a person could have."

"Nineteen thousand dollars!" Mike's blood pressure jumped. "What the *Hell* for?"

Jack remained calm and began his pitch; "Twenty eight days of room and board, medications, laundry service, etc. You will get three awesome meals a day, prepared in our own diner, served buffet style. You get around the clock monitoring and health checks if you fall ill, plus all the materials you will need to complete the course."

"That's it?"

"Well, it also covers your physiological exam and therapist."

"No way partner… I'm not seeing a shrink!"

"It's part of the program. You skip it and you fail. I'll be your guide through all of the processes and even your group leader, for most all of your group therapy sessions." Jack opened Mike's file again and tried to ripple the water, to see what to expect from Mike. "Says here your ex-wife blames booze for your divorce."

"That's incorrect, she… I…" Mike didn't know what to say. "Who told you that?"

"You did-when you checked in-don't you remember?"

"No."

"You were examined by a nurse; your things were checked for sharp knives, razor blades, shampoo, aftershave, other things that can hurt you and things that can hide alcohol. Then you were stripped searched…"

"What? Aftershave?"

"Contains alcohol…"

"I certainly wouldn't…"

"You wouldn't believe who does…"

"Anyway, you were conscious the whole time; you even were making jokes with the nurse."

"Oh."

The session lasted for thirty minutes and Mike was sent back to his detox room, where he would fill out numerous forms and then wait for two more days to be transferred to the general population.

Mike leaned back on his detox room bed and closed his eyes. He mentally reconstructed Jack in his law enforcement molded mind. The man looked about forty-five; he was graying around the edges of his hairline. He dressed casually as Mike had observed every employee so far, Jack wore a snap-up style western shirt with a very expensive bolo tie in the shape of the state of Oregon, black Wrangler Jeans and shiny black Roper cowboy boots. *Wasn't much cowboyin' in Northern Oregon...* Mike thought.

He would share a room with another man, a guy named Roger B. Later he'd have all the privileges granted the others, nearly everything as normal, except television-it was banned. He would then rise at seven, do fifteen minutes of group meditation, have a chance to read the paper, eat breakfast and then the day would be filled with AA classes and therapies.

It took a week, but Mike eventually fit in and things were looking good for him, he got along well with everyone, there were a few eccentrics though, a couple of guys with very rough edges and somewhat neurotic behaviors; Mike was told this was one of the many side effects of someone who had been drinking heavy for many years, so he considered himself lucky.

There were a few things that bothered Mike, like the psych exam and his therapist. In the world outside the center, Mike was the man with all the questions, it was his job, in here *she* was the one with all the questions and she responded in a peculiar way each time he would answer-probably trying to get some kind of body language out of him-he thought. Her name was Ann T., and Ann-like Jack-had a half dozen diplomas and certificates lining her walls, fewer photos though.

Another thing Mike had trouble with was the honesty part, he held tight and kept to himself the real reason that brought him here, he swore to himself that he would never tell another soul about that night, and even the deeper prodding forced him to be silent.

After a few days Mike took a liking to Jack, his counselor. He learned that Jack too, was a recovering alcoholic, a very bad one from the stories he told at the meetings. The booze had driven him the lowest levels of human feelings and depression, his *sobriety* drove his wife of ten years away-and she took his daughter. Jack explained that in many alcoholic and drug relationships spouses tend to become "co-dependent", meaning they are just as hooked on the addict as the addict is to his vice. When an addict sheds his or her dependency, the spouses have a hard time handling the "new" version of their husband or wife. They no longer are needed as a crutch or tool, they are no longer the primary source of thinking or rule making. It drains a family-especially the spouse-when an addict gets their life back in order. They no longer rely solely on their spouse to make important decisions, the reformed addict becomes independent. This causes major problems in relationships. Especially if the couple meet during the addiction, the spouse never met the sober version of their partner-and they generally do not like the person their loved one has become.

In the third week, a period called *family week* for the patients, family members were allowed to come and visit for the first time of the treatment. First off the loved ones are given an indoctrination meeting that lasts two days, to give them a better understanding of their loved one's problem and to warn them, that person here in treatment, was not the same person who they brought in three weeks ago. The newer, more fragile, but less dependent person who was receiving the care was learning to take care of themselves, to develop philosophies that would help them steer clear of alcohol or drugs, and may not be the person that they wanted back.

For the addict and families; friends had to be changed, some were even forgotten-especially the ones who liked to party-jobs might have to be changed and in extreme cases, the addict must uproot and move away from the source of their problems. The treatment goes way beyond what the families are told, but they leave that for the patient and extension services like Al-Anon and recommended outside counseling to explain. At the end of the counselor/family session, the final advice to the families is given a little contract of sorts that the families have to sign as a show of good faith:

"Your loved one has changed. They are no longer dependent on many things you provide to make them happy; they may all-together be a different person. You have to accept this, you have to understand, if they feel conflicted they might relapse and if they do, they can and many do-die. Your whole life will change from this day on. This is simple information given the families, the education the patients received is far more detailed and more in depth, after all, the patient was given fifteen hours a day seven days a week of therapy, the family had just one day."

After orientation day the families were encouraged to spend a lot of time with their recovering addict, encourage them and show them they are still worth something on the outside. They eat together, walk for hours and talk about many things, except one major rule: there is no discussing other patients, there is no talk of therapies or what is discussed in group and names may never be mentioned; in fact a disclosure statement is mandatory at check in. If a patient reveals information about another, there could be federal charges, if not just local and financial lawsuits brought. This included the families-the treatment community was very strict about protecting the privacy of its patients-by law.

Mike had been prompted by Jack to call his ex-wife Lisa to come down for family week. Mike was very hesitant, knowing of course that the call would probably end in an argument-like most of their conversations did. He found the lone phone booth in his dorm to be cold when he entered it. He took out a phone card from his pocket that Kelly had left for him and his trembling fingers pattered at the cold keys on the old pay-phone.

"What for?" An impatient voice asked.

"I'm in treatment here and I need to share some time with you, it's all part of the program. If you can't make it, then just send Mikie."

"We're very busy."

"Didn't you get the check for six hundred dollars to fly up here and bring him?"

Mike's dad in Idaho had been one of the first he'd called after his incarceration; his father was very supportive of the treatment plan, since his own life was marred by alcohol and eventually pain medication. Clark Greene wasn't rich, but he did have a vast amount of savings from owning his own trailer-house and living a simple life in a small town with few expenses. He sent the money as soon as Mike had asked for it-a loan of course-and Mike would pay him back as soon as he was out.

"Yes, and we'll just take that from your child support this month; you know the one you missed?"

"I've been here; I have limited contact with the public."

"Maybe they should keep you…"

Mike hung up the phone on her, he knew she wasn't coming, neither was his son.

A day later he told Jack of his conversation with his ex and her refusal to come.

"Maybe it wasn't just the alcohol then, huh Mike?" He responded softly. "Few here see that the alcohol hides a lot of things, from both parties involved. Trouble in a relationship can be hidden with a couple of drinks or a hit of pot. Hiding simply because we didn't want to deal with the problem. We drank or used because we were afraid that the truth would surface, that we were in a bad relationship or a bad place as things got worse, we used more and more."

Then Jack had a suggestion, it was a gamble and against usual regulations, but he had an idea to help Mike through the family week ordeal. Mike would be allowed, by special order of the center therapist board, to talk to one of the other patients on the *other* side.

"Excuse me?" Mike wasn't sure he had heard right.

"Mike, you have been very good at following the avoidance order, but we've noticed you capturing glances from one another once and a while; then there was the incident in the laundry room…"

"That wasn't my fault! The monitor said the women were done, I went to do my clothes and she was in there…"

Jack raised his hand and smiled, "I know, I know. Relax, everyone steals looks at the women and the women grab a glance in our direction when they can, too. It's just a little joke to think men and women will stay totally apart. You are only human. Anyways, this visit with young lady can only be for three days actually. It is an experiment." Jack took a small breath and then leaned forward to Mike, "There is this one girl here, her name is Rika F. She's been released after her ninety day treatment program and she's been a good help around with other patients, giving good advice and so on. She's going home in a few days and I want her to help out with a few more people before she does. She might make a good counselor if she doesn't feel like returning to her old job.

"But both of you could use a dose of friendship this week with the other families hanging around."

"Okay. I'll be good."

"Remember the rules, no touching, kissing, or contact of any kind. You can talk with her, but that is all. Be careful, she is fragile in a way, but has made great progress. You can spend the whole three days with her, sans the nights of course, even eat together, but you can't ask her any personal questions about where she lives, why she is here and things that might send her into a relapse mode. Clear?"

"Yes, Jack. I promise."

The next day Mike met the young lady he was told to ignore for three weeks, at the front steps of the center.

"Hi."

"Hi…" The hesitation in her voice told Mike she was nervous, even when you are told to break a rule by the people who give them, it is difficult.

"Name's Mike, I'm an alcoholic…"

"Rika, I… I'm an addict." She offered her hand and then retracted it quickly when she remembered the rules.

"If this isn't the most awkward way to meet a girl, I don't know what it is." Mike smiled big. Rika mirrored his smile and sat down next to him on the steps.

"I guess we're rats today." She twirled her shoe in the gravel at the bottom of the steps.

"Yeah, rats in a maze." He picked at a glob of paint on the railing.

Mike looked her over, as if he hadn't already since he had been released to general population-a prison term Mike hated-she was a beautiful young girl, probably about twenty-eight or a little more, blond hair with a brown strip on one side, brown eyes and a frozen sadness to her thin face. She was lean all the way around; no breasts to speak of and her arms were thin like matchsticks. She was frail looking, but pretty and Mike noticed Rika always had a look of wonder mixed with the sadness on her face, that is what drew his attention to her.

There was silence for a few minutes, neither wanted to push the rules, but it was hard to sit next to the opposite sex and not talk about things in their life. The most common question was the same as it was on everyone's mind: *Why are you here?* But there was the fine line… the house rules.

The rules were established on his first day out of detox: *"There are no women here, got it? There are only patients, clients they were sometimes called-were androgynous in every way. You are not to look at them if it can be helped, you are not to engage with them any conversation, and "Hello" was a conversation. You were not to touch them, if they brush against you-you are too close."*

If you think having forty men and twenty five women basically in the same building for nearly a month and no looks would be shared, think again. But for the most part everyone followed the rules; that was until today, when two were allowed to break them.

"Want to go for a walk?"

"Is it okay?" Rika asked, quietly.

"Sure, they didn't say anything about walking together in the rules."

"Right."

And they shuffled off, towards the large grassy center quad.

Mike was happy around Rika; she was a veterinarian's assistant and had become addicted to Diazepam, an animal tranquilizer. She was sad all of her life, as far as she could remember and the drug eased her pain.

"You know I'm not supposed to hear of your past…"

"You hear it every day in AA, or don't you listen?"

"Well, sometimes. Mrs. Hanna says…"

"You have Hanna as a psych too?" There was excitement in Rika's voice.

"Yeah, she kinda scares me."

"Me too."

Mike led the way to the courtyard from the quad and out into the open back area of the complex. Of course it was fenced in, the barbed wire was facing out, which meant it was to keep people out and not from getting from the inside to the outside. The whole area was about a half-acre; small hills of short grass and a gravel path that ran the fence line for those who wanted to jog, a small creek running off of the Tillikum River that passed to the west of the buildings. The creek was filled with newts and small fish.

Every day for the next three days, Mike and Rika were inseparable. They would walk together everywhere and chat about life, breaking a couple of rules about each other's private lives-but they kept from touching, that was until the last day, when Mike and Rika were at the end of a long path that circled around the grassy areas, over a little wooden bridge and into a line of tall lodgepole, ponderosa pine and fir trees. The gravel path had little markers with the *Twelve Steps* carved on them. The trail was at the far end of the compound and they stopped to look at some salamanders in a little creek with the wooden bridge over it. A slight breeze lifted Rika's hair gently off her face, Mike had become intoxicated with her now, and they practically knew each other fairly well. Under a huge pine tree on the little wooden bridge over a small babbling creek-Mike leaned over and kissed her.

At first he thought she would jump back in horror, but she didn't. She accepted the kiss and leaned against him, holding him tight along her small body, the slender figure trembled at the fear of being caught, but she desired human contact so badly, as did Mike. It lasted only a few seconds and they pulled away from each other and started walking back towards the compound, with warm red faces and soft smiles… identical smiles.

"I guess that'll be a secret, huh?" Mike asked.

She smiled up to him and nodded as they approached the compound.

"I've been here ninety-three days."

"Why so long? I only have twenty-eight total?"

"I'm a veterinarian's assistant. He insisted that I do the whole course, and my mother insisted. I hated her for putting me in here. Now… well." She paused and looked at the parking lot, "Now that I'm getting out, it seems like it was worth it. I like helping people here, it makes everything so rewarding for myself. It's like I'm not alone in this stupid world."

"You feel alone a lot?"

She shook her head too fast.

"I'm coming back in a few weeks, after I adjust to normal life and then I'm going to help others out here, make them better like they did me."

"And like me?"

She smiled warmly and rubbed his arm with her soft small hands. "Yes. Maybe we can see each other after you get out? I have a boyfriend but we can be friends. We can call each other and tell each other how we've helped others like us."

"I'd like that."

They stopped at the diner and had dinner on their final night together. One and a half weeks later, Mike noticed that Rika hadn't come back to help the other patients like she promised. He knew she was going to readjust first, but she seemed so eager to come back to help others here. Mike missed seeing her at the dining hall, even thought they were separated by a wall and a small stair case, he could still sneak a peek as he walked in. He'd hoped he see her one more time before he left. He felt alone again but he knew he had only a few days left and the docs plus his psychiatrist all gave him raving reviews. Mike was able to hide the incident that brought him here in a roundabout way and was proud of that; he knew he could keep it a secret forever.

On his last night Mike was called to Jack's office, it was late and he knew something was up. There were a few stares at Mike as he came into from the dorm off the hallway into the counselor areas. He walked up to the door and knocked, the door creaked on its hinges slowly. Mike pushed it all the way in and saw Jack sitting there with his head in his hands. Jack was solemn looking, his office was barely lit. Jack motioned for Mike to sit down. He took a deep breath and turned his chair facing Mike.

"Mike, you're a policeman and you are going to find this out anyway..." There was a look of pain in Jack's face, a sadness etched in his cheeks and under his eyes, almost like he had shed a few tears recently.

Mike fears rose. "What is it? It can't be good news, you look so sad..."

"Mike… Rika, your friend. She was found dead yesterday; she committed suicide at her house."

Mike's world of happiness and freedom from the bounds of the poison alcohol began to end. He wanted a drink. He was mad, no-furious that she'd made this decision to take her life with asking him for help. He would've done anything for her. He would've stopped at nothing to see she was alright; he would've hurt people to protect her. That's how much of an impact she had on him, she was there when he needed it the most and now, she was gone. A tear formed in his eye on the left, the right eye was burning to release more.

"Do you think this will have an effect on your sobriety?" Jack looked up at him.

"I… I don't know. God, Jack, *why*?"

"Good answer. You were close to her, we know. She meant a lot to you these last two weeks, I think her being with you over family week pulled you out of the basement. If you had said her death would have had no effect, I would have to recommend another four weeks for you."

"*Why*?" It was all Mike could think to say.

"No Jack, *why* did she do it?"

Jack shook his head and bowed it. "I don't really know. No one will. She was a shining star, bright and we had great hopes for her."

"Why would it matter if I lied to you about wanting a drink? What if I said I didn't want one?"

"Because you cared for her, if you said you would be all right with it then you would be lying and we practice rigorous honesty here, right?"

"Yes."

"We will stay in touch; you call me if anything goes wrong. Kelly has our number and has been instructed to do the same thing, if you say it is all right."

"I do." Mike rose from his chair and started for the door, without looking at Jack he turned the handle and paused; "How?"

Jack sat looking at his desk and answered, "Gunshot, she had gone home and had a few drinks. Not what she was here for, but the alcohol caused a relapse, she took a syringe half-full of Acepromazine and that caused extreme depression. The police think that maybe she'd had a fight with her boyfriend and he left her. Or something like that. Loneliness. Remember HALT Mike?"

Jack made it sound as if the ends didn't make the *How* matter. The results were what counted.

"Hungry, Angry, Lonely, Tired." Mike said without batting an eye.

Keep those in mind, recognize the signs. Get help; get to a meeting if you are anxious over one of those symptoms. Do it before you end up like Rika."

"Was there a note?"

"I'm afraid not." Mike pulled the door open, and behind him just before the door closed he heard Jack tell him, "She cared for you too." Then a pause just before the door closed. "Keep in touch Michael."

A dejected Michael Greene headed back down the hall towards his room. In the common area a crowd was gathering for the send-off ceremony for him, he passed by and acknowledged that he would be out in a few minutes-he just needed to be alone. He went to his room and cried for Rika.

With dried tears and a choked up voice, Mike celebrated his departure from Future Frontiers by drinking a traditional shake made with orange juice, ice and sugar. All the newbies and the next-in-lines to be released toasted him, and then Mike received a coin with a small portion missing. This symbolized the part he left behind at the center, after hugs and thanks he made a little speech-shortened by tears welling behind his eyes for the young drug addict who became so lonely she decided to die alone-then he was given a little silver camel pin. The pin meant that a camel can go more than a week without a drink-so now a newly sober man can go longer.

He landed one day later in Reno and returned home, sober, sadder but he felt better. He knew he could resist alcohol… but something was missing. He felt re-energized, he followed the daily routines as much as possible; meditation, avoiding the bars and friends parties-even a welcome home one that was planned and later cancelled. He walked the streets around his home at night, near the Truckee River that ran just a few hundred yards from the front of his house. He wished there was a little bridge over the river, so he could walk out and stop in the middle and gaze down into the murky green water and think about Rika. He followed his recommended regimen until he left for Australia.

Mike told his tale to Shannon -he figured mentioning Rika would be okay; she died without any friends or relatives around other than a mother she mentioned, no one to sue him if the word got out. He knew Rika would have probably wanted it this way anyway, to remember her-her pain and struggle. Her loneliness.

Mike didn't even mention how hard it was on a daily basis to avoid the things that tempt you, how coming here to Australia was a bad idea-the culture was beer oriented in a way after all. Then to end up hiking around God's country with a bartender? Jack G. would have a coronary.

But it felt right to talk to her-Shannon-it just felt as if the world was better if she knew, he felt right telling her almost everything, he could talk to her-she was that kind of person-he hoped he wouldn't fall in love though. But all in all, for what it was worth, Shannon took it all in as she heard this all the time. She made him feel comfortable and that made him… uncomfortable.

CHAPTER SIX

SYDNEY HARBOUR

Shannon sat quiet through Mike's story, she had to brush a tear away discreetly during the last few minutes of it, her cheeks were still a little red. Even though Mike had given her many of the details of his stay, nearly every one of them, a few he kept secret. First he had never told Shannon about his job as a cop, he thought it best to keep that secret as long as possible, at least till he could think of a way to tell her. He skipped the particulars and just gave her the meat of the story. He tried to be un-dramatic as possible, but he managed to convey his feelings.

He never told Shannon about his first week home from the Center, how he cried for nearly three days, how he couldn't eat or sleep, how he felt the whole thing was his fault, how he nearly fell off the wagon. He didn't need to mention that he had been given six months leave for medical from work, and he planned to take it all, Mike even thought about quitting and moving up to Idaho, where his father lived; just like they had suggested in treatment, '*quit your job if you have to, change your whole lifestyle.*'

Shannon placed her hand on Mike's thigh again, higher this time, it wasn't a sensual touch, it was an understanding hand. She rubbed it a little and whispered to his ear, "I'm so sorry. I don't know how you can do it. You are a very strong man, Michael Greene, the strongest I have ever met, both inside and out." And she meant it, not even Mathew had the fortitude Mike had. "Do you want to go back now?"

Mike shook his head no. He rose from Mrs. Macquarie's Chair and started walking down the path back towards the gardens, his head was hung low. Shannon followed along, little tears of sadness in her eyes. She pulled his hand to a stop at the edge of the point, and she pointed over the Harbour to Dawes Point.

"Look over there Mike, to the left of the point." She called him Mike for the first time, "There's a sight that would make anyone feel welcome and happy to be alive…"

She was indicating the Sydney Opera House.

After they had come to a central area of the park, an area laden with grass. He had seen this patch on the way up to the Chair and noticed how it resembled the quad at Freedom Frontiers, how it reminded him of Rika but not until he thought about the loneliness Mrs. Macquarie had over her lost home. Seeing the Lady Governess in his mind staring out over the ocean lonelier than any human should be, he thought of Rika more and how lonely she must have been at home that day. Mike had wished to god that he could have been with her that night, the night she gave up on life, the night her loneliness forced her hand.

Mike dropped his backpack off his shoulder onto the ground and sat down, hard, Shannon followed suit and sat very close to him, not enough to touch legs, but close enough to put her arm around him. "I'm very sorry."

"I know. You said so already. Where are we going next tour guide?" He could feel her radiating body warmth raising his temperature a little.

"I think we have dug enough graves today, don't you?"

Mike nodded lightly, and then he turned his reddening eyes towards her. "Can I ask you a personal question?"

"Anything."

"Tell me about your boyfriend, Marty?"

"*Mathew*. How did you find out about…?"

"Natalie told me, she said you two were very close, right up till this last him he was here." Mike tried to keep from over-smiling; "She said that you were a little distant after that."

"She did, did she?" Shannon felt a little warm rush of betrayal.

"Yeah, she said she was glad I came along, that I put a little steam in your step."

"*Oh, she did, did she?*" Shannon thought for a moment, Mike had just told her a story she was sure no one had heard before, maybe not even his friend Kelly, so she acquiesced and rose to her feet. "Make you a deal. We walk, and I talk."

"About Matt?"

"About *Mathew.*"

And she started to walk towards the north end of the park, towards the shortest route to Circular Quay; she knew where to take Mike to make him feel better and herself a little too. They were a good fifty paces into the walk, the sky was turning a little hazy as the sun was hiding behind a small bank of clouds, it would be dark in about an hour and a half.

She was close to her element here, her home and her work. She was not a man chaser nor was she desperate as Natalie, but she found Michael to be so intriguing. He seemed protective, he built his trust with her and she was able to discern that he was reliable and not a serial killer or maniac. She'd made a bad choice in Mathew, but now she felt as if she were making amends, in some twisted sort of way. She was buying this guy's sob story, hook line and sinker, but at the same time she knew he wasn't just searching for a night in the sheets or maybe a week of female companionship, it seemed to her he was avoiding that, but he was lonely inside. He needed friendship.

"We met in Kuranda Queensland. That's where I'm from, mostly. He was selling some trade print at a local shop in Cairns-he's a record producer you see-Cairns is a city just below my hometown. I was working at a resort called the Cairns Colonial Resort."

"Bartending?"

"*Barmaid*, do you want to hear the story or not?"

"Sorry, no more interruptions…" Mike was beaming.

"He sat at my end of the pub one night and ordered a Rocket Fuel…"

"A what?"

"I thought you said you weren't going to interrupt?"

"I just have never heard of one of those before and I work in a town that prides itself on funny drinks."

Shannon took a deep breath, she skipped over a swollen piece of turf and continued, "There is this band from here actually, called *INXS*."

"I've heard of them."

"One more ear bashing and I will shut up for the rest of the walk." She said sternly. Mike smiled at her and nodded. "Anyways, they have this song which is popular here and in Perth, where my friend lives. It says something about Rocket Fuel, about a drink." Shannon paused and looked at Mike. She waited for him to ask a question, and then continued when he finally kept his promise. "You take a chimney glass and move it from one liquor spout to the next, pouring a little of each of the fifteen into the glass. Very powerful, very expensive, about eight dollars seventy-five I think."

Mike nodded. Shannon continued, "Mathew was cute, a lot shorter than you but cute. He asked me out, and as I have told you before about American men here in Australia…"

"No you haven't told me anything about American men here in Australia."

"Oh. I'm never going to get to the end of my story with you asking stupid questions all the time." She smirked.

"But…"

"Another day, okay then?"

Mike nodded it was. "We went out for the three weeks he was here, I fell in love and when I moved here he would still spend his three weeks of holiday each year here. I would visit him once or twice in other parts of Australia when his business took him there; we'd chat twice a week on the phone and write all the time."

"How long?"

"Four years."

"Wow..."

"Yes. Anyway, when he was here last time things didn't go well, he was chippy and cheeky and I was... well I was not in the best of the moods either. We argued his last day here before he went back to the States and that was it."

"You haven't spoken since?"

"No, we haven't. He left two weeks before you arrived and put my life in turmoil..."

The walk took them to the outside of the Royal Botanical Gardens; Mike noticed for the mile or so the large crow like birds circling over their heads. Fact is Mike didn't remember any bird that was out flying so close to sundown...

"What kind of bird is that?" He asked, eyes looking straight up in the trees, where many of the birds had landed...*upside down?*

Mike knew the answer just as Shannon proudly announced it, "Those birds, are bats."

"Bats..."

"Yes, they are called flying foxes, they are quite large eh?" She giggled at the word *birds*. "Notice the little red-orange tufts of fur around their heads? They are adorable little buggers, aren't they?"

"Yeah, adorable..."

Mike hated bats, the largest one he had ever seen up close was about the size of your hand, and these were about the size of a Chihuahua, with wings...

The last bit of the Gardens behind them, Shannon guided them west towards Millers Point, where the view of the Harbour Bridge was coming up. They slowed as Shannon told the history of the "Coat Hanger" Bridge, a nickname given to it because of the way it looks; how it once was the tallest structure in Sydney and is still the largest steel arch bridge in the world. She said they would venture that way on the tour tomorrow. Mike was excited that she had planned a second day.

"Where are we going now, if not the bridge?"

Mike was still glancing up once and a while to see if any of the monster bats had followed them, there was a true fear in his eyes, he was really afraid of the bats. Shannon saw his concern and the look on his face. She smiled to herself.

"The Opera House, of course." And under her breath but loud enough for Mike to hear, "*Big baby*."

As they passed the Quay and neared Dawes Point, Mike could see the tell-tale sail shaped roofs of the most famous building in the world across from them. They were walking slower now-Shannon had slackened the pace-she was smiling again, she was thinking of Mike more than she was the tour and her pace reflected that.

Mike and Shannon neared the Opera House; the daylight began to fade as the sun dipped behind the land and the city of Sydney. Night was fighting day and the end result of the night winning at dusk was a brilliant pink-orange sky that extended from the western part of the skyline, then the colors enveloped the bay. The color glowed off the tall glass skyscrapers and the concrete pillars, darkness had nearly won completely by the time the travelers from Rushcutters Bay had arrived at the base of the Opera House.

When they approached the massive monument to the sailors and the sea, Shannon took her light windbreaker from her pack and put it on, Mike was too engrossed to feel anything-he was in awe-he was finally standing at the front door of the building he would have never dreamed of seeing a few months back, only images on television and the occasional photograph. But he was here, now. He reached out and touched the concrete structure in front of him and turned with a childlike smile to Shannon.

"It's real. It's really here, I'm really here."

He walked around in circles behind Shannon, then in front of her, trying to get better views of the famous roof that was designed to look like sails on ships long past. She saw his eyes were misty. He was finally in the midst of the Opera House. Made mostly of pre-cast concrete, the sails or shells as they are called by different eyes of different people are covered in a bubbly configuration of over one million white and cream colored tiles that rose two hundred and thirteen feet into the air above Sydney Harbour. Maybe this is why the confusion over the shape of the most prominent feature was either a shell from a giant mollusk or a tribute to the sea and the sailors who brave it. The complex area itself covers over four acres. Construction began in 1959 and ended in 1973, with the grand opening hosted by Elizabeth II, Queen of Australia on October 20th, 1973. Jørn Utzon, the Danish architect was not invited, nor mentioned.

The structure itself is actually anchored to the seabed with over five hundred pillars driven into the ground eighty feet deep. It's more of a podium, not unlike Liberty Island where the famous Statue of Liberty rests in New York. And the Opera House is much more than that; it is several houses dedicated to music and the arts.

Shannon took Mike's hand like a mother would do a child and guided him from the forecourt around to the western side of the building where there was a terraced area and a pub on the lowest one. Shannon led Mike to the lesser terrace, the closest to the Harbour and they sat on a long concrete bench that ran the length of the lower promenāde, behind the seat back was the Harbour. The tall light posts around the walkway held little globes that gave off a soft white glow, not enough to disturb the ambience of the night sky, not bright enough to take away from the brilliance of the spotlights that illuminated the side of the curved gables. Mike was trembling; Shannon could feel it when she rested her hand on Mike's thigh again. In front of them was The Sydney Opera House.

"Are you okay?" She asked, knowing the answer. Knowing that he was beholding a life's dream and could reach out and touch it, something that Shannon took for granted, each day she passed within view of it-some days she looked-others she forgot it was there.

"I'm… so happy… My god, it is the most beautiful thing I have ever seen, more than I could ever imagine."

Shannon leaned against the back side of the bench and could feel the warm misty air coming from the sea just a few feet below them. She saw Mathew's face, her smile went blank and she was thinking about why he hadn't expressed such emotion over the bridge-as a matter of fact-Mathew was always in quite the hurry to get through the Quay and to her flat. Mathew was always in a hurry to just be with her, not do things with her outside her flat-Shannon realized that she needed a man like Michael. He was innocent in so many ways; he was indeed a child of sorts. He loved learning, he had the power over himself to keep from pushing himself upon anyone-she knew he had taken a liking to her-she wondered when he would make a move, if ever. He was so shy.

"…inside?"

Mike's face appeared in front of hers breaking the spell.

"What was your question Michael Greene?"

"Can we see inside?" Mike's eyes were as wide as saucers under a tea cup.

"Well…" Shannon's eyes darted left then right and she then put an index finger to her lips. "Follow me…" She whispered. They walked to base of the building again, the sky was completely dark now.

As they came to one of the entrances Shannon stopped and looked left and right again as if to see if there was any security around. She pushed on the bar to the door and it opened, she put her finger up again and gave a wave of her hand and whispered, *"Follow me…"*

Mike felt the rush of adrenalin, the thrill of being in a place he wasn't supposed to, that is; until he saw the sign on a stanchion in the entrance to the main hall.

ALL MAY ENTER MON–THURS
UNLESS A PERFOMANCE IS SCHEDULED
NOON TILL 9PM
PLEASE RESPECT OUR HOUSE
BE SUBTLE AND QUIET
MIND THE VELVET ROPES
SYDNEY OPERA HOUSE TRUST

"You made it look like we were sneaking in…" His voice deflated, Mike placed his hands on his hips.

"Sshhh! You think I'm a criminal?"

"Well it was exciting for a moment."

Mike began his stroll down the first hall towards the stage. He did as the sign requested and walked between the purple velvet ropes; as he walked he began to feel small. The concert hall was intensely large-the largest of the three main venues-from his position the stage below looked the size of a hatbox lid. The whole room sunk at least a hundred feet or so from where he was standing, with more than two thousand seats almost circling from wall to wall. The proscenium made even the largest man feel minute; "acoustic clouds" that hung above the audience resembled long rounded and stacked boxes-dozens of feet from the ceiling, flat on the bottom and running to the side walls; each with an opening for stage lights on the foot.

The whole room looked like a giant ocean wave cascading from the back to the stage, from side to side, like two walls of rising water were ready to crash together in the center at the crescendo. Then the Grand Organ that graced the back of the stage seemed surrealistic. Mike had never witnessed anything like it. According to the pamphlet Shannon had taken from the tour starting point, there were ten thousand one hundred and fifty-four pipes ranging in size from one half the size of a No. 2

117

pencil and producing a sound unlike a dog whistle that can be heard to the very back of the auditorium.

The concert hall offered a unique odor of fresh clean carpeting, upholstery, Birchwood and curtains. It would be a smell that Michael would never forget-each time a similar one wafted past him, he would think of tonight and the most beautiful building the world.

A quick tour of the Opera Theater that held fewer seats and a smaller stage was still spectacular, as was the even smaller Drama Theater. Then Shannon and Mike walked to the main hall as Mike found his breath.

Shannon moved closer to Mike, her face showed the expression of satisfaction, she wrapped her arm around his shoulder again-this time in contentment-not like a few hours ago, which was in pity and sadness for him. Mike turned and gave her a hug, his body warmth gave Shannon a shudder; he thanked her for his experience today and he took her hand and led her outside. Back on the concrete walk Mike pulled lightly on her hand back to the benches that lined the Harbour.

They sat there silent for a few moments, he was still reeling over the experience he would never forget, Shannon was warm from her pride over how she turned a man who was upset about his life, into a child who was excited as seeing Disneyland for the first time-as she was when her family took her-she thought that must be how Mike feels now.

She felt warmness around her chest and arms, the breeze had stopped and the air inside the Opera House was warm, so she slipped the windbreaker off. She returned her arm to Mike's shoulder again, this time she felt a shot of electricity as her skin touched his, the warmth of his neck, the slightly sweaty sensation, the coolness of her arm, whatever it was she tingled inside around her middle and sides; her head swam just a little. She didn't know what else to do so she pulled him a little closer, and Mike pulled back. They were inches from each other's lips. The temptation was agonizing, for both of them.

Mike then looked away.

"Is everything all right Michael?"

He sighed through his nose lightly and then turned to her; "This has been the most wonderful day of my life, I swear it."

"But…"

"I… It's hard to explain." He looked into her eyes, past the bluest of blue, to the soul that reflected the image of the Opera House as it reflected off the water behind her, "When you flirt with me, it feels so… I feel so young. But then a few seconds ago, when you put your arm around me, I felt old. So old, older than you. You are over a dozen years younger than I am, you are a beautiful woman, young with the power of youthful spirit and playfulness, I'm growing old inside from the world that has burned me."

"I'm sorry Michael, I was just… I just felt it was the proper thing to do."

"Don't be sorry. This was the most spectacular day of my life, ever. I have you to thank, and I so look forward to the next day with you I think I can die in my sleep next week and they will never be able to remove the smile from my face."

Shannon leaned forward towards Mike's face, his stomach turned knots, and he started to shiver from anticipation as Shannon kissed him on the cheek. She sat back on the concrete bench and remained quiet for a moment, thinking.

Finally she spoke; "Let's have bite to eat shall we?"

Mike was amazed at her power, her looks and now… her ability to use Australian dialect and American English so easily, there was something hidden under that façade of beauty and smarts. It comforted him.

"Sure."

They walked down to the Opera Bar, a restaurant that one can dine inside or out, Shannon chose out. They were seated next to the railing of the Harbour, overlooking the beautiful bay and the ships that passed. It had grown dark, there was a chill in the air and Shannon donned her windbreaker, Mike did the same. The smell of the sea wafted from the water below, salty and brine with an overtone of animal.

J Jay Ross

The little bistro was romantic, there was quiet music playing over hidden speakers, umbrellas open even at night to give the place a closed in café look. Little glass bowls with etched glass and white candles in them to light the tables. Soft upholstered chairs with high back beckoned the weary walker or tour tourist from the walkways to come and sit.

There was soft lighting provided by lamps on poles, simple opaque white globes and low wattage bulbs. Pathways around the place and around the stairs that led up to the main level were lighted by small vented fixtures in the concrete.

They ate in near silence, glancing at each other as they took small bites of a delicious appetizer they decided to have instead of a full meal. A small selection of cheese sticks and dressing to dip them into, a couple of spare ribs in a tangy barbeque glaze, chips (fries) and scallops in a creamy white wine sauce. Shannon ordered a Coke and Mike had a coffee.

They were contemplating dessert when Mike noticed Shannon was a little pale, her color drained very fast and she seemed very uncomfortable all of a sudden.

"Are you alright?" Mike asked.

She smiled as best she could under the circumstances.

"Yes, of course. Haven't been on this long of a walk in a while. I'm… tired."

Mike picked up the check and laid out a few notes from his wallet, then rose picking up both their packs, hoisting them onto his shoulder without any effort. He held a hand out for his friend and she took it with a smile of appreciation, albeit a throbbing was aching her side, she was not very happy about the pain. It was making things a little less-romantic.

"After you." Mike said.

Shannon stood back against the lamppost that held the Bus Stop sign and watched as Mike tried to flag the bus down. She had a smile on her face, a pained one though; as the conversation just before they walked here was solemn, sad. She had made a flirty move and was rejected, by a man she felt so much for inside. But he was afraid and she knew she was trying to make up for the fight she had with Mathew perhaps... But there was something about this man, sure he was more than a decade older, but he had a spark of a new formed star in him. She would have to see if she could get closer without hurting him, without hurting herself. And speaking of hurt, the pain had receded but only marginally. She would have to look into it in the morning. Her suspicions made her uneasy; this kind of thing would make a mess of her life.

The first bus came close to the curb and Mike stepped forwards as if he was ready to board and the driver nearly struck him as he passed.

"That's the second time this week!" He shouted back towards Shannon.

She stepped in front of him for the next bus and looked him in the eyes.

"I'm sorry I offended you Michael. I wasn't being fresh or cheeky, I wasn't even feeling randy... I just felt the moment called for me to..." Shannon heard a bus approaching and she put her hand out to Mike to indicate she wanted him to stand back, a shot of fear rushed through him, for a second he thought she was going to step in front of the bus...

She did. The driver spotted her and slowed to the curb then opened his door. Still in a little bit of shock, Mike was pulled up into the bus by Shannon, who paid the fare and led him to the back for the ride back to Rushcutters Bay and the Bay Point Hotel.

"*Oh*! That's how you do it."

The bus pulled away with the same fervor and driving skills that Shannon displayed earlier in the day, he even navigated the same way. Mike was happy the driver waited till they were seated before igniting his rockets and taking off, he then looked at his tour guide; she was folding up the notes she used to pay the driver from and was in the process of putting them in her front pocket of her cutoffs.

"You scared the hell out me back there." Mike was nearly panting.

"Sorry. The only way to get a bus here in Sydney is to get the driver's attention. You have to flag them down like a cab in America or they will run your feet over."

"Oh."

"Michael Greene, can I ask you a personal question?"

"Of course."

Her expression was dry and curious, not foreboding but she hindered a thought of suspicion in it. She asked, "What do you do for a living, back in the States?"

Mike swallowed a dry knot in his throat; he scanned the back of the bus for eager ears and then turned to give the answer to the question he had dreaded for the entire time he knew her.

"I'm a cop."

"I suspected as much…" Her expression never changed.

The bus arrived six blocks from the Bay Point Hotel, most of the way Shannon and Mike were sloshed around the back seat together, into one another and apart. The driver's maniacal operation seemed suicidal at times, the rate of speed he was attaining rivaled that of most NASCAR tracks. Shannon had been quiet for the trip, since Mike revealed to her his occupation back home, Mike suspected that it was because she was debating whether he still was a worthy friend or maybe he should be locked up like the cops in L.A. were going to be.

He wondered if he should have poured a little of his soul out to her at Mrs. Macquarie's Chair-what the little glimpse of it he gave-he would never give more to a somewhat stranger than he did today, a moment of surrender, but Mike felt he needed to get the pressure off his chest, the pain that still kept him awake at night, nearly a month later.

Mike closed his eyes and he could see Rika's blonde bangs dropping below her eyes and the swift involuntary move she made with her hand to put it right back into place on her forehead, where it held for a few more moments; till she had to do it again-it was almost flirtatious at times. The way her dark clothing contrasted with the grass they were stretched out on, the way her hair and eyes conflicted with her clothing, the way her life was dissimilar to her lifestyle; which made Mike feel younger when she spoke to him, but the conversation was intelligent, which made Rika diverse from others her age.

Shannon, on the other side of Mike when she wasn't being pulled against the side of the bus by the g-forces, was not on the same level as he was. She wasn't concerned the least bit he was a police officer; in fact it seemed to fit him like a tea-cozy, he was a big man, had very hard features in regions and was a quick thinker. He also reminded her of a few policemen she knew by the way he asked so many questions, he never backed down with married Joey at the bar and he handled the little drunk American sailor like a pro.
What concerned the young barmaid turned tour guide was the fact Mike excited her so.

She wasn't looking for a new beau, nor was she looking for a replacement of Mathew, but Mike was a breath of fresh clean air. He was innocent in the ways of the Australian culture, which made it easy for her to tease him, he liked to follow along on her little fantasy charades; playing the part as well as any child would, but with the intensity of well-mannered man.

But his *story*... Shannon glanced at Michael, who was watching the bus driver initiate a curbside maneuver to stop at their appointed locale, he was strong and full of life, but the girl he liked so very much who had killed herself over loneliness? And it was Shannon's fault for exhausting him, then placing him a position like the Chair and telling him the story of a lonely Mrs. Macquarie, no wonder he felt out of place right away. But then she saw the other side of the older man, the soft pleased soul who loved the styles and structure of the Opera House. He was like a child in his observations, like an explorer on his first discovery. Excited, jubilant, ecstatic, *tender*...

Shannon exited the bus first after the deranged driver managed to come to a stop barely fifteen feet from the actual spot they were supposed to, she insisted that Mike go first, but as any gentleman would do he simply pushed his hand out in front of him opened palm and nodded with a smile. Shannon thanked him and proceeded. They were still a good five minute walk to the Bay Point and this place was awfully close to the reaches of the dark folks of Kings Cross, they would have to step lively to keep from being molested. After about five minutes, she broke the silence that had shrouded them since they left the Opera House.

"Michael, have you ever married?"

"Yes." His voice was low and solemn, he didn't hesitate to answer, but there was a slight disapproval in his voice. "Once." He looked over to her as they walked.

"Was she a nice woman?"

"At first, but she turned out to be a little *bit*... uh, neurotic."

"Oh." Shannon chose her question carefully, she wanted to know more about her friend, but didn't want to seem prying. "Were you happy, at first?"

"Yes, I was; we were. It was a whirlwind romance, engagement and wedding. Then after Mike Jr. was born, things changed; she changed."

"You have a son?" She chided herself for not asking about children after inquiring about a wife.

"Yeah. He's sixteen now, just turned. He lives with his mother in Sacramento, I bet he would love it here..." Mike let his voice trail off; after he said the words he actually found doubt in them as he gazed around at the darkened streets, the high rise hotels and the chatter of traffic.

They were nearing the final three blocks to the hotel and Shannon felt pressed to find out more about Michael. Traffic had lightened; many folks had no need to be this far into the tourist sections this late in the evening. A slight breeze blew the odor of briny seawater across Rushcutters Bay past Mike and Shannon, she slowed her pace.

"Tell me about him-your son." She asked this question first for a reason.

"He's bright, a little lazy though. He likes to sleep in for hours past sunrise. We have little in common now, but when he was younger we did everything together."

Mike's voice was a bit unsorted; he had a lump in his throat. He didn't mind answering Shannon's questions, he was just apprehensive about his replies.

"Like what?"

"Fishing, hunting, those sorts of things. We liked going to the movies a lot," Mike smiled widely "We both loved *The Man from Snowy River*."

"Oh I just adored that picture! I love the end when Jim says to Harrison about coming back for the horses, he looks at Jessica and says to her father; "*and whatever else is mine…*" I cried for nearly an hour over that ending." Her voice warbled a bit, she was reliving the ending in her mind, the romantic time the old Australia must have been. "Did you see *Return to Snowy River?*"

"Of course, the day it came out in theaters. It wasn't the same as the first though."

"Yeah." One more question, she told herself, and that will do for tonight. "What happened? With your wife I mean."

"We fell out of love. Like I said, she went a little weird after Mikie was born, she was possessive of him, everywhere she went and everything she did had to be with him. After he was about eight or nine, he was tired of it, he wanted to be with his dad a lot too and Lisa seemed a little jealous, she would start saying hurtful things about me to him. After a while I guess he believed them, in the end he moved with her. He rarely talks to me now and she only calls when she wants money for something that the child support can't provide."

"I'm sorry." Shannon truly was. She felt she had time for one more, although Shannon knew she was pushing her luck, she had to know. "How did you and Lisa? Is that her name? Meet…"

"Yes its Lisa, well we were…"

"It's a pretty name. I like it."

"Do you want to hear the story or not?"

"Oh yes, *dreadfully* sorry…" Shannon beamed a smile at him.

Mike continued with a little smile of his own, the memory of his first encounter with Lisa was a good one. "I was in San Francisco for a training exercise in riot control;" He looked at Shannon and slapped his fist into his open hand, "You know, beating poor criminals in the street?"

"Very funny. Please continue."

"Well the guys and I had the this one night off and we were just walking the streets, looking for a good time I guess, I wasn't in the mood for a one-nighter or anything; I just wanted to see the sights. We walked past this little café in Little Italy and there was the most beautiful woman I had ever seen; drinking an espresso. One of the guy's I was with was from San Francisco P.D. and he knew her, so he introduced us. For the rest of the week I was there for training, the young lady and I would meet for coffee or something. When I returned home I called every night I was off shift, and we would talk on the phone for hours; we even sent letters to one another for months. In between work days I would occasionally make the four hour drive just to see her."

"How romantic. Did you have to threaten her with your billy-club to get her to marry you?" Shannon added a soup of sarcasm to the words.

Mike frowned frustration so Shannon took the hint that the joke was getting old and made a little zipper motion across her mouth and pretended to throw away the key behind her. He continued.

"One night, after dating for three and a half months and forty dollars a month in long distance phone bills, I had the idea on my mind to ask her to marry me. I bought this little quarter carat diamond ring, but had no plan for a romantic enough evening. We were to meet in Ghirardelli Square, at the end of the Cable Car route at Hyde and Beach; I think it was supposed

to be around six o'clock. I waited and waited, three hours had
passed and she hadn't shown up yet. I was getting worried-
Frisco was known for its crime rate-so I boarded the second to
last Cable Car to North Beach, which is where she lived, to look
for her. She wasn't around the end of the line either, so I
returned to Ghirardelli and waited. About nine thirty I saw this
woman sitting on the bench by the round-a-bout, that's where
the gripmen turns the cable car around, and there was this pissed
off look on her face."

"She was angry?"

Mike pursed his lips, but at the corners of his mouth was
a smile. "She thought I said eight, to this very day when we
argue about something she always brings this up-but anyways I
sat down beside her and hugged her tight and apologized for
losing her. '*I thought I lost you forever*' I said and she sobbed in
my ear that she loved me. We stood up to take the last car of the
evening north again, the line was a little long so we had to wait
for nearly an hour so Lisa and I just stood in line talking about
things, I had my arm around her and there was this tall thin black
dude-a street performer, the ones who play music or do artsy
things for cash-anyways he was all dressed in Rasta clothes."

"*Rasta?*"

"Jamaican."

"Oh, how quaint."

"*Anyways*, he had this electric guitar all made up with
stickers he had collected I guess and this little amplifier next to
him on the ground. He was playing some god-awful version of a
Doors song and I was racking my brain, trying to find a romantic
moment to ask Lisa the question. Then suddenly, there was this
little gust of warm air-it was about fifty that night-and my hair
sort of stood on end. There were little goose pimples on the back
of my neck and I could smell the pong coming from Aquatic
Park towards the area we were in. Then this guitar guy starts to
play *Stairway to Heaven*. I got all misty eyed and squeezed Lisa
tight; I pulled her face to mine and kissed her like I had never
kissed her before." Mike smiled upwardly towards the Sydney

127

sky to try to catch a moment of remembrance. "It was then I asked her to marry me."

"How… idealistic." Shannon had to turn her head towards the street to wipe a single tear from her left eye. She was moved.

They were now at the front steps of the Bay Point and Tommy, the doorman, came out of his little cove near the inside door.

"G'day lovers!" He simpered.

Shannon shot him a look of disapproval and he nodded and looked downward.

"Hi Tommy. Fancy giving me a lift home?" Shannon returned at him with a warmer tone.

"Of course Miss Shannon!" His smile returned. "Be just a few as I check off." The man turned and walked back into his little glass cubicle.

"I'm going to walk Mr. Greene up to his room and return." She added.

Shannon prodded Mike in the direction of the lobby, then the elevator and in.

"Why didn't we ride the bus back to where we left the truck?" Mike asked with a tone of concern in his voice.

"It's okay Michael Greene. No worries, all right? Tommy has given me a lift home many times, we live within a few blocks of each other, I don't drive at night very well and I'm tired. I had an incident once and since then if it gets dark or I am too sleepy, then I catch a ride and retrieve my truck later."

Mike looked down his nose at his shoes, wondering what he did to have the evening end like this. "But what about your truck tomorrow? Are we still on for tomorrow?"

"Of course, you still have the second half of the tour to fulfill. As for my truck, well… do you remember that I asked you to look around to see anything different?"

"Yes, the Sydney Lace."

"Very good, you remembered. But you also didn't notice that there was a little flat right in front of you, Mr. Policeman; a nameplate that read *Hunter*-by the gate; did you?"

"You live there?"

Mike sounded surprised, then a little hurt. Hurt because he didn't remember quite where they parked the truck and now Shannon's confession of her home's location made Mike feel a little ticklish inside. *She drove us right to her house and you didn't even know...*

He smiled at himself and nodded at Shannon. "Very tricky Miss Hunter."

"You have to be more observant next time Mr. Copper." She smiled.

"I'm going to bring my notepad tomorrow."

"Too late, you had your chance, I doubt I will let you that close to my place of slumber again..."

Mike frowned, "That is sad..." They arrived at the second floor and Mike glanced into the pool enclosure, there was a family swimming. He said, "There's something more, to my story, that is."

"What is it?"

"Lisa didn't act all that bad all the time, she was over the top of course a lot, but the real reason she left me was because of my alcoholism. We divorced because of it."

Shannon nodded and thought alone for a moment. They reached Mike's room door and he paused in front of it, holding the key. They smiled at each other uncomfortably and Mike opened the door. Just before he closed it, Shannon spoke quietly.

"Sometimes people see something in another that is not there."

Mike nodded, hoping for a reprieve.

"Other times someone sees what no other can see."

Mike smiled.

Shannon returned the smile two-fold. "Your rehabilitation has made you a different person, not the one that

married Lisa. You are who you are and I see *that* side of you.
You're a good man. I feel it."

She lunged to the tip of her toes and planted a kiss on his
lips and escaped to the elevator.

"G'day Michael Greene. I shall see you in the morning,
eleven sharp, don't forget swimming trunks, eh? No excuses this
time. If you're late I will take Tommy to the Harbour Bridge
instead."

Mike wanted to follow her down discreetly, to see that
she was all right with the little doorman, but he realized he was
acting jealously-they weren't dating-and she was just a friend.
*But wasn't this just like a date? She told you about her ex-
boyfriend, you told her about your ex-wife and son.*

Mike frowned as he headed into his room. He thought
about why he had told her of Rika, and rehab. *Yeah, it was just
like a first date, you confessed a deep feeling to her…*

He picked up the pack of Australian smokes and shook
one out into his hand. Lighting the cigarette, Mike stepped in
front of his window overlooking Sydney; what he could see of it
anyway. The Tower was blinking its anti-collision lights at the
top, and he thought for a moment of Shannon, she was on her
way home-with Tommy-and Mike was right there in front of her
house, she led him there; then she told him about it.

*This was more than just a little tour of the town, this was
a glimpse into her life here…* Mike lay back onto the bed and
stubbed the butt out in the ashtray on the nightstand, he thought
for a moment about turning on the television, but declined opting
to close his eyes and rerun the day-the good parts. He leaned
over and turned off the lamp and the room went dark, except the
lights from the Tower. Mike began to doze immediately,
thinking of Shannon Hunter, her house, her face, and the way
she liked to tease at him.

He saw the tail of her hair floating on the little breezes
that blew across the bay and over the short rolling hills to the
Gardens; he could smell the ginger-lemon grass shampoo,
occasionally the wafts of sea air found their way to Shannon's

long bangs that escaped her ponytail knot. He smiled at how the wind would wave her hair back and forth around her brow and she would scrunch up her face in frustration then use her middle finger protruding down between her index and ring fingers to pull it back to the top of her ear, only to have the wisp of hair fall down a few seconds after.

He liked the way she acted serious at times, but he could see her eyes glimmer in felicity, the little tear of joy she shed when he first went inside the Opera House, even though he was beside himself with excitement, he still had time to see the look on her face; a look of satisfaction. Mike then fell asleep…

Tommy left Shannon off at her flat and went his way home; he lived close, just a few blocks away on Judge Street. She gave him the traditional kiss on the cheek, let him inhale her faint perfume-as she always did in payment for the ride-and walked up to the slightly modest two-story in front of her truck.

Inside Shannon peeled off her cut-offs and her tank-top then went to the bathroom to run the shower. As she passed the mirror she looked into it and into her eyes, then surveyed her facial features, and finally after making a face at herself, smiled and took off her bikini. The shower was warm and cleansing, the day was full of adventure and Shannon had a little pang of happiness that was not for her boyfriend in the States. She was intrigued and the smile she wore the whole twenty minutes in the warm water spray was not for him, it was for Mike Greene. The goofy American policeman and his wonder of the city, the sights she took him to and the last bit of tease, her apartment.

She shook her head in the towel she had wrapped her hair in thinking of the look on his face when she revealed they had parked the truck in front of her flat. She was falling for this bloke-Shannon knew he was feeling for her too, that was bad…

CHAPTER SEVEN

WINDS OF CHANGE

Mike woke to the sounds of the folks from next door banging their luggage on the walls on their way down the hall to the lift. He panicked and looked at his watch, it said nine forty-five. For a second Mike wondered if he had set it for Australian time, then he remembered doing so yesterday in the restaurant before going on his tour.

Sighing, he lifted his body off the bed and swayed a little to the bathroom to shower, his daily routine. Lisa, his ex, liked to shower just before bed each night; it was an odd ritual, for an odd woman, most folks like to shower in the morning to wash the sleep off. Some like to shower in the evening to wash the day off, or some problem they were focusing on. The hot water relaxed the body as it did the mind. But Lisa wasn't relaxed when she left the shower at night; sometimes she was just getting wound up. One of the many things Mike thought she was a little off about.

Out of the shower, Mike spent a few extra minutes in front of the mirror; making sure his hair was just right. He took the trimmer out of his kit and plugged it in; the hotel had both 220vac and 120vac for tourists and ran the clippers to the hair on his neck. He then touched up his little goatee around the frame of his mouth, then running a razor over the rest of his face. He splashed on a little after-shave and rolled deodorant under his arms, adding a little extra in case they would travel farther today.

It was ten fifty-five when Mike was sitting outside the hotel on an iron bench, a fresh cup of coffee in his hand and a rolled up *Sydney Morning Herald* under his right arm. He had a look on his face of a man that was about to go to the moon; excitement tickled his insides as he imagined the look of surprise on Shannon Hunter's face as she pulled up. When she did, it was five minutes after eleven.

"Waiting for me Michael Greene?" She said with a smile as she stood from the doorway of the truck in the street.

"No Ma'am. I'm waiting for my tour group. The leader gets very cranky if I am a minute late; let alone *five* minutes…"

Mike crossed his legs, pulled out and opened the *Herald* and raised the paper to his face.

She narrowed her eyes at him, pursed her lips, and then nodded in an apologetic way; she closed the door to the truck and walked around, taking the backpack from beside him.

"I'll get your bags, sir…" She plopped the pack into the back of the Mazda and turned to meet Mike's face. "I had an unexpected phone call, I'm sorry." She whispered to his ear, close enough to make Mike's neck hairs tingle. As she slowly pulled her head back she grazed his cheek with her lips and gave a little smack sound. She hadn't made full contact; just enough to change Mike's expressionless face to a warm smile. "I'll explain on our way there."

"*Where?*"

Mike handed the paper to the doorman before his feet touched the ground after his leap from the bench.

"It is a surprise… Michael Greene with three E-s. We are going to the beach first, then to the surprise. Did you rest well?" She asked as she rounded the front of the truck and entered the driver's door, Mike joining her from the left side. Mike told her he had…

Shannon pulled out into traffic like the crazy driver she was, but today they headed into the opposite direction than yesterday, driving east-north east on Expressway 76. A little pause at Watson's Bay, and then drove the same road towards the south. Every few minutes Shannon would point out a new bay and explain its name's origins and a little history on it. Finally, after about an hour and a half in the cramped truck they arrived at their destination. She crisscrossed the motor lot to find a space and pulled into one about twenty yards from the beach walkway, pulling the shifter into the neutral position she tapped Mike on the leg.

"This… is Bond*i* Beach…" She pronounced the '*i*' hard like eye. "We walk from here."

She hopped out of the truck and grabbed her pack from the box of the truck and slung it over her shoulder; Mike did the same, without a word. He followed her down a little cement path that went from the lot to the edge of the sand wall, about a forty foot walk. Mike paused and looked around, he smiled at the architecture, it reminded him a little of Santa Cruz, in the way the outbuildings were constructed with the high archway doors and the little round lamps on tall light posts. The beach wall was built up about seven or eight feet above the sand line, with a staircase leading to the beach that ran down and along the wall. Near the center of the beach there was a little house that was shaped like a pilot house on an old tug boat, oval round in the front and squareish towards the back. The back nested a few feet behind the wall and the front protruded out onto the sand with a rounded base. It was the secondary lifeguard shack, or as Shannon told him in Australian slang, "Second*ree lifehouse post…*"

The beach was well groomed before people arrived in the early morning, Mike noted; by the rake marks where the empty spots were. It was still over two weeks till May and the sun hadn't warmed enough to attract huge crowds. But the ones that braved the sixty degree heat-Mike used to tan in fifty degrees at Lake Tahoe-were partially clothed in warm climate swimsuits and the surfers wore wetsuits.

Shannon stopped Mike at the base of the wall to remove her boots and socks. Mike noticed how beautiful her feet were; perfect with a light pink polish, Mike saw himself rubbing them after a long day walking, to ease her cramps. He sat his backpack down, retrieved a bottle of water and took a sip. A vision yes, but he was beginning to look for things he liked about Shannon, her little traits that most others would ignore. She picked up his bag, stood and gave it a look inside as they walked on.

"Not a fair turnout today, eh?" Shannon said as she shielded her eyes from the sun, when she turned to look at Mike. "I'm a bit disappointed at that, I was hoping for you to get the peeps."

"The what?"

"Peepshow…The north end of the beach is usually filled with white pointers."

"White what?"

"Mommies showin' their Mammies!" Shannon laughed as she looked down at her chest, back up to Mike's eyes and winked. Mike felt startled in his own clothing, startled and a little overanxious, he wanted his bag back to cover some... areas.

"How very disappointing…" Mike replied, mocking Shannon. "Would you like to demonstrate for me?" His tone half serious, half creaky like an adolescent boy in the onset of puberty.

"No." She tossed Mike's bag to his feet. Shannon didn't even break her stride when she looked over her shoulder at Mike and said; "Sorry, I didn't bring my sunscreen lotion." She turned back towards the direction they were walking, and smiled widely.

After they walked from one end to the other, Mike stopped to look around again, to gain a feel of a place he was certain he would probably never see again, like the Opera House the night before. He wanted to take it all it in a have something to remember when he returned, at this moment he wished he had brought a camera; if not for the pictures of the scenery and the buildings, but to have a few snapshots of his pretty guide.

Shannon laid out a blanket and set out some food she'd purchased still in its wrappers. Kentucky Fried Chicken, from the store near her home on George Street. They ate and watched the brave cool weather beachgoers play and swim in the surf. Mike watched as Shannon removed her shirt and shorts to reveal the bikini that had been winking at him for the past two days, he removed his shoes and top and followed her into the cool water.

They swam and played for an hour and then went back to the warmth of the blanket and towels. Shannon had brought two large beach towels, one for both of them and as Mike dried his head he could smell the sweet tangy aroma of her laundry detergent. Another glimpse into her life. He finished as they sat next to each other and watched some kids playing with a Frisbee.

"Now, this is a vacation." Mike said firmly.

"Are you sure you wouldn't like to sit in a hotel pub somewhere and drink colas?"

He rolled his eyes at Shannon, who was retying her long fair ponytail. She watched as Mike's chest rippled as he pulled his shirt on, her insides tumbled as his forearms and biceps flexed when he wrangled the clothing into place. He caught her stare.

"What?"

"It's been a nice weekend for me. I feel anxious about going back to the pub, summers almost over. School starts soon, and I've decided not to go back."

Mike felt ambushed. "Why not?"

Her face faded into a grimace and then turned towards him, leaning back on an elbow. She was thinking of the right way to say it, the decision she made last night, and confirmed this morning after her appointment with the doctor. Things didn't go so well after that and she was one the phone to her parents in Kuranda, explaining her choice to return home. They were broken hearted, as she feared they would be. She was in no small amount of distress over the early diagnosis. She could do something about it if she wanted to, but she'd seen what others had suffered through after treatment and with a heavy heart decided not to go that route. Michael would never be allowed to know of her fate.

She looked up and caught the sun waning.

"Michael! What time is it?"

"Five forty."

"Oh lord, we'll be late!"

She jumped to her feet and began a half maniacal cleanup of the picnic spot. The blanket was rolled up and the leftovers were all piled into the white and red bucket for the tin at the bottom of the motor lot. She donned her shorts and top, then began packing everything that could fit into her pack. Mike was dumbfounded and silent as he helped. He put on his boots and Shannon stood and began a rush to the parking area.

At the end of the beach Shannon cut a ninety degree angle towards the steps up to the motor lot and Mike followed, she seemed a bit hurried and it took a little effort to keep up with the barefooted woman, he was wearing his hiking boots.

"Are we in a hurry?" He asked panting up the last few steps.

"A bit. I promised someone something tonight and I've ticked off a few too many minutes here."

She said without looking back at him. She could hear the lack of proper breathing and smiled a little, to think of how big and intimidating he looked, yet he was in rather poor shape.

When they reached the truck Shannon opened her door all the way and set her pack on the seat. Mike did the same a few seconds later when he reached the vehicle, and grabbed one of his water bottles he didn't need yesterday, but was dying for today. Shannon turned her back to Mike and he saw she was untying her bikini top from under her tank top. She slipped the top off and out from under the bottom of the shirt and quickly ran a blue and light green tube top over her head. She pulled her arms through the arm holes of the tank top and one by one slipped them through the new article of clothing, and then pulled it down over her body. She then removed the tank top and tossed it onto the front seat, when she caught Mike's gape.

"Be cautious here Mr. Greene, the animal control man will mistake you for a slobbering dingo and lock you up tight..."

"Oh, please continue... it'll be worth it." He grinned mischievously.

137

"Sorry. I'm just a bit chilled, and where we are going it will be a little cooler tonight."

She reached into her pack and pulled out a beach towel and unrolled it, wrapping it around her torso. She selected another clothing item from the bag; a knee length skirt that was navy in color, with a little silver snaps at the waist. She gave a quick look left then right and then with one hand slid off her jean shorts and bikini bottom in a single motion. While she reached down to pick them up and start her feet into the skirt, Mike noticed a little scar that ran from the top of her buttocks to the middle left of her back. Shannon wriggled a little under the towel and unwrapped it from her waist and rolled it back up, Mike hadn't realized he was still staring where her behind was.

"Mr. Greene, if you don't mind…" This time her voice was a little terse.

"Where did you get that scar?"

She turned as if she could see it and then looked at him over her shoulder. "Here, I'm afraid."

"Shark attack?" Mike had heard of Australia's famous shark attacks.

"Skateboard…" She pointed to a couple of kids riding along the sidewalk on a pair of them.

"Skateboard? You ride?"

"A bloke toppled me as I was coming out of the store." Her face turned a little blush, "Why are you staring at me bum?"

"I think it's cute. Besides, no one but my wife has ever undressed in front of me before."

"Ex… wife." Shannon corrected.

"Yes. Ex-wife."

"Shall we go? We have a bit of trip ahead of us."

Without waiting for an answer she put her clothes in the pack, zipped it up and tossed it in the back of the truck. Mike tumbled in, he had to pick up his left leg, it had cramped up on him. The drive back was a little more than suicidal if not just plain heart stopping at times, and Mike had to brace himself against the door several times to keep from flying out the window. They traveled back towards the City of Sydney on Expressway 76 then onto 40 North. Thirty minutes later they were at Darling Harbour, more specifically the Darling Harbour Marina. Shannon parked the Mazda near the Powerhouse Museum at the end of the marina and stepped out, running her hands down her skirt to flatten any wrinkles.

Mike made a once over of his attire and pounded the dried sand from his shorts, he hoped the butt had also dried. He felt a little out of place, Shannon had planned ahead and brought something more formal, he had his polo shirt and khaki shorts with the billowed pockets, and he taken them into the ocean for a swim. He bent over and laced his hiking boots up tight, he hoped that the light tan boots matched his shorts; he'd seen a lot of folks wearing the same kind of set up elsewhere, at the Opera House and on the beach. But this place seemed, rich.

"This is it." She addressed no one particular.

"What is?" Mike said, relieved they were done driving for a while.

"Berth 32, down there…" She pointed down into the harbor, to then end of one of the piers inside the marina.

"What is?" Mike repeated himself again.

"Your surprise, silly." She giggled at Mike's concern.

"Are we going on a boat?" Concern flooded Mike's voice.

"Of course, if we wanted to fly somewhere we would have gone to the airport…" Shannon let her sarcasm stab at his concerns.

"I… haven't been on many boats." Mike protested.

"You're a policeman; you're not supposed to be afraid of anything." Came the reply, she had gained a few steps on Mike; who had slowed down.

"Yeah, in the desert two hundred miles from the ocean…" Mike was begging to sound like a child that didn't want to go get his first haircut.

"You said you like to visit San Francisco all the time."

"But I never went out into the bay."

"Relax you big policeman baby. We won't go far."
Shannon picked up the pace, hoping that by hurrying, Mike
might not have time to think about it anymore. "We're almost
there."

Mike had caught up with Shannon at the gate; she had to
use a pass code to gain access to the marina, then they walked
down a long narrow staircase to the docks, fifteen feet below. As
they approached the end of the jetty, Mike noticed they weren't
turning into any of the smaller pleasure boats that were docked
here, and the only ones left were the big yachts, the kind you see
on the *Rich and Famous* shows. Ten feet to go before sea, Mike
saw what looked to be a fifty-plus foot luxury boat, no-a ship, at
the end of the pier.

"Here we are." Shannon said, and once again ran her
hands down her skirt, and then tugged at the bottom of her
halter/tube top to straighten it. Checking to make sure nothing
was hanging out or peeking, she put on a big smile and raised
her voice to the boat, "Ahoy *Stella*!"

"Ahoy! Welcome aboard!" Came back the woman's
reply. Shannon reached back and took Mike by the hand and
walked slowly to the little staircase that led over the rail into the
fabulous yacht.

He helped her to steady herself and she kissed him on the
cheek and said, "Sorry."

"For what?"

"You'll see."

Shannon walked towards the stairs under the immense
flying bridge.

Mike's mouth dropped a little as he looked over the
immense boat, it was all white from bow to stern and the light
reflected from the little lamps of the shoreline off the water and
gave the paint a pearl-like look. There were three windows up
front and two along each side, all were tinted black and made the
boat look sleek and fast… He could see a series of oval shaped
portholes below the dock-line, because the boat stood twenty
feet beyond the end of the dock, Shannon and he stepped off the

little stairs onto a deck that had an overhang coming down from the flying bridge, there was a little spoiler shooting skyward, for looks no doubt. Mike could see forward into a room below the flying bridge, a set of controls that rivaled an airplanes, and off to the left of that was another little staircase that ran down another four or five feet to the main cabin. He could see a pair of female legs; crossed and the top one was kicking back and forth slowly.

"Down here!" Another call-it appeared to be coming from the owner of the woman's legs.

"Coming!" Shannon replied, this time there was a little excitement in her voice.

Mike saw her practically jump the last few feet down and he followed as fast as he could, careful not to bump his skull on the overhead. A very pretty young woman stood, with a glass of wine in her hand, met Shannon's embrace, wrapping her arms around her-glass and all.

"My God it has been so long since I've seen you!" The woman bubbled as she kissed Shannon on the cheek. "How are you doing, really?"

"Just wonderful, just like I told you this morning." Shannon's voice had yet to drop much.

"Well, we were far out yet. I couldn't hear all that well on the radio-phone." The woman turned her attention to Mike. "Is this him?"

Him? Mike thought nervously

"Oh, yes." Shannon stepped back and took Mike's arm, "This is Michael Greene, from America."

The woman curtsied slightly and took his hand, "How do you do? I'm Paula, and somewhere floating above us is John, my husband. He is *trying* to read some navigational charts; he'll be down in a flash." She turned and sat on the U shaped couch that ran the interior of the second deck, then she patted her hand on the sofa next to her; "Come sit next to me." Mikes face flushed a little as he did as he was told.

Paula was a forty-something trying to look like a thirty or twenty-something. Her clothes were tight, a blue skin clinging Moschato Mini Tank. The neckline exposed a chest that was probably an extension of some sort, Mike was slightly aware of enhancements, but Paula was sporting some serious extra cash around. She was warm when he sat next to her, she was radiating in beauty and body heat.

Her skin was creamy chocolate tan, obviously not from the southern regions where the sun was cooler than the northern tropicals; her hair was red and so where her thin brows above two large almond shaped eyes of blue that mounted a thin cheek line and small chin. Her lips were red from lipstick, but full and not duck-billed like so many stars wore this day and age. If it weren't for the Australian brogue, he'd sworn she was full blooded Irish.

"I thought you were going to be here an hour ago!"

A man's voice said as his legs appeared, stepping down the stairs. He was wearing white Dockers, a blue collared pull over and was carrying a rock glass full of brown booze. He shoved his right hand out towards Mike smiled at him, the way he had seen all the locals do so far. His face was a little older looking, maybe mid-forties; he had dark brown hair styled into a curl in front, like a Dean Martin wave and deep brown friendly eyes that sparkled, like most everyone else here in Australia. His face was small and pleasant looking, he was no macho model, but he wasn't Marty Feldman either.

"Name's John. You can call me Cap'n John or just John, whatever ya like mate except a bloody son of a bitch! Welcome aboard the *Stella Ursus*."

"Thank you; it is a very nice ship." Mike said after taking John's hand.

"This isn't anything really…" John put his hand to the side of his mouth and whispered to Mike, "It's my father's boat actually, ours sits in Cairns." He pronounced the name with a heavy accent so it sounded like *Cans*.

"Oh."

"Yes, I thought you were bringing the *Missy* along with you." Shannon cut across the conversation.

"Oh, I wish we could have." Paula grinned, she had dimples the size of ladybugs in her cheeks when she did so. "We couldn't bring her here… She won't fit under the Pyrmont Bridge."

"At least not without waiting a half hour or so for them to raise it." John chimed in. He had whispered again, like it was some big secret "Mast is too tall."

Mike nodded as if he understood.

He had sized up John; he had money-probably his father's-and he was very friendly with strangers. A great combination for Mike, he thought to himself.

"What do you do Michael?" Paula asked, trying to change from the subject of the sailboat.

Mike pulled at his collar and sat back down next to Shannon, "I'm a policeman."

"Oh! How delightful…" Her face went south for a second, "You aren't with those whomper blokes that beat that poor black man are you?"

Mike tried to smile the question off a little and then replied; "Nah. We wouldn't tolerate those types where I come from."

"Oh!" Paula exclaimed and nearly scared five years out of Mike, "Were you ever on *COPS*? I love that show!"

"No ma'am."

John and Paula laughed together; she rubbed her hand on Mike's leg and generated a little uncomfortable heat. Her hand was strong and soft. Shannon pursed her lips at Mike and gave her head a little twitch as if to convey '*Told you I was sorry…*'

"*Ma'am*! Did you hear that John? He sounds the bloody part!"

"Where you from then Mike?" John continued the questioning after the guffaws dropped off.

"Nevada. Near Reno."

Paula almost hit her head on the roof when she heard this and again Mike was startled, "Reno! We were just there last month!"

Mike looked at John and he was nodding his head.

"Yeah! Traveled on holiday with my father there, went to a gaming vendor, to one of your manufacturers, I forget the name…"

"Gaming Manufacturing Technology?"

"Yes, that was them. They made a set of back plates for my father's machines and they flew him over there to inspect their plant. My father was gracious enough to order a few dozen machines from them."

"Your father owns a casino?"

"Yes, three of them actually; in Perth. We're Westies."

"*Westie?*" Mike wondered.

Shannon jabbed him in the ribs softly, "That means they're from the west coast of Australia. John likes to use his *strine*; though it can be vulgar at times." She tilted her head in a mock apology.

"I see, I need subtitles …" Mike whispered back in a defeated tone.

"How terribly rude of me," John began. "It's my shout and I have yet to offer anything to you Mike." He stood and walked towards the port side, where a small bar was. "What is your preference?"

"Mike will have a Coke, and so will I." Shannon answered before Mike could. His eyes drifted towards hers and she smiled back at him, Mike realized she was protecting him-in a way-from having to answer questions about his choice of drink. "I want Michael to be on his abilities."

"Very good; two tea-totalers. Would you like a second honey?"

"Of course. I'm not sailing out of here tonight."

"I'm just going to let the *Ursus* drift out of the slip myself…" John stated with a straight face as he poured another drink for himself, then looked at Mike and Shannon and burst out in a belly laugh. "Better not, if we smash my father's best yacht on the rocks, after he is done with me, all they will ever find will be bum-nuts."

Mike sat back more in his seat, brushing next to Shannon. She stiffened and whispered into his ear again, "I'll tell you later." Mike was satisfied with that, and happy that Shannon caught on to his lack of knowledge in Australian vernacular.

"John Wright! How *dare* you talk like that in front of our guest?" Paula turned towards Mike, "I'm sorry dear, he gets a bit carried away with himself when he is sipping."

"Sorry mate. I know you aren't the typical American who comes here expecting to see every Aussie man wearing Khaki brush shorts and an oiled bush hat saying things like *"throw another shrimp on the bar-b"* or singing Waltzin' Matilda right?"

Mike shook his head, not really having a clue what John was talking about.

Shannon took over the conversation for a moment. "I'm heading home in a week, is Missy going to be in port?"

Paula looked at John and then back at Shannon and a smile crossed her face. "She is; we won't. Jeremy," Paula looked at Mike, "That's John's father…" Then she returned addressing the room, "Will be meeting us; we are flying to New Zealand to look at land for a possible hotel. Dreadful business thing." She frowned as she took a sip of her drink John handed her.

"Why from up there? Why not stay here and fly out?" Shannon asked.

Mike was beginning to feel like a third wheel on bicycle.

"Can't. Jeremy is looking over his cane fields and will be up there. Family business stuff, and he wants Johnny there too for a couple of days. We are going to leave Missy there." A flash of enlightenment crossed Paula's face. "You want her?"

Shannon smiled broadly back at her companion. "Why yes, if that is all right with you John."

"She's yours. But beware; she is in a bit of a mood these days."

"Of course, I'm off on holiday short of a week and would love to take her out. Nothing fancy, maybe the reef."

"Very good then. Oh, you might tell your folks that she is for sale if you like. Maybe they could buy you an early Christmas present, we left the deed with your man Kurran when we were there last."

"For sale? Why?" Shannon asked John.

"Dad's looking at a new one. A little bigger than Missy, about fifty-five or sixty."

"You'll need a full crew for that!"

"Yes and a larger slip in port."

The banter about sailboats-Mike assumed-continued over the next twenty minutes, so he sat there with a smile on his face and nodded when addressed and answered with yes and no's when questioned. He was bored out of his mind for the most part, but he did like watching Shannon engage in the conversation, it made her face light up and she looked as if she almost glowed. Mike didn't know why, but he was beginning to enjoy just watching her chat so casually, she was always teasing him or using her "guide voice" with him, so he rarely had the chance to see her engaged in a full conversation with anyone until now, and he liked it. He hoped he could have the chance to do the same with her soon. But then a flash of troubling sadness hit him, he remembered Shannon said she was going on holiday-vacation-next week, even though she told him she was returning home and not school. He saw a slight deception, obviously her friends weren't privy or he was misunderstanding what was going on. That depressed Mike and his face showed it. He quickly brightened when the conversation was steered towards him, offhandedly.

Shannon glanced at Mike and his face had turned a bit sour, she knew he wasn't having the cheeriest of times with her friends, she thought he might at first, but realized that strangers don't always connect the same way. She also came to the conclusion all this talk about sailboats and traveling around the world dragged Mike down; he was of a different class, the one she was taught to grow up in. John and Paula were of a higher set, mainly because of John's father Jeremy, who owned and operated the casinos around Australia, plus a sugar cane plantation near her home. The look on Mike's face was that of stalemate-he wouldn't complain, but he wasn't part of the whole conversation-and Shannon thought it would be best to let him off the proverbial hook and get him back to the hotel; she glanced at her watch.

Shannon listened for a while longer to the chatter, Paula and John were tag-teaming each other with Mike, who was oblivious to most of the conversation. She watched as he managed to keep in the conversation, even though a lot of it had to do with sailing, casino ownership, life in Perth, having more money than they could spend in a lifetime and seeing the world. But Mike smiled when he was supposed to, he laughed at the right times and added something useful once in a while. She was feeling something inside that she hadn't in a very long time. Something that tickled her insides as well as sent shivering jolts up and down her spine and legs. Every time Mike answered a question, she warmed, he was happy and honest. She wanted that. She wanted to know why she felt as if he was sweeping her off of her feet, he was so... innocent and shy, but at the same time he managed to fit in and not become overly controlling of the conversation. Mathew would be driving the chat towards his career, what a brave and noble man he was for the things he conquered in the world and he would've blown his chest out in triumph as those around him acquiesced their topics for his.

Mike never nudged her; he didn't squirm around like a child at the dentist's office nervously waiting for his name to be called in for a filling. She stared at his face as he answered questions about his life and job. For the first time since she knew them Shannon noticed Paula and John listened to someone without trying to sound better than thou.

She was falling in love with him. Hard and fast. This troubled her and excited her at the same time. He was mature and still a child inside. She wanted to change things about him but knew that she would never be successful, and that was the sticking point of it wasn't it. She knew changing him would make him something short of the person he was, she would be trying to make a fine masterpiece into an art class sketch of a fruit bowl, turning the sea to fresh water. If her only objections about the man seated next to her was there was things that intrigued her to the point of frustration, then she would have to be in. All in.

She felt a flinch in her side, reminding her of her appointment that day, earlier, and she felt her body sicken as she realized she was sitting here dreaming like a smitten teenager in science class over the kid with the big glasses and charming whit. The one who would be successful in life, not because he thought of himself the smartest man in the room, but because he understood everyone else's place in the world. He didn't have to try and fit in, he just did. Another pinch told her it was time to go. Her body was conflicted as was her feelings.

"Lord save me, would you look at the time! Its way past dark and I should be getting Mr. Greene back to his room at the Bay Point."

"Awww. How terrible you have to trot off." Paula's face turned down.

"You can't wait?" John insisted. "You can flag a bus anytime…" He turned his eyes to Mike; "She can't drive well in the dark. Did she tell you?"

"I think she *mentioned* it once." Mike smiled back at John, realizing the issue now. Shannon had parked her truck and they rode the bus home from the Quay last night; now he knew why. He smiled next to him, at Shannon.

Paula chimed in, "A terrible thing that happened too."

Shannon raised her hand and cut both of them off. "We won't discuss this now please. I'll do fine, but we do have to *bugger*, I thing they say in American." She looked at Mike and he nodded slightly. "I can't tell you what that word means in Australian, but it is very vulgar."

"You'll be okay to drive then?" Paula asked.

"Sure, been practicing." Shannon answered, carefully.

"Okay." The room stood almost at once and hands were shaking.

Paula stepped forward and hugged Mike and whispered in his ear, "Take good care of our Shan; she is our little one-well almost." She giggled as she ran her hand down Mike's buttocks and back of his thigh.

"They seem very nice."

Mike thought out loud as he and Shannon made their way up the gangway towards the gate that lead to the street level. He didn't want to mention the fact that he was *manhandled* by a woman a several years older than him, or that he wasn't really the type of person who knew anything about sailing. Both embarrassed him.

"They are. John's father is a good friend of my father; they have known me well for nearly ten years." Shannon replied, not looking up from her steps-small and paced slowly as they fell in front of her.

"Very nice indeed." There was a tinge of fear in Mike's restless and nervous words.

They stopped at the Mazda. Shannon glared at it for a few moments, her mind at work making decisions. She looked to Mike, who kept looking from the truck to her and back. He sensed what she was going to ask and he was feeling a little nervous inside.

"I have to ask you a big favor, Michael Greene."

"Yes?"

"I need you to drive."

Mike swallowed painfully because his throat had dried together, he'd feared this. "I... can't."

"Sure you can. I know you have the skills. I can't drive in the dark, I had an accident once a few years back, people got hurt and I have been afraid to drive after dark ever since." Her eyes were misty looking in the glow of the globed lights of the marina.

"I don't know how to drive on the wrong side of the road." Mike was half joking, a nervous sentence of jovial appeal, mainly he didn't like the sudden morose tone of Shannon. He hadn't seen this side of her; it frightened him a little, knowing she had a dark side. Shannon just nervously smiled back at him.

"We can take the bus then." She turned her head towards the main street and looked for the stop.

"No need lass; I'll give it a good show."

Mike tried his imitation of Sean Connery.

"You mean a proper go." Again a fearful smile, but there was relief in her eyes, which had stopped watering. "I told you, your new accent is troublesome. Speak your language please."

"Whatever, how about the keys."

Shannon handed him the keys after unlocking her side of the pickup, Mike then did the same and slid into the driver seat. Everything felt different; the steering wheel was out of place, having to look left to the passenger side; the shifter was uncomfortable in his left hand-this just didn't feel right. The transmission hump touched his left leg ominously; he was used to resting his right leg on it, next to the gas pedal-not the clutch.

Traffic was another issue; instinctively Mike looked out the left mirror and found the sidewalk, not the street. After shaking his head in fear, he managed to gauge the oncoming cars, on his right side. He tried to figure out the best way to enter traffic, join in on the bustle of the left side of the road, without serious injury.

He looked at Shannon with wide eyes. "You're sure about this?"

"It was a terrible accident. I hurt people, we could bus it if you rather…"

"No. I'll give it a try. Don't I need a special license for this?"

"No. Yours is just fine; I have an American license."

A little bit of hidden honesty that took Mike by surprise.

"How?" He was stalling.

"Just get us to Woolloomooloo and I'll tell you." She winked.

"Wooloomullah? Where?"

"My flat, do you remember where it is?"

Mike winced his brows for a second and shook his head, then looked her in the eyes; "No I don't, sorry. I was so full of the drive yesterday I forgot."

"Never mind, I'll direct you. Just remember, everything is opposite than what you are used to. If you make a mistake, just take it easy. That's all; I'll direct you through the off-streets instead of the expressway. It will take longer, but at least you won't have to deal with fast moving traffic."

"Okay."

Mike pulled out slowly, his hands were shaking from the nerves and the wheel was a little slippery from his sweat. He managed to get into the flow of the traffic with only one finger wave from another motorist.

"*Watch where you're bloody going dopey bastard!*" A man shouted after he managed to stop his small car in time to avoid a collision.

After a few moments, Mike was getting the feel for left handed roads and shifting with his left hand. He ground a few gears, but the clutching was steady and a little jerky; like a new driver.

Shannon gave him instructions on navigating away from the expressways like she promised, using the side streets and residential areas as the main route, rounding the south end of the Royal Botanical Gardens and then north to the area Mike would start to recognize: Woolloomooloo. The fear in Mike subsided as he began to remember the beautiful tall homes with the Sydney Lace in the front, the ornate ironwork in grates, railings, and fencing. A few more turns guided by Shannon and Mike almost felt comfortable driving-down Wilson Street, to the end; he remembered where he was now. He managed to park in front of a flat with the name *HUNTER* on a porcelain and brass plate near the front door.

Mike and Shannon walked from the well parked truck and were giggling like a couple of high school kids.

"I thought that copper was going to wet himself when he saw your badge."

"Well, I think he was more interested in the way you were laughing at him after he pulled us over."

"Who knew that you could make such a turn, I nearly thought we'd spin completely around!"

Mike patted his chest, "Years of police training."

Shannon stopped at an iron gate. She nodded to it as she wiped a tear of mirth from her eye. She felt serious all of a sudden.

"I'll be damned, it is here." Mike sighed, almost sadly.

"What? Did you think I materialized each morning in front of the hotel, out of magic then?"

Mike thought for a moment, something was troubling him. "Where do I catch the bus at? There is no way I am driving."

"You're staying over." Shannon said, quietly; but without a coyness to indicate any other intentions.

Mike rotated his head agonizingly slow towards her as she snicked the key into the lock and opened her front door.

"*What?*"

CHAPTER EIGHT

THE SLEEP OVER

The door opened with a little squeak, like a mouse that had been surprised by a room light. The room was cool, Mike felt goose bumps rising on his neck as he entered the flat. His stomach was tingling inside, this was a prospect he had never figured upon; going into the home of a beautiful Australian girl, just less than two weeks into his vacation. Shannon gave a tour from the foyer.

"Up those stairs are the rooms, the one on the left is mine, you are not allowed in there. The one on the right is yours for tonight-a kind repayment for services rendered-you will find it is quite comfortable. There is a bed and the loo… I mean *bathroom* is at the end of the hall. Kindly do not occupy it all morning."

Mike nodded his head at the instructions to signify he understood them. He smiled at Shannon's back as she led him through the flat, noting what she thought was important to mention.

"If you wish, you can make yourself comfortable on the couch, while I change into my relaxing attire."

Again Mike nodded to her and she spun quickly and headed up the staircase, while he slowly made his way into the living room and finished his examination of the apartment from the couch as he sat down.

The whole place from front to back was probably about twenty-five feet and around fifteen feet wide. Even though it looked smaller on the outside, the inside was larger-probably because of the lack of furniture-there was a white wicker chair with a toadstool shaped wicker ottoman, the couch was a high backed tan of the same style; heavy pillows arranged around the seat and back made it look and feel very comfortable on Mike's tired body.

The coffee table was wicker also; Mike was beginning to see a theme. On the wall behind the couch was a giant Chinese fan with a watercolor painting of flowers and birds; done mostly in blue and light green. On the opposite side of Mike was a mural that consumed the whole wall, it was an ocean scene of some type, he loved the serenity the image set off in the room. Odds and ends on various sized wicker cabinets and curios filled the rest of the space; but were placed neatly-to give the room its natural size.

Mike leaned towards the left arm of the wicker couch to get a glimpse of the kitchen. He could see just the end of the small table and one chair; Mike surmised that there was an identical chair on the other side-just like the one in his house in Nevada-he could see the beginning of cabinets and a tile covered counter that must have ran to the sink area. The wall to his left obstructed his view into the full area, so he imagined the stove and refrigerator were behind this wall, side by side.

The dark mahogany hardwood floor was expertly clean and shined brightly. Mike could make out the reflection of the ceiling features and the image of the slowly spinning fan that was suspended above him. Under the coffee table, jutting out three feet on each side was a beautiful Persian Isfahan Rug; it seemed a little out of place at first, but if you took the whole context in of the room, it just fit. The entire room and wall to the adjoining kitchen was decorated with photographs of friends and family-Mike again supposed-some of the same people appeared in the pictures, he recognized John and Paula from several. Others were of a huge sail boat and various ones of sea life; shot by Shannon-Mike bet.

The room beheld a light odor to it; it was foreign to Mike as he tried to inhale slightly-not to overpower his sense of smell-it seemed flowerish; maybe rose or some kind of tropical flower. He knew he had smelled this kind of aroma before-he just couldn't place it. The fan blew a cool breeze around the living area and Mike stood from the couch to give his muscles a stretch, he was still a little rigid from his driving experience. He could hear light rumbling upstairs and then a sink running for a few seconds, he returned to his seat when he heard footfalls coming towards and down the staircase.

Shannon was nervous as she had ever been. She had never brought a new bloke to her domicile-not even Tommy-who had sacrificed to her many rides home. She paid him with a little peck on the cheek or a rub of his leg, his marriage would never suffer from an infidelity brought on by her.

She was searching her armoire for something fitting for her guest, she didn't want to imply that he was welcome to touch her or feel open to serious discussion about their relationship. She also didn't want Mike to think that he had not gone un-noticed by her, after all he did scare the hell out of himself driving her home, after a protest of course-but he did do it for *her*. She wanted the oxymoron equivalent to provocative-relaxed, she settled for her jeans and white cross over top halter. Shannon also debated bra or no bra-and firmed her immediate thought of being conservative. She hadn't brought him here for sex; nor was that any of her intention. He was a good friend that deserved femininity and no notion of freelance opportunity. Shannon had nervously made up her mind; she was not going to be available for him or his advances.

Shannon passed by her perfume tray, knowing that any scent might start something she didn't want, they were just friends. She went to the bathroom and lightly brushed her teeth-the cola had left a filmy taste. Then she headed downstairs, nervous-she knew why, she was feeling like it was date night.

Mike stood as she softly ambled down the last few steps of the staircase. His heart beat rapidly for a few seconds as he adjusted to her new look. She was dressed fabulously earlier tonight, with the little dress she changed into at the Harbour, but now she had returned to a simple kind of everyday look and Mike was astonished how beautiful she could look in anything. His heart finished tap dancing on the wall of his chest, then it sunk into sadness, a low slow beat; knowing this look was not intended for him, he knew Shannon probably liked to dress up a little when relaxing at home. Besides, she on more than one occasion reminded him of their plutonic relationship-even though he had tried no advances-and he feared that he might lose his second best friend in the whole world right now if he did.

"You hungry?" She asked quietly, but her voice still echoed around the furniture in the room.

"A little. It has been a long while since lunch."

"Sorry, I got caught up in the excitement of seeing Paula and John. It has been so long." Shannon walked past Mike-who discreetly breathed in as she passed to catch an aroma she might have. There was none noticeable.

"That's okay. I had fun today, even though I didn't get to walk across the Harbour Bridge."

"Sorry again Michael. Things went a little disorderly today, would you like me to recommend a new guide?" She remarked coyly from the kitchen. Mike noticed just the slightest hesitation in her voice, he knew if he said yes it would break her heart.

"Of course not. I can never thank you enough for what you have done." *To my heart…* He didn't have the nerve to say.

"Outstanding then. Is Vegemite, bacon and lettuce greens okay?"

"Pardon?"

"Never mind. I think you Americans call it a BLT." She said over the tinkering sounds.

"Oh, that would be wonderful."

He took the opportunity to walk around to the mantle and get a close up at some of the photographs. He found some with what he assumed was her family, her father and mother; she must be an only child. He saw pics of a huge plantation style mansion and photos of masses of green land. He stumbled upon the last picture on the marble hearth.

It was a young man, in his twenties. Fair hair and skin, someone who spent little time outdoors, deep blue eyes behind round wire rimmed glasses, the kind that *Radar O'Reilly* wore on *M*A*S*H*. His smile was the not-so-honest look of a used car salesman, the kind someone wears when they are out of their element, probably the kind Mike wore all night at the Wright's yacht. The boy was handsome, no-he was stunning. Definitely a woman getter.

"Who's the Spicolli looking guy?"

"That would be Mathew." Her voice echoed off the walls of the kitchen.

Mike crunched his lips together and bowed his cheeks out. "*Nice.*" He said sarcastically.

Mike returned to the wicker couch and sat down.

A few seconds later Shannon returned with a tray of several triangular shaped pieces of a sandwich, neatly cut and served with a little toothpick in each. She had a glass of light brown liquid in her hand and set it in front of Mike.

"It's tea." Shannon announced, when she saw the quizzical look in his eyes.

"Thank you. But bourbon would taste great right now."

Shannon rolled her forehead down at him; "*Michael Greene.*"

"Sorry, just joshing."

"Just who?"

"Never mind." Mike picked up a slice of the sandwich and took a small bite, he didn't know why at first but as the taste hit his tongue he realized there was something different, and he was right not to chomp down on the whole thing at once.

"What's this...?" He didn't want to say *funny*; "...peculiar taste?"

"Vegemite. I thought you could use a little culture." She smiled at the pun.

"And what is Vegemite, exactly?" Mike was able to chew the rest of the morsel and swallow; *it wasn't half bad,* he thought.

"The epitome of Australian cuisine Mr. Greene. It is made from brewer's yeast, veggie extracts and various wonderful spices."

"Oh." He smiled.

"You don't like it?" She pretended to be hurt.

"Actually, it is different; but all right. I was just a little hijacked by the sudden taste. I was expecting mayonnaise." Shannon wrinkled her nose at him at the word.

"Yuck. I hate mayonnaise." She offered.

For the next few minutes, few words were spoken as Mike and Shannon both ate the sandwiches and drank warm tea. Shannon realized once again her breath was probably a little off; she smirked at herself for wasting time brushing them earlier.

Shannon picked up the plate from the coffee table and went back to the kitchen while Mike rubbed his stomach in a gesture he had eaten enough, he had. The meal was quite good, new spread and all.

He smiled at her as she walked by, she returned it-nervously. Definitely like a first date-the room was full of tension, they both were drawing closer-but had to be careful.

When Shannon returned to the living area, stopped at the stereo on the bookshelf and turned on some very light classical music; then sat down in the easy chair next to the couch. Mike's face lit up next to her.

"What?" She was puzzled by his expression.

"I figured you for a classical music type." He replied with a quiet whisper, in order not to interrupt *Brahms' Symphony № 2*.

Shannon stiffened in her chair; a moment of interest overtook her. She had to know something about this man who was making her feel slightly uncomfortable all of a sudden. It was his mannerism, his aloofness to her infatuation with him. She was having trouble controlling her feelings and that bothered her.

"Mike." It was the unusual occasion she abbreviated his name. "May I ask you a personal question?"

"Of course. I owe you, anything." He was judging a portrait of her from what appeared to be a high school pose, on the shelf behind her.

"You said you were in rehabilitation for alcohol. But what made you go there? What could have driven a strong individual such as yourself to drink so much you needed help?"

Mike's face turned somber, he looked away and down from the picture he was examining, and away from Shannon's gaze. He paused for a moment and then returned with a proposition for her.

"I'll tell you, but you have to tell me something personal too." He had a bargaining tone to his voice; he tried to hide the pain with it.

"All right then, I suppose I owe you." Shannon said, emotionless. "What is your question?"

Debussy's Clair de Lune began to fill the room from the stereo.

"You have a very light accent; you seem to know a lot about America. There is something about you that is familiar to me, I can't quite put my finger on it, but it seems like your hiding a little tale inside. Perhaps something you wish to share, but are afraid to. You drift in and out of the slang here, and the slang we use in America.

You said you had a driver's license in America; you also seem to have a grasp about my country, you rarely ask me questions pertaining to it. So that means you know a little more than any average Australian woman. Even Natalie asks me stuff about my home."

Shannon drew a long breath; she smiled at Mike and started to feel a little more relaxed. "My name is Shannon Christine Hunter; I was named after my aunt-my father's brother's wife-they live in Montana. A beautiful place called Thompson Falls. My father was an appointee of the President of the United States. He was made ambassador to Australia fifteen years ago, coming from Montana as a State Senator."

"I thought I recognized your accent." Mike said with a laugh, imitating Shannon's quip about his accent a few days prior. "You're American too."

"Indeed. I was born there, I have dual citizenship."

"How is that possible? I thought the immigration laws of Australia were very strict, can it be possible?"

"It is. My father made quite an impression on some very influential people in Canberra." Shannon pronounced it rapidly-Can*burr*ah.

"Where?"

"Canberra." She said it like an American; "Can-*bear*-ah… It's the capital of Australia. Therefore, when he retired after your-*our* President was replaced; many folks who knew him offered him and my mother a place to live. He had made so many contributions to both our countries that they were impressed with him and Parliament still uses him once in a while in negotiations with America."

"So your folks live in Canberra?"

"No. The have moved to Kuranda, a few years back. I live there myself during the dry season. This is their place too…" Shannon looked around the room to indicate the flat; "…they keep it for guests and friends who visit, when I'm not living here."

"So you grew up in Montana?"

"I moved here when I was ten." She smiled.

"So you visit the states often."

"Not as often as I should. Australia is my home now, I love it here. There is always so much to do. Diving, fishing, sailing, just walking around and seeing the sights, everything all in one place."

"They are remarkable." Mike added. "Seeing the sights, that is…"

"We go there to Montana for Thanksgiving on the odd year and they visit for Christmas on the even." She took a small breath and then asked with a slight hesitation, "Have you enjoyed your last few days here Michael?"

Her voice was relaxed, not the smart sharp toying one, but softer, more intimate.

"Yes. Thank you so much, I don't think I would have been able to see so much of the area. I wish you could accompany me to the Northern Territory and Victoria; uh-to be my guide of course."

"Of course."

Shannon let off a small easy looking smile, she agreed with Mike. She would have liked to go along with him and help fill him with her vast knowledge of her adopted country, but she had to return to her home in Kuranda-as a favor to her mother and father. *There was no variation on it, but maybe?* Shannon's eyes narrowed to the ground, deep in thought.

"I really don't want to return home." Mike said, prompting a curious look from Shannon.

"Why?"

"I don't know, I just don't feel comfortable there any longer. I hate my job, I hate the place I live, it's just not for me anymore. I guess since I sobered up, I have lost my way in the world. You spend so many years drinking that you hide your life deep inside of you, when you sober up you see that every year, every moment you spent drinking, you've lost something. All the feelings come at you at once, the depression that so many years were wasted on drink and you'll never get that back." Mike sighed and looked at the pricey Persian Rug. "When you do sober up, then you try and find things to fill that void. I'm not supposed to, not all at once anyway, but there's one thing that's been missing from my life since I began to fill my heart with booze instead of love."

Shannon thought she knew the answer, "And that is?"

"Someone who needs me as much as I need them. I guess some call it a soul mate, but I wonder if such a thing exists. It someone who just can't exist in this world today."

"Mike." Shannon began in her most serious and normal sounding tone he had ever heard, "Tell me about you problem, would you? What happened, why were you required to be

161

institutionalized for drinking. I mean half of the male population of Australia needs a rehabilitation of sorts. I hate the way the men separate themselves from the women when they go out pubbing, the women left to talk amongst themselves while the men drink hard and even dance with one another. It's like living in the Middle East."

"I don't know if you would understand." Mike thought she might, it was just he didn't feel well enough to share *the* story; after all, this was the story that put him over the edge-sent him into a free fall of drinking hard and daily.

"Try me Mike."

Mike's eyes locked into hers, three times now she has called him Mike instead of Michael-the name she has addressed him by ever since they met; now she was in her home and calling him out on his drinking problem, using the same tone and look and the counselors did in Oregon.

"This is very sensitive stuff, I mean, I don't want you afraid of me, thinking I might be a crazy person."

"I promise I won't." Shannon crossed her chest like a child in a schoolyard would.

"I… killed a young woman."

Shannon froze in her chair. Her face went white with anticipation, not the good kind.

"Michael Greene that is something you should've brought up before I invited you into my home!"

Her response was aimed as a tension easing joke and at the same time part of her meant it.

"I think it happened that way. I was hung over, badly…

It was eleven thirty p.m. one warm March night and the shift was ending for Michael Greene, patrolman. It was a typical Sunday swing shift-about three calls total-a domestic dispute, the most dangerous situation a cop can be involved in. Another call was a drunken fight in front of the Lockwood Inn and Casino, where the parties involved were long gone by the time anyone made it to the location, and a dog barking complaint a few blocks from Mike's home. He threatened to write a citation if the lady who owned the dog didn't keep it inside unless it had to go to the bathroom. Easy and routine.

Mike returned to the city garage; where he fueled his patrol car before taking it home-something that was allowed by small town police and deputies because of parking constraints and vandalism. He was sitting in the car smoking a cigarette when his radio crackled to life.

"351, 376." Mike's call sign-351- and the person who was calling him and the "3" signifying the shift. One was graveyard, two was dayshift, and three was of course swing, the preceding number made for less confusion to overlapping patrol units on the same shift. The caller was Mike's best friend since high school and boss; Kelly Daniels or 376.

Mike picked up the microphone and returned the call. "351; go ahead."

"Hey Mike. Gonzalez is running late-seems a car parked behind his cruiser and he had to have it towed. So could you cover for him for an hour?"

"Sure. I just got fuel, so I'll hang close to home. If they need me I'll go *code two and a half.*"

Mike knew he could get in trouble for using 'Code Two and a Half'. It meant he would hurry, not using his siren but just his lights-a clear violation of company policy-but overlooked because of the size of the patrol areas and the Chief frowned upon using code three all the time. It made the citizens edgy this late at night; many noise complaints came every time a fire engine, police car or ambulance turned their siren on after ten p.m.

"10-4. See you tomorrow afternoon."

"10-4 Sarge."

Mike shook his head about Gonzalez, another victim of a late night at *The Bison Range*; the local hangout for cops. The most important of those was the Chief and even the Sheriff would stop off on their way home and have a few belts frequently.

If you were looking to get ahead in the law enforcement community in the area, you would hang out there too. Buy the Chief a few drinks and talk shop for a few hours. That's how Kelly made it to sergeant, and that's how Gonzalez was trying to break into the supervisory ranks. Mike wasn't the boss type-the watch commander had too many hats to wear-and being the shift commander, also known as the shift lieutenant, was even harder.

Mike liked patrol; it was simple and even boring sometimes. Some nights like Sundays and Mondays there would be hardly any calls at all; once in a while a husband would come home drunk; beat the wife, slap the kids, and kick the dog-which was also known as a *10-16* or a domestic dispute. This was the most dangerous of all police calls, where most policemen lose their lives. Spouses will beat upon each other until nearly unconscious; then when the police arrive to break up the fight and take the husband to jail for spousal battery, the wife becomes upset her meal ticket is going away, so she pulls a knife or even a gun and injures or kills the policeman. A sad duality of peace keeping.

Traffic stops were slow some nights also, Lockwood was a small town-it had only three stoplights-the big patrol areas like the Sparks industrial and railroad yard had burglaries to stop and vagrants to herd, making it prime time entertainment for a patrolman.

Tonight Mike would just meander around the *back forty*, an area of railroad track crossings and spurs at the edge of town. It was close to his home, so he wouldn't have to return to the city garage to top off his tank; if you take the patrol car home you were on call and might need a full tank for the occasional high-speed pursuit over I-80 east or west, for a hundred miles or so. The desert offers many miles between towns and bad guys like to run on the endless track known as Interstate 80; they think they can outrun a police car-but they can't outrun the police radio and the half dozen of sheriff's offices and police stations along the late night deserted lanes of freeway.

Tonight would have been the perfect night to overlap a shift, but fate had a path lined up for Michael Greene he never anticipated, or wanted to begin. It all started about ten minutes into Gonzalez's shift.

"351, Lockwood." Dispatch broke the reverent silence of the evening over the radio.

"351." Mike yawned back into the handset.

"351 respond to the Lockwood River Trailer Complex. Cover Fire, en-route to a reported structure fully engulfed. 176 advises-for traffic control only of the south entrance."

"351, ten-four; '76 code three." Mike responded, *76* meaning en-route. He reached down and slid the mic back into its holder and then over a few inches to the accessory switch panel. He flicked the overhead lights on and moved his hand up higher to the Federal Interceptor Siren control to *WAIL* and stepped hard on the gas pedal; the 1987 Crown Victoria roared to life, but the engine sound was drowned out by the high pitched alert of a police car in action.

Four minutes later Mike arrived at the south entrance to the trailer park. It was an older park, with the residents mostly elderly and infirm. Kelly referred to it as *"God's waiting room."* Although there were a few younger residents, mostly low income and government assisted housing, the park was rarely a problem.

Mike could see the flames on the other side of the park, not too bad-just a few flickers that reflected off the mountains just a few hundred yards south of the park itself. Mike placed his car in a position to block any incoming cars, and to keep *rubber-necks* from getting in the way of the fire trucks and any other emergency vehicles. Another big problem with a small town, nearly everybody had a police scanner and would listen to the damnable box for entertainment, even Mike would listen in on occasion on his days off; it was just like listening to a ball game on the radio when he was off duty. But the lookie-loos were trouble, getting in the way of the help people needed, even wrecking their cars on the freeways and side streets because they were more focused on the excitement at the scene than the traffic ahead of them, yeah; law abiding citizens were a real problem sometimes.

Mike switched his siren off as he skidded to a stop, placing the car in park and reached over to lock the shotgun rack. He stepped out and heard the rumbling of the fire engines in the distance; the trucks would idle high as they pumped water from the hydrants. Looking around to take in the scene, Mike noticed just a few lights were on this late at night; a few older folks who had stepped out on to their porches to see what the commotion was all about, a few of the younger residents peeked out their windows, not venturing outside for fear of an arrest; the park held its fair share of druggies and ex-felons. Mike just leaned on his open car door and placed one foot on the door jam. It was going to be boring…

The park was on the south end of the Lockwood area, against the hills that led up to Virginia City eventually through Lagomarsino Canyon. There were six streets with ten trailers on each street; the mobile homes were not so mobile-sitting on cinderblock foundations with sheet metal or freight pallet skirts around the bottoms. The homes ran side by side with a forty-five degree angle to the street, each one had a car port. Some had cars.

At one time the homes had to pass annual inspections for safety, a sticker was affixed to the front window of the trailer to identify that the owner had met the fire and health codes and many of the older trailers had several years of stickers accumulated in the windows.

But as with many things in the latter years due to budget cuts, inspections were stopped and as a result many of the trailer homes became unsafe and dilapidated. Fire were frequent, as were infestations of bugs and once in a while a serious case of food poisoning from a block party would cripple several residents for a week or so. The homes were in several layers of disrepair, from one needing a serious coat of paint, new roofs, new windows (often just plywood in place of glass), new stairs, etc. To places that should be condemned outright before someone was killed or several people are killed.

Twenty minutes into the incident, Mike had his attention turned to one of the trailers about twenty yards to his left. There was a light on in the large kitchen window and some movement, which always caught Mike's eye; he was always on the alert. He turned his head and saw a young woman in a light blue robe, probably in her twenties, in front of the window apparently washing dishes. She looked up and saw Mike watching her, so she smiled a warmly back at the policeman-whose face was lit up by the yellow glow of the fire and the flashing blue and red lights of the rotators on Mike's patrol car roof.

Her hair was golden yellow, she wasn't very tall; Mike guessed about five foot three or four-it was hard to tell from the distance and half of her body was hidden behind the sink. The window was a bay-view type, common in the smaller trailers, to give them a larger-less confined look on the inside.

The young girl watched him for several minutes, her hands occupied with drying a dish, then retrieving another from the sink. Mike watched back, from his location he could tell she was rather pretty, although he couldn't see her eyes well enough, he noticed they were light colored; maybe blue. Mike continued to smile affectionately, even though he knew this would lead nowhere, he was a cop and this young woman probably had some issues if she was living here, and that would lead to complications later on. The girl just kept looking at him, his heart kept a slightly higher beat, over the prospect of having a pretty girl just staring at him with a warm smile.

Mike looked down for a moment to adjust from one foot to the other on the running board of the open door; when he looked back up the young girl's face had turned to a pale, with a frown. Mike focused his attention on her, even turning his body to face her, something was wrong.

Her eyelids started to flutter, her eyes rolled back white and she collapsed straight down. Mike could see she hit her head on the sink as she fell, knocking her head backwards.

Mike slammed his patrol car door shut and began running towards the trailer. He quickly grabbed his Handi-Talkie out of its holster and keyed the transmitter button.

"351-I have one down. South entrance trailer number uh… twenty-seven. I need a *10-52* code three!" He shouted, panting from the run and adrenaline.

"351; 10-4. *Ambulance* is 10-76." Dispatch called back, though Mike's attention was distracted.

Mike reached the young girl's trailer door and found it locked. In a life or death situation he had full authority to kick it in, but he knocked first, shouting to anyone inside.

"Is anyone home? This is the Lockwood Police Department! Open the door!"

Mike counted to ten and then raised his leg. Mobile home doors are as about as thick as cardboard and twice as flimsy; the first impact of Mike's combat booted foot sent the door crashing open on its hinges, smashing the glass window in it as the shaking door struck the wall inside. A quick look to see if anyone was coming at him with an object-heavy sleepers didn't like their doors kicked in, in the middle of the night-and Mike rushed to the kitchen.

The first glance at the scene was awful. The young woman did indeed strike her head as she fell-just above the eye-and it was bleeding profusely. Mike rushed over and clamped his hand around the wound to stop the bleeding. He placed another hand on her shoulder and shook her a little.

"Can you hear me?" He was sweating from the run. "Hello? Can you hear me? Are you all right? Miss?" He was shouting; he could hear the echo off the walls all the way down the hall of the trailer. There was no response.

Mike took his hand from her shoulder and carefully pushed open her right, then her left eyelid. He could see she her pupils were dilated and not responsive to light; she wasn't breathing. Mike ran his hand down from her eye to her neck and looked for the carotid artery, feeling around for it. He couldn't find a pulse. A little panic ran through his spine, Mike was a trained first responder or Basic E M T (emergency medical technician), but the girl's pretty face had shaken him. He had never performed CPR on a young woman; many drunken vagrants covered in their own vomit and urine, sometimes old men and old women-but never a *young* woman. His hands started to shake and his mind drifted.

Mike shook his head and focused on the limp body in front of him. He remembered other pulse points and quickly checked the brachial artery under her right arm, then hesitantly her femoral artery, having to reach below her groin through the open robe to her inside her thigh made him uncomfortable. Nothing.

Mike pulled her warm body close to him to listen for breathing, he felt her body tremble for a second, then it shuddered and he heard rush of air come from her lungs. She was dying, right here in his arms. Mike began to coldly shiver.

He started to panic again when he heard his radio crackle.

"351-ambulance is seven minutes out."

"That's not good enough! I have a female, down and she's not breathing and I have no pulse. I'm starting resuscitation." Mike dropped the radio next to him and took a split second to think about what he was going to do.

He opened her robe all the way at the top, exposing her chest. Now he felt completely out of place and unnerved, he knew you can't do accurate chest compressions with clothing on, but he had to fight off his urge to cover her out of decency. Next he ran an index finger along the bottom rib on her right side, the side facing him, and traced the rib bone to the bottom of the sternum -the "V" shape between the rib and the pointed bottom of the sternum bone. After his index finger bumped between the pointed shape and the rib, he held his finger in place as he took his other hand and aligned four fingers, starting with his pinky and marked off the spot from the bottom of the rib cage to the area he would place his palm. Her skin felt warm to the touch of his hand and Mike began to feel dizzy, he knew what he had to do, but he didn't want to hurt her any more. He took a deep breath and began the compressions.

"One-two-three-four-five." Mike counted out loud, just as he had been taught. He leaned forward to hear if the girl was breathing; she wasn't.

Mike leaned over her and placed one hand under her neck and elevated it in the center, tilting her head back. Using the thumb and forefinger of his other hand he pinched her nose closed and gave two sharp breaths into her mouth, turning his head to the right to see her chest elevate and contract. Once again he used the same method of placing his hand in the perfect spot on her chest above her heart and gave her thirty more compressions, counting out loud on each one.

Time stopped, the world stopped moving. Mike was locked in a battle to keep this young woman alive till help came. He knew deep inside that CPR only kept the blood flowing to the brain and the blood full of oxygen by exhaling his breath into her lungs. The chances of her heart restarting this way-without a defibrillator or meds-were slim to none. He continued without fault for five more minutes.

After the five minutes Mike looked at her face, her eyes were open now, and Mike had confirmed in tragedy that they were indeed blue-green-just as he thought he had seen from across the lot. But the beautiful eyes weren't full of life now; they didn't glisten in the moderate light from the kitchen. When eyes see things they glow with life, they are focused or *looking*; now this young woman's eyes looked forward, not focusing on anything. They appeared dry, accusatory. With the compressions the blue-green eyes seemed to follow Mike's every move, with every push downward they seem to turn just slightly enough to follow his eyes. Tears started in the police officers own eyes now.

Then it happened; one of the girl's ribs snapped. Mike could feel it under his hand. He fought off a wave of nausea as it rolled across his body and settled in his stomach. He kept pumping, knowing that this had to be done-broken rib or not. He had to keep her blood flowing. He did thirty compressions and two breaths. He checked her pulse; nothing. Again the cycle started.

Mike saw his sweat dripping off his nose and forehead onto the woman's stomach; his head was burning, his muscles fought for oxygen of their own; "Where's that damned ambulance?!" He shouted to the empty trailer.

Fifteen minutes later, Mike felt a hand on his shoulder-it was the paramedic. The only way you are supposed to stop CPR on a person is if you are relieved by someone. But Mike kept going; he didn't want to take the chance of this young girl dying.

The medic calmly told Mike; "I've got it…"

But Mike unconsciously continued the compressions.

The other ambulance attendant began opening tackle boxes that contained medical supplies, breathing kit, EKG monitor, and a defibrillator. He placed a breathing bag over the young woman's face and told Mike to slow the compressions to five so he could push air into her lungs.

Mike was exhausted, but he kept the chest compressions coming; he was working on pure adrenaline now, nothing was going to stop him from allowing this girl to die. The first medic once again placed his hand on Mike's shoulder and told him he was relieved, but Mike didn't stop. Finally, under protocol, the driver of the ambulance pushed Michael backwards, off of his knees and up against the nearest wall-then began hooking the EKG up to her through sensor pads to points on her chest and started to warm up the defibrillator.

Mike used his feet and last little bit of energy to push his body against the wall. He looked to his right and saw a mirror on the door just down the hall from the kitchen, he saw his graven image; it frightened him.

Staring back down the hall six feet away was the reflection of a monster; its face was covered in the young girl's blood-from her face-its hands were also crimson red around the edges. The eyes of the creature were sunken hollow and had evidence of tear streaks flowing from the glazed-over eyeballs down the cheeks through the blood and off the chin to its uniform shirt.

The dark vision of Michael Greene cast across the room and back to the owner revealed the look of a frantic man; a man who just died inside a little, who lost a battle with death, the fate being that of an undeserving young woman who's only chance was a thirty-eight year old cop. Mike pulled his knees up close to his face, he placed his blood and tear stained cheeks on his knees, and he wept. He cried from exhaustion, from pain, and for the young girl. A hangover added to his misery, making his emotions flow more easily, paranoia less subtle. He was worried that he hadn't performed the procedure right. He felt the rib break and it nauseated him, that never happened before.

The sound around him faded, all he could hear was the whispering of the medics to one another, an occasional beep from a portable machine, the crackle and snap of electricity running from the paddles of the defibrillator into the chest of the young woman. A pause would follow the shock, then compressions would start again and the little machine's capacitors would whine like a flash on a camera as it was drawing energy from the batteries for another try at starting the girl's heart. The sounds became muffled even more, the room started spinning, the smell of iron and copper flooded Mike's nostrils and throat from the woman's blood. Mike saw a paramedic plunge a hypo/syringe of Epinephrine into the young woman's chest. Mike leaned over and threw up on the floor next to where he was curled up, and passed out.

The next thing he knew, someone was trying to smother him; *no*-the man was trying to put something over his face-a mask. An oxygen mask was being shoved over his nose and mouth. He was lying on his back, one of the medics and a cop-

Gonzalez-had Mike's shirt open and his ballistic vest off. The ambulance drive kept saying; *"Relax...breathe deeply...take it easy...you had a spell..."*

Mike asked through the plastic mask; "Is she okay?" But the rushing air and device that covered his mouth drowned out the words. He reached up and pulled the mask from his face, only to be met by the hands of the medical technician who fought Mike's strength to place it back over his mouth. Mike shot the man a terrifying glance; the man froze for a second. "I said; is the girl all right?"

The medic gave the tired cop a grave look and said quietly, "She's being transported." Another gurney arrived into the kitchen, Mike surmised this was for him and he fought off the men attending to him and sat up.

"I'm going with her."

"You can't." Gonzalez responded.

"Like Hell! Just try to stop me..." Mike rose to his unsteady feet and propped himself against his fellow cop. The medic took his other hand and step by step they made it out the door and down to the idling ambulance.

The door to the vehicle was already open; Mike was helped up the step and inside, what he saw next was horrifying. The other gurney was locked in place, a sheet covering the top. The young girl-the young woman-had died. All of Mike's Herculean efforts had not paid off.

Mike didn't look at either man helping him; he sat down hard on the cushioned attendant seat and again placed his head in his hands. He didn't cry though; he sat there; thinking of the bright blue-green eyes that shone down through the bay window towards him as he stood outside. That is how he wanted to remember her, not the lifeless faded eyes that glowered at him as he pushed down on her chest, trying to force her heart to keep pumping blood to her brain.

A thought hit Mike. He felt the rib snap; *did he force the broken bone through the young woman's aorta?* He heard of it happening before, a rib breaks and punctures the largest artery in the body-sitting next to the left side of the heart, making any attempt to keep blood flowing impossible. Had he done that? Did he kill this young woman? The girl with the blue-green eyes that beckoned him from the safety of her home?

Twenty-four hours later Mike was drunk.

He had gathered his blood-stained uniform from the closet in the emergency room and dressed himself half-hazardly; leaving his ballistic vest and gun belt on the chair next to the bed he was placed on. It took ten minutes to get a cab, one pulled out front of Washoe Medical Center to drop off a relative of a patient and Mike slid into the seat and gave the driver his address.

The driver looked at the face of the man, then lower to his uniform and thought better of asking what happened and drove quietly the fifteen minutes to Mike's Lockwood home.

What happened next, Mike could only put together from what Kelly told him over the phone at Future Frontiers and some other friends who wrote. Mike had gone into his house and dressed in a pair of jogging shorts and a running shirt. He pulled on a hoodie-type jacket and walked a mile and a half to the nearest bar, the River Inn, and drank beers with some friends until six in the morning-since bars and casinos didn't close-then he managed to get from there to *The Wonder Bar* on Wells Avenue near downtown Reno, eleven miles away.

There he bought drinks for the quaint little place for three more hours, building a tab of over one hundred dollars, then he managed to stumble towards the downtown core of Reno-and it's never ending bars and casinos that had an endless supply of booze.

A check written at one of the casinos gave Mike all the cash he needed-three hundred dollars-but when it was deposited it would leave him with thirty-two dollars in his checking account, for the rest of the month.

For two more days Michael Greene bought drinks and accepted free ones for his police duty-he made sure the bartenders who didn't know him did-and eventually his luck ran out. He was on the three day bender, eating only when he felt ill, and drinking until he passed out. A police car was called by the bartender at Whiskey River, Mike's final destination.

Mike had passed out in a booth in the back by the stage and was left there for eight hours, before the bartender called. When the patrolman from another department arrived Mike was slightly combative in his semi-conscious state and flashed his badge demanding special treatment, also known as the brass pass.

That's when Sgt. Kelly Daniels was called.

"Sixteen hours later, I was at the Future Frontiers Detox room." Mike ended his story. He took a deep breath and gave a half heartwarming smile to Shannon, who was in shock.

"It wasn't about being drunk enough to forget. It wasn't about feeling sorry for myself, it was about one thing. Caring. I didn't anymore." He sat upright in the wicker seat and pulled at the seams of his shorts, "I didn't care if I died. I didn't care if anyone got hurt around me. I didn't care if the world blew all to hell and burned every soul alive. I no longer wanted to be Mr. Protector, the policeman, I wanted to be left alone, hell, I was alone. Especially after my cash ran out. I was lucky enough to be sufficiently wasted before passing out, otherwise I would've found a way to get more cash and drink more. As long as I was awake, I would drink.

"I had no one. My ex was gone with my kid. My family was all but gone, my dad was ten hours away in another town and we hadn't spoken in months. My friends at work abandoned me when they heard about my binge. A young woman smiled at me and it warmed my heart, I killed her because I couldn't save her. I was through.

"But, there was one person that cared enough, cared more than I did about myself and he took a chance with his job and career and gave me a boost. And here I am."

Shannon had pulled her legs up to her in the chair and sat through the story, her eyes were red and swollen, and the backs of them were aching to flood. She tried to keep from sobbing loudly, and her chest was burning from sniffling. She imagined the young woman lying on the floor of her trailer and the relentless Michael Greene trying to keep her alive. She imagined herself ever needing help, and the man in front of her-the man with red eyes and sweating while telling the story-saving her life.

"I…" Shannon had no words for what she just heard.

Mike just continued staring at the floor, his eyes fixed on the same spot since the story began. "Hmmmmnn" He cleared his throat and looked up. He saw that Shannon had been fully engaged into his story and felt sorry for making her cry. "Sorry…" He whispered to her. "I think I should be getting back to the hotel now."

Shannon sniffed back a tear and stood up. "I think not!" She walked over and kissed him on the top of the head. Then walked to the kitchen with her empty glass.

"If you're sleepy then you can retire to your appointed guest room." She used a softer version of her "tour guide" voice from the kitchen. She put the glass in the sink and then placed her hands on opposite sides of the sink, lowered her head and wept, quietly.

Guilt washed over her as she recalled Mike's story over in her head. She could imagine him trying to bring that woman back to life; she could see his face contorted into a frenzy of fear, and a fight to save her. She felt guilty for letting herself get to this poor person, why was she playing with him as she was? At first it was just making friends, but was she playing a game with him and now his emotions had spilled over onto her?

"Where do I find the blankets?" He called from the upstairs.

"Just a moment."

Shannon had forgotten, she had taken the blanket off the spare bed to wash a few weeks ago and hadn't replaced it, she really never expected visitors anyways, her intention was not to bring Michael here. But as darkness fell over the city and her choices were limited and she needed a ride, she didn't think her little pickup-as bad as shape as it was in-would survive the drive back to the hotel with Michael at the helm alone. She brought herself to composure and went to the closet, finding the freshest smelling bed cover and slowly walked upstairs.

"Here, this one will do." Mike noticed she had dropped the pretense of the tour guide voice.

"Thank you." He took the blanket and whipped it in the air and allowed the blue fleece float to the bed, nearly covering all four corners.

Shannon paused before she made it to the door. "Michael, I'm sorry if stirred up any hard feelings."

"It's alright Shannon. No worries, I think you say here." He smiled at her, the room warmed with it, Shannon stepped forward and kissed him beside the ear, Mike could feel her warm breath brush past. His heart accelerated in pace as he felt the room spin a little. "Can I ask you another question?"

"Of course."

"Why won't you drive at night?"

"A terrible tragedy, not as bad as the one you carry with you, but it was horrific for me and I can't seem to find the need to operate a vehicle in the dark, it's a fear." She turned and walked back downstairs. Shannon wanted a drink, but she knew she shouldn't in front of him.

So she walked quietly as she could across the living room to the kitchen and poured herself a large glass of Australian Syrah. She stepped backwards from the counter and looked out the window to the small courtyard outside. '*I wish you could be my guide…*' Mike's voice resonated in her head.

CHAPTER NINE

TRAVEL AGENT

The phone rang in two short bursts, a little less annoying than the constant American ring, Mike shuddered from his sleep. He fumbled for the noisy thing on the nightstand next to the bed, but he remembered he had moved it to the floor a few feet away, to keep it from being stridently knocked over if he had another nightmare. Lately the nightmares hadn't come.

Mike fumbled to his feet as the ring ring-continued, he wondered who the hell was so bent on getting him up so early. *Maybe it was Shannon!* The thought of her calling him the day after she left woke his mind and body straight up.

Shannon and Mike had returned to the hotel the day after his little sleepover, nothing happened-just as she had predicted, but he was happier for it. It was the first time he had the chance to relate his experience to another person, a caring and concerned one at that.

Even though she made it seem she was slightly aloof about his plight, he could see in her eyes softness and a caring sadness, which meant he had gotten *to* her heart. They ate lunch together at the restaurant and a few of the employees stopped by their table to say goodbye and good luck to Shannon on her holiday. Mike-although he didn't show it too much-was saddened by her leaving, he knew in just a few days he would be off to the Northern Territory and the last day he would ever have with Shannon was today.

He knew he was getting *inside* her heart too, because she refused to let him see her off at the airport, he was allowed to give her a kiss on the cheek as she left the Bay Point Hotel; he placed his lips semi-affectionately near her ear and he could smell the *Ocean Breeze* perfume she wore. The smell lingered around him all day, prompting Mike to smile often and think of the young blonde beauty that made his life a little more interesting-even if was for only less than two weeks. Her eyes and smile would light up his life for a long time, her scent would be close to him-he would know the light odor from now on, he would remember the young beauty Shannon Hunter for the rest of his life.

Mike found the phone and fumbled with the receiver to get it to his ear. "Hello?" His insides tingled as he half expected the caller to be Shannon, calling from Kuranda.

"Mr. Greene?" It was a man's voice.

"Yes." Mike sounded disappointed.

"G'day, I hoped to find you in your room. I need you to pop by the concierge desk this morning to verify your travel plans."

Mike shook the cobwebs from his head and remembered he was heading out in the morning, tomorrow. "Of course. I'll be down in a few hours."

"Very good then. Look forward to seeing you. Ta-da."

Mike stood and stared at the phone on the floor for a few seconds after hanging up, he sighed heavily as the thought he might have fallen too deeply for the much younger woman barkeep. He was saddened that the caller was the man downstairs and not her, even though she said she couldn't call, he half kind of expected her to. For all intents and purposes he wanted her to.

When she left, there was a sadness about her, a distant hurt-probably coming from her relationship with Mathew-but none the less, she was different than the first day he met her in the bar, she had changed a little after she had met him and Mike had changed too, he was a different man. He wanted to be with her so badly it hurt, it took hours to get to sleep last night, all he could think about was her, he dreamt she was calling him and saying she missed him, that she was returning and would spend the rest of Mike's travels around Australia with him. The rest of the vacation was going to be pretty boring, it was going to be hard to outdo these last two weeks; that was for sure.

It was less than an hour after the phone woke him, Mike was already downstairs reading the local newspaper and semi-enjoying his breakfast. He did have a better appetite now, a lot of the burden and guilt he carried around with him had been shrugged off onto the shoulders of someone else and his world seemed brighter because of it-or maybe it was who he shared his inner most secrets with.

He left almost a clean plate and paid for his food with a smile and five Australian dollars, then casually walked towards the concierge desk. He smiled as he passed the trinket shop, thinking of Shannon and her cinnamon gum.

Mike arrived at the desk; behind the wooden artsy looking work station was a uniformed man, with the same smile on his face that most everyone had here in Sydney-maybe the whole of Australia had that same type of smile-he didn't know, but he noticed it on everyone now. It wasn't bland or even fake, like a salesman in a car lot in America would wear; it was genuine happiness and a willingness to make others happy. A week ago, that kind of attitude would have made Mike repulsed, he wasn't happy with the human condition of emotion, but his eyes have been opened recently.

"Hello."

"G'day sir. How may I help you?"

"Name's Mike Greene, someone called me here from my room this morning. Says I have to verify my travel plans for tomorrow."

The man looked down at his register and smiled back up at Mike and nodded, "Of course sir. If you would be so kind as to just go over this itinerary, sign for it here." He pointed to a blank spot on the paperwork.

"Of course."

Mike took the paper and looked it over effortlessly, until a word caught his eye. He stopped and looked over the schedule completely, noting that there were several changes made; that his route was not going to be through Alice Springs-he was to get off the plane in some place called Cairns-he remembered he heard the name somewhere, but he couldn't put his finger on it right now, it ambushed him as he read it.

"Excuse me sir. Where is this Cairns, and why do I get off there?"

"I'm not quite sure. But the travel arrangements were verified by me this morning, this is the current schedule."

Mike looked over the paper a little more closely, and noticed a return flight back to Sydney after nearly two weeks. It made no mention of either the tour to the Northern Territory or Victoria. He began to get frustrated; when he applied for his Visa he knew and was warned several times that he cannot deviate from his route for fear of detainment by immigration authorities. His itinerary was approved by the Australian Consulate and he was not allowed to change it without their endorsement; Mike intimated this to the concierge.

"Oh, I have no doubt you know the regulations sir, but the schedule came in last night. I thought you were the one who made the changes, but it seems here…" He pulled a small piece of paper from a file folder marked with Mike's name on the front. "…umm, your authorization is allowed by the embassy and the consulate. It bears the signature of one Marcus Tittenblaum. Ah yes, here we go-the request was made by Shannon Hunter, right here at the hotel sir."

"Shannon? You mean…"

"Yes, she is authorized to make this change isn't she?" The man looked a little full of fear he was the victim of a ruse. "I guess I could have these plans checked if you prefer."

"No. I… guess she was doing the right thing. I mean how did the approval of my plans go through so quickly? It took me weeks to get the original…" But then Mike realized how it had happened. Shannon said her father had a little political clout. She must have used that clout, at least she was thinking of him.

Mike's face turned up bright, his heart started pounding hard against the wall of his chest, the young bartender had made arrangements for him to travel outside of his plans, and again she demonstrated her unpredictability. She had to have had her father pull strings to change his status, and nearly overnight. But where was he going? Shannon said her folks lived in Kuranda, not Cairns.

"Excuse me, how far away is Kuranda from Cairns?"

"Just a bit. One hundred and thirty kilometers or less."

Mike frowned, he had no clue what the conversion from miles to kilometers were, the conversation was becoming one sided and Mike was finding it hard to contain his excitement over the fact Shannon had changed his flight reservations and he had no clue-other than maybe it was to be near her-where he was going. "Is that less than a day's travel?"

"Oh, yes sir. About forty minutes-actually Kuranda is in the mountains outside of Cairns so it might take a bit longer."

"Wonderful."

Mike's face was beaming now, he felt a little shiver of anticipation streak down his spine, and he knew that his adventure was just going to be continued. A small pang of sadness struck Mike; he wondered why she had changed the schedule to be with her. After all, she made no qualms about the fact she was not looking for romance, even though he felt he was closer to her than her ex-boyfriend was at this point, Mathew having really pissed her off for something or some silly reason before he left last time. His nerves crept up on him next, the itinerary only told him which flight he was coming in on, he had hoped that Shannon had made arrangements to pick him up or at least showed herself. He didn't want to be stranded in a strange airport in a strange city-even if strings were pulled to bring him there. Mike looked back at the concierge and smiled big at him, in the same ingratiating smile the locals had given him these last two weeks; until he stumbled upon the sleeping arrangements.

"This says I'll be staying at the Cairns Plantation Resort?"

"Let's see....Yes. One of the finest accommodations in the country mate. I'll personally vouch for the resort, you won't be disappointed."

But Mike already was he had assumed he would be staying with Shannon at her folks place-or at least in Kuranda somewhere. Now that he knew he would be nearly an hour away from Shannon he felt saddened by the thought she might be just sort of teasing him again-keeping him at arm's length while dazzling him with her charms-either to amuse herself or fill some inner need of plutonic companionship. Mike nodded to the concierge and neatly folded his copy of the itinerary. He walked forward towards the front glass doors and out, stuffing the paper into his pocket as he went.

The streets were rather busy today, with the weekend coming up and Mike noticed a larger crowd than usual in the restaurant as he passed by the window. Mike's mind turned rapidly to his next adventure and Shannon. Why does she haunt his thoughts so? He smiled as he forced his thinking to how her slightly sweet perfume smelled near her ear as he kissed it, the gentle and nearly inaudible sigh she gave him as he did so. This tingled Mike's stomach as he walked. *Why does she intrigue you?*

He kept running scenarios through his head as to why, when he approached the dangerous bus stop, the one where he nearly was run flat a few weeks ago. Unconsciously he boarded the bus, being able to leap in front of it at the perfect time to signal the driver to stop-just as Shannon had taught him to do-after paying the driver, he sat down as his mind was still trying to feel out why Shannon had changed his plans.

The bus circled around the Harbour, by late afternoon Mike had made the ride he did the first time-without Shannon-nearly in reverse. The cab ride from the airport actually, when he noticed very little of Sydney's beauty and glamor; the scenes of people walking and working around. The beautiful *lace* of the front of many of the smaller flats, the shops that were bustling in the warm evening air.

Even though the bus made dozens of stops, and each one had a particular interest for Michael, he had already seen what he came to see with his makeshift tour guide and her somewhat sinister sense of humor. He saw the Opera House across from him and Mike could not take his eyes off the sail-like structure, then the Harbour Bridge.

Dark was settling over the skies as he watched the pink-blue hue turn to purple. Mike craned his neck around as far as the windows in the bus let him, he wanted to see if there were any bats flying in circles like he witnessed the first evening in the Royal Botanical Gardens-with Shannon. Everything was with Shannon.

Mike realized for the first time he had come to Australia with a closed mind, he didn't want to get away to see the sights here, he just wanted to get away from his home and the life that had become poisonous to his health. But then this beautiful young girl named Shannon Hunter opened his eyes to the beauty around him. She allowed him to tell his tale of woes about why he was placed in a rehab; she heard his story of the saddened poor young girl named Rika who had suffered from the worst fate anyone could think of-loneliness. She taught him to look around him and see the world for its splendor instead of tarnish.

A slight breeze moved the leaves on the thick green treetops and smaller ferns that scattered around the entrance to the Gardens; a few folks walked slowly-meandering in the chill-some holding hands, women shuffling their feet along as the men held their arms around their shoulders, very close.

The bus turned south onto Bourke Street from William Street, a shudder of happiness tickled at Mike's chest, he recognized some of the streets off to the side as the ones Shannon took him through. He could hear her voice over the rattle of the bus's interior, telling him what to look for and what historical significance the area held. At the next stop a young couple boarded the bus and walked towards the back past Mike. The young woman was wearing the same kind of perfume as Shannon, stronger-obviously some women needed more-but a few moments after the youths sat in the back seats, the aroma lingered.

Mike felt a little tear form in his right eye, he wasn't feeling sad, but he knew why it was watering. He was feeling lonely. Even though he knew in a day or so he would be right back with Shannon-at least all things seem to point that way-he sighed deeply knowing that it was just for companionship, not to be engaged as the two lovers were as they passed.

He closed his eyes and slightly inhaled the scent of the other woman, he didn't want to overload his senses with a big breath, he just wanted a mental illustration; as soon as the fragrance passed his sinuses he saw Shannon, and her blue eyes and brilliant smile. He saw Shannon in his mind smiling at him, her perfect little smile that drew the corners of her mouth ever so slightly upward, the little quarter-moon circles forming from the corners, how her eyes sparkled like white surf crashing on a blue water beach.

Mike pinched his eyes even tighter as the feeling of sadness grew, he saw Shannon's face-but she was with someone else-and Mike knew that her love was with that someone else. Now his left eye watered up and they both leaked a little out of his clenched lids.

The flight was on time and the ride to Kingsford-Smith International was pleasant enough for Mike, the Bay Point Hotel providing a shuttle bus free of charge, it seemed to him because of the company he kept-namely Shannon. He wasn't expecting a ride; in fact he even rose earlier than usual just in case the hotel had trouble getting a cab. He ate breakfast at the restaurant as was his usual daily regimen, a few of the regular customers said goodbye with a handshake, but Natalie came over with the check and hugged him tightly as he sat in his seat, then gave him a peck on the cheek as she said, *"Take good care of her…"*. Mike just smiled back; he felt he would-take good care of her-if given a chance he would-she would never hurt again if he were hers.

Mike felt the wheels thump into their bays and heard the tell-tale whine of hydraulic pumps pulling the wing flaps back into place, as he searched the seat pocket in front of him for a magazine to read, or at least a shopping book to occupy his time. He began to get fidgety, nerves began to take control of his mind and a little of his body. His hands were slightly shaking, his foot bounced incessantly. His insides tumbled and he felt a little air sick-for the first time in his life.

What if this is just about more touring? What if Shannon needed to use him for jealousy bait for Mathew? Both sadness and fear replaced anticipation and adventure, he wished he had a drink-for the first time in a week he craved a beer, something that his mind told him alcohol would take the edge off-instead Mike just closed his eyes and tried to meditate, another tool he was taught in rehab, an escape from taunting of the mind.

With his eyes closed he remembered waking in the morning at her little flat, the bed was way more comfortable than the wicker couch, the soft pillows bore the essence of Shannon-at least of the laundry detergent he smelled on her clothing the few times they were in close proximity-the sheets were silken and his body felt it was sliding around in a pool of warm water, the sensation made it hard for Mike to even consider getting up. He could see the sun shining in the widow and after fumbling around the nightstand for his wristwatch, he determined that it was eight a.m.

He heard subdued clatter downstairs, in the kitchen he believed, and then the smell of coffee wafted around him forcing his mouth to water. He flipped the pillow over and pulled it onto his head; he liked feeling the cooler satin on his face, and the redolence of Shannon's household around him. The way she could talk serious one moment then joke the next, the way her eyes locked with his after he told her his tale last night, the warmth of her sad smile, her tearing eyes when he had finished.

He was falling in love with her...

Mike knew it in his heart, he couldn't help but feel alive inside when he thought of holding her as a lover, he could not imagine his future at this point, he knew that he had very little chance of ever fully explaining his feelings toward her, Shannon always had a way of diverting the conversation away from that-for a good reason-Mike assumed.

He dressed and slowly walked downstairs, looking at the photos of Shannon in her early childhood-now he knew why she eventually had to tell him her secret, that she was from America, many pictures were of a very young Shannon and her family in places like Yellowstone, Yosemite, Little Big Horn, at Washington D.C. monuments, etc. If Mike had not been told last night, he surely would have learned it today, just by looking at the pictures on his way down, which he would have done-it was just the curiosity about other people and places that made him more attentive-a cop thing.

Shannon was standing in front of the stove barefoot, wearing a *very* interesting snug pair of cotton pajama bottoms, light turquoise with blue flowers, and a white tank top with a blue flower arrangement print on the back. Her hair was pulled up into the usual ponytail, with a little blue butterfly clasp holding it in place, there was no makeup this morning-not that he noticed much on her-her eyes were a little sleepy looking, but when she turned completely and smiled at him her face lit up like the soft glow from the moon, bright and cool. Mike felt his face flush a little, for some reason he expected her to be wearing gym clothes, his heart ached even more at the sight of her, he wanted so badly to just softly say; '*I love you!*'

"Good morning sunshine." She said first, breaking Mike's concentration.

"G-Good morning Shannon." He stuttered.

"Sleep okay?" Concerning and soft.

"Oh, yes. Those sheets were wonderful, very soft, best sleep I've had in years."

"Tell me Michael Greene," Her serious tour guide voice again, "do you always greet your host with an inside out shirt in the mornings?"

Mike looked down at the tee shirt he was wearing and sure enough, in his dreamy state this morning he had pulled it on the wrong way.

She returned her attention to the stove. "I don't recall Natalie mentioning it to me that you came to breakfast like this, I'm sure she would have said something…"

Mike just smiled with a little blush on his cheeks and then pulled the shirt over his head and off, exposing his torso to Shannon-who was peeking over her shoulder. Caught off guard by his action, Shannon's face immediately felt warm, her eyes were locked to his chest. He had very little hair, but the abs were definitely six-packed, his pecks were muscular, not what she had expected to see, she imagined him a little out of shape-after all he had been out of work for nearly two months-she hadn't thought he still might be working out during all this time. She felt herself mentally comparing Michael to Mathew again; the policeman from Nevada was building an edge to the music bloke from L.A. She lost concentration on her solid thought, she was very distracted.

She began to feel nervous about her sensations. Last night, after she had gone to bed she had quietly wept over Mike's story again, then she cried a little for herself too and her predicament. She tried to formulate a plan that had been on the edge of her mind for a few days now, she wanted to be able to pull it off as secret as possible. She really liked the man named Michael Greene; he was nearly fifteen years older than she was, but somehow being with him just felt right.

From the moment in the hotel lounge he defended her, to him showing his weaker side last night, she knew what love was about-and this was brewing like a pot of coffee-slowly, when she first decided to take him on a tour of Sydney, then drip by drip she was falling for him-but he showed little if no sign of any love interest in her, Shannon was old fashioned. She wanted him to make the first move; maybe she had scared him off with all the talk of Mathew. But she couldn't recall talking that much about him, just when Michael asked, that was it. She turned back to the stove before Michael caught her gazing at his mid-section.

Shannon spooned the scrambled eggs she had been stirring onto a plate and then added some sausage from the saucepan next to the eggs, she extended the plate to her side-careful not to turn her head towards him as he reached for it. She was feeling ashamed for herself, the plan she worked on nearly all night was a long shot, Shannon no longer thought about Mathew Wright as much, and she wanted to spend more time with the American bloke that stumbled his way into her heart-in less than two weeks.

As she unconsciously stirred the browning eggs, Shannon's eyes welled with tears; her plan was going to fall apart. She knew this man was never going to fall for her the way she was falling for him, he would never leave his home in Lockwood Nevada or even the United States for *her*, and she felt as if she were trying to catch the wind with a butterfly net. Sure, he said he wanted to, but in the end all the blokes are the same inside. Afraid of change, even if she could Michael here would he want to leave everything? And then there was the possible future, the one that was dark and cloudy. The one the pain reminded her of each day. Once she got home, she'd check and make sure. Second opinion and all that. If it were positive, then she'd have to forget her future with Michael Greene. Any future she could think of, as a matter of fact.

Mike sat quietly at the small kitchen table and ate his breakfast, hoping Shannon would soon finish cooking and sit next to him. He waited till she rubbed her face with a dish towel before he said anything.

"You okay?"

"Sure, why do you ask?" Her back to him still.

"Are you going to sit down and eat?"

"Yes. In a moment, I like my eggs cooked thoroughly, if you don't mind."

She forced the words out un-sarcastically, she didn't want to play the part of a hard woman anymore-even though that was her personality, and she was going to try to be the softer spoken, frail, and vulnerable one. Maybe she could get more results from that course of action.

"So," Mike broke the silence again, "when do you leave?"

"Three in the afternoon tomorrow." She slowly turned towards the table and sat down across from Mike.

"Can I see you off at the airport?"

"I… no you can't." He voice sounded sad. "I want you… to… I can't have you there okay?"

She started to cry; Shannon stood and left the kitchen, then stopped in the living room. Mike sat for a second after she left, stood slowly himself and walked towards the living room. When he rounded the corner he saw her standing with her back to him, she was looking at her portrait on the wall. He was shaking.

"I… I…" *Come on you ass, say it…* He pursed his lips, finding the courage. *I love you.* As he took a deep breath and opened his mouth to force the words out, Shannon cut him off, her back still to him.

"Michael, I'm afraid I have made a terrible mistake inviting you here. I have been very sad lately and I'm afraid I've brought you down with me."

"No! Not at all Shannon, look…"

She turned and her face was red; "Michael Greene. We both know that I must return to Kuranda, I can't change my plans; you by law cannot change yours. The best thing for us to do right now is shower and I'll take you to the Bay Point."

"But Shannon, I…"

"Please Mike. There are fresh towels above the toilet on the rack, please be kind enough not to use all the hot water."

With that she turned and walked back to the kitchen, picked up the plates and began washing them in the sink. Mike followed her. Shannon realized he was standing behind her and spun to meet his eyes.

"Have you forgotten where the bathroom is?" Her eyes burned.

"No. Listen to me for one minute will you?"

"One second, then off you go…"

"About Matt…"

"Dammit! Why do have to do that? You know I loved him and I know what you are going to say, he's not the reason, okay? I must go home; I can't stay any longer here. This flat will be rented out in a week."

Shannon was starting to feel angrier now, things were going too fast to find a stable point in the conversation-her ego took over and she was blocking out what she should have heard, she now was only hearing what she was scared to hear.

Mike sensed a change in her demeanor; he felt this was his chance… "About that, look-I know there is a huge difference in our age, but you know as far as getting together, maybe we could work something out, maybe you could come home to Nevada…"

Shannon froze, isn't this what she wanted?

"Michael, I can't live in Nevada or the States any more than you could move here. Why are we talking about his? We aren't an item, we aren't a couple, I have…" Before she could finish her sentence, Mike broke in.

"I don't care about that right now. We are getting close right? There is something…"

Shannon was full on angry, she had been up all night trying to think of a way to tell Mike what the most important thing to her was right now, but he broke her concentration and now she was becoming frustrated with his constant interruption.

"Please shower. We must be off in a very little while." She lowered her head, and then turned her back to him.

Mike stood silent for a moment, he pursed his lips and gave his next move some very deep thought and he acted. First he reached for the back of her flannel pants and pulled lightly at the waistband, not too much, he just wanted a simple reaction. Shannon spun immediately towards him. He grabbed her underneath her arms and placed his hands on her shoulder blades and pulled her to him, he slowly moved towards her, he could feel her resisting slightly, not as much as a person who wanted to be left alone should.

Mike kissed Shannon for the very first time, his trembling lips touched hers just so ever slightly; Shannon felt lightheaded for an instant and then wrapped her arms around him and pulled him closer. The kiss lasted only a few moments, but it had served its purpose, the room was less tense, Shannon was slightly less tense. As he pulled his mouth from hers he lowered his head onto her shoulder softy and whispered to her ear; "I think I'm falling in love with you."

He felt her shoulders slack, he didn't know why, but he knew this wasn't the reaction from her he had hoped for.

Shannon's mind was spinning; this is what she had dreamed about. The kiss twisted her insides to a ticklish tingle; it was all she could do to keep from giggling a little from the sensation. Then, as Michael slowly and romantically pulled back, he whispered the words she wasn't fearing-but knew were coming. She thought of her future instantly, the future which had been predetermined by a twist of fate, he wouldn't accept her knowing what she was going to go through in the next few months-definitely less than a year, she felt it. Things had moved too fast, now this man was falling in love with a woman he knows little about, and how if he stayed with her now, his life would be different in a year, he might not ever forgive her for not telling him now. Shannon had the option to tell him, she felt she had the obligation, she was saddened and was no longer in control of her destiny-her body and God now structured her future-Shannon didn't want the burden. If she only knew for sure, she could give him a glint of hope.

She pulled back from him after he said those words, realization hit her that things had gone too far now. And now she had to slow them down or put this to an end.

"I… can't love you."

She turned away. Immediately she saw an image of Michael flash in her mind, he was standing just a few feet away-his face turned down eyes slightly flooded. When she opened her own eyes and looked back at him-the picture was complete.

"I…" Was all the trembling man could think to say.

"Michael, things are going to happen soon, things that you would not understand right now. You have a bright future-now that you have shaken your demons, but…"

"But…"

"But, my path has been chosen for me, I can't change it. My life…" She burst into tears, wishing she had the ability to change what was going to happen to her. "Please understand, I would have never taken you on those tours, invited you here if I didn't have some kind of feelings for you."

"But now those feelings are gone?"

"No, but…"

Mike was becoming frustrated.

"But what? We aren't teenagers; you can tell me what is going on, really. I won't be mad, I won't yell or anything at you, but you should to tell me now!"

Shannon looked into his eyes, those hazel eyes were turning dark, he was being torn down by her and she had to stop this. "Michael, you wouldn't understand." She stepped towards him and reached her arms out towards him. He took a step closer and folded his hands into hers. She could feel them trembling. "I must go back to Kuranda; there is something that I have to do there. I don't wish to do it, but I must. I will spend the rest of my life there, from the time I land in Cairns-to the time I pass-Kuranda will be my home, as far as I can plan ahead anyway. Do you understand that?"

"No."

"Then let me finish by saying I've had the time of my life with you, no man has ever touched me the way you have in these last few weeks, and you did it all by just being you-not a flashy record producer or a drunken sailor or even a newlywed construction worker from New York."

Mike broke a small smile at the references. "But?"

"You can't stay with me, the law says so, my family would never understand completely. I can't love you fully, ever. Please understand…"

"I don't, why can't you come with me?"

"Aren't you listening to a word I am saying Mr. Greene? Is your head so thick I have to overstate what my intentions are? Do I have to just say *go away*?"

Shannon's heart snapped in two at that moment, the pain rushed from her chest to her head and the tears were building, she had never wanted to hurt him, but it seemed he cared for her so much that wouldn't listen to a simple brush off-he needed to be kicked in the center of his being-and she did just that, '*Do I have to say just go away?*' She fought off the tears, if she broke out crying, he would see she wasn't serious, and her attempt to free him from the pain he would face in the future, would fail. Shannon stood her ground.

"I… I'm sorry…" He turned and slowly headed upstairs towards the shower.

Shannon cried for ten or fifteen minutes, she wasn't sure, but when she heard the water being turned off upstairs, she knew it was time to clean her act up; she didn't want Michael to see her this way. After straightening her back, Shannon held her head up a little higher and left the kitchen for the upstairs, passing Mike who was making the bed in the spare room. She knew he had heard her pass, but made no sign of talking to her as she did.

Shannon turned the shower on and felt the soothing water wash the tension from her body; she closed her eyes and submerged her head completely under the shower head to get the full effect of hot drops rushing over her ears and cheeks. With her eyes closed she reached for the lemon-grass and ginger shampoo, the scent relaxed her. After the second rinse of her hair, Shannon thought about what she was trying to say to Michael, she tried to force herself to remain calm when she talked to him next-of course she had to, it would be a very short goodbye if she hadn't-Shannon thought about the way she would let him know what she wanted.

But she had wanted this. And now she couldn't make up her mind. It was so confusing to her. What could she get away with? Could she find a way to stay with him, for a short time more anyway?

Then another plan entered her head. Shannon smiled as she turned the faucet off, opening the curtain and reaching for the towel, a tear of relief dropped from her right eye. As she dried herself off and applied lotion to her legs, Shannon self-approved of her new plan, it was devilishly sneaky, not to mention borderline legal.

Mike, on the other hand was totally frustrated with himself for not being able to tell her how he felt, or how much he was falling in love with her. Every time the chance arose he felt he needed to justify what he was going to say, instead of outright saying it. He wasted precious seconds trying to explain his feelings first, when he should have come right out with '*I love you Shannon Hunter.*' and explained himself from that point on-if she wavered. He knew he was out of his league, Mike had succumbed to his fear and let it drop; he would carry his pain, and never repeat it again to Shannon or anyone about how he felt for this young barmaid. He feared for her, and what she had said to him-*her future...*

The drive back to the hotel was quiet and a little banter here and there over the sights kept the conversation pleasant, Shannon and Mike both pretended the incident at her flat had never occurred it seemed, they were where they started out two weeks ago; Mike felt.

The plane bumped over turbulence and Mike's meditation was broken by the voice of the captain telling the passengers to remain in their seats and stay buckled for a few minutes until they passed the layer of instability. Mike looked out the window over the wing and noticed how beautiful the sky was, the clouds slowly passing under the aluminum structure were soft and billowy, he thought of the pillow at Shannon's place and smiled at the thought of her again, making these arrangements. Maybe her future wasn't set in stone yet...

Shannon spent the three-plus hour flight worrying about her predicament. She had made the arrangements for Michael just hours before she left, she really wanted him to be able to see her off at the airport, but she had to sneak around him to make a phone call to her father-who would do almost anything for her without question-then she had to submit an itinerary change; acting as a representative of the hotel, an infraction that could bring legal action-and make a few other calls to get the results she wanted. She did want him to stay at her family's bungalow in Kuranda but strict immigration laws, even ones her father couldn't persuade to be bent, prohibited a foreign traveler to stay in Australia without permission and confirmed hotel reservations. Since her father was given no time to fill out the proper paperwork for Michael's stay, Shannon went ahead and booked him at the Colonial, a mainstay and beautiful resort outside the jungle home of her parents.

But it wasn't the fact she had to pull strings to get Michael's schedule changed, that was an effortless no worry, neither was her concern over whether Michael Greene would want to visit her at her home, her worry was over the *main* reason she invited him. Her plan was not fool proof, she knew deep inside he liked her a lot, but she also saw hesitation when it came to her small but testing advances.

She grew concerned he would not respond to her the way she hoped, her plans included him in the rest of her life-if he wanted-but Michael seemed distant at times. She had met aggressive men before, they took advantage of situations; a well-planned kiss in a moment of closeness like at Mrs. Macquarie's Chair-he opted out, an affectionate hug in a warm moment which could have come at her place after a sad story, which he didn't do; maybe even his try to advance himself upon her before she left for Kuranda, not knowing of course the whole truth. Even though her father and mother knew little details about the truth; Shannon wasn't even convinced herself that her new plan would work, *if Michael Greene found out first...?* She shrugged the thought away and tried to sleep, the nagging pain in her side made the task difficult-at best.

The plane touched down at Cairns Airport and Mike had to be roused by the flight attendant. He could hardly believe he had slept on the-he looked at his watch-three hour flight up. Mike shook his head as he pulled his carry-on from the overhead compartment; on a map Australia seemed so small, even though in true size it is about the same as the United States it just didn't look like a twelve hundred mile flight or '...*one thousand sixty naawwtical miles*...' as the pilot had described on the preflight.

"G'day and thanks, sir..." The pretty flight attendant offered as Mike ducked to keep from hitting his head on the doorframe. He nodded to her, he might have said thank you in return but right now his insides were turning faster than the day he woke up at Future Frontiers.

Mike took in a breath of fresh air as he passed between the plane and the gangway tunnel, his nausea egging him to do so. He walked the ramp up to the concourse and into the seating area. His eyes darted left to right to find Shannon-*she had to be here to meet him after all, right?*-but to no avail, the lovely young woman was nowhere to be seen. He waited for several minutes before walking to the luggage area, glancing at the customs checkpoint, and thankful he didn't have to go through that nightmare on this flight.

Mike waited patiently as his bag finally made the round on the conveyor belt towards him, he picked up his bags and started towards the front doors, fear filling him as he kept looking for Shannon, and not seeing her. Just before he cleared the baggage claim area a man in uniform stepped up to him, Mike's heart sank. *What now?*

"G'day sir. May I see your claim ticket?"

Mike sighed a little relief, then he wondered for a moment if he should ask the man about his plight and the fact he might be stranded here, as he was beginning to think he was. He reached into the back pocket of his jeans and pulled out the itinerary to show the man.

"You seem in a bit of a quandary, may I be of some assistance?"

Mike smiled sheepishly at the baggage attendant and shrugged his shoulders.

"I was expecting a ride from a friend and she hasn't shown up yet."

"Ah, American eh? Well welcome to Australia!"

Michael Greene from America, you have a call on the white line…

"Where's the white line?" He asked and the baggage checker pointed him in the right direction. His stomach loosened a bit now, knowing at least someone was looking for *him*. He tensed his fingers as he picked up the receiver.

"Hello?" Again in anticipation of hearing Shannon's voice.

"G'day sir." It was a man's strained voice. "I've been searching for you for a bit. Can I ask your whereabouts?"

"Just outside the baggage claim, by the doors." Once again Mike couldn't hide the disappointment in his tone.

"Fantastic, please do not move sir, I'll be there in a twitch…"

"Okay." Mike said, but he heard the line click off just as he answered.

Seconds later a man dressed in a casual suit and bolo tie approached Mike, he had a huge smile and his hand was extended before he was in front of him.

"Are you Michael Greene from America?" The accent was American, broken in itself.

"Yes sir."

The smaller man, about five nine or ten, shook Mike's hand; reluctant as he was to offer it to a stranger, and reached for Mike's bag and carry-on.

"I'll handle those for you sir."

"Thank you?" Mike was trying to be sure there was nothing notorious about this new development.

The man whisked the bags up and started walking. "This way if you please, sir." Mike followed, his brow wrinkled in bewilderment.

As they passed the baggage agent the stout man in uniform leaned over to Mike and whispered, "*She*, needs a shave." Then walked off guffawing in his own humor.

Mike surveyed the man a little, he had the notion he'd seen him before; the man's short brown hair had tinges of grey around the temples, probably around fifty, maybe fifty-five years old. He wore round glasses that made him look intelligent, his polite vocabulary seemed to back it up. His cheeks were a little flushed but all in all, the man seemed in outdoorsy type, rugged in the shoulders and strong moving. Like he had an important task ahead.

Outside the man stopped at a large limousine parked in the red zone in front of the airport terminal and opened the trunk, then he went back around and opened the passenger door for Mike; again he returned to the boot and hoisted Mike's bags inside. Mike slid far to the door as he could, and turned his body towards the driver's seat, he wanted to keep an eye on this guy. The man slipped into his side and started the long car. He fired up the air conditioning, it was only eight a.m. but the humidity made it feel around three or four. It was hot and wet.

"Did Shannon send you?" He couldn't wait any longer.

"Yes and no."

"Excuse me?"

"Yes I'm here for Shannon, but she didn't really send me. She became unavoidably detained and I was able to get free and come here for you. She thinks the chauffeur is picking you up."

Mike's hands tensed. "You're not the chauffeur?"

"Afraid not."

"Okay, who are you?" Mike felt a drop of sweat roll down the center of his back.

"My name's Ted and I'll be driving you to see Miss Shannon."

"*Miss* Shannon?"

"Yes. While she is not quite royalty, she does deserve the respect owed to her, don't you think?"

Mike was growing ill in his middle again. "I… guess so."

"I mean, I couldn't believe that she had made arrangements for you to come here. After all, she was very into Mr. Wright you know."

"Mr. right?"

"Yes, Mathew Wright. Didn't she tell you about her former boyfriend in America?"

"Oh, Matt. Yeah, she told me about him. Could you do me a big favor?"

"Certainly, after all a *big favor* was asked to get you this far wasn't it?"

Confusion washed over Mike like a wave crashing into a shoreline, he felt ambushed by who knows who this guy is; he felt intimidated and was short of using his angry policeman voice to get quick results, instead of this game-playing the man next to him did.

"If you're not the chauffeur, then who the *Hell* are you?"

"Oh, I'm sorry. My name is Ted, didn't I tell you already?"

Mike felt his face rush warm, but then the image of Shannon's smiling face swept over his mind and he calmed a little.

"So you're a friend of *Miss* Shannon?"

"In a way; look my friend, I care deeply for her, if that is what you are getting at. Sometimes that little flighty girl gets a weird idea and things like this happen."

"You mean like, she changes a man's schedule around in a foreign country and then abandons him with a stranger who sounds more like a psychotic than a chauffeur?"

Mike cracked a smile; he hoped this new tactic would change the direction of the conversation, or at least get better results.

The man exhaled sharply through his nose and chuckled. His face was concentrating on the traffic and Mike surveyed him carefully, looking for something he couldn't quite put his finger on, he felt *sure* he had seen this man before and now was wondering where and when.

For the next ten minutes the drive was quiet, Mike studied the driver, the driver studied the road. Mike resigned after a minute or two and looked out the window towards the new city. The limo took a street that departed from the east of the airport terminal towards the Coral Sea, along a road that was surrounded by greenery. Mostly small flat brush and a clusters of trees; palms, eucalyptus, oak and thicker varieties Mike didn't know the names of many of them, though he did see their examples in the Royal Botanical Gardens in Sydney. After a few more moments the road turned southwest and followed the coastline towards the city.

Cairns was flat. Mostly, as they came closer to town Mike noticed cane fields everywhere, and a tropical theme. Obviously this city was closer to the equator that Sydney and it reflected in the foliage everywhere. Not as much in palm trees than in thick heavy teak and almonds, gums and mangroves. As they rode from the airport exit, the thoroughfare was called the Captain Cooke Highway or Highway 1. They turned south onto the semi-busy bypass and kept a good clip going for about three minutes until they reached Arthur Street, turned right and then Arthur became Greenslopes Street and a left onto Macnamara

Street. Mike saw a sign that read *Manunda-Endeavor Park*. Finally the driver Ted broke his silence.

"Miss Shannon does do things impulsively at times, she can never be predicted. It has been one of her slight imperfections, though almost all the time those situations seem to work out." Ted changed the subject abruptly; "Now you may have been told that you cannot stay with Miss Shannon or her parents, so she has made dozens of phone calls to get you set up here…"

The man pointed out the front window.

The front of the resort looked like something out of an old movie set in the jungle. Ted pulled the limo in front of the place, at the bottom of the stairs to the entrance. Mike slid out of the car, looking to his left then his right marveling at the sheer size of the main building around him.

The resort's appearance to Mike was a huge old French Style Plantation; several buildings in fact had the same look, two stories with columns and a wraparound deck on the second floors. There were dormer windows every dozen feet on the roofs, the entire compound-a dozen acres or so-was covered with rain forest foliage and palm trees giving the appearance of the jungle plantation right out of the movie *Bride of the Gorilla*, an oldie Mike saw with his father once.

The foyer was immense outside as well as inside, white wood columns shooting up two stories with decorative supports fanning out in on both sides of the façade; on top of the 'A' frame gable was smaller wooden slats also in the shape of fans and a beautiful stone entryway made a path through glass doors to the front desk. Mangrove trees hid the fence-line around the property and tall eucalypts stood like giant pillars surrounding the outbuildings and openings into alleys that accessed the inner compound.

Mike was in awe as he stepped from the car and shuffled towards the entryway. Inside the air was cooler, just as good as in the limo, but it was still muggy. Mike felt as if he needed a second shower. Ted carried Mike's bags in-he insisted-and set them on the floor next to Mike's feet.

"G'day sir. How may I help you?" A man dressed in khaki shorts and a white polo shirt embroidered with the resorts name and a green multi-vined banyan tree asked.

Mike looked at Ted and the man just nodded to him. "You have a reservation for Michael Greene?"

The clerk searched the records for a moment and nodded with an emphatic smile; "Of course sir. Do you have your passport?"

Mike handed the man the document and sighed, relieved that this part of the journey was over. The desk clerk handed Mike a key on a long paddle-like piece of plastic, about three quarters of an inch wide and four inches long.

"If you will follow our man here…" The clerk pointed to another shorts and short sleeved shirted man on the other side of the hall.

"That's okay Billy. I'll take him to his room, been in that wing a few times."

"Yes sir thanks." The clerk nodded at Ted.

Mike just stood next to Ted with his mouth open. Ted picked up the cases and jerked his head towards the back of the desk area.

"Follow me Mr. Greene."

Mike did, the desk clerk winked at him as he walked by.

He followed Ted closely, still wondering about the man, who he was, where had seen him before. Being a policeman, he was supposed to remember these things, but Mike assured himself he probably was a little off, due to jet lag.

They walked down along a walled area that held a series of rooms to the left of Mike, and a courtyard that was as big as small university campus. The building's colors were all of a calm pastel; mostly browns and tans with some sharp contrasting mahogany frames and window dressings with small planters hanging off of an overhang above them, filled with bright large flowers.

A quad with more jungle trees filled the areas up to the rocky ledge of a false granite lagoon-style swimming pool, complete with ten foot waterfall and a rickety wooden bridge spanning across one thin end of the pool's expanse. They stopped at door 1112. Ted opened the room and gestured Mike inside; the room was dark, and Ted set the cases at the foot of the first bed in the modest room.

"Look here Mr. Greene…"

Mike turned after surveying the space and nodded. He sat on the edge of the bed near the suitcases, staring at Ted's back. Ted moved near the door.

"Take this key ring here see…" Ted took the plastic strip and slid it into a slot that was next to the door. The room lights came on, as well as the television. "This keeps you from forgetting your key, and saves a few dollars in energy for the resort."

"Wow."

Ted gave the rest of the tour from the front of the room's bay window after he opened the blinds. "There are three lagoon style pools; you'll find the main pool the most relaxing, it is also next to the restaurant veranda, a great place for your meals…"

"Ted?"

"Yes sir?"

"How do you know this place so well?" Mike folded his arms in front of him.

"I have been to many conferences here, by the way the resort would like you to muster at the conference center Friday night, they have this traditional orientation dinner and drinks thing, and you'll love it."

"Great. Thanks. One more question; will Shannon call me here or do I get secret instructions on the mirror or something?"

Ted smiled widely, and very friendly at Mike's joke.

"She'll come by, *Double O Seven*." Ted in a mock *Q* voice from the popular movie genre.

He stared at the cop for a moment, looking him over Mike thought, and he pulled a wicker chair from the stationary table and sat down, still giving Mike an appraisal.

Mike stayed on the edge of the bed, he was tired after all, but he sensed this is what Ted wanted. He gave him a little smile and opened his mouth to speak, but Ted broke the silence first.

"Mr. Greene, uh Michael…" Ted sighed, "…let me level with you. My name is Theodore Hunter."

Shock struck Mike in the chest. "Shannon's father?" *Of course*, the photos in Shannon's flat and the family portrait… he knew he had seen the man before.

"Yes."

"Of course, I knew I knew you!"

Mike fought off a moment of queasiness, stood from the end of the bed, walked over and offered his hand. Ted took it and smiled.

"Pleased to meet you, sir."

"Likewise. I have heard so much about you in the last three or four days. Forgive me for my theatrical entrance, but Shannon would never approve of something like this."

"It seems to me she would probably *do* something like this."

Ted let go a belly laugh and wiped a not so pretend tear from his eye. "Yes, I suppose she would. I see you know my little girl better than I first thought, you are a very perceptive man Mr. Greene."

"Please, call me Mike."

"Mike, I'm here for two reasons: one, I didn't want to wait to see who she was making such a fuss over. She had me making backroom deals to get you here, at least to Cairns."

"I hope it wasn't any problem. I mean I had no idea she was doing this until yesterday."

"She mentioned it was going to be a surprise for you." His smile turned down a little. "If you don't mind, Mike, may I ask how old you are?"

"Thirty-eight, sir."

Ted sighed. "Yes, she said you were a *little* older. I have to temper myself here next, Mr. Greene. Shannon's mother and I have met her other boyfriend from the States, Mr. Wright. He was more her age…"

Mike winced slightly, *here it comes…*

Ted looked out of the bay window at the children swimming in the lagoon pool and again sighed, "Children. They drive you to think you'll kill them the first chance you get, but you realize that they are only growing up. Trying to understand life. They are our last great resource."

"Sir, I…"

"We don't care for the young record producer you see. He is a real pain in the backside, every time he goes home to America; our Shannon is a nervous wreck. This time is no different. She says she's in love with Mathew, but her mother and I doubt it. She says that she's broken things off with the man from America-Mathew-and that she wants to entertain you as a friend here, and at our home in the mountains outside of town."

Mike nodded.

"This time she had a request that I make it happen so you were allowed here. I would do anything for my little girl. I trust her feelings, and I trust her heart."

Mike smiled slowly; he was getting nervous about the direction this conversation was heading.

He said, "Sir, I have no expectations from Shannon. I'm happy she brought me here, to meet you especially, but we are just good friends. Really. Nothing more than that."

Mike felt as if he were defending a suspect the way he was acting.

"No need to explain yourself Mike. She's twenty-four, an adult, in most respects. I do like your approach though. You are a gentleman; maybe what she needs is a little maturity to settle her down. I will say she seems to care for you more than Mathew."

The color slowly returned to Mike's face. "Can I ask where she is?"

"Then we come to the second reason I came here. She thought she could go behind our back and get our driver to bring you to the resort here. I think she was just biding time, trying to think of what to say to us when we met you. But she unexpectantly came down ill and had to go see the doctor here in town, her appointment time was the same hour your flight arrived. The chauffeur tattled-he knows who pays the bills-and I came instead. I'm glad to say I did. You seem to be an honorable man."

'An honorable man?' Mike could see a request coming, one that usually started with '*I need you to swear...*'

"Mr. Greene... sorry. Mike. I need you to make me a promise, I know you don't know me from anyone, but as Shannon's father; I need you to keep a secret."

"I promise." It made no sense to say anything else, Mike thought.

"Please do not tell her that I said anything about the doctor. I'm not even supposed to know. Her mother and she keep secrets, but I always find out. Also, don't tell her I picked you up, at least until we are all together. She will eventually figure it out."

"Is Shannon okay sir?"

"Ted. She has been ill, for a little while Mike. It shouldn't be anything that comes between you right now." Ted stood and dusted his suit. "As a father Mike, I have obligations. Obligations to my family-you understand."

Mike nodded again, a hint of sympathy in his eye. It covered the fear welling in his insides over Shannon's health.

Ted continued, "Her health is our main concern of course, and we don't need any complications. Any. But you should've heard her voice on the phone when she called me to make your adjusted arrangements. You should've seen her face when she came home and knew you'd be on your way."

Ted smiled and his face reflected a man given a dozen years back from the love he felt inside.

He said, "Well. That said I shall see you in a day or so. Maybe tonight, remember you don't know me for Bob? Right."

"Right… Bob."

Ted chuckled and offered Mike his hand again. Mike shook it more profoundly this time, full of thanks and pride. "I do very much like you Mike. Please don't let us down…" Ted nodded and reached for the door handle, giving it a twist he said over his shoulder; "The driver was to tell you to meet her out front at seven tonight. She said something about your habitual tardiness?"

"It has been fixed sir."

"Ted."

"Ted."

"G'day Michael Greene."

"Good day to you Ted. And thank you very much."

Ted just nodded and closed the door behind him. Mike noticed there was a slight smile on the man's face as he walked in front of the window on his way out of the courtyard. Mike sighed heavily, both with anticipation and sadness. He knew something was bothering Shannon back in Sydney, something she had to take care of here. His heart grew heavy. He unpacked his bag and headed for the shower, it was two hours till seven and he wanted to make a great impression. Still, he was worried about Shannon.

There was a cool breeze flowing over the tropical treetops, Mike inhaled the air and noticed it was sharp with freshness, crisp with sweetness, light on his lungs and it made his head swim a little. Darkness was enveloping the city and the resort's clandestine lighting scheme was flickering on here and there across from his room. Bright blue lights illuminated the lagoon pool from underneath the surface of the water. There were people gathering from their own rooms and collecting on small porches in front of bamboo cabanas on the quad. A quiet murmur resounded off the walls and foliage. Mike felt like a million bucks, hell a hundred million bucks; this was the best night of his life to date. The atmosphere was astounding and relaxing and vibrant-all at the same time and he was growing more excited with each passing minute, he smiled, of course it was all he could do to keep from crying in emotional release.

After about twenty minutes at the front of the resort he felt a twinge of the excitement leaving him. It was seven fifteen now, he was growing concerned. Shannon would never stand him being this late; a flash of worry hit his heart. What if her appointment turned to a hospital stay, bad thoughts drifted through his head, Mike was starting to fear the worst.

The humidity had not increased into the evening, so a chance of rain was probably slim, but the moisture didn't drop significantly either. Mike was still clammy in his charcoal grey chinos, white polo shirt with purple crown-the Bay Point logo-on the left breast. He bought the shirt just before he left in the small gift shop next to the pub, he wanted one last look into the place he'd met the most beautiful women ever. Mike was excited and worried.

After a few other cars passed by on the road out front of the resort, a blue Toyota 4 Runner pulled to the bottom of the steps. Shannon stepped out onto the sidewalk in the semi-circle driveway. Mike was sweating slightly, he woke inside, he was stimulated-so alive right now and the foreboding vanished.

"Sorry I'm late Michael. It has been a terrible day."

Her smile grew as she spoke, the little dimples at the corner of her mouth made their small crescent shape. Mike's insides melted and his heart beat out a tingle of sharp notes, she was so damned beautiful.

"I guess so. Don't worry; I've had the resort summon a cab for me." His expression was flat.

Shannon's eyes darted behind her, looking for the taxi. "I'm really sorry. Please forgive me." She let a mock frown appear and then it melted into a full blown pout.

"I forgave you before I even saw your car..." He broke into a bright smile and hopped four stairs down to the ground level. "I've got a Toyota too."

"Really?" Shannon broke a huge smile.

Shannon almost ran to him and they met in an embrace. Shannon kissed the side of Mike's face and he did the same, to that special spot he liked-just in front of her ear. It was like he was home; the sweet aroma was the same, her warmth felt just right. Mike was happier than he had been in a very long time. He could feel her pulse thumping on his cheek as it lay against her throat after his kiss.

Slowly breaking the hug, Shannon stepped back and winked her eye at him. "Are you expecting someone important? You are dressed so quaint."

"Yes, someone very important indeed. But she is late, I'm afraid I may have had a wasted trip." He looked over her dress, nodding at her beauty.

She ignored his remark and said, "Thank you for coming Michael, this meant a lot to me. Please understand though, this doesn't mean we are going to be very close."

When Mike's face turned down she added, "Tonight."

Mike's smile turned to a half-frown. He felt a rush of emotions at that moment. In an adoring tone laced with some sarcasm and self-pity he held her at arm's length.

He asked, "Why did you invite me Shannon? I can't get a good read on you."

"You made me feel happy when we were in Sydney, you know, I could tell you some fancy stories about a man I met there. He was a sad bloke; divorced, down on his luck, just out of a rehabilitation center. We became good friends and he made me smile a bit. Do you know him?"

"I do. But he started to fall in love with you. He says he's sorry, he didn't mean to scare you."

"Tell him I'm sorry too. I think you and I can be terribly good friends. We must proceed slowly though, we don't want to break any hearts."

"I agree." Mike thrust his hand out in front of him. "Friends first?"

"Absolutely. Are you hungry?" She shook his hand firmly.

"No, I had time for a few steaks while I waited."

"Oh how terribly sad, would you like to come along and keep me company while I grab some tucker?"

"I would love that more than anything else in the world."

"Follow me then mate."

"Would you like me to drive? It's getting dark."

"I think the resort would be unhappy if you drove my father's car into the lobby."

"Oh. We're eating here?"

"Best food in town. If there are any steaks left." She turned her head slightly and gave Mike a sly smile. "I'll ask Billy if he'll park the car."

"That's your father's car?" Mike asked as he opened the resort's glass door for Shannon.

"Yes, what do expect? A *limo*?" She giggled.

"Well… as a matter of *fact*…"

Shannon walked ahead of him and made her way to the counter to talk to Billy, who smiled and nodded with charm at her. Mike noticed she was more beautiful here than in Sydney, the proximity of home must have given her a glow-happiness, peace, and serenity.

She was wearing the same style of dress she wore at the Harbour when they encountered John and Paula at their yacht. The tube top was replaced by a matching lace and silk blouse.

Her hair was pulled to the side this time though, the traditional ponytail was missing. It flowed over her shoulder and lightly touched her skin and glittered in the indoor lighting, Mike liked the way she wore it down. For the first time Mike could see the blond locks in their true form, shimmering in the bright foyer flood lamps, it made Shannon look unusually rounded-like a conservative woman, a lawyer maybe-she looked mature and secure with herself.

J Jay Ross

CHAPTER TEN
KURANDA RAIN FOREST

The restaurant overlooked the main lagoon pool, Mike and Shannon had seats near the small piano alcove on the patio. The dining deck extended from the back of the resort lobby into the quad area, the same square where Mike's room was located-the main courtyard.

The deck area itself was surrounded by wrought iron fencing, allowing the fresh air to waft around the dining guests who generally were enjoying the scenery of the quad, a series of large three bladed horizontal ceiling fans made from bamboo and grass stirred any remaining stale and tepid moist air. Filled with jungle foliage and trees like mangroves and palm, hundreds of ferns and shrubbery-a lagoon pool that boasted a ten foot rock wall waterfall, the square kept the theme of a rain forest jungle.

Shannon and Mike were seated facing the pool, the piano behind them tinkled sonatas in the background, children laughed and screamed while splashing each other below the diners in the lagoon. The waiter just finished lighting a candle in a cut dish in front of them and Shannon was tearing into a piece of fresh baked bread. She raised her eyes to Mike, remembering the last night they spent together at her place in Sydney. Her eyes lowered, thinking about what she said, what he did, and the way the week ended. Moisture built a little haze around the corners of her eyelids; she pinched the oncoming tears away.

Mike was engrossed in the menu, he had not seen the little moment.

"How about… steak and lobster. And a nice red wine for you."

"The meal sounds fine, but I'm not going to drink around you."

Shannon found a smile when he looked at her.

"It's okay, really."

"No. Just order what you want, I'm sure whatever you desire will be right for me too."

"Why do you talk like that? Do you have a long college background?"

"Like what?"

"Always proper, then at time you say things that are so funny, in slang. I love that about you." Mike's tone was bubbly.

"No. Only one semester, next year… well *maybe* not. Either way, I was just properly raised by my family."

"I can't wait to meet them, they sound wonderful."

"My mother will love you, she says she can't wait. My father on the other hand… well, he might not take to you right away. Be patient, he takes a little while to come around." She looked at Mike. He had the strangest look on his face. "Why are you looking at me like that?"

"I'm sure your father and I will get along."

"Don't count on it." Shannon firmly said, looking back at her menu.

Another long pause forced Mike to think back to his conversation to Ted.

"Shannon, will you be honest with me for a moment?"

"Of course."

She tensed, he was going to ask-*just say what you rehearsed*-she told herself.

"Is everything okay? You're…" Mike almost spilled the truth himself. "You look a little pale."

"I'm fine. Maybe a little tired from getting everything set up for you."

"Thank you so very much."

"You may have been better off in the *Outback*."

"I doubt it. I would have spent the whole time in my room, thinking about you."

"You would?"

"I meant what I said…"

"I know. Shall we eat?"

She avoided the conversation, but Shannon knew it wasn't going to last. She eventually would have to tell Michael that she was falling in love with him, that Mathew was a thing of the past. She had to make the choice-past or not, Mathew was bound to her in way she could never explain to Michael, she had to find a way to tell him but implicate her availability. She would want a nice week or two with Michael. She could handle that much.

"You look down." Mike said, after taking a bite of bread.

"Just feeling a bit under the weather. I'll be fine."

After dinner Mike and Shannon decided to walk around the courtyard, through the mangrove trees, palms and smaller ferns, the small plants were mainly *I. coccinea* also known as jungle geraniums, some of them forging the course of the path the couple walked. The air was cooler, the humidity had subsided a tad and Mike had forgotten to bring a warm sweater or jacket, Shannon had nothing warm on either. He suggested that they go by his room and pick up something cozy to wear.

Shannon just smiled slyly. Mike opened the door, reached in and grabbed his windbreaker off the bed and his blue sweater off the back of the chair by the door. He swung the door closed just as Shannon was walking towards it.

"Aren't you going to invite me in?" She said with a twinkle.

"Nah, I got what we need right here. Sweater or windbreaker?"

"Sweater."

Her face turned down a little like she was disappointed at the answer. Mike helped her put the blue knit over her shoulders and pulled her hair out from underneath, then he gently laid her blond mane back into the same place on her shoulder. He stood behind her for a moment and rubbed her neck softly, and then he massaged her back a little with his thumbs, Shannon closed her eyes and softly moaned to herself.

"Michael?" They began walking around the path.

"Yes?"

"Am I not allowed in your room?"

Mike didn't answer immediately.

He put his hands in his pockets and Shannon looped her arms through his. The pathway was wide enough in some spots to allow them to walk side by side, every once in a while they'd have to scrunch shoulder to shoulder to allow another passing couple or maneuver around a bush or shrubbery.

"It's a little messy."

"Oh."

"Truthfully, I'm a little gun-shy since our last get together."

"Gun-shy? Why is everything with you Americans firearm related?"

"I guess because that's how we were raised, you know, kicking the Redcoats butt and all. Heritage, killing Bambi for dinner, shooting raccoons."

He smiled.

"Oh." Her voice was solemn; she missed his humor at first and thought he was serious about it. She recalled the conversation and returned to it. "I guess you mean since I practically threw you out of my flat?"

"Well, you were a little rough on me. But it was my fault."

"I never said it was your fault, as a matter of fact, I was a little testy. I was the one who yelled at you, you were nothing but sincere."

They ended up outside the restaurant, below the deck area. A small dock went out over the lagoon pool; a few kids were still swimming. The soft sound of the piano was drifting around the courtyard on hidden speakers in the brush; Shannon pegged it as *Mozart's Sonata № 11*. Mike stopped at the end of the small pier and Shannon put her head on his shoulder, she exhaled softly, waiting for the rest of his answer.

"You were not in the position to hear what I had to say; you know the *Love* word? It had been so long since I was that close to someone who made me feel the way you did."

"Did?" Her face rose up and she lifted her eyebrows. "You mean you don't feel that way about me any longer?"

"I don't know what I feel. I don't know if I can feel like I did that morning again."

"I upset you."

"No, I shamed myself. I should have never been so bold as to kiss you; I should have never said what I did. I knew better, it was my fault." He looked down into her eyes.

Shannon thought to herself for a moment. "I believe it was I that had the issues. I felt so spurned by Mathew that I was afraid I had pushed you into something. I was at fault, we could have…"

"Yes, that's why I didn't let you into my room." He waited a second till the words were thought through.

"Michael Greene with three E-s!" Shannon let go of his arm and stood back.

"Sorry. Just kidding." He said through a belly laugh. "I don't want to put either of us in that situation again. So… the room is off limits to you."

"Where am I going to sleep tonight?" She asked, seriously. "It is too dark to drive; you know I don't drive past twilight."

"Maybe I could drive you home. I'm pretty good, I had a great teacher."

Shannon shrugged off the compliment, she was a little panicky, and she couldn't tell if he was joking about the room.

She protested, "But I paid for the room. I made the reservations and brought you here in the first place."

"I know and thank you for that. I'll find a way to repay you *in cash*." He smiled confidently at her. "I mean it, I can drive you home."

"I live an hour away, on a mountain road. Letting you drive would mean I would die younger that I… well, there's no…" She caught her own breath. "You just can't…"

Mike felt bad at himself for putting her through the torture, he would welcome her to his room, and they could talk more there. Mike loved talking to Shannon; it was like talking to his new friends back at Frontiers. When they talked he felt relaxed, open, unafraid.

It took a second but Mike realized Shannon had again avoided finishing her sentence; he was beginning to see a pattern. He knew from training, she was avoiding a subject; it was usually about her health.

Mike's voice lowered a little and an octave, "Are you sure you are alright? You sound a little… shaken."

"I'm a little worried…"

"Yes?"

"About sleeping on the wicker couch in the lobby."

She crossed her arms and pouted-like a child-with all the intention it carried.

"Okay, look. You promise to tell me what is wrong with you and I'll let you have the other bed."

"Deal." Her face brightened. "Do I have to tell you now or later?"

"Later would be fine, if you're in no hurry."

"I'm not."

They finished walking around the entire resort, once around inside the courtyard and then onto the other pathways around the smaller buildings. Mike unlocked the door to his room around ten thirty. The lights clicked on when he put the key in its holder.

Shannon had to use the bathroom, so Mike took off his shoes and windbreaker and tossed them on the stationary chair, then lay back on his bed. He flicked on the TV and after a few minutes of channel surfing, he found a movie that made his heart skip several beats. This *was* fate.

Shannon came from the restroom and slipped out of her shoes, Mike's sweater, and relaxed on her bed also.

"*Man from Snowy River.*" She said, looking at the TV.

"Yep."

Both of them fell asleep before the movie was over, Shannon managed to talk Mike out a pair of his sweatpants and a T shirt then changed in the backroom. She went back to the bed and rolled to her side after a few minutes, she didn't want Mike to see her cry. After Shannon had rolled over, Mike was able to wipe his misty eyes constantly, without having to make excuses- he loved the movie. When the point in the movie came that Shannon said she loved, Mike felt like waking her, but instead he mouthed the words as they were spoken on the screen:

"*...and whatever else is mine...*" He wiped his tears of happiness and dozed off just after the end.

Mike woke at six a.m. to the TV. He rolled over to see how Shannon slept, but she was already out of bed and in the shower. He went and knocked on the door.

"I'm going down to see if I can get us some coffee." He heard the shower turn off.

"No need Michael, just open the front door."

Mike did just that. As he looked outside he saw a tray in front of his door, complete with a decanter of coffee and a plate of Danishes. Rolled up on one side of the tray was the local newspaper. He smiled to himself, feeling like a king; he lifted the tray and turned his head to gloat at the other rooms, but each one had the same morning surprise.

"Nice, great place." He said as he closed the door.

Shannon was just coming out of the shower and had a towel wrapped around her hair and his T shirt on, she wasn't wearing a bra. Mike spun back around towards the door and he could feel his face heating up.

"Shannon, uh..."

Instantaneously she got his drift, grabbed another towel and wrapped it around her torso. "Sorry Michael; gave you a little start didn't I?"

"Yes. And come to think of it, we never did have that talk last night. You fell asleep pretty fast."

"Sorry, I must have been really tired." *Mostly true...* "But right now I need you to shower and get ready to meet my parents."

"But…"

"No time to waste, we can talk in the car on the way."

"All right. What should I wear?" He asked as he opened the case to show her the contents.

"Anything is alright, just be sure to pack everything."

"Why?"

"You're spending the week at my mother and father's bungalow in Kuranda."

"What?"

"I hate to repeat myself. You heard me. Shower, now…"

Mike knew he would lose this argument, as he seems to have lost every one they had to this point. He lowered his head playfully and walked to the bathroom.

"So you just had to be late that's all?"

"Yes. Does that surprise you?"

"I'm sorry, but you just looked-well you seemed a little out of it. I do worry about you, I want to be sure you're feeling okay, you went through a lot of trouble to bring a *friend* here."

Mike and Shannon had been driving for about twenty minutes before he started the conversation he wanted; Shannon's health and why she was late yesterday. He couldn't reveal his source or what Ted had told him, so Mike tried to trick it out of her. She would make a good cop, Shannon exposed nothing.

"What about the room?"

"Billy will keep your name on the book. The room is paid for. It was all prearranged."

"You seem to know what you're doing." Mike smiled at her; her focus was the road ahead. He looked back out the passenger window.

After leaving the city Shannon began the trek from Cairns north to her home. Mike looked out the window to get a view of the city and what Shannon had described to him after he got out of the shower as the "*most beauty you shall ever see in your life.*"

Heading north off Esplanade she made several-or it seemed to Mike's stomach-U turns and they started gaining elevation. After increasing speed north on the Captain Cook Highway, they rose to the mountains that gave a panoramic view of the immense valley below, thousands of acres of green field, and the city of Cairns. The sea even farther east.

"Sugar cane." Mike noted; he had seen a pamphlet in the resort's lobby.

"Yes, very good. My family owns a small plantation, one of the few ever owned by a non-resident."

Higher the road went and Shannon gracefully along with it, every turn gave Mike a different view. Eventually she changed roads by way of an enormous round-a-bout. Shannon made the third left expertly, just as professionally as Mike would have made a right turn at a stop sign, and the Kennedy Highway lay ahead. From this point, palms and ferns and cane fields soon gave way to the jungle. Giant trees of all types rainforest such as gum and eucalyptus, banyan and oak created canopies over the road, making it grimly dark in places. A quick turn on a small one lane dirt road and Shannon pushed herself back in the seat.

"This is my father's private road. The plantation is just a few kilometers ahead."

"Great. How far is that?"

"I don't remember my schooling on miles, Michael. You Americans, I understand, have been taught the metric system have you not?"

"A little, I think. I wasn't paying much attention that year." He smiled at her.

"You'll see it."

Just as she spoke the canopy cleared a little and the sky broke through. Ahead was a little miniature of the Cairns Plantation Resort or so Mike had thought. There was the same Cajun-French style house, two stories with a small one story building jutting out on each side of the larger one with one false dormer on each roof. At least a hundred yards of rolling green grassy areas surrounded the home in every direction, with hundred foot trees and maybe a hundred mangroves in and around the open area, Mike thought some of the trees had to be over three hundred years old. A driveway of soft grey gravel circled the front of the little palace, around the side towards what Mike thought would be a garage of some sort, and then back out towards the jungle. Shannon stopped the car directly in front of the home. She exhaled quietly, butterflies were battering her abdomen.

"This is it. Home." She turned to Mike and smiled, there was a flaw in the confidence she was showing.

"Nervous?" Mike smiled.

"No, you?"

"Terrified."

Shannon opened the Mazda's door and gave a quick outside tour from where they stood in front of the immense home. She pointed out the wing to the left of them was to be his, at least the first door was, it had all the amenities. Mike looked at the short statured but long building; it was perhaps forty or fifty foot long but only ten or twelve feet high-one third of the main house was tall-and extended from the main house with an obvious mating that occurred during remodeling at one time, long ago. It had four windows in front, three were stained glass mosaics and one pebbled glass, Mike assumed this was the bathroom.

He inhaled and whispered, "We won't be in the same room?"

"We aren't even in the same building…" Shannon said.

As she was directing his attention to the other side of the small in height, wide in girth stairs, where she would be staying; an older woman, about fifty or so opened the door with a rush and stepped to the concrete portico. She had blonde hair, intense as Shannon's and blue eyes. Mike knew it had to be Shannon's mother.

"So, this is Mr. Greene?" The woman spoke with a sweet American accent-a twinge of Australian.

"With three *E-s*..." Shannon helped, while she retrieved Mike's luggage from the boot. Mike just shook his head in mock disgust. "Her name is Lisa."

Mike walked to the steps and reached out and took Mrs. Hunter's hand, lifting it to his lips he gently kissed it and gave a little bow. He had never done that before, but it seemed the proper place.

Mrs. Hunter blushed slightly and gave a little curtsy back and smiled at him. "Well, you are the gentleman Shannon described. But I'm not royalty Mr. Greene. We are simple cattle ranchers from Montana, with a bit of good luck."

She smiled artfully. Mike immediately saw Shannon's smile on her face. There was the corners of her mouth that made little crescent moon shaped dimples, the wider and humble looking larger half circles like little ripples spreading out from the tiny ones. Her eyes squinted a little, there was true mirth in them, and her nose wrinkled just a little at the bridge. She was a future Shannon, one could not go wrong in finding these two related-one could even be tricked into believing that Shannon and Lisa were sisters.

"Pleased to meet you." Mike responded.

A few moments later a familiar man walked from the immense double front doors and cleared his throat. Ted was wearing a grey business suit with a peculiar western style cut, a white shirt underneath a nice leather vest and black cowboy boots. They looked snakeskin or maybe ostrich, whatever they were, they *were* expensive.

"Oh! Mike this is my father, Ted. Just call him Ted."

She walked up to the stairs and next to Mike-to come to his defense-if she had to.

Mike reached out his hand to match Ted's motion and they shook vigorously.

Ted said, "Good to see you again Mr. Greene."

Mike blushed, but immediately responded. "Mike, please…"

Shannon turned red. "You know each other??"

Mike's face warmed also and he started to explain; "We…"

Ted inhaled and readied himself for the barrage that was soon to follow, "Randall had an emergency. I took his place, besides; someone had to be there to make the arrangement with Billy."

"I told Randy to do it!" Shannon's color was still warm, her answer hot. "You had no right…"

"Shan, I did nothing wrong. I met Mr. uh, Michael at the airport and drove him to the resort. We chatted a few minutes and that was it, he is a very nice young man and I approve of him." Ted smiled as honestly as he could.

A lighter color washed across Shannon's face. "You do?"

"Yes. We understand each other." Ted said as he shot Mike a look.

Shannon turned to Mike and lowered her voice as her parents led the way into the main house.

"*We'll talk about his later, Mr. Secret Keeper.*"

Shannon hissed a coarse whisper from her lips to Mike's ear. She told Mike to leave his bags on the porch and someone would take care of them for him, then they followed Shannon's parents inside.

"So you see Michael we have been blessed with this little place here in the jungle-as it were-and this young beautiful daughter." Ted had been talking since they had seated at the dining table for lunch. "I repay the government with my expertise in matters of State with the Oval Office and we have been the happiest since."

When they entered the house at first Ted had given Mike a history lesson of the Hunter clan from its roots in Montana in the eighteen hundreds to the present much like a docent would in a museum. Mike felt little was left out, but he wasn't going to yawn or do anything to ruin his "better than Mathew" status with the Hunters. Mike was seated on a fine leather sofa that had a matching love seat across from him. Shannon went into the kitchen with her mother.

The room just inside the door was small, small compared to the other rooms, Ted had said. This one was about fifteen foot from front wall to back, thirty foot long with a small fountain on Mike's right and a spiral staircase on his left. The woodwork was impressive, it was cut and polished to look like marble, fine expensive Italian marble. Above him where the stairs met the balcony in front of the bedrooms the bannister whirled down to the first floor with a glow of bright white glossy paint and very soft carpeting on the steps it encircled. It was impressive to say the least. When they'd all gathered at the long dinner table of maple covered in fine linen and adorned with four silver candelabras, the finest China and silverware, Ted had resumed his story of the past.

The former Ambassador had talked of his brother, who still ran the family ranch in *"The second most beautiful place in the world, next to Kuranda..."* and how the families traveled back and forth once a year to see each other. One year Ted, Lisa and Shannon would travel to America, the next his brother and wife would come here. Shannon, Ted explained, has been to her old home more than a dozen times since they moved to Canberra in the early eighties.

Mike shot her a look and raised his brow at her, Shannon just shrugged her shoulders at him and merely replied, "You never asked how often..."

Then the tensest moment of the night for Mike came; Ted and Lisa wanted to know what Mike did for a living. A small bead of sweat formed on his brow, but Shannon nudged him from under the table and he acquiesced.

"I'm a policeman." He might as well have said, serial killer, the reaction from the table nearly would have been the same.

"A policeman!" Shannon's mother explained. "Here that is not a very bad job, but policemen in America are in a lot more danger, aren't they?"

"Yes ma'am. But I'm very careful."

"I should hope so…" Ted added.

There was a few minutes of silence as they all finished eating, Mike was worried he had lost his '*in*' with Ted; Shannon was worried her father would begin a lecture of the importance of knowing the boundaries of the sleeping arrangements, as he had done once with Mathew, the first and only time he visited.

After lunch, Ted stood and asked Mike to follow him out to the back of the house, and they walked-Ted slowly going to point out artifacts and family portraits-Mike nodding his head and taking it all in, just in case there was a quiz later. Ted was especially proud of his stuffed Cane Toad on the fireplace mantle. The specimen was eight inches long and weighed nearly four pounds, Ted had explained.

It represented-Ted clarified-man's failed plight to control nature. The cane toads were brought here in the nineteen thirties to control a beetle that eats sugarcane. But the toad had trouble getting to the beetles because the bugs live higher in the cane stalk than the toad can reach. Looking for alternative sources of food the cane toads started to consume other predators of the area, growing larger, and basically becoming a pest themselves.

"This particular one was killed by a local, for the Hunter Plantation after one of its kin killed a dog of ours by eating it. They are very poisonous…" Ted patted the plastic looking thing on the head before continuing the tour.

The "backyard" was immense as the front, a larger open grassy area that ended the bottom of a cliff of mountains that went up hundreds of feet-even that was at least several hundred yards from the back of the veranda, which in itself was no small deck or patio. It was at least twenty yards round, off the back of the house and then ended on one side with a pool; kidney shaped-the edge of the decking following the edge of the pool evenly-and a raised hot tub next to the pool's staircase. To the right of the pool was a circular path that followed areas of small bushes and flower gardens, which eventually surrounded a large four tier fountain of white marble. Well manicured mangroves provided a perimeter on both sides of the path and around the fountain, keeping a close constrain like a few dozen soldiers with their raised swords would a procession underneath. Ted used his hand to point to a small wet-bar that was located to their left, a dozen feet in front of the pool area.

"Have a seat Michael. Would you like a drink?"

"Cola?" The urge to have a beer was very strong.

"Yes." Ted reached over the bar and grabbed a can out of ice and opened it for Mike and handed it to him-Ted did the same for himself. "Shan says you don't drink. I like that, alcohol affects thinking."

"So I've heard." Mike wondered what else Shannon's parents knew.

"Mike, thank you for not telling Shan about the trip to the doctor. She's mad at me already for sneaking you away from the airport."

Mike nodded.

"But, what I have to say now is more important than any secret about a limo ride from the airport to the resort."

"Yes sir." Dozens of scenarios entered Mike's head.

"On the first day after Shan returned from Sydney she spent most of the night in my study arguing with that Mathew fella on the phone. It breaks a father's heart to hear his daughter cry so much-at all even, mine *is* broken. The next day Miss Shannon asked me for another favor. She wanted me to find a way for you to stay in Australia, she said you intimated to her that didn't want to return home to America, that you wanted to live here and she would be very happy to see you adjust."

"I didn't mean…"

Ted raised his hand, Mike silenced. "I wish I could fulfill my young daughter's request, but I just don't have that kind of power here. I have friends, but I can't burn every favor I have coming, for you-no offense-I might need those for later, and getting you here was a challenge to say the least."

"Thank you, I'm grateful."

"No need Michael. Shannon's happy you're here, I'm happy she's happy. My heart smiles when she looks at you and her face glows like her mother's did when we met so many years ago at a livestock auction in Kaycee, Wyoming. But there's more." Ted shifted his gaze from Mike's eyes-out over the fields of grass, towards the tall mountains. "I love this place; it sort of reminds me of my ranch back home in America."

"It's beautiful." Mike agreed.

"You should see the old place. Anyways," Ted continued, "I just can't help you stay. There is the matter of marrying Shannon for immigration status, but I believe that is not on your radar right now is it?"

Mike could feel his face growing hot, he knew Ted could see him blush, he was cornered. "I haven't even thought about that."

"Good. Let me explain why…" Ted told Mike of Australia's strict marriage laws and how they apply, he nodded at everything, and he knew he was not going to get the chance to marry Shannon anyway, Ted's lecture solidified it.

"He loves Australia though mom." Shannon and her mother were in the study listening to *Chopin's Nocturne* on the CD player. A newer machine and very expensive, but the music was crystal clear and perfect sounding.

"Shannon, there is something other than that, something that concerns me."

"Yes?"

"What did the doctor say? Your father and I are very concerned, you returned home sick from Sydney, but it appears you haven't said anything to your friend."

Shannon lowered her gaze from her mother, she folded her hands in her lap, a nervous tick she had done since childhood. "It… didn't go well."

"Please tell me." Her mother sat down next to her.

"You have to promise not to let on to Michael, or dad. I need to tell them, it would be better coming from me, I want them to hear it from me…" Shannon's eyes flooded, tears streamed from her cheeks to her dress. "I need you to promise."

Shannon spent the next fifteen minutes explaining what the doctor told her, the doctors actually, she had been to see one in Sydney, but he said it was too early to make any diagnosis. She had been feeling ill for a while now, and finally she had the news.

Lisa Hunter held her daughter as tight as she could, crying along with her, she felt the pain her daughter was feeling, the confusion, the now uncertainty of the future. Since she had been born, Shannon had been the dream child for Lisa; she had everything she needed in her little girl. But she wasn't so little anymore, now she was thrust into the adult's world, having to make adult decisions and to make things worse-as her daughter just confided in her-she was in love with their new guest out on the veranda with her father.

"Your father tells me Michael is a bit older than you are." Lisa wanted to take the conversation away from its present course.

"Does that matter?"

"Of course it does, there's barely two years between your father and I."

Shannon heard the "voice of reason" coming from her mother. She didn't talk like the people Shannon had met on her visits to America, Ted had paid for four years of college for his new bride and her mother had the best vocabulary and mind anyone could ask for, and most of it rubbed off on Shannon. She knew when her mother was right, when she was telling her not only from experience but education, the best education a millionaire cattleman turned Senator turned Ambassador could buy.

Lisa Hunter took her daughter's young soft hands in hers. "If you love this man, you have to tell him now, before he finds out about… well, the *other* situation on his own. In this small place a secret can't be kept and he would be devastated if he found out from anyone else."

Shannon was still wiping the tears that wouldn't stop. "I know but not now. I have to do it my own way, on my own terms."

"Then I won't tell your father, like asked, either. He would certainly blab it to Michael, I think he likes him."

It was the first moment in nearly an hour Shannon's face lit up. "Really?"

"Don't get your hopes up honey." Her mother's eyes began tearing up, she was having a hard time pretending that the news her little girl told her was so easy to hide. "I am so sorry Shannon. I love you so much; this is going to hurt all of us…" She broke down and cried on her daughter's shoulder, who in turn sobbed over her mother's slightly greying hair.

"Maybe there is something we can do. Have you thought about that?" Her mother spoke, her voice slightly muffled from tears.

"I've given this much thought. I know, maybe we *can* do something, it is my life after all."

"I understand Mr. Hunter." Mike sat, expressionless, facing the jungle and his future. None of which was going to be here, and more than likely not with Shannon.

"Don't be angry Mike. I wish it were so easy, or even possible. You are a much better person than Mathew; your job is even more honorable. But I can't change the world for my little girl I would if I could, but as you see, I can't." Ted put his hand on Mike's shoulder. "Maybe things will fall into place… someday."

"Maybe." Mike almost whispered; he was watching the water fall from the top of the fountain, trickling down from the first scalloped bowl to the next and so on. "I hope so."

Shannon knocked on Mike's door. Mike was sitting alone in the nearly dark room, he felt sad inside, like he was getting divorced all over again-and his wife, the meaner and bitchier Lisa, was telling him she was taking the child-his son-with her and moving two hours away to Sacramento. Mike jumped at the rapping.

He quickly moved to the door and opened it, seeing the red swollen eyes of the woman he had surely fallen in love with, made his mood even sourer. "What are you doing here? I thought we were banished from sneaking into each other's room."

"We're not prisoners here, Michael. You and I are both free to see each other; we just aren't allowed to sleep in the same bed."

"Or room…"

"Well, we just won't tell them about last night, will we?"

"I have this feeling your father knows." Mike said flatly.

"Can I come in?" Shannon put her hands to her shoulders, indicating she was cold.

Mike gestured her in.

"Now. Tell me what the big secret meeting at your room was all about."

She had a scolding look in her eyes. Mike knew he had better tell the whole truth-well most of it anyways.

"Your father was playing the oldest game in the book for fathers: he was checking me out. He wanted to see me on his terms, he wanted to be sure his little girl… have you been crying?" Mike's chest started to hurt.

"A little, don't worry about that now, what else did my sneaky little father say to you?"

"Are you sure you are alright?"

Mike tried to act like he was frustrated with her avoidance of the doctor visit, the fact she did appear ill once in a while. He didn't have to act much.

"Michael, please!"

"Ted wanted to make sure I knew how he felt about you, about hurting you, about your future…"

Shannon's eyes began watering. "He is such a great father."

"Yes. Are you sure you won't tell me…"

"Later, please?"

They sat together on the edge of Mike's bed. Shannon placed her head on Mike's shoulder and closed her eyes and smiled. She was falling in love with him… hard. Mike leaned his head on hers and smiled too; he knew he was in love-even if he would never be able to act on it; he would love this woman the rest of his life, no matter what.

Silence filled the room except the little breaths each was taking and was enjoyed by the other. If lovers were real and as romantic as described by poets-the room was overflowing and spilling away.

Shannon had to break the silence for nothing else than the nagging in her heart and the small pain in her side.

She had a plan. Another one.

CHAPTER ELEVEN

PLANS

"So you see Michael, they aren't against us being friends or even maybe closer, but things grow difficult from this point on." Shannon had spent the last twenty minutes talking to him; she filled him in on most of her conversation with her mother and answered questions Mike had about her father.

"Yes, I do. It just makes me sad, deep inside."

Shannon seemed distant for a few minutes, the room fell silent and she finally broke the thickness with a lighthearted question.

"Have you ever been sailing Michael?"

"All I know about sailing is watching the America's Cup on TV." He replied with a sheepish grin. "Pretty boring."

"Remember John and Paula? They have one of their boats at the marina in Cairns."

"I think I remember you folks talking about it, which was a long night…"

"Yes, sorry. We can go for a cruise, just you and I."

"Where?"

"To the reef, maybe farther. I called Paula about an hour ago and she's says she would love for us to use the Missy."

"When?"

"Day after tomorrow, say for the better part of a week?"

233

Mike was excited, everything he had done to this point was a new adventure, Shannon had not steered him wrong at anything they had done previously together, she felt he needed his spirits lifted and she did just that, but then he fell in love with her. Maybe she would tell him the big secret while on the boat.

The night before the big sail, Mike and Shannon sat at the dining room table with her parents eating a wonderful version of sea bass that the cook had made for Mike. He loved it, even had seconds, and felt more comfortable here in this huge mansion than he did with a few of his friends. Mike had his face lowered a little to the table to keep a bite of food from falling off his fork when Shannon played her hand.

"Michael and I are going for a cruise this week." Shannon announced.

The room froze; it was colder than when Mike told them what his job was in the States. Ted had a cup of tea in his hand; it began to shake a little. Lisa was cutting a piece of bread and the knife stopped its sawing motion. Mike's face was in mid-catch of the morsel he was aiming at his mouth and after seeing the reaction from his hosts-stopped moving entirely-he felt ambushed. Ted cleared his throat and sat his teacup down with a rattle. He had the look of a man who just had his feet stepped on.

"Do you think that's a wise thing to do?"

Lisa had pulled her hand from the knife and placed both of them into her lap under the table. "*Especially* with your…" A look shot from Shannon stopped her cold from finishing her sentence.

Ted looked at Lisa, then at Shannon and then finally at Mike, who looked pale and pasty, sweat had formed on his brow. Lisa looked at Ted then Shannon and Mike also, the *slightly older than their daughter* man was the centerpiece right now. He felt a little grumble in his stomach, not the good kind.

"Shan, you've just had a rough relationship end. Your mother is right…"

Shannon pursed her lips at her father, she wanted to make sure he didn't spill the truth; she hadn't yet told Mike and wanted that for herself. When she told her father-after he wept with her-he promised not to break the news to the man, he respected him and his daughter's decision. "…you are so very vulnerable."

"Daddy! Not in front of Michael!"

Ted's face reddened and a surge of need enveloped his face. He curled his lips just as his daughter did in act of defiance and nodded his head at her as he spoke, in a very stern tone.

"He should hear this too. He needs to understand how I feel right now. What you are about to do can be very dangerous in this situation, things happen and things can go wrong, just understand that your mother and I disagree with your intentions. That being said," his tone and face softened into retreat, "is there anything we can do to help?"

Shannon began to ask for a ride to the Marina, a few dollars for diesel fuel, and their reluctant blessing. Ted said those things would be alright, but Lisa shook her head with a tear in her eye; she wouldn't even go along with the blessing.

"I am totally against this… *trip*…" She turned her head towards Mike, "…and you should be too."

Mike opened his mouth to tell Shannon they were right, but as usual he was cut-off mid-inhale with a sharp blow to the top of his knee under the table.

"This is my cruise; Michael is going along for the ballast and as a hand. I can conduct myself properly with him, he has been nothing but a perfect gentleman since I have met him, Michael has helped me out of a couple of scrapes and for anything else I trust him with my life. There are two berths on the cruiser, one for each of us. There will be no *close-proximity broken heart taking the advantage of*; father…" She spun her head to her mother, "We talked about this earlier, this is what I want to do, if only for this last time."

235

Mike was still in agreement with Shannon's mother right up until the last sentence her daughter spoke, his insides crumpled to near nothing; "*if only for this last time*".

Ted looked at his daughter and repeated that he was unhappy about her getaway, but he would help as much as he could. Then he looked across the table at his wife and narrowed his eyes at her, the way they solved many of their arguments.

Lisa looked down, her opinion obviously heard but unheeded, "I understand how you feel Shannon. Remember, your father and I love you. Please be careful."

"Mike will take good care of her, won't you Michael?"

The look Ted was giving the policeman was nothing short of tendered murder if anything else happened. Mike nodded emphatically.

After dinner Mike was sitting on the veranda with Shannon leaning on his shoulder watching the water in the fountain twinkle in the multi-colored lights surrounding it. He could smell the moisture of the heavy rainforest air, the decomposing leaves and ever-fresh flowers. But the air was still, a little cool-even though the dry season was coming on-and Mike felt the young beauty shiver a little. He wrapped his right arm around her and tilted his head so it just rested easily on hers.

"Thanks for *that*, by the way…" He said with a tinge of sarcasm.

"Very welcome. It is a ritual you see, they always give in, but I have to ask. It shows I respect them."

"Yeah, well the look your father gave me would have any other man wetting his pants."

"You should be a little startled, sleep lightly this evening Mr. Greene with three E's, my father owns a gun."

He felt Shannon's hand rub the inside of his thigh, his temperature shot up ten degrees.

"Stop that!" He whispered forcefully. "Are you trying to get me killed?"

"Are you afraid of my father? A big policeman like you?"

"I'm predictably nervous around a man with a gun and a daughter who flaunts her father's ability to use it."

"You should be frightened, a little. You stole his daughter's heart."

Mike looked at her with adoration. "Seriously, it was not my intention to…"

"Michael, I'm falling in love with you."

The sound rippled off Mike's head and he felt a tear forming. Even though Shannon had whispered the words that tickled Mike's spine, he felt a deep foreboding on the horizon.

"I…" He was in shock, he half expected Ted to come out and throttle him, he looked around quickly for the sign of an angry father and his gun.

"But I have to tell you something. It won't be easy so you must promise me that you will respect my wishes."

Mike had hoped there weren't strings attached to the words he wanted so badly to hear. This was her first time openly admitting to him her feelings, now she wanted something in return. He promised.

"I have a problem that no one can fix, understand."

He nodded, his throat was drying rapidly and tears were forming and causing his eyes to hurt.

"But I am not going to talk about it before or while we are on this trip. I know it will be hard on you, but I want you to understand that whether I tell you or not, I want you to act like you feel. Not because of something I told you, or because you feel sorry for me, or because you feel you have to." She pulled away from him and scooted a few inches away to get a good look in his eyes. Shannon noticed they were watering and it was breaking her heart to hold back the one thing that will end their relationship, as if it were going to last anyways when he went home.

"I promise. I love you Shannon, please don't make me wait though…"

"There you go, breaking your promise already!"

Mike shut up and returned his gaze to the fountain with a sour face, he lowered his voice and said, "This trip is really going to suck if you die on me out there."

"I promise I won't if you promise never to say something like that again."

She smiled and put her hand on his. Shannon slid back beside him and kissed near his ear, like she did the first time in Sydney at the bar. Shannon could feel his heart beat faster through his hands.

She sighed slowly and forcefully as if content, "Please understand my feelings; I just want you on this cruise."

The sun was rising and shining through the small stained glass windows of Mike's bungalow. It had taken him hours to get to sleep, his worry over Shannon and her condition, but he finally succumbed by running her words over and over in his head, "*I'm falling in love with you…*"

There was a knock at his door; the blows were hard and bordering on obnoxious, it was insistent and the sound annoyed Mike as he slipped on a pair of shorts and opened the door slowly. Outside was a tall aboriginal man, holding some boomerangs.

"G'day! Name's Akama Janna."

"Yeah?!"

Akama hefted a large black hand out to Mike, who was still startled at the sight of a man at his door holding ancient Australian weapons. The man had the obvious trait of the bulbous nose, large forehead and very curly hair both on top of his head and in a small beard formed around his chin. A large grin with shiny white teeth reflected the morning sun that was finding a path through the thick of the jungle shined in Mike's eyes and he held up a hand to stop the glare from the sun and the teeth. He was menacing at around two hundred pounds and six foot tall.

Akama was wearing a loose fitting polo shirt with the name HUNTER CANE embroidered over the right breast and khaki shorts. His Australian was heavily pronounced, as Mike noticed the aboriginals seemed to be prone to, but there was that damned laughter in the dark brown eyes that everyone Mike had met on this trip here had.

Akama took a step towards Mike and Mike retreated a step back in surprise.

"Miss Shannon says to entertain you whilst she's away with her father shopping for the sailin' trip."

"I'm sorry, your name again?"

"A K A M A-pronounces it *Akama*. J A N N A-*Janna*. Means great whale… It's Murri thing." The man said again with a bright wide smile. "You ready yet?"

"For what Akama, uh Akama Janna?"

"Toss some boomerangs. Made 'em myself, got a lot here…" He lifted his hand to show Mike the wooden V shaped boomerangs and some other L shaped instruments.

"I'm sorry, I just woke up and I don't have time to learn."

"Don't take much time mate. You'll learn real fast, for you know it, you'll show me. Eh?"

"I…"

"Sides, Miss Shannon say you gotta."

"I'll be right out."

Mike knew he was on the losing end as usual, now he was giving in to a man who carried dangerous sticks in his hand.

Akama had led him to a secluded area of the plantation where they wouldn't be disturbed, about one hundred yards from the back of the house. The grass was soft and long, and filled most of the hundred yards from the house to the line of mangroves that lined the back side of the property. Several gum trees and a few large oaks gave the place an arena look, sans spectator seats, as the big trees separated the jungle from the grassy area. A bench was placed at the foot of every large tree, about eight in all, two trees had a tire swing and one had a tree house the size of Mike's trailer house in Nevada. The wooden flat and curved stick flew out a hundred or yards or so, Akama Janna ran to his side ten feet to meet up with the returning boomerang.

"See, no problem." He walked over to Mike and stood behind him, showing him how to stand with his free hand in the air to feel the wind, to determine which way to throw the thing. "Gotta feel the wind, mate. There you got it!"

Mike held the boomerang in his hand, it was light and he could feel the beveled edge, much like that of an airplane's wing. He hefted the device to eye level, the long end pointing away '*at your dinner mate*' the man told him.

"Just feel the wind, point it at your tucker and let fly..."

Mike reared back and swung the thing like he was pitching a baseball, the boomerang twirled away and landed in the jungle brush twenty feet away, in the wrong direction.

"No worries, that jumbuck gotta way, pretends another one right here..." Akama Janna pointed and handed Mike another boomerang.

"I'm not very good it seems."

Mike was smiling, he was having fun, he was learning to kill a sheep or something with a simple wooden stick, he felt as he were privy to some secret ancient tribal ritual. He followed Akama Janna's instructions carefully each time he couldn't make the flying wing return.

"Relax mate, just give it a whirl, not tossing a rock at a stray. Just like you was castin' a line out fishin'."

Mike did his best and the boomerang went out thirty yards and retuned, landing three feet from Mike. Mike shouted for joy and the tall aboriginal man clapped his hands, which were full of boomerangs so it made a loud clacking sound; Mike picked up his new toy and launched it again, this time it went even further and he had to run just a few feet to catch it. After a half hour Mike was tired from the running and excitement, he sat down on the grass to catch his breath, Akama Janna sat next to him.

"Thank you. That was fun." Mike studied the boomerangs and noticed the different designs on each one and asked the native about them. "What are these?"

"This a goanna; very sacred, then there is water-turtle; also very sacred, then I painted the duck-bill, the croc and the roo. All are very sacred. I paint them myself, which one you want to buy?"

Mike laughed, he knew he was had, how could he refuse the man who spent an hour teaching an uncoordinated bloke like him to toss a boomerang? Mike thought he should reward Akama's infinite patience.

"I'll take the platypus."

"Very good mate, they're sacred ya know."

"I know."

Mike sat with the man for a while longer and chatted about simple things. He found out that Akama Janna worked for Mr. Hunter around the plantation, and he was a member of one of the local tribes called the *Murri*. Akama had a wife and four children that lived nearby in a local village, his two oldest sons worked on other plantations around the area and his youngest helped around the house. His one and only daughter was three years old and "helped" her mother around the house they lived in. His family had lived here for five generations; each one had worked for the sugar cane plantations in one capacity or another, some as house servants, others as field workers.

Akama was a little of both, he explained that he helped out in the fields like a foreman and was in charge of many workers, and he was also part of the house crew that worked around the yards and kept the gardens and trees trimmed and weed free. Akama was also the Hunter's security man. Even though Mike was three inches taller and about forty pounds heavier, he'd be intimidated by Akama if he didn't know him. He had a look that could stun or kill, a way he narrowed his eyes and set his jaw in a way that would strike fear in many a vicious animal. Mike wished he had the ability to display such a look; it would help out with drunks.

"Hey Mr. Greene…"

"Mike, Akama, please."

"Whatcha do for work Mike?" Akama asked with a tight little inquisitive smile.

"Copper eh?" The man nodded. "Know a few of them I do. Lots of my friends are cuffed for getting pissed. Kinda like your Indians in America."

"My friend, you sound educated." Mike smiled back.

"Of course mate, gotta be to stay alive and outta jail. We were once proud, we lived off the lands, and we belonged here. But like your Indians, we have been moved to the back of society."

"Sorry."

"No worries, wasn't you mate." He flipped a boomerang in his hand. "Worse they coulda done though was give us the dole."

"The what?"

"Free money, you know they *dole* it out. Many blokes just buy plonk with it." He looked Mike in the eyes. "I don't touch the stuff mate, I work hard here, I feel like a man."

"What is *plonk*?"

"Wine liquor, tastes bad. Lots of buzz though. I can get you some, if you wish mate."

"I don't drink Akama."

"Very wise man."

"Yeah, thank you."

Mike was in the back practicing his new found talent when Shannon and her parents returned from the store. Shannon placed the boxes she was carrying on the table and looked out the window, she smiled softly to herself. Almost every time he would throw the boomerang he'd have to chase it down, but he'd throw it again, every now and then, it would return to him. His successes seemed to be outnumbered by his failed attempts.

"What are you watching honey?" Lisa asked quietly.

"Michael, trying to throw a boomerang. Being a fool with a foolish grin on his face."

She smiled over her shoulder at her mother, who walked up to her and placed a hand on Shannon's shoulder. She watched for a few throws and wrapped her other arm around her daughter and squeezed, carefully.

"He keeps trying, even though he isn't very good about it. It's a good quality, it shows he has fortitude. It's a strong suit."

Shannon placed her hands on her mother's arms. "I love him mother. He's like a kid sometimes, so alone others."

"You see what he's doing there?"

"Acting like a fool?" She smiled at her mom.

"He's throwing that infernal thing away and hoping it comes back. You think he would do the same for you?"

Shannon's feelings sank. "I don't know mother. Let's hope he does."

"I do hope so for your sake honey, I have faith in him."

Mike sat on the veranda after playing with the boomerang for over an hour, even though he was tired of chasing it, he believed he was getting better at it, just like Akama Janna promised he would..

"Hey." Shannon said from behind.

"Oh hey. Thanks for the play date. I had fun."

"I know... I watched you from the window. Are you packed?"

"Of course. I put everything in the duffel bag you told me to, plus the pair of deck shoes in the closet. Whose are those by the way?"

"Never mind, are you ready to go?"

"As I ever will be."

The Toyota 4 Runner pulled up to the main entrance of the marina in Cairns, the hatchback popped open and four people got out. Ted went directly to the back of the car and retrieved the baggage, setting the four duffels on the sidewalk. He hugged his daughter tightly, and then kissed her on the cheek.

"Please be careful sweetheart."

"I will dad."

Lisa Hunter walked over to Mike as he was hefting the four bags on his shoulders. She threw her arms out so Mike set the bags back down with a nervous smile and hugged her.

"Take good care of my little one. She is very precious, I trust you Michael to make the right decisions; you know what I mean."

"Yes Mrs. Hunter. I promise."

"Call me Lisa."

"I... can't. It was my ex-wife's name, you are such a better person, and I don't want to associate the names. If it is alright with you of course..."

Mrs. Hunter smiled at him, "It is. I didn't realize it meant so much to you."

"You are a wonderful person, you deserve the respect anyways." He nodded with a little smile on his lips.

Lisa Hunter lowered her voice and looked at her husband hugging her daughter and then she quickly looked back at Mike, who was again lifting the bags.

"You would do best to listen to me real quick; never give up, just like the other day when you were throwing boomerangs, this will take great work and a huge sacrifice-but if you endure-you will be rewarded, eventually. Not right away, but your dreams can come true."

Mike flashed a look towards Ted and Shannon, he too wanted to be sure that they hadn't heard; "That is very poetic, did you just make that up?"

"A little, but most of it comes from a very old tale of love and loss. For the first time in my life I have a reason to use it." She leaned forward and kissed him on the cheek, it took longer than the usual peck, and this was a statement in itself. Lisa Hunter rubbed Mike's arms and then walked to the back of the car and hugged her daughter, and in a slightly louder whisper said; "Take good care of him honey, he needs your guidance."

She pulled away and winked at her, she mouthed the words *good luck*.

Ted rolled a portable cart down to the dock, full of supplies for the week long trip to the boat. Shannon followed Mike with her hands full of weather prediction charts and a small coffee cup.

Mike was amazed at the beauty of the harbor in itself. The Marina was surrounded by green thick forested hills all around; the light to dark green was in contrast to the blue water. Blue water-so beautiful, calm here, but the smell of the sea was already hitting him.

There were several slips on the side they were facing, nearly every one that was occupied had a huge sailboat in it, and Mike began to get nervous; he was in way over his head if he thought he could help Shannon drive one of these monsters.

"My god... All that boat for us?"

Mike had stopped short of the slip; he was amazed at the sight before him. The *blue water* was long and sleek, navy blue and white with a mast as tall as Mike could crane his neck upward, the duffels stopped his progress. A cabin lay just a little forward of the aft, sunken deep into the boat via access stairs downward. A deck that was just below the railing had a cockpit for the tender (tiller) and a big silver wheel in the center with a console fitted with a half dozen gauges, most of which Mike didn't recognize, except maybe a compass. The fantail was about four foot in a half round wrap of the stern with stanchions and a rope railing.

The rest of the deck was up a couple of feet from the cockpit, the mid-deck ran to where the mast ended at the base and an arm extended where the mainsail was kept in a zippered bag, it was called the *boom*. Every few feet wires ran from the deck to the mast at odd seventy degree angles, the wire whistled in the slight breeze. These were called *stays*. Fore was a little higher even, about a foot and a half with the anchor point on the bow and a shiny golden fluke anchor in its holder on top of that was the *pulpit*, a short cage that gave an observer an over the water experience. The jib rig had the same wires from the deck, only two ran from the mast to the nose. Another zippered bag held the jib sheet or sail. Winches and cleats held miles of white nylon and cotton rope, wrapped to precision. More rope was coiled into perfect circles on the deck.

"Not a *boat*, it's a deep ocean cruiser." Shannon replied.

A man was stepping down off the 1974 Coronado 35, wiping his hands on a rag. When Ted got close enough he helped set boxes of food and supplies on the mid-deck; as Shannon approached he nodded at her.

"G'day Miss Shannon. Everything's checked out then; everything is in fine order with the electronics. She's full of diesel, fresh water and ready for a proper sail."

"Thank you Kurran. Did Paula or John leave anything for me before they left last week?"

"Oh, yes of course-how silly of me." The man reached into his pocket and pulled out a rolled stack of papers and he handed them to her.

Shannon took the papers and immediately gave them to her father, who had just hefted the last of the five boxes to the sailboat. "These are for you to look at dad."

Ted took them and unrolled the papers and glanced at a few pages, he raised his brow at his daughter and frowned. "Ownership documents?"

"She *could* be an early Christmas present. I'd hate to have Missy in someone else's hands after the end of the month."

Ted shook his head and knew he could never reason with her here, it would have to wait for her return. "Come back safe and we'll talk."

"Who is *Stella*?"

Mike was standing on the slip looking at the stern of the boat and noticed the finely hand painted name on the transom.

Shannon smiled at him and smiled, "It's Italian, it means star."

"And *Taurus?*"

"Bull."

"*Star Bull?* " Mike frowned.

"Actually, the name refers to the constellation Taurus. In Greek mythology, Zeus assumes the form of a white bull to protect the princess Europa of Phoenicia."

"Oh." Mike looked at the name again and lowered his head, he hated being unaware of these things.

"Then Taurus carries her out safely to sea on his back…"

"Okay. Bulls can swim?"

Shannon saw his expression and hugged him, then whispered into his ear; "I'll give you explicit lessons later." Then she kissed him on the ear. "Better get aboard."

Mike nodded and decided on the best place to enter the boat, as he placed one hand on the railing he felt a pat on his back. He turned and saw Ted with a look of determination on his face. Ted offered his hand to Mike and he shook it with confidence and a little smile.

"Be careful, do what she says, keep you head on a swivel-that boom flies around often." He said pointing to the mast. "Don't argue with her, you'll only lose. Bring her back to us." He added quietly, out of earshot of Shannon.

"I promise." Mike meant it.

Shannon grinned at her father who made sure the moor lines were clear of the cleats and he waved back, a look of concern in his eyes, Shannon noticed it and nodded. She reached to the control console behind the rudder wheel and pushed the starter button for the diesel engine. The *Stella Taurus* fired to life.

"An engine?" Mike asked as he sat behind her on the transom.

"Can't raise sail in port silly. You sure you know anything about sailing?"

Mike smiled back at her. "I knew a diesel engine when I heard it; I know that isn't part of sailing."

"Wind can be very intermittent. We might need to move in a windless condition. Then on the other hand, the engine charges the batteries and serves as a generator."

"Lesson number one." Mike drew a one in the air with his finger. "Got it."

The breeze was blowing over Mike's face as the cruiser cleared the breakwater, he could smell the briny air-not the heavy pong like on the west coast; lighter, mystic and a tinge of moisture. The sky was cloudy to the bow of the boat and a slight worry washed over Mike's chest.

"Are we going to run into that?" He pointed.

"No. I've charted the storm and it appears to be heading south. We're heading north. In a few moments I need you to move and sit over there by the main." Shannon was looking up at the wind indicators on the mast. "I'm going to shut off the *iron spinnaker*."

"What?" Mike looked confused, which he was.

"The main is the mast, the big one. The iron spinnaker is slang for the engine…" She smiled at him as he shook his head and moved towards the center of the boat.

Shannon gazed up at the indicators again decided that lessons should come first, or this man was going to get wet or hurt. She pulled back on the throttle a little and tied off the wheel.

"This is a Coronado sail cruiser. She's thirty-five foot long and has a deep weighted keel, meaning there is sufficient weight added to the inside of the keel for ocean cruising. Do you know what a keel is Michael?"

"The thing that sticks out the bottom?" He smiled at her; he was going to be a rough student. Shannon just smiled back at him.

"Okay, come here." She motioned him towards the cockpit.

He complied.

She took his hands and set them on the wheel, at two and ten o'clock. "You take the wheel."

"I…"

"Quiet and learn." She untied the wheel. Using her own hand she showed Mike the motion needed to keep the boat true, using the little indicators on the stays running from the deck to the top of the mast.

"Just try to keep the face of the compass-see that 'N'? Keep that white needle between the N and the 30 degree mark here. And…" She continued; "Watch the indicators, those little flaps on the wires, up there to keep us pointing in the direction of the wind. The wind is blowing north to south right now, so just keep us going north, into the wind." She said, training.

"Got it." Mike was nervous as he moved the large wheel back and forth with the surge to keep the cruiser sailing as Shannon directed.

After a few seconds, Shannon knew Mike would do okay as she stepped out of the cockpit and onto the mid-deck, checking the running stays she grabbed the halyard from its clip and looked up making sure it was free. She put the halyard end in her mouth as she unzipped the sail bag, once open she started tying the halyard to the headboard on the top of the sail, Shannon stepped back into the cockpit next to Mike, untying the flat straps to the mainsail as she went. After opening the canvass sail cover she stepped back and loaded the halyard into the winch and began to raise the sail, then shut off the engine.

Mike watched as the huge sheet came out of its bag and slid up the mast, the head on wind caused the sail to flap making the sound a flag does in heavy breeze, she then tightened the line down. Using another line and the winch she hauled the sheet taught causing the boat to pitch to the right. Mike fought at the wheel to keep from falling over-the sudden changes made him lose his balance.

"Turn her a little to starboard!" Shannon yelled as she scrambled to secure the boom lines.

"Huh? Right or left?"

"Turn it right! Just a little, there that's it!" She was beaming as her insides told her how excited Mike was right now.

She finished with coiling the halyard and making sure all the lines were secured and stepped beside Mike in the cockpit again.

"Hold on!"

Shannon gave the wheel to port and the cruiser leaned even farther over. The smile on her face told Mike he was safe-at least he hoped so.

The wind was blowing over the high-deck and into their faces as Mike stood back and watched Shannon steer the boat almost west. Shannon pointed to the left of the sailboat, "Left-port. Right-starboard. Left has four letters, port has four letters. Right has more than four letters, starboard has more than four letters. Simple as that."

"You're kidding." Mike stared at her with a blank look.

"Nope. Now, comes the tricky part. I'm going to open the jib sail, while you keep her pointed like she is now. Can you do that?"

"I…"

"Good. Oh, keep your eye on the boom, if it goes port, it will take your head off."

"Right." Mike said aloud over the wind. *Whatever that means…* he said to himself.

Shannon performed the same ritual on the diagonal jib, the sail unrolling from the forestay and eventually flapping just like the mainsail did. Shannon took the line back to the winch through a series of pulleys and wound the sheet tight. The *Stella* lurched harder to the starboard, but before Mike had the chance to make any corrections, Shannon was next to him and trimming the *Stella* again, then slowly releasing the boom tension. She kissed Mike on the cheek and he sat back against the cockpit rim. Shannon turned the boat westerly, towards what looked to Mike as large white waves in the distance.

The *Stella* was racing at nearly eight knots when Shannon shouted above the rushing winds at Mike.

"Look at the bow, over the side-here!"

She was pointing from the cockpit towards the front the boat. Mike stood and leaned over the side-what he saw brought mist to his eyes: a dozen dolphins were chasing the wake coming off the bow. Like a fancy game of leapfrog, the thin mammals were crashing through the waves created by the bow as it sliced the water and pushed it off to the sides, it was a game. They were playing like children. They would leap into the air and dive back down into the whitewater created by the front of the boat, keeping pace. Mike laughed out loud and turned back at Shannon, he had never seen anything like this before-Mike was the happiest man on the sea today; his life had been again filled with wonder.

As the winds stabilized and Shannon was sure there was little chance of Mike getting injured, she began a simple lesson on sailing. She taught him what she was doing earlier, she even stalled the sails a few times to teach him how to regain the powerful force that was wielded above and around the seas, she showed him how to turn the *Stella* to make full use of the sails, all the while explaining the lingo he would need *"to be a proper sailor"*.

When he said floor she corrected with 'sole'; when he said window, Shannon stressed 'porthole'. The divisions of the decks was an easy lesson with the high-deck being above where they would sleep, the mid-deck is where all the mast lines or 'stays' were attached and the low-deck or below deck was going to be home for almost a week. She let him control the cruiser for another hour, until she could see he was tiring from the constant turning in the now shifting winds.

As they drew closer to the "stationary waves" Mike was curious, he had never seen waves just stay in place before.

"Why don't they move?" He asked Shannon, pointing to the phenomenon.

"Those are breakers. That's the reef Michael."

"The Great Barrier Reef?" His voice rose.

"Of course, do you think I would take you to the '*Little lesser known reef*'?"

251

Mike's insides were churning with excitement. He had seen TV shows including one titled *The Great Barrier Reef* as a kid and now he was just a few miles away from being able to see, feel, and just plain be in the presence of the most beautiful living thing in the world. The reef *is* alive; millions of sponge, corals, thousands of morays and tens of thousands of species of colorful fish swam, ate and lived within the reef and its surrounding waters. The unmoving waves were caused by the current washing over a sub-current pushing up from the reef and rolling across the usually barely submerged top.

"Twenty six hundred kilometers long, mate." Shannon said when she saw the look in Mike's eyes. "We'll be staying here."

Mike walked towards her, "How?"

"Watch and learn." Shannon stepped back and asked Mike to take the rudder. "Steer her into the wind again. And watch your head!" Just as she spoke the wind shifted and Mike wasn't able to control the pitch from starboard to port, then the boom shifted sides-swinging like a ninja swings his sword. He was able to duck just as the aluminum pole swished past his head and snapped tight on its slack ropes. He clipped the side of his head on the wheel as he went down, a flash of bright light went through his head and he felt dizzy. He could hear Shannon shouting at him-but he couldn't make the words out.

Shannon hurried to stow the jib and scrambled back to the cockpit and tied down the wheel after correcting the course back into the wind. She then released the mainsheet line and the sail went slack, flapping again in the wind. The *Stella* went slack and began to slow, the keel straight down. She reached down to Mike, who was sitting on the deck holding the side of his head, a little bump had formed.

"You okay?"

"Yeah, what did you hit me with-I promise I won't do what I did wrong again…"

Shannon laughed and hugged him to her chest, "No worries now. I'm putting the sheets away."

Mike breathed in her scent. Citrus, sweet and her bosom was warm. He felt exhilarated. He swallowed tightly.

After stowing the mainsail back into its boom mounted shroud, Shannon fired up the engine and entrusted the wheel to Mike, she walked around the cruiser to make sure everything was secured and stowed. She padded back behind Mike and put her hands over his on the rudder wheel. He could feel her slightly sweaty palms, he could even smell a hint of the faint metallic smell of it on her, and he felt a little aroused.

"Have to be careful here. The keel will damage the reef, so we have an area set aside just for us. Look." She raised her arm and pointed around the high-deck to what looked like a big white ball floating on the surface. "See that long pole there? I need you to take it forward."

Mike knew she meant go to the front-so he did, with the pole; which had a sharp curved hook on the end. When he reached the bow he looked back. "Can't we just drop anchor?"

"No. Everything is alive around here-we don't want to damage anything. So the buoys are permanent moorings. We just hook to them. Now what I need you to do is point the end of the pole towards the buoy, yeah, hold it in the middle. Now as I get close raise the back of the pole to show how close I am, since I can't see over your bloody backside..." She chuckled.

Mike knew what she wanted immediately and began performing the task. He thought he would help out by calling out the approximate distance. "About thirty feet..."

"In meters-if you please mate."

"Ten?" Mike remembered a little of the metric system.

"Very good." Shannon cut power to one third.

"Six..."

"Okay Michael, I need you to reach down and hook the line to the *Stella*. There should be a line from the top going to a carabiner attached to the chain just below the surface. When I say."

"Okay." Mike remembered boating with his uncle at Lake Tahoe when he was a kid, many things started to come back to him-except the fear he had. "Three…"

Shannon cut the power and gave it a little reverse till the Stella almost stopped.

"Okay now." There was a tinge of excitement in her command-for Mike.

Mike leaned over the small pulpit and using his arm anchored himself to the cruiser. His heart was pounding a thousand beats a minute as the white ball with blue stripe got closer and bigger. On top of the ball he noticed a small nylon line attached to the top of the buoy; the boat slowed with the current and Mike was counting down the distance in his head-in feet, then inches. He stretched as far as he could with his hand out and grabbed the line off the top of the ball. Rapidly he pulled the line upward and just as Shannon had said, there was a locking hook on the end. He slipped the *'biner* over the bow eye hook and let go, almost falling face first into the sea. He pulled himself up and returned to the cockpit with the grappler.

"Well done First Mate Greene." Shannon then grabbed what looked like a canvass cone with a line out of one of the stern lockers and tied the loose end of the rope to the stern cleat and tossed the drift anchor over the side. Then explained its purpose; "The current fills the cone shaped bag and keeps us from swinging back and forth with the wind."

"Simple." Mike smiled.

"How's your head?"

"Just a bump, look the swelling is going down…"

Shannon ran her hands across Mike's forehead with the slightest touch, her hand felt warm, sensuous, it made his head tingle. Shannon withdrew it when she noticed his eyes fasten on hers, they had a look of ardor, she didn't have time for this yet, and there were things to be done before nightfall.

Mike smiled as she pulled her hand back, then he turned and looked out over the railing to the vast openness of ocean all around them, not a dot of land visible.

"I forgot to ask Shannon. Shouldn't we be wearing life jackets?"

"I like to live on the edge…" She smiled and winked at him.

"I noticed."

"Too late now anyways *chicken of the sea*."

"How far out are we?" He asked as he studied the reef.

The wind had all but died off, there were some scattered clouds building-the white harmless looking ones-Mike didn't want to endure an electrical storm his first time at sea. The ocean was a deep blue in most areas away from them heading northwest; where the reef was the sandy bottom could almost be seen clearly from the surface with moving objects below-fish. Then closer to the *Stella* the cobalt water gave way to the submerged coral, which lighter was in color.

"We are about two hundred twenty kilometers northwest of Cairns." She said matter of factly as she scurried around securing items. Tying the main into its bag and the jib into its protective covering. "If you'll look in that locker next to you there should be some items we will need for our next adventure. After we eat of course."

Mike looked down, opened the box and inside was four pair of swim-fins, four masks and snorkels, and an array of skin suits. He looked up at Shannon who was finished top-side and heading towards the gangway.

"You mean we're going diving?"

"Of course. Once again Michael Greene, did you think I brought you all this way to stare at the top? Everything is below us, like that wrasse to your right."

Mike spun expecting something was about to eat him, when he realized she was pointing towards the water. "What the Hell is that?"

"A wrasse, we call her Mary. She visits us every time we moor here."

Mike looked at the size in comparison to the side of the *Stella*, the fish was at least eight feet long, and so round you couldn't wrap your arms around it. "We're diving with things like that?"

"No worries, I won't let anything eat you. Besides she's harmless, she just hangs around waiting for us do dump our scraps from meals. Every now and again she follows us around under the water…"

Mike swallowed hard in a dry throat. "Are there any sharks?"

"Sure. You'll see black tips, white tips."

"And Great Whites?"

Shannon moved next to Mike and put her hand to her head to shade her eyes from the sun; then she pointed way out from the boat. "See that dark area?"

Mike nodded.

"Great white, big shark. Stay away from there if we get separated."

After lunch Shannon changed into a red and blue one-piece swimsuit and Mike put on a blue and white striped pair of trunks Shannon had purchased for him earlier. After a brief lesson about the do's and don'ts of skin diving, what coral to stay away from, what animals bite and finally she told him to never really touch anything, just look; they slid off the fantail and into the water. Mike was shaking slightly, he had never been out in the ocean-when he couldn't see land-and the sensation of the warm water eased him only a little.

They then paddled about seventy yards to the reef itself. The vision below had Mike almost hyper-ventilating. The floor was littered with fish and lobster, crab and zillions of starfish. Mike spied a few giant clams, but they didn't seem all that big from twenty feet up.

Mike was shocked by what he saw, at every turn of his head. When he would snorkel up in the frigid waters of Lake Tahoe, the sound around him was calm, peaceful. Occasionally a boat would pass nearby and the sound like a distant electric saw would reverberate in the dense water, but nothing else really. A small clicking noise as air trickled from his mask, but otherwise-silence.

Here, the sounds were almost deafening. Snapping, clacking, sounds of sandpaper on sandpaper, a low and high pitched hiss, hundreds of other noises he couldn't make out or accurately describe. The world under the sea was communicating. Sound travels four point three times faster and farther in water because of its density, so it was if Mike had had his ears next to a speaker and the cacophony of communication was directed at him, waiting for him to answer. With the crowded water around him full of every kind of fish he could imagine, and thousands more he couldn't, the bombardment on his senses wasn't over with just the rock opera fish-talk that sparkled like static in his ears.

Colors from every end of the spectrum occupied one part or another of Mike's vision. From purple blue hues, ultra to dull violet, yellows that nearly hurt his eyes for looking at them with their brilliancy in tone, to reds and greens, oranges and pinks, even brightest whites and various greys. And that was just the coral!

Small living creatures that inhabited tubes of tube coral, the wavy and eerie look of brain corals, stag-horns and hundreds of others, including the famous (made so by Shannon's account of her accidental brushing against of) fire coral. The red and orange looking self-descriptive nodules that extended from its base were full of *nematocysts*, which were little booby traps. Similar to the soft jellies and other sea life such as anemone, these little balloon-shaped cells had inside of them a spear with a barbed end surrounded by a protein based poison. Coiling around the barb was a spring like mechanism which was triggered by a minute hair on the outside of the lip of the balloon cell. A brush up against this hair shot the barbed arrow into the agitator along with the poison, and when an animal such as a fish or a person even touched one of these creatures that had nematocysts, they set off thousands or dozens of thousands of these traps all at once. Box jellies and Portuguese man-of-war carried millions of these on their dangly tentacles; the reason most of their victims, including humans, can go into shock when they brush up against one.

Shannon had given Mike a heads up on the Fire Coral as well as the other little (or big) things that can stab you, stick, you, jab you, or impale you in their home environment, and he resolved himself to just not touching anything and being careful not to let his legs touch the coral or bottom.

At one point Mike was hard pressed to follow Shannon, she'd seem to be on some kind of tear, he feared for a second that she was trying to get away from some huge animal that was pursuing them, but moments later he saw what she swam off so fast after. The Reef is littered with thousands of *swim-thrus*. A swim through or thru was a little arch or hole surrounded by coral on all sides and dozens of other plant life and multi-colored nudibranch (a very colorful slug-like animal). Along with other sea life, small and medium sized, some swim throughs resembled arched doorways under the long and living reef. Mike was almost within touching distance of Shannon when he saw why she had come this way.

Just about four feet into a large five by six foot swim through, Shannon paused. Mike was feeling a little low on breath and resurfaced, then dove back down to where his guide was. In about ten feet of water Shannon had her arms crossed in front of her like she was waiting for something, Mike was amazed on how long she could hold her breath, then almost like out of a horror movie; a sharp nosed animal slowly inched its way out of a hole in the side of the reef. Mike felt a chill run along inside his stomach; he felt a small panic coming on as a moray eel addressed the small crown in front of its den. Mike's eyes went as wide as they could possibly go without physical pain.

Based on the size of the hole, which Mike figured to be two feet across, the eel's head was about one foot eleven inches thick. But the shock was to come, as the eel decided to take a closer look at his new neighbors, and swerved side to side as he left his house in the sea. Mike knew he was six foot three, and when out of his hole the eel had outstretched him by at least three feet.

Now, common sense would tell Mike that if Shannon wasn't scared of this fish, then he should feel safe. But when you encounter an animal that ate Louis Gosset Jr.'s face off in the movie *The Deep*, then common sense goes out the window as fast as a flicker of light. Not only was the size of the eel what bothered Mike, but the teeth that looked like stacked daggers-even the two crooked ones on the bottom of the mouth-seemed ready to bite his face into pieces.

Shannon looked at Mike and smiled, then signaled to head for the surface. Mike didn't break eye contact with the eel all the way up. After a few sarcastically kind words directed at his docent, and a few giggles from her, they both took four very deep breaths and held the fifth and slipped under the surface again.

Shannon kept close to the surface this time, playing a make-shift game of tag with Mary, the three hundred pound food disposal. Thousands of brightly colored fish schooled around them, they would brush up against their legs and swim under their arms as the snorkelers made a large circle away from the *Stella* and out towards open water. One more breath stop at the surface and Shannon was leading Mike deep to the reef once again, her speed and purpose told Mike that they were on course for another animal or something she'd seen, and Mike missed.

Mike was still largely impressed with the clams, the six foot and even larger shells that sat open, its million eyes staring up towards the surface. He wanted so badly to get close to one, but just as they were close, Shannon made a b-line for the reef and away from the sandy open bottom. Mike was looking over his shoulder at a clam when he bumped headfirst into Shannon's behind. It was an accident, and she seemed to understand this in her eyes, but she placed her hands on her hips as if to accuse him of some form of underwater sexual harassment. She gave him an evil eye for a few seconds, then slowly turned, her eye direction giving away what she was darting for in the first place.

About ten yards in front of them was a school of sharks. Mike felt uneasy again. Shannon didn't move towards the toothy swimmers, which Mike took to understand that these scroungers of the sea were not the happy-go-lucky type. Shannon raised one arm and opened her palm out, then gave a slight wave as she went from a vertical stalled position to horizontal and began kicking with her fins, Mike followed, keeping an eye on the sharks as they circled below. Mike found himself drawn to the spectacle of the beautiful animals under his kicking feet and floating body, the seemingly emotionless drudgery of their routine as they swam in circles, the smaller fish scattering from the path of the teeth-filled mouths as the Black Tip Reef sharks flicked a head once in a while at the prospective meals.

After a few minutes Shannon signaled for him to follow her and he did-reluctantly. She made another pass on the reef to give Mike time to adjust to holding his breath properly; and then she dove deep. Deeper than they'd been before, almost to then sandy bottom, then on each successful dive she went deeper. Shannon was right, Mary followed closely, hoping for a snack. After each dive Shannon checked to make sure Mike had enough energy for the next, they would sometimes hold on to one another to keep from treading too hard, Shannon was becoming aware that Mike was touching her more and more each time they surfaced.

Mike was wondering why they were doing this up and down routine, he was getting tired and he found himself having to use Shannon's help to stay in place on the surface and more than once he'd bumped into her, unintentionally of course, but he was aware that her breasts were receiving the brunt of his clumsiness.

She decided it was time-after all they had been out for over an hour-she made one last deep dive to twenty feet and Mike struggle to keep up, but he did. This time the clam didn't look so small; thousands of "eyes" surrounded the shell's purple-blue velvet outer lining or mantle, the clam itself was about three feet across, when Mike's body cast a shadow over it, it closed-slowly-not like you see on the cartoons. Mike was a little disappointed.

After returning to the *Stella*, Mike found a pole and reel in the cabin and asked if he could do some fishing. Shannon showed him how to rig the line with some thawed squid she had bought frozen earlier in the day, he went topside and cast several times. After his tenth cast Mike reeled in a nice Spanish mackerel, then another one ten minutes later, then another. On his last cast Mike felt the rod almost yank out of his hands, with a little help from Shannon who came above to see what he was shouting about-pulled in a large cod. They ate well that night, with enough left over for the next couple of nights.

Shannon sat on the deck with her legs crossed under her, Mike sat opposite. He was dressed in his swimming trunks and a T shirt that read *G'day Mate!* Shannon was chilly so she wrapped a sarong around her waist and pulled a sweatshirt over her. She was tearing at the mackerel with enthusiasm and smiling at Mike with each morsel she put into her mouth. She took a sip of soda, even though she preferred whine on her sailing voyages she respected Mike's sobriety, and wiped her mouthy with her sleeve. She had been waiting for a while to dig deeper into his psyche, she was so very curious about his stay at rehab.

"Mike, tell me about rehabilitation."

Mike smiled at her and looked down at his plate. There was not enough food left to feign taking the time to eat, so he took a breath and looked around at the creaking rails of the *Stella*. Memories came flooding back. Some happy, some sad. A warmth of familiarity overtook his chest, he'd grown accustomed to living in a small place with sixty-five other men and women. In fact, going home from the center was harder than the stay itself.

"Sure." He cleared his throat and decided the best path was truth. "After drinking myself into oblivion for a week or more straight, I woke up in a small room in Oregon…"

The details of his incarceration followed, from his first recollection to his group sessions. A moment of relief rushed over him, glad that he was sharing it with someone who would listen without impatience, as so many regular people did.

Someone would ask "*How was your experience?*" and then quickly change the subject when the tale became personal, or even detailed.

"At first, I was scared. You know, big man syndrome. I would act belligerent and pretend that I wasn't afraid of their tactics. I'd finally passed the one week waiting period they determined was needed for me to dry out. Funny," Mike laughed, "they kept me on drugs to minimize the effects of the alcohol."

"Why is that humorous?" Shannon asked quietly.

"Well, once you're in there for drinking too much, they give you drugs to counteract the effects of the alcohol. Then they tell you stories about addiction, and you're sitting in there with drug addicts, who were given the drug too."

"Sounds, confusing…"

"Oh it was. But, after a while, I was allowed to walk about on the campus on my own. That's when I started smoking again. I hadn't had a smoke since I was about twenty; anyways I would wander out to this little courtyard where everybody was sitting in the afternoons, after being locked up for a week and then trying to be tough at the same time, few of the others wouldn't talk to me. So one day I walked over to the smokers area and bummed a cigarette, started a conversation and I had made a friend."

"Not a healthy relationship, might I say. And you should reconsider using the word *bum* here, it means ass."

"So bum nuts are… *oh!*"

"Yes Michael, back to the subject at hand. You met friends while polluting your lungs with cigarette smoke, weren't they worried about nicotine addiction?"

"Not as much." Mike shook his head. "But they were more concerned with me triggering something else, '*One addiction at a time*', they'd say. They could only cure one addiction at a time, if they tried to get us to quit all our bad habits at once, they figured we'd rebel. Or worse, relapse."

"Sounds simple enough. But I don't understand addiction, I know blokes who live for the drink and shout all night long until their dollar notes run thin. They show up for work the next day after a few hours sleep and start all over again."

"Sure, that can happen. Happened to me. Remember the girl I told you about, the one who I thought I killed?"

"I don't believe you actually killed her Michael..."

"I was really hung over that night. I still believe that affected my decision making, maybe if I was sober the night before, she might've had a chance."

Mike looked out over the water. He could smell cocoa butter on the wind, of course the breeze was blowing across Shannon's legs and they were smothered in the oily stuff. An uneasy feeling hit Mike in the abdomen, one of desire and lust- the other of patience and love. No matter how he looked at Shannon, no matter what expression her face was in, he knew he could love her the rest of his life.

"Michael, you can't save the world then." Shannon said, noticing he was staring at her legs, she drew them underneath her behind and slowly looked up, trying to catch his eye as she did, "Michael, you can't change everything about your world, you know."

Mike smiled as he looked into her eyes, the deepening light from the sunset that was hovering a distance above the horizon reflected in her iris' and the deep bright blue had an eternity to them. He felt if he stared too long, he'd see right through to the other side of the world.

263

Mike said, "No, but the things I can change I intend to."

She smiled, "What do you plan to change?"

"I'm going to make an effort to get my son back, at least get more time to spend with him. I'm going to think about quitting my job and finding one that I love, without the drinking or the worry about things I've done right or wrong. Things that could get a person killed, if I'm not careful."

"Your policeman's' job? Michael, you love that job!"

"Not as much as I used to." He sighed out a laugh, "It was almost like one big party after another with those guys. I loved it then, but now that I'm sober…"

Shannon nodded as his voice drifted off. She knew what he was trying to imply.

Mike laced his fingers together then cracked them in unison. "I do miss the center though, it was a great place. After I was put in *mine*."

"Really? What was *your place* Michael?"

"They get so many patients there, so many men and women who are going to 'fight the system', but in the end, the counselors know how to handle everyone, in almost any situation. You're not fooling anyone but yourself."

Mike looked around again, this time he felt at ease.

Shannon asked, "Do you think it was the fact that they cooked, cleaned and told you what to do that made you favor the place so much?"

Mike focused on her eyes, "Yeah. It was easy. Except for the fifteen hours a day we spent in class, group, counseling meetings or seminars. We had an hour a day each for lunch, breakfast and dinner; then we had some homework from the classes to do at night, which meant working till eleven o'clock or so. Then we were awakened each morning at six to be at meditation by seven." Mike smiled sarcastically, "Oh, did I mention we had to do our own laundry too?"

"I wasn't being condescending, Michael. Sometimes people favor being looked after, I reckoned you had also. But I didn't know it was that intense." She looked down at her knees, "I'm sorry."

Mike felt guilty about how he'd just laid it upon her; she was right, she wasn't being condescending, Shannon was merely saying what a half dozen other people had said when he talked about rehab. He was almost tired of hearing it, a reason he stopped talking about Future Frontiers to just anyone, temperate people or 'normies' rarely understood addiction and what it took to remain sober. For them it was simple, have a couple of drinks, eat and go to bed. For an addict it was have a couple of drinks, skip dinner and drink some more, drink a little afterwards and then when you run out of cash, go somewhere that either serves drinks for free to cops, or find someone who is still buying and leech onto them.

For drug addicts, it was much worse. Mike spent time in the best rehab center on the west coast, so the clientele was higher end. Doctors, dentists, lawyers, musicians, poets, comedians, movie stars, etc. were all attending pretty much the same time Mike was, so he had full-on exposure to those who lived in the limelight, until they ran out of luck or nearly died from an overdose.

The scariest were the doctors and dentists. Many of the men he was with practiced medicine while drunk, stoned on pot or even worse, self-medicated on self-scripted drugs. Mike was part of the general public that didn't know what so many professionals did behind closed doors in hospitals and offices, until his second week there. Many of the nurses and doctors sounded like rock and roll musicians with the list of drugs, women (or men) by the busloads, and parties with mirrors that spent most of the time on the counter than hanging on a wall. It was a lifestyle few patients knew about, but at least the docs and nurses were in rehab getting help. There were thousands more out there, which still thought they had no problem.

Mike swallowed a bit of pride with his side of guilt and said, "No need to be sorry Shannon. In a way, you're right. It just hurts to hear it."

Shannon smiled; Mike stood and walked to the quietly creaking railing on the starboard side, the side the sun was going to set on. He took a deep breath and slowly let it out; his nose tingled at the ardor for the big open ocean he was developing. The water was so deeply blue that it hurt to think of seeing dry land again. It hurt to think he was going to have to use his feet to plow him around the piles of humanity and downtrodden, the sick and homeless, the husband and wife who can't get along so they fight until the neighbors call the cops. He knew the pang he was feeling in his heart was jealousy, envy, selfishness. He envied Shannon for her ability to live here. He was jealous that Mathew had the power and money to come here when he wanted. He was selfish, because he wanted Shannon for his own. He wanted the deep blue Coral Sea just a few meters below his feet to be there every time he looked down for the rest of his life.

And he wanted to share it all with Shannon.

"What about you Miss Hunter?" Mike said after a very long pregnant pause. "I suspect you have great plans for the rest of your life…"

Shannon had been listening with a smile, until the last words left his mouth. When she heard '…*rest of your life…*' a tear welled up on one eye and the other could feel the burning sensation of floodwaters being held back. She wiped at her face quickly with a hand as if she had swiped away at a rogue mosquito.

"No, well…" She cleared her throat, "…I have plans. But one can never tell when things won't go their way." She tried to smile confidence, wax happiness, but there was a hollowness to her face. A deception, not outwardly to someone, rather inwardly. A self-lie meant to dissuade oneself from breaking down into tears and cries of deeply hurt feelings.

"I'd like to hear your plans." Mike said, noticing she was not herself.

"Another time, Michael. Let's just enjoy this evening, shall we?"

Mike let it drop.

After dinner Mike went below to wash up and Shannon was gazing out at the setting sun. She felt at ease with the world right now, she was no longer angry at God-who had given her a warning in a way-and she was content to live her life out with the man from Nevada if she were allowed to, she would pray extra hard each and every night she could for her wish. Then it hit her, the twinge in her side and the sudden nausea told her that the kind of thinking was just that-just dreams-there was not going to be a man from Nevada in her life soon, he was going home. What little time she had left with Mike she had to make the best of...

It also meant she couldn't tell him her secret, not until he was safely home in the States. He had enough grief in his life up to this point-Rika, Lisa-his ex, the young woman that died in his arms. She could not stand to see the pain in his eyes again, she knew it wasn't fair of her, but she had to wait till he went home.

Shannon went below; this was going to the night they had both waited for since she knew she was in love with him. It had been a long day, from her early start to go shopping with her father, to watching Mike practice boomerang for a half hour in the backyard, to loading up and sailing. Watching Mike's eyes light up when he saw the dolphins chasing the bow, to the amazement in his shivering body as he controlled a thirty-five foot deep blue cruiser for the first time.

Shannon knew she had affected the course of this man's life-she knew she was going to let him down eventually-he didn't deserve her, but he loved her, she knew it.

It was time to share a part of her that so many wanted, but only a lucky few ever enjoyed, her love. She was going to make Michael Greene feel wholesome and manly. She knew she had *the* power. But she didn't swing it around or brandish it like a weapon, it was a reward for those who were worthy of her love. Her passionate self was almost animal at times, she wanted

Michael more than anyone in the world, and Shannon knew he loved her enough to share himself with her.

As she passed the first smaller berth she saw his feet hanging out into the gangway-he had fallen asleep…

CHAPTER TWELVE

NIGHT TWO AT THE REEF

The sky was filling fast with stars. From a distance, the *Stella* was hard to see, even her white hull and blue decking, but a tell-tale sign was the moving star just above it, swishing back and forth with the swells. The anchor light, mounted on the top mast to warn approaching vessels there was a boat parked here, swung lightly like a pendulum against the coal-black night sky that was encroaching on the twilight.

The sun was waning, a few light clouds drifted towards the horizon as the sapphire-blue hue of the sky turned darker and pinkish yellow. Mike was sitting on the high-deck with his knees to his chest, his arms across them and his hands were folded neatly in front. He was wearing a pair of sweatpants and a horribly colored Hawaiian shirt and had a smile of contentment on his face, happiness that only could be had here-in this place-on this boat, with this beautiful woman. A separation had been placed between them. But Mike didn't mind too much, sure he ached to hold her, but he would settle for a close friendship, closer than he was with his wife in many ways, and certainly better acquainted.

He wondered what had happened between her and her ex-boyfriend to make Shannon so cautious of him. It must have been a good argument, she's been sick all week. *And the visit to the doctors?* Even though Shannon wouldn't tell him outright, it had to be a tragic secret; a deep down fear told him the worst was coming, but after he'd learning to sail in this vast open nothingness of blue ocean waters and the world below he had experienced snorkeling off the reef, life seem so short for anyone.

Shannon, sitting directly across, glanced at Mike above her book every now and again to see him smiling. She liked his soft warm smile; he looked like a child that was well rewarded from ice cream and chocolate. Happy, gratified, at ease with the world. She smiled behind her book at the sight of him, just looking off the side of the sailboat into the fading sun, waiting for the stars to appear. She was dressed in flannel pajama bottoms and a sweatshirt with flip-flops on her pretty feet.

She was worried that her fight with Mathew before they left would spill over to this trip with Mike; her father warned her it was a bad idea for a young lady to take a man out alone for a sail, directly after such a prognosis, and especially just after she had a terrible argument with her former beau.

He'd called coincidentally just before she had told her parents about the trip at dinner that night, he was his usual threatening and abusive self and he'd set resolve into Shannon that she was going to everything she could to make herself happy and forget the imbecilic record producer. He was on his own now; Shannon had fallen in love this time, not just a crush or a sexual encounter. Not what she ever felt about the little man Mathew had any bearings like the feelings in her gut and heart now. Something about this man in front of her was right; she was at ease-at peace with herself.

Her father's voice filled her head.

"*Your feelings might be compromised, Shannon. You might give in to urge and availability, to take the moment of sadness and use it to feel something for this older man. He might take advantage of you, too. You should be cautious-he might be aggressive.*" Ted said, while they were shopping.
"*But…knowing him as I have these last few days-I believe you are alright in a sense with him-just be mindful of your own feelings…*"

Shannon's smile turned to a frown and she lifted the book above her eyes to shade the sadness from Mike, he looked so peaceful right now-there was no reason to let him see her down.

She acknowledged to herself that her father was right; this was a bad place to be when you are sad and lonely. Mike was so close, and she did love him; but she had to block the loneliness out. She had to resist the urge to tell Mike what she fought with Mathew about and she was very desolate inside right now. The previous day had been so wonderful, so full of discovery for him. He was smiling so big and bright as he tried to help her navigate, to set the sails, to run the rudder. Like a kid in a toy shop, he was enthusiastic about helping, even though he failed miserably at so many things yesterday-he excelled at others. Mike would be a wonderful sailor if he kept at it, he would be wonderful at so many things.

Today was filled with more snorkeling and Shannon kept her distance, a bad dream the night before made her feel exposed, she wanted Mike, but now her feelings were causing her to sense she was losing her battles-she needed to be stronger-for both of them. Her plans to this point had failed; she had wanted her father to bring Mike permanently to Australia. She wanted so many things that would make them both happy; but her good hearted attempts had failed; now fate had to play a hand. She needed Mike, without reservations-but he would eventually find out about her and how long she had before…

She *needed* to feel needed. Conflict ravaged her.

"Mike, what are you thinking about?" She asked.

"Just how happy I am right now. How the world is not even on my mind, there is no land within sight and I just want to be here forever."

Mike didn't want to push his luck, again. He drew some fear in his mind since he last kissed her-passionately-in her flat in Sydney. Her response and uncertain future in his mind made him very cautious.

"It is remarkable, isn't it?" Shannon put the book to her side and pulled her legs to her chest-just like he had his. She was sitting a few feet in front of him, but felt compelled to be closer, again fighting off the urge to hold him. "I often dream about doing this all the time; sailing that is. I just want to leave everything behind and never look back."

"What about Mathew?"

Shannon frowned at the name; she didn't want him in her daydream right now. "*He* won't be there. Just I, and maybe a pet dog or something. Company you know, just to chat with."

"Woof." Mike did his best dog imitation.

"I'll keep you in mind, if I feel the need for fleas and ticks."

Her heart was pounding harder now, she could have easily said she wanted him to go with her. *But Mathew… Her parents… her future…*

"Thank you, I'll bring my own flea powder."

He smiled at her and turned his attention back to the sky. He could almost hear the sun crackle like ice melting when the yellow dot touched the blue-green water ahead of him.

After several minutes of silence, the sky was nearly black. Mike was moving his head slowly back and forth-side to side-up and down. He was searching for something.

"Missing something eh?" Shannon broke her gaze of him and looked where he was looking.

"I can't find the Big Dipper."

He said, like a little boy who had lost a quarter or something.

"There is no Big Dipper here silly. You're in the southern hemisphere; the Dipper is in the northern. But you will find the *Cross*."

"The what?" Mike turned and looked at her.

"The Southern Cross. Look over there…" Shannon rolled beside Mike, a little behind him and pointed at the stars over his shoulder. Her breath was warm and made him feel anxious as she spoke in a whisper as she pointed at the stars one by one and drawing an imaginary line between them; "…see, up over there. It looks like a giant cross."

"Yes. I see it." His voice became a little excited, he was learning again from his favorite teacher. "It's beautiful."

So are you... He wanted to say so badly as he smiled at her.

"It is that, isn't it?" Shannon tried to hold her next few sentences back, but she had to tell someone. "I have this dream, of someday sailing away."

"You told me." Mike said with a laugh.

"No, dopey. I see myself just drifting away with the tide, with the evening breezes. As the sun sets, I raise anchor and let the boat drift along south. I would *follow* the Southern Cross."

"Where would you go?" Mike whispered, not wanting to break the mood.

"Anywhere the Cross goes."

"It sounds beautiful." Mike looked back towards the sea. "It's so dark, no light from land. The sky is like one huge dome of stars, from this side to the other." Mike looked from the port side of the sailboat to the starboard.

"Drift the tide on dusk's calm breeze, to a land once was lost. You can reach the shore there, just follow the Southern Cross. Swells swallow your bow, gusts push your silk, across the whitecaps you will toss, but ne'er fail to follow the Southern Cross."

Shannon looked upward and sighed after reciting the sonnet.

Mike sat up, straight. "That's one of the most beautiful poems I've ever heard."

"I want so badly to follow my dream, to have nothing but a star to follow."

"It's a great dream." Mike said as a compliment.

Shannon was aching now, aching to kiss Michael Greene. She needed someone who understood her; she wanted to be held the way he held her in Sydney. She tried to change the subject again.

"Michael. Have you ever been in love?"

It was all she could think of. *So much for changing the subject*, she scolded herself.

"Once, I think. You mean other than…"

"Michael, just answer the question. Just once? You don't need a very vivid imagination to recall one love now do you? Didn't you love your wife-I mean…"

"Of course, we were in love at first, but we drifted apart; both of us thought we could change what we didn't like about one another, but for my first real love?" Mike paused; his eyes reflected a sudden change in mood. He was gathering the will to tell a story he'd nearly forgotten all about, a tale that made him sad thinking about it was heartbreaking and defiant of everything he'd made himself to be. It made him wish himself back to a different time, a different place in time.

"There was this girl, in the neighborhood I grew up in."

"Sounds like true love to me…"

"Do you want to hear the story?"

"Sorry, please continue."

"Anyways, we lived on this little street not far from where I live now in Lockwood. There was this beautiful home across the street from ours, sort of kitty-cornered. I don't remember anything but she'd always been there. Always been across the street."

"Sounds romantic!"

Mike glared at her, "This young girl barely noticed me at all. I mean, we just never connected."

Mike looked at Shannon to see if she had any comments on the subject, and continued; "I liked her a lot, we played together like kids do you know; jacks on the sidewalk, hopscotch. Her eyes were always looking around, she was always using her eyes to convey her thoughts, now that I think about it…"

"Were they as pretty as mine?" Shannon joked sarcastically.

"Yes, when I did get a chance to look into them, they were just as pretty as yours. Can I finish now?"

"Oh please do. I wish to hear all about my competition in the States."

"We never got very serious about anything, we'd play with her toy Noah's Ark and joke about the river overflowing and how we'd be able to survive because we knew how to save ourselves, we'd hide on a neighbor's boat and let it take us away, safely."

"Sounds, familiar…" Shannon said with an air of suspicion about her own tale.

"It was quite the same idea I suppose. When you're a kid, you just want everything to be better for you. Easy, like the way parents pretend that being grown up is so much better than being young. It's kinda like a lie. Childhood is so much better than adult life, so innocent, so unrequired."

Shannon adjusted her butt on the deck and leaned forward to Mike.

"I told her if anything ever happened to our city, I'd protect her…"

"Always the policeman…"

"It's in my blood from birth. We parted one year, I went to live on my uncle's ranch for a couple of weeks and she went to stay with her father-her mother and father were separated-no big deal today, but in the seventies shacking up with someone was almost sacrilege."

"You never saw each other again?"

"I kissed her on the cheek goodbye, you know, like you see your parents doing all the time. But it felt strange, it was wonderful and confusing at the same time, I spent the next few weeks thinking about her every day."

"I should say you were very brave. I so much haven't received a cheek smack."

"You scare me."

"I do?" Shannon's voice raised an octave.

"Yes." Mike smiled and then he pecked Shannon on the cheek, she pretended to blush.

He sat back on his haunches and looked up at the stars. "When I returned home from vacation, she was still gone. She never returned. It bothered me for weeks. I never saw her again."

Shannon smiled widely, her eyes glowing in the little cone luminance that trickled down from the anchor light on the mast. "What happened?"

"I don't know. Custody thing or something like that. It was hard for me to understand at that age, I can't even remember the details now. But I still see her face in my dreams sometimes, the good dreams. I still hear her laugh and can smell her cheap kids perfume. I can still see the nearly invisible hairs on her soft skin as I kissed her.

"For the best part of the rest of my life until now, I still think about her. How she made me feel comfortable inside, how that little kiss on the cheek made her smile. The last time I ever got to see her smile."

A moment of silence felt like a weight on the both of their shoulders, finally Mike asked, "Remember your first time, your first kiss?"

"Yes, it was a little frightening. I was eleven, this young bloke named Martin and I were playing *Wee Willy Winkie* and he stopped for a moment, then we embraced and he kissed me, French style. I was floored; it took a week before I would even look at him again."

"Wee Willie Winkie?"

"It was a game we made up from the old Scottish nursery rhyme."

"Of course." Mike sighed as he returned to his memories, "Now that I'm getting older, I wonder about her even more. I don't know why, I mean there were several girls in the neighborhood, but why just this one? What made her so special? It makes me wonder sometimes if there isn't a soul mate for everyone."

"I would like to believe there is." Shannon said unceremoniously.

Mike cleared his throat, "It's just that I wonder, sometimes for days at a time; where she is, how can I find her, what's she like now, does she have kids…"

"Perhaps she thinks the same things about you?"

"Maybe. But this is really kinda small world, in a way you know. I would like to think we'd run into each other one day. Just to say hi or catch up a little."

"No gratuitous sex?" Shannon smirked.

"I'd settle for a: 'I'm sorry we lost each other, I'm married and have five kids and my husband is a rocket scientist' or something like that."

"I'm sorry. '*But if it isn't for love that leaves us needing another, we shall never need anyone else…*'"

Mike's eyes perked up towards his lovely host, "Wow. That was very nice."

"Yes? Remember '*Drift the tide on dusk's calm breeze, to a land once was lost. You can reach the shore there, just follow the Southern Cross. Swells swallow your bow, gusts push your silk, across the whitecaps you will toss, but ne'er fail to follow the Southern Cross*'."

Mike smiled with a satisfaction. "You are the poet! I can never get enough of that one; it feels so… so…"

"Right now? Us?"

"Did you write that?"

"I'm afraid not. This was a poem taught to us in school when I was young. But it did inspire my dream of sailing off to the horizon on the *Stella*."

"And a true dream it is! '*All I ask is a tall ship, and a star to sail her by…*'."

Shannon giggled, "John Masefield, *Sea Fever*." She threw her back in a very intimate way and looked up at the darkened sky. "Perhaps one day, you'll discover the love of the sea that I have."

Mike smiled, then the thought of the young girl from his past caught up with him and he lowered his head. "I guess she was just a part of my mid-life crisis. Wanting something that I know I can never have, nor ever will."

Silence overcame the sailboat, only the slight creaking of the wood and metal railings expanding and contracting in the rocking motion of the captured air and soft churn of the surge.

"I'm sorry."

It was the only words Shannon could think to say, the only thing that seemed appropriate.

"I only wish I could kiss her one more time, even if she didn't want me too. I keep thinking about using my police powers and find her I guess, get her phone number, sort of stalk her…"

"Michael Greene the copper?"

"I guess if were meant to be together we would." Mike smiled and rose again to face Shannon. "Can I have your number?"

"I'll be sure to write it down for you." Shannon looked back at Mike, whose smile had frowned. "Can I ask you a question?"

"Of course."

"Back at my flat in Sydney last week…" Shannon began; Mike could feel his stomach tighten. "…you said you loved me."

"I… guess. I'm sorry I didn't mean to."

"My father didn't understand."

Mike gulped; he had a promise to keep for Ted Hunter. "Uh oh."

"He was quite, well… unsettled…"

"I didn't mean to upset him…"

"I wouldn't worry about it; he just knows that you've made a special place at our family table now."

Mike smiled, "Really?"

"Yes." There was sultriness in her answer, then acerbity, "I *would* keep my eye on him though, my father, he still thinks of you as a threat. Of course, he thinks I'm still fifteen."

"Yes I know, he owns a gun." Mike finished.

"I love you…"

"I know."

"Michael Green with three E-s... I love you." She exhaled hard and a tear appeared in the corner of her right eye.

"I don't know what to say."

"Say that you love me too."

"You know I do. But your mother and father-I think your mother likes me but your dad acts like he wants to skin me alive and set me on the mantle next to his stuffed frog."

"Toad." Shannon took a deep calming breath. "My mother adores you, she always liked the strong, silent, protective type; you see what she got..."

"Your dad is cute."

"I love him more than anyone, but he can be a bit overprotective. He likes you though." She said with derision.

"He does. Did he tell you that too?" Mike made fun of her.

"Sure, he told me before we left that he trusts you, from doing anything that would jeopardize his deal with you."

"That's reassuring. Trusts me from doing what?"

"*This...*"

As Shannon finished the word she slid quickly to Mike who was rising to his behind, startled by her sudden movement towards him. She made the connection as he grasped her around her shoulders and fell onto his back, Shannon's kiss searching Mike's lips, then face and just under his cheek on his jaw. Towards his ear her breath washed a tease of warm air; and the tickle of the cool night air made goose bumps form all along his neck. Mike squeezed Shannon closer to him, as close as they physically could go, and he felt her arms searching his silly looking Hawaiian Shirt for the buttons.

When she managed to get three of them off, she became frustrated at the last one and the rush of adrenaline allowed her to rip the last button out. Shannon ran her hands and arms inside Mike's shirt and massaged his shoulders. Then she moved her arms to his sides and behind his back, her fingers flexing and contracting with her breath. Finally she lowered her hands to his waistline and wound her fingers in Mike's sweatpants.

Mike's breathing grew rapid and the taste of Shannon's skin as his kisses began to glide to her neck drove his passion even more, he could smell the ginger-lemon of her shampoo and a tang of sweat. When her fingers reached his belt line, Mike began to tremble uncontrollably, Shannon sensed this and stopped short of going any farther at the moment then she broke the kisses off as she slowly pulled away from his searching lips.

"Are you okay Michael?" She was slightly out of breath.

"I… I'm afraid…"

Shannon sat upright with a bolt. "What??"

"I mean I hope your dad thinks you're old enough to… you know…" He sat up and pointed his hand out towards her, palm open and up.

"Why is my father on the top of your thoughts right now?"

"I think he could kick my ass…"

"Probably, but mother would thump him for it. Would you like to go below deck and see your sleeping arrangements?" She smiled slightly; in the faint anchor light Mike could see a sly quirk in her eye.

He would play along.

"You mean we are sleeping in separate bunks?" Mike faked surprise.

Shannon rose to her feet and beckoned Mike to do the same, then teasingly she slid down to the cockpit and to the below deck doors.

"Separate berths Mr. Greene. There are two in this cabin, one for you and one for me. Yours shall be the one closest to the cockpit stairs, the aft-berth. The fore-berth here…" She pointed as Mike looked over her shoulder from the louvered companionway door, towards the open door of the master bedroom, "…is mine."

"I know, we slept here last night, remember?"

"Yes, you were out cold, from exhaustion."

"It was hot down here, that fan didn't do a good job of keeping it cool…"

Mike felt the warm rush of air coming from the small fan above the galley stove, it pointed towards the doorway on a self-rotating arm. "It's a little warm down her right now, don't you think?"

"Yes. I think we should…"

Shannon turned her eyes towards the upper deck above the cockpit for a second as she was responding, when she felt Mike's hand on her cheek, his fingers on the other hand were tasseling with her hair and he put slight pressure forward on the back of her head, pulling her face to his.

He could feel her hair blowing from her ponytail up against the side of his face in the gentle breeze downward, along with the smell of sea-salt and her lotion, Mike's passion amplified. He made a move to get her attention turned towards the small hallway, she didn't resist this time. They slowly walked back to the fore-cabin, eyes locked together, Mike driving Shannon as she retreated backwards, her hand feeling above her to make sure she didn't bang her head on the overhead or ceiling beam nor any suspended light fixtures, her bare feet made little thumping sounds on the sole towards the forward berth.

Shannon landed with a soft whump on the bed and Mike used his arms to take the weight off the small drop not to crush her, he then lowered himself so very carefully to her; his eyes were locked with hers, as the glow of the down light above the bed made Shannon's glisten like a sapphire in the moonlight.

Her body was warm to his touch, her face inched closer to his, her sweet breath dazzled his head-it was swimming with excitement and the world between them slipped away, the love they felt for each other took the place of fear and the future.

"I never want to go home…" Mike whispered.

"Home?" A whisper came from Shannon, her heart pounding blood through her ears.

"I…"

"To an empty bed?" She closed her eyes; she could feel him pull closer.

Her upper lip touched both of his first, she slowly let it brush Mike's trembling soft lips, and he slowly closed them to hers.

This night had brought peace to their aching hearts. Mike's kisses trembled with the fear inside of him over the young beauty, her small body compared to his and the excitement of the time he anticipated so, being with Shannon, his breath rose and fell with the *Stella*, as the waves from the sea generated thousands of miles away in an unseen place washed around the hull, as the swells slapped the side of the boat gently like a breeze over a grassy warm meadow.

Shannon could feel the anxiousness of Mike shudder against her body-she had to smile, while she was nervous as he was, she wanted to make love to him for a week, enticed by his strong muscular body and sad distant eyes. He had told her stories of vulnerability, his weakness over the world he couldn't control, Shannon had decided that he was no fluke; the man that held her tight against his skin was human and needed real love from someone who needed him as much as he needed her.

Shannon drove the thought of her new condition from her mind, she required that a man that loved her as much as Michael did receive reward for his efforts-effort of protection, constant semi bumbling attempts to show how much he loved her by just being himself, by showing concern over her health even though she had yet to reveal the truth to him. Her body numbed with his kisses and her breathing became short and shallow-the lovers had become a single part of each other-rather than having their lives circle each other. True love from hearts of both.

The early morning sun shone down through the small flat oval portholes above the master bed, the blankets had been tossed to the floor and only a sheet covered the entangled bodies of Michael and Shannon. Each morning for the last week they'd been out here, the sun always came in the same way and each morning Mike felt deeper in love, but today was different.

The rocking sailboat still was creaking as the gentle waves brushed past the side of the boat, and the crying of a seagull flying around the mast kept stirring Mike. Shannon's arm was over his chest; his leg wrapped around hers under the cover, his right arm was under her head and left was holding her arm close to him. Mike surveyed the small cabin from where they lay in the bow; he looked towards the stern and the small stairs that lead up to the cockpit several feet from the edge of the bed he was so comfortable on. Mike then noticed the coffee pot on the small galley stove. Time for his daily ritual.

After a few minutes of small movements designed not to disturb his sleeping beauty, Mike managed to neatly crawl to the galley, where he stood and promptly hit his head on the cross beam above. Wincing in pain with sparking shafts of white light in his eyes he found the coffee grounds in a pantry cabinet off to the right of the stove; he used the fresh water pump handle and filled the pot, placed the grounds in the filter and lit the burner with a wooden kitchen match that was next to the sink. Satisfied he had accomplished something important; he pulled on his sweat pants and walked quietly above deck, to survey the morning-and the new world that was bound to be out there today.

It was the most incredible week ever had by Shannon, she smiled. She was drifting in and out of consciousness when she heard Mike thump his head on the ceiling. She fought back the urge to giggle and managed to keep her eyes closed when she knew he briefly glanced over. She could smell the dark roast brewing in the kettle and decided she wanted to see what Michael was doing but she didn't want to bother him, so she snuck out from under the sheet and tiptoed across the crumpled bed covers on the sole then slowly made her way to the stairs. She tried to get a glimpse of where he might be standing from the shadows, but he wasn't in sight. She slipped up into the cockpit and glanced over her shoulder above the high-deck to the bow. He wasn't there. Suddenly she felt a chill on her back like someone was watching her and she spun around.

"Morning."

Mike said from the small fantail, he was sitting down watching the sun rise and was unable to be seen from the lower deck or the cockpit.

Shannon was startled and let out a little yelp, then her face drew into a tight smile, her eyes reflected the sunlight light like blue mirrors.

"Good Lord, Michael. You startled the life out of me."

"Sorry."

"How long have you been spying on me bum?"

Mike smiled widely and let his eyes drift south on her.

Shannon watched his eyes move from hers towards the deck, when she realized she wasn't wearing any clothes. Her smile turned to a crooked frown and she bit the corner of her lip.

"How dare you spy on me while I have no clothing on, sir?"

"I'm sorry; again I was just minding my own business here."

Shannon smiled back teasingly at him and lowered herself back into the cabin and hustled to her cabin drawer and found a sweat suit. Just as she was pulling on her deck shoes the whistle on the coffee kettle went off so she made them both a cup and placed the steaming mugs on a tray, along with a banana hanging from a basket above the sink and an orange for her. Again she walked slowly up the stairs to Mike and found him this time sitting on the high-deck, port side looking out over the water. Shannon quietly stood there watching him, how at peace he looked with a smile on his face, how the slight morning breeze fluffed his hair, the air seemed to be happier today; she could breathe easier.

Mike was watching the reef create little white-capped waves off of it as the seawater washed over the top; he could smell the briny air and realized there was not a better place on earth right now. He remembered he had asked Shannon to return with him to Nevada, to live with him-marriage was his real intention-happily ever after there; he would go to work at night being a cop and she would have nothing to do all day. That is what flashed through his mind at the time.

But now, after seeing this expanse of ocean in front of him, after snorkeling the Great Barrier Reef with Shannon yesterday, after the dolphins and Mary and everything else including Akama Janna the boomerang maker near her home made Mike realize he would be taking a beautiful entity away from paradise. He might as well take the reef home or the dolphins, it would feel the same to him, he would be removing something that was not his, nor should it be, and it certainly doesn't belong in Nevada or anywhere else but here. A decision had to be made and he had to make it right now before things got any closer between him and Shannon, before she agreed to do something that would make her shining beauty go dull as a sanded wood floor.

Then Mike pondered the possibility of him staying here, he could do that without any prompting. All that had to done was to ask him; and he would have everything sold at his home and he would stay; but he knew from Mr. Hunter's tone the other night that a prolonged stay would be impossible. Ted made it clear that he couldn't even interfere with the strict immigration policies that Australia had, he conceded that an immigration marriage could take years, and then there was that thing with the doctor.

It infuriated him that Shannon made him promise not to ask her about the trip to the doctor the day he arrived, he wanted to know if she was going to be alright, if maybe the reason he keeps running into a dead end is her diagnosis but why wouldn't she tell him? Maybe she thought after all he had been through, he would have trouble handling this, and she cared enough for him to keep his spirits up.

Shannon sat the tray on the top of the high-deck, where they lay last night gazing at the stars before bed. She handed Mike a cup of coffee and he continued to stare out over the Coral Sea.

"Are you pretending to be Mrs. Macquarie?"

"Am I facing east?"

Shannon looked briefly over the side of the boat and the way the reef was pointing. "Yes, you are. Why do you look so down? Earlier you had this look of content on your face, like the whole world didn't exist, but us."

"It didn't then, but it came back."

"What came back?"

Mike sat his cup down on the deck and looked into Shannon's inquisitive eyes, the early morning sun reflecting off the blue water made her eyes seem unending inside, tunnels of blue infinity.

"Tell me the truth."

"What truth?"

"After this week, we won't see each other again will we?"

"I couldn't say for certain Michael. What brings this up?"

"You make me the happiest person in the world Shannon. What happened last night will never be matched, ever in my life. But, you seem hesitant when I ask about our future, your eyes go distant-to a faraway place without me-I can't seem to get you back for a while."

"Michael I…"

"The truth, if you please. If you love me."

"I do love you, and that is the reason I can't predict our future together. I can't make promises beyond next week, after you leave…" She turned her gaze out over the water, looking towards the east, Mike did the same; "…you have to go home, I tried everything I could to keep you here. But your visa expires soon."

"In five months." Mike said defiantly.

"I know that, my father went over that with me last week."

"It's for sure he doesn't see any future for us."

"He doesn't want to get in any trouble either. As I was saying, you can't look for work, you can't afford to pay for hotel rooms or resorts for the next five months, and I would never ask my parents to care for you too."

"Too?"

Mike almost broke the promise to her right there, he wanted so bad to know why she had to go to the doctor, why her mood had changed, why her beautiful eyes lost so much luster the day she met with him, his first day in Cairns. He wanted to ask her if he could stay and take care of her if things weren't going to go well for her, the revelation in Cairns that she had sold her Mazda to Tommy the doorman at the Bay Point Hotel convinced Mike that Shannon had no intention of returning to Sydney. That made for a bad sum, all the factors combined-but he promised the little man with the greying temples, the man who fooled him at first just to get a glimpse of what Mike was, to be sure his treasure, his only daughter, would be safe with him. Mike knew Ted did not like Mathew at all, even Ted himself told Mike that, so Mike felt her father trusted him more than any other person in Shannon's life right now, he had to keep the promise-but he had to know; why did Shannon act like she had no certain future?

"Too, as in also. They live an idyllic life in Kuranda; they want me to stay with them for a while anyways, at their expense. I can't ask them to make room for you for five months, then after that? We are right back here at this same conversation."

A tear formed in her eye closest to Mike, he would have seen it but for the tears that had collected in his. He looked down towards the water, the deep blue beneath them, where just yesterday he was exploring the reef with Shannon, skin-diving for the second time. The life that was so abundant around him, so huge and continual, there was so much peace and beauty here,

287

now he felt as if it all meant nothing. How could he feel so sad surrounded by the most beautiful place in the world, with the most beautiful girl he ever met and fell in love with. It was because Mike realized she was right.

He would never ask Ted and Lisa if he could stay, that would be a burden. The law says he can't look for work or he'd face immediate deportation. He only has several hundred dollars left in his savings account back home, depleting that to keep a room here would leave him flat broke when he returned and he would have to return because a new visa had to be issued to him after six month stay back home, another immigration law. He needed that money until he decided whether he was going to return to his cop job.

Shannon sniffed back a tear and looked at Mike. "What are you thinking about?"

"How much I love you, how hard it is going to be to say goodbye."

"We have two more days out here; we can make them last a lifetime."

"Yes, that would be wonderful." Mike raised his eyes to hers again. "I would like that. Promise me one thing."

"Anything."

"Let's not talk about me leaving again, till I'm packed and on my way to the airport." He smiled, sadly.

The question of her father's promise burned in him like acid. But he would keep it, if he left here with anything else, it would be he kept the promise he made to the man whose daughter he loved more than anything else in the world, someday that trust might be useful.

"Agreed."

Shannon wrapped her arms around Mike and laid her head on his shoulder, wiping her tears away with a hand. They spent three hours holding on to one another there, staring out to the east-just as the lonely Mrs. Macquarie did over a hundred years ago from her hand carved sandstone chair.

Mike steered the sailboat without as much fear as he had the first time Shannon made him learn it. She worked the riggings and sails; she barked orders at him as she danced around between the high-deck and the cockpit. She would teach him new words like *tack*, *windward* and *leeward*, *mizzen* and *ketch*. She would show him the meanings of the words as she worked, eventually on the last day, Mike would work at deck-hoisting the jib off the primary winch, attaching snatch blocks to the toe rail, every command Shannon shouted at him from the helm sounded as if he were on a pirate ship.

Mike laughed as he tried to imitate the actions Shannon made as she whisked around the decks making adjustments and tying down ropes, using tackles and dodging when Shannon would yell *"jibe all standing!"* as the boom went from one side of the cruiser to the other, switching with the wind and the waves.

At one point in the afternoon on the last day in open water, the west wind was set fast in the sails and the boat took a starboard keel, the *Stella* was going as fast as she could without a spinnaker sail, a little over eight knots. Shannon called for Mike to stand beside her, he slipped in to the right of her in the cockpit and she lifted his right hand and put it on the wheel, showing him how to keep the sails full and speed going by using the rudder. He placed his left arm over shoulders and pulled her close to him.

The wind that billowed around them, the speed of the boat as it slid through the seas ahead of them, the passion of learning about sailing and the adrenaline of the ride made Mike feel small, he wanted this every day. He kissed Shannon on her ear, she turned towards him and they made contact-lips first-as their kisses motioned around each other's necks and shoulders, smelling the salt on their bodies from the spray coming over the sides as the *Stella Taurus* kept her course.

On the last night, the sunlight faded as it came through the portholes below deck, Mike was in the galley preparing some

Spanish mackerel they had hooked earlier in the day. Shannon stepped out of the shower just a few feet from him with a towel wrapped around her hair; she was rubbing another over her legs as she headed to the berth for some clothes. She took the turban off of her head and shook her mane free as she bent over.

"Wow!"

"What?" She stood up straight, startled.

"It's just that I love seeing you with your hair down, you're beautiful."

"Thanks. But I hate it this way."

She responded by taking her right hand and twirling her damp-darkened hair into a little ball and set it in place with a quick tying motion.

"How do you do that?"

"It's a girl thing. Now how do you like my hair?"

"It's okay. I just wish I could have had a chance to run my fingers through it." He smiled sheepishly.

She sat on the edge of her bed after retrieving a pair of white slacks and a warm sweater and pulled them on. "Dinner smells good. What are you making to go along with the mackerel?"

Mike raised his hand to his chin and rubbed it thoughtfully. "Well, we have canned pork and beans, canned dried beef? Wow, that just doesn't seem right. Canned milk, canned cans…"

He waited for a response, and then turned his head when he didn't get one; he saw Shannon staring out the oval porthole outside. He turned towards her and noticed her eyes were glistening. His head dropped, he knew she was thinking about the same thing he was; tomorrow they would return to the port, that night he was to catch a flight to Sydney, then he would have to make his connecting flight to LA; after that he would go home.

He knew her well enough; he knew what was on her mind. "Hey, I asked if you wanted canned can."

He elevated his voice to make it sound cheerier; Shannon looked over from the porthole.

"That would be fine." Her voice revealed no emotion.

Mike turned the burner on and opened a tin of asparagus tips, set the can directly on the burner and lit it. He made sure the flame was low enough not to scald the vegetables, then he slowly walked over to Shannon, who was brushing the end of her ponytail while she still gazed out the porthole. He sat down next to her softly and placed his arm around her, using his other he softly worked his index finger to lift a stray strand of bang to her ear.

Shannon turned to smile at him, but her eyes were pink with sadness, her heart was aching, she had to tell him the truth-maybe there was some way he could take care of her until...

"Hey, have you lost your hearing?"

Mike gently kissed her neck.

"I'm sorry, I was just thinking about what you said two days ago. You were right; this is going to be difficult."

"I know. I promise I'll call as much as I can. We can still be friends."

"It costs more than one dollar fifty a minute, *U.S. dollars* Michael. Trust me, Mathew complained all the time about it."

"How long does it take to say *I love you*?" He kissed her forehead gently, Mike could feel her strain. "Or, will you marry me?"

Mike could feel Shannon shudder at that moment. She pulled back away from him and bumped her head on the side beam over the berth.

"This is no time for jolly humor like that Mr. Greene..."

Her eyes were darkened to a deep cobalt instead of their traditional sapphire.

"I know, I was just kidding. A little anyways..." He reached for her hands and clasped them in his. "If I were ever to get married again, it would be you."

"Really?"

She could have him right now, Shannon thought. But did he really want her? How could any man go through what she was about to? Shannon remembered watching a friend of hers in Sydney who had to take care of her elderly sick mother-in-law. Feeding her, bathing her, changing adult diapers. She had to watch the woman every second until she finally passed away, dementia had set in. All this and the woman wasn't even hers. How could a man want to take on the responsibility if it wasn't even his to assume?

Then she thought of her condition, it was changing constantly, she had to know.

"Michael, what if you and I couldn't have children? I mean right away? If at all, if we were to be married."

Her eyes began searching his; she would know the truth when he spoke it.

"I have a son already."

Mike thought about how things had turned out so bad for him and Mikie, how his ex-wife had turned his young son against him. Mike thought about how happy he was when his offspring was born, how he was so careful in raising the child, taking him fishing and hunting and teaching him to play street hockey at three. How they grew so close, watching movies and just plain talking boy stuff; until the divorce, maybe a little earlier than that, but Mikie had changed. He hated doing things with his father, he would argue over the simple things that he and his father had agreed upon so earlier in his life. The boy had-*was*-changed, Mike thought about living that way with another child, he knew if he ever did marry Shannon, there would be little chance they would end up like his last marriage did. He felt he knew way more about Shannon than he did his ex, he knew for sure he loved Shannon more…

But still, he had been ultimately burned by Mikie, he didn't know if he could chance it again, not right now anyways. He knew what to say.

Mike looked directly into Shannon's eyes; "I see no need for children right now."

Shannon lowered her head and nodded. "I thought so." She let go of his hands and used her feet to push her farther back towards the bulkhead. "I sort of knew, just from listening to you talk about your wife."

"Ex-wife."

"Ex-wife; that you had been terribly hurt." She looked away from Mike and stared out the porthole. "I would never expect you to go through that again."

"I…"

Just as Mike was about to further explain his feelings, the solder on the can of asparagus tips melted completely through and the packing water flowed out and onto the burner with a loud hiss and the flame went out.

Shannon looked over Mike's shoulder, and he saw her eyes grow wide.

"You had better shut the gas off before we suffocate!"

Mike rose to the stove and turned the knob to the off position. He spun and started to walk back towards the berth, but as he did, he saw the door close to the head. Shannon had locked herself in the bathroom.

An hour later Mike was sitting on the high-deck, eating his cold dinner and staring out over the dark water. He tried to get Shannon to eat with him; after he was able to coax her from the bathroom she laid down, claiming illness, so he eventually went topside to eat, alone. The small waves lapped at the side of the sailboat, the slight swaying back and forth soothed his pain, a little. It felt to him like the rocking motion of a cradle, even though he didn't remember being rocked in the cradle as a child, but the rhythmic motion seemed to ease his sadness, for some reason.

He wanted to be mad, or at least depressed, he knew the answer he gave Shannon was not the one she was looking for. She had been hinting around about marriage, never about having children and now he thought she acted if she wanted one, just not right away. Mike had dreamed of marrying Shannon and moving here to Australia-a very difficult task filled with miles of paperwork and tons of bureaucracy-he had run the scenario through his head. It would be difficult at best, he would probably not get to see his father again-alive at least-he was sure that Shannon and he could attend a funeral, she wasn't that cold. But what could he do for money?

First he had to leave the country, his visa would expire before the paperwork could even be started plus he was not allowed to seek work or immigration on a visitor's visa, Ted claimed he had used his last few favors, so the possibility of anymore rule bending was out. Then he had to apply for a new one, after a few months, and give the consulate a very good reason for returning. If he could prove he was the right age, health, a good risk, had the required skills, and the biggie: financial resources, then he could get another visa to return and apply for immigration.

If he just married Shannon instead, he wasn't allowed to work here for at least two years, at least not legally. He had to wait that long to become a citizen, to prove that he wasn't using his marriage to Shannon as a way of just gaining citizenship; they had to be together for at least two years-no problem there-but to get employment Mike had to have some employer advertise a job he was interested in locally and nationally in the paper, and in the local employment offices.

Then, if no Australian citizen was interested in the job Mike could be hired on a temporary basis, as long as no other person applied for that position until Mike gained his naturalization papers. Difficult at best.

Then there was his job at home.

Mike flicked the bones and head from his mackerel over the side of the boat and watched for squid coming up to graze on it.

The job at home; he was a veteran of eighteen years, he became an Explorer Scout at fifteen, at eighteen he enlisted as a cadet for three years extending his training, then at twenty-one he was officially sworn in. In Nevada, P.O.S.T. school was given at each department, Mike had all he needed, and qualified for many of the programs-including the new S.W.A.T. Team that was being formed at the end of the fiscal year with a new budget. He had worked half of his life for his career-a career he loved-now he would have to change it, if he wanted to stay.

Shannon's father was quick to point out that Australia had no room for *"overzealous sorts who carried guns* (Australian Police carried them) *or billy-clubs"*, when Mike inquired. Ted wasn't mean about the way he said it, it was just matter of fact. Mike doubted he could become a cop here anyways, he hated the uniforms. And the work would be about the same, arresting aboriginals who were drunk off of the money the government gave them for stealing their land from under them. Mike hated the way life treated others.

So here it was; all around him Mike could see no real reason to stay here other than Shannon, and how long could their relationship last if couldn't find work, how deep would his love have to be for her to rely on her family's money to exist? Love doesn't go that deep, he felt. Eventually it would strain their love to the breaking point, and then he would be stuck in another country alone, if he wasn't deported.

Shannon lay curled up in the master berth, her arms wrapped around her legs. She was weeping slightly, the pain in her side was a small factor, and she knew that her excuse of feeling ill put Michael off, but it was the truth. She was feeling ill a lot lately, the nausea came and went, but the pain in her side-the reason she was seeing the doctor in Cairns-was constant.

But that was the least of her worries right now.

Shannon wanted so badly to hold Michael right now it hurt worse. He was above deck eating, probably thinking to himself how he could have gotten so mixed up with this wild woman who wanted to marry him and not have children. She heard in his voice the hesitation when she mentioned the part about becoming pregnant; she saw the pain in his eyes from his previous relationship. *But it was he that mentioned marriage, wasn't it? Why would he ask her-even if it sounded humorous when he did-if he wasn't half way serious?*

She realized that he may be just thinking about skipping out of his job in America and settling down here with her, but even as her father explained to him, that would be a long and difficult thing to do, no matter how serious he was about it. As another cramp hit her, she winced and her tears rolled down her cheek onto the bed covers.

Shannon's weeping became crying, and several minutes later she steeled herself for what she knew she had to do.

She heard footfalls on the deck above and knew Michael was probably headed below deck and she didn't feel like any confrontations right now. The pieces of her grand plan, even though it was the second plan, hadn't dropped correctly into place-simply-it had failed. She would have to think this one out, the final plan; one she knew would work even if it did end their relationship, as far as it had come in nearly a month. He had to go home tomorrow, after a stop down in Sydney first, but he would have to return to the States. There was no way of stopping that, she had to be brave and look him in the eyes, those sad hazel eyes that had seen so much pain in the last year, and let him know they were not going to see each other anymore.

She heard Mike close the gangway doors behind him and shuffle to the first berth, the thin door closed softly behind him. For only the second time on this week long sailing trip, they would sleep in separate beds. Shannon pulled the sheet to her face and cried some more, angry that she had no choice, angry that her world had thrown her such a terrible curve-ball, as the American she loved so much and was just ten feet away in the other room, would say.

She cried till the gentle rocking of the *Stella Taurus* lulled her to sleep, her mother's words echoing in her head, the day they watched Michael throwing the boomerang in the back of the plantation house. Throwing it away, hoping it would come back to him…

Follow the Southern Cross

CHAPTER THIRTEEN

LAND and HOME

The sun broke the surface of the water around six thirty a.m. They both rose around the same time, Mike using the head just after Shannon had finished. They would collide a few times below, hug and kiss little, then continue to pack for the sail home. Mike made them both bowls of cereal with banana slices and cream, they ventured above deck to eat and stare out over the blue water and sky. Very little was said, occasionally there was the obligatory "gonna be nice today" and "looks like smooth sailing", as they walked around the deck preparing the *Stella* for sail.

At nine-thirty Shannon fired the diesel engine up to maneuver the cruiser out of anchor, they had moved the boat three times over the week and the second to last day they used the anchor off a small flat sandy island. Once the heavy chain and fluke was stowed Shannon turned the *Stella* into the westerly wind and began the rigging, this time with Mike's apprenticeship. Once the sails were set Shannon guided the boat east, again making Mike dive out of the way of the boom on the transition.

With a half hour left before the *Stella* has to be switched to engine power again so Shannon can put her into the slip, she looked at Mike, who was standing next to her in the cockpit. He had his arm around her, his hand flexing on the curve of her arm at the shoulder.

"Sad, isn't it."

"Yes. I had the best time of my life this week; hell, the whole month." He kissed the top of her head gently. "In the last year, I've known nothing but pain and suffering. But you made it all worthwhile, I would go through all of it again to be with you for just one more week."

Shannon wiped a tear from her eye. "Thank you." She rested her head on his arm.

The *Stella* quietly slipped into the Marina, the small chug of the engine only heard by Mike and Shannon. After her first turn, Shannon felt a little cold, a chilling sweat crossed her brow, she wiped it quickly, then the cramps hit her again-a touch more intense than the other night-the boats around her began to darken and spin.

"Shannon!"

Mike was placing the fenders out when he looked back and saw her collapse. He dove over the decking and landed on his knees in the cockpit, a sharp pain rippled through his legs, but he ignored it as he pulled the young girl to him. Her eyes were rolling around, she was experiencing dizziness Mike knew, there was a small cut on her forehead from striking it on the winch; there was a little blood. Mike scooped her up into his lap and remembered they were moving so he reached up and pulled the gear handle back, grinding the transmission into reverse. He felt the *Stella* lurch to a stop then began to shudder backwards a little and Mike simply shut the diesel off in frustration.

"Shannon! Can you hear me?"

The flash of the young girl in a bathrobe bleeding on him in a small trailer. His eyes watered, he began to shake her a little and he felt her neck for a pulse. It was strong. His own body was shaking violently-afraid that a part of his life would replay again...

After a few seconds her eyelids fluttered, Mike knew she was going to retch so he pushed her as gently as possible to the rail so she wouldn't foul the deck and she began to throw up. Mike turned her on her side and made sure she wouldn't choke. He was cold; Mike was on the edge of panic-he had to steel himself-Shannon needed him now. After what seemed a half hour but in reality was only minutes, her eyes opened and she looked up and smiled at him.

"Did I fall asleep at the wheel?" She joked through tears and a cough.

"Yes. You almost hit a whale, boy is he pissed."

Mike's eyes glistened with fear and relief as he spoke to her.

"A drunken whale?"

Her eyes fluttered open and closed, her body relaxed and Mike shook her again.

"Stop that Michael, you're going to make me sick."

She reached for a rail to pull herself up.

"I just don't want you to pass out again."

"I'm alright. Get me up; I have to dock the *Stella*."

"Sit right here, I've already stopped her. What do I do?"

"Watch closely."

She stood using the wheel to pull herself up, started the engine and moved the cruiser towards her berth. Mike watched her closely as she asked to make sure she didn't fall again. Shannon made the last few turns a little wide, and then bumped off the left side of the berth and slammed a little hard into the fore board. Mike jumped over the rail and tied down the stern just as Shannon had taught him, crossing the line over and over, and then twisting a loop over the end of the cleat. Mike stood to tie the bow off... and bumped directly into Ted Hunter.

"What happened? Were you driving? You hit that dock a little hard."

He was panting, Mike assumed he saw the *Stella* hit the dock and ran all the way down.

"It's okay dad..."

Shannon was coming to the side of the cruiser to get off and Mike broke Ted's stare and helped her down.

As she crossed the railing line, she collapsed again-conscious this time-but out of sorts. Ted rushed to Mike's side and helped him lower his daughter to the wooden deck.

"What happened?" He demanded.

"I don't know… I was getting the fenders out of the locker and she just fell. I ran over to her…"

"I knew this would happen, we warned her not to go out with you." Ted snapped, worry set fast and he was almost crying. "She falls for you blokes all the time and ends up getting hurt."

"I…"

Just as Mike was trying to explain further Lisa Hunter ran to her daughter's side and helped lift her to her feet. Shannon was trying to walk now, she was mumbling, "*It's not Michael's fault…*"

Lisa and Ted took a side and walked her up the runway to the car. They placed her in the back seat, carefully laying her down and Mike was trying to get in alongside.

"No. You go down to the boat and make sure it's tied down tight. There's no room for you. I'll have Randall come pick you up in an hour."

"But…" Mike felt helpless.

"*GO!* There is nothing you can do, just go…" Ted was in a rage; he ran to his side of the car and screeched the tires speeding out of the marina's parking lot.

Mike stood there with tears in his eyes; he was shaking-visibly-and received stares from people who had witnessed a little or everything in the last few minutes. He lowered his head and through tears, walked back down to the *Stella Taurus*.

Mike's flight into Kingsford-Smith Airport into Sydney arrived at ten thirty that night, he was expecting a layover till one a.m., but the world had changed because of a trial in Los Angeles. Two policemen in the beating case that made national news were found not guilty and the city erupted into violence, riots broke out, fires were started, and people began shooting at airplanes as they flew over. As a precaution, LAX ceased all incoming and outgoing traffic into and over LA. All night flights from Australia were postponed till late morning to give the Americans time to control the riots and shooters.

Mike was stuck. Even though he arrived, his luggage was held so he didn't have to check it in again.

"Michael Greene from Nevada… you have a phone call holding on the white line."

Mike found his way to the in-house phone bank and raised the phone.

"Michael, this is Ted, Shannon's father. I heard your flight was delayed."

"Yeah, how's Shannon?"

"She's quite well. The doctor said she was a little dehydrated and overstressed. She wants to talk to you. She'll call you later at your hotel."

"I don't have a hotel."

"The shuttle bus to the Bay Point Hotel comes through there every hour. Just look for it."

"Why can't I talk to Shannon now?"

Mike heard Ted sigh on the other end of the line, he wasn't testy or short with him, he sounded tired, very tired. He knew in his heart that Ted couldn't blame him for what happened, but Mike still felt responsible. You just can't let things happen to those you care so much about.

"Relax Michael. I'm sorry for yelling at you at the Marina, I truly am. I was upset as you can imagine."

"I'm sorry too."

"For what?"

"For not keeping my promise, if I would have known she was going to get sick on the trip, I would've done more to stop her from going."

"There was no way of knowing. She would have gone anyway, I'm sure you know by now you can't force the young woman to things she doesn't want to. Or the other way around."

Mike just sighed.

"I've made reservations for you at the hotel. Shan will call you when she's feeling better, we'll have the room number after you check in."

"Thank you."

"Thank you for taking care of my daughter." And Ted hung up.

Mike stood at the courtesy phone for a moment, trying to figure whether or not Ted was serious about thanking him. Things didn't end well. Then he realized he didn't ask Ted for their phone number.

"Dammit!"

After finding the shuttle and checking in, it was past one a.m. now. Mike was lying in his room on the soft bed, wondering when Shannon would call. He should have asked if she was home or had to stay overnight. He had forgotten the line of questioning he used at his job; he compromised over Shannon's diagnosis and forgot to ask for a number or when she would call. He forgot to ask Ted if there was anything he could do-or if he could change his plans and stay a few more days-maybe fly back to Cairns and help. If they needed help. He fell asleep wondering why everything he touched seemed to rust away in front of him.

Breakfast was buffet style as usual; Natalie served him with a smile and a pat on the shoulder.

"Sorry to hear about Shannon, sick and all. She call?"

Mike shook his head no.

"She'll get in touch mate, she adores you."

"How'd you find out?"

"It was written all over her like ink on a cheap bill."

Mike pursed his lips and shook his head, "*No*, how did you hear she was sick?"

"Tommy the doorman chats with the receptionist all the time. When Shannon's father made the reservations, he told her about the little one's condition."

Mike looked up to Natalie, "What condition?"

Natalie smiled grimly as if she was trying to make the news as painless as possible. "She's in for a rough patch I'm afraid."

A customer at another table motioned for Natalie and she darted off, first giving Mike a kiss on the forehead and she ran her fingers through his hair.

"She'll call mate. If not, you come back and see me."

Mike had been in the air for three hours now, the desk clerk at the hotel refused to give up the telephone number for the Hunter family or where he had called from to make the reservations, regulations were cited.

He knew once he was in the air heading for America that he would never see or hear from Shannon again, at least the chances were next to nothing. In less than half a day he would be on the ground in San Francisco-his flight was rerouted because of the rioting in LA-then he would rent a car with his last few dollars he taken with him.

Mike smiled out the window, more of a frustrated smile; he intended to bring some Australian cash home with him as a memento, but was surprised to find out he had to pay a fifty dollar departure tax before he boarded his flight. That was the end of the paper notes, he had a few dollars in coins, but it was the cash he liked-it was beautiful. It reminded him of Shannon.

Everything reminded him of Shannon; he refused to watch the inflight movie, a comedy-love story called *Father of the Bride*, for obvious reasons. The flight was booked solid because of the previous flight delays to Los Angeles, so Mike couldn't stretch out; the smoking section was booked solid so he couldn't have a smoke. Mike was feeling the true definition of miserable. He wanted to get home, and wait.

Shannon was forced to spend the night at the hospital, they had run some tests and most of the results wouldn't be back till the next day. She hadn't slept but for a few hours; she felt the full force of the world on her shoulders now, Michael had to go home and was on his way. Her father refused to let her make the call in the middle of the night, after hours of tests and exams she was detained long enough into the early morning to have slept through a reasonable time to call before he left for America. Her mother slept in the room with her, having cried for over an hour together. The first diagnosis was that she was dehydrated, anemic, and was drained physically by her previous condition.

Distraught over Mike leaving without her being able to say a proper goodbye was hard enough, but her father was adamant that she get rest, or he'd ask the doctor to administer a sedative.

"But I love him…"

"We know, but think of Michael. Maybe it's best this way, he will heal after time."

"And me? What about your only daughter? Will I heal before…?"

"That's enough you two." Ted broke in. "You can call him in a few days, after you are out of here, after he has a chance to get home."

"I don't have his number." She lowered her head. "I never got a chance to ask him, we were going to say goodbye at the airport." Tears started to fall. "I never got to say goodbye, mother. I love him dad. I really do! I wanted to at least feel him hug me one more time, I got cheated."

She rolled to her side on the bed and put her pillow over her head.

"I'll try and get his number. Don't worry. Everything will be alright, you'll see…"

Her voice was muffled by the pillow, "It'll be too late."

Mike took a cab from the rental car drop off and slowly walked up the familiar drive way, not the two hundred yard long one he hoped to see one more time in the jungles of Kuranda and the familiar old Landcruiser in the carport. Mike thought of Ted's Toyota 4 Runner. He slowly made his way up the steps to the front door and opened it, taking a breath of home. Kelly's wife had taken care of the place, she put the mail on the kitchen table-except the bills-she paid those for Mike with money he had given her to do so.

His three houseplants were still alive… and looking better than when he left; the room was cold, Mike figured Kelly set the thermostat to fifty-five degrees, just enough to keep the pipes from freezing and to keep Mike from fainting when he got his power bill.

Mike set his keys on the kitchen table and looked at the phone. He picked it up to make sure there was a dial tone, he didn't know why, but he hoped that Shannon would call. Even if she had planned to break it off with him after he left, she should at least call to say goodbye and tell him how she was doing. That's when the feeling hit him.

Mike began shaking, his stomach felt like it was ready to explode inside of him, he felt a cool rush over his body and he had to sit down. She was sick; they kept talking about her condition… *What if she had passed away?* That would explain why she didn't call him at the hotel, why she didn't call before he left-she knew he was leaving. Mike imagined that her parents were so overcome by grief they would not think to call him. Mike picked up the receiver and dialed 0.

"Hello?"

"May I speak to Shannon please?"

"Michael? Is that you?"

Shannon heard a heavy sigh on the other end, and then she thought she heard sniffling. "Michael, are you okay?"

"I am now."

"Do you know what time it is here?"

"No. I'm sorry, I had to call; I had to hear your voice again. I had to… to know you were alright." He was almost hyperventilating.

"It's four in the morning. How did you get this number?"

"A little mutual respect between policemen. I called the local constable in Cairns; I lied and told them you were a victim in a case I was investigating. They called my department and Kelly took the call. They gave him the information. It took two hours, but I got through."

There was a long silence; Mike took it as Shannon passing him off but Shannon was trying to hide her crying. She and her father had a heart to heart after she was released, and the outcome didn't favor Mike.

"Shannon, I miss you. What happened?"

"Michael, I…" He heard her sniffing. "I miss you too, but I'm okay. Just a little insomnia and dehydration. It was my fault for not drinking enough water and getting more sleep." Her voice cracked with a little laugh. "I should have gotten more sleep, that's all."

Shannon was sleeping; her parents were out for the weekend. They were assured by the doctor and Shannon herself that there would be no danger in doing so. Shannon had to beg.

"Michael, I have to get some sleep now. If I don't test better in a few days then they are going to put me in the hospital. I don't want that."

"I don't want to hang up. Not till you tell me that everything is going to be okay, that you aren't dying, that you will live to see me again."

"Of course."

"You don't make it sound sincere."

"Michael, it is four in the morning. I haven't had much sleep in the last few days, I need my sleep. I can't say it to you in any other way. I'm going to be okay." He heard rustling with the phone. "Give me your number; I'll call in a few days, around six o'clock." Mike gave her the number.

"I don't know the country code or anything like that."

"You're not the only one with resources. I'll figure it out. Now, goodnight."

"Goodnight. I love…"

Mike heard the phone click off before he was finished, which frustrated him even more.

Shannon rolled over after hanging up the phone, she cried herself to sleep for having to put Michael through this one more time-but it had to be done-it would be easier on him than the alternative.

Three weeks went by and not a call from Shannon. On the fourth week he called her again, only to have a slightly angry Lisa Hunter answer at nearly midnight-he had forgotten how do to the time in reverse. Another week after that, still no call. Worry racked Mike daily. His job became monotonous, he hated going.

Kelly called him to his office one night and talked to him about recent events of pure thoughtless work, a bad traffic stop, an irate mother complaining about the way her son was treated.

"Any other time Mike, I would laugh it off with you. But you *have* changed. What's going on?"

"I'm thinking about retiring." Mike said coldly. "Take my early pension of eighteen years and get out. I need out of this place, this town, this life."

"What the *Hell* does that mean?"

"It means boss; that I'm going to quit."

"Where would you go, what would you do?"

"Maybe up to see my dad in Idaho. I could get a job up there as a logger."

Kelly Daniels laughed. "You hate heights. Why would you leave here anyways? You've lived here all your life."

"I know; that's the problem."

"I could call up there and talk to the sheriff, maybe poke around for you, if you're interested."

"Thanks boss, but no. I need outta this line of work. I need something that keeps me from having to deal with the public; I'm just not in the right mood now for people."

Mike left the office and went back to work.

The problem was he never really lived like he had in Australia, before he met Shannon. They had done so many things together Mike felt alive after so many years of hiding under his bed from the monsters of life; Lisa his ex, his son who hated him and wouldn't even talk to him on his birthday, his job which he had no taste for any longer, and his alcoholism recovery more recently. He wanted to be alive, he cared again for the people and the world around him, and he felt they saw him as he was.

But now things had changed again, he was in love but he felt cast aside by her and her family. She was six thousand miles away now, separated by an entire ocean. She acted as if she wanted him not to love her, she didn't even say it the last time they talked on the phone; she acted cold, distant in more ways than just geographically. Mike's heart was broken.

Mike didn't quit. He took another week of vacation, approved by Kelly for health reasons, and took his Landcruiser to San Francisco for the week. He had no money in checking any longer. It had been over a month since he had talked to Shannon last; his phone bill for talking to her for ten minutes was sixty-five dollars. In his pocket after paying this month's bills was a meager eighty-five dollars and forty-one cents.

Mike stayed at the hotel he and Lisa honeymooned in: *The St. Francis Hotel*-the same place that jazz singer Al Jolson died while playing cards. Mike didn't even didn't feel a pang of regret for his divorce. That chapter of his life was over, all he wanted to do is see his son one more time; if nothing else than for himself. He knew another chapter of his sad story was coming to an end, the last chapter he thought. Mike made no qualms about never having to look for love again, he couldn't take the pain of the loss-even though few would match the one he just experienced between him and Shannon-the loss, that was.

Mike sat at the writing table in his small but nice hotel room and wrote his son a letter, his first letter in years. He put all of his feelings down, how much he was sorry for being a terrible father, for being a drunk. Mike apologized for not be able to buy his son a nice expensive car, but explained that he would never learn the value of his money if everything was given to him.

The second page of the letter spelled out his time in Oregon at Freedom Frontiers, the friends he made and the one he lost. The next four pages were of his experience in Australia, how he met Shannon and what they did together-well, the PG rated version anyway-and how much he loved her. Mike opened up about that more than anything else, he felt he was hurting so bad on the inside because he never had a chance to say goodbye to her.

Mike ended his letter by telling his son the same thing. How horrible he felt inside that he never had the chance to say goodbye in person to him, how that would be the only thing that he would change in his life if he could. Being man enough to make a stand to be there for one last hug and offer Mikie care other than the monthly child support check. He finished the letter and mailed it on the way out of the hotel.

Sitting on a high point of the sand dune at Baker Beach on the west side of the peninsula he stared out over the sea towards the west-towards Australia-Mike wondered again about Lady Macquarie, he knew *now* how she felt, longing for home. He watched as the fog rolled towards shore and in the distance he saw a blue sea cruiser, full sail and heading out beyond. Mike's eyes began to tear up, he was lonely, and he missed Shannon terribly. The sailboat disappeared into the fog bank.

Mike sat up straight; he would have to forget her. He would have to or in just a short time he would be institutionalized for drinking again, or worse. He would get someone killed at work if he were distracted. He would get himself killed. He would not be the same unless he found it within himself to forget the best part of his life in experience. Other than the birth of his son.

He would use his new found tools of sobriety. He couldn't change the world; he had no control over how things went outside of his life. He recited the Serenity Prayer. The bag of weapons against his enemy, addiction, and he needed it more than ever now, because other things in life are just like addiction. He knew he would not have Shannon as a wife or friend anymore. He knew all this and he also knew he had to move on.

"God, grand me the serenity to accept the things I cannot change, the courage to change the things I can, and the wisdom to know the difference."

Mike returned home a few days later, feeling better about his world. He had the chance to love the most beautiful woman he had ever met, young and full of life. He reasoned that he could carry on, few others in this world would have the chance he had, few others would feel the love he felt Shannon give him. It was just bad timing and bad placement. Australia and the loves he held for it-was too far away.

Mike returned to his job, Kelly didn't have to call him in for any more butt-chewing. Mike had returned to normal, sober and happier.

CHAPTER FOURTEEN

BAD NEWS

It had been over six months now since Mike had left Australia. Not one day went by he didn't think about Shannon Hunter and how she was doing. It saddened him for sure, but he didn't feel helpless anymore. He wondered if she was even alive sometimes, he knew she was sick, at least that was the impression he was given. He had put her behind him; he had hoped she was alright. He dreamed of her once in a while, afterwards he was saddened by his dreams, but he moved on.

Mike was on the final hour and a half of his swing shift when the call came in.

"351, Lockwood."

Mike picked up the handheld mic. "351."

"351, 21 dispatch for phone message a.s.a.p."

"Ten-four"

Mike hated these kinds of communications; it meant to call the office for an important message. Last time it was because Lisa his ex-needed some cash for a doctor bill. Mikie was hurt in a bicycle crash and had to have a cast put on. Mike was expected to pay for half. Maybe Lisa had read his letter to Mikie and was upset at his revelations as a bad father and wanted to let the two speak to each other. Humph. Hardly.

Mike found a phone booth and made the call to dispatch; Jackie Jackson was the communication supervisor on shift. She had a thing for Mike, but the fact she was married kept anything from happening. They still flirted once in a while, but not since his return from Australia.

"Yeah this is Mike Greene."

"Oh hey Mike, one of my girls passed me a note from a phone call earlier. You have a number to call, important message. That's all the slip says Mike."

"Okay, give me the number." Mike wrote the number down, he knew it was a local one, but just couldn't put his finger on it. "Thanks." And he hung up.

Picking up the receiver again he deposited fifteen cents and dialed the number.

"Ace Car Rentals"

"Hi. This is Officer Michael Greene, Lockwood Police. I was told to call this number."

"Just a moment please."

There was a brief pause and he heard rustling on the other end as the receiver was being passed to someone else.

"Michael?"

Mike's heart pounded. Cocoons of butterflies opened inside of him as he recognized the voice.

"Shannon?"

"Michael, it is so good to hear your voice again. How have you been?"

He stood up straight in the phone booth.

"Just fine and you?"

"Alright. Really. Can I meet you somewhere?"

"You're in town?"

Mike should have realized this, he called a local number after all, but shock was settling in. He was not in the proper mind for this assault right now, he'd not thought about her for some time, maybe not at all today. He felt ambushed all of a sudden, he felt betrayed by his feelings for her. He was making progress and now she was on the other end of the phone, here in America. Less than twenty minutes away from him.

His cop intuition told him why she was here, sort of; she was on her way to see her uncle in Montana. But why stop here? Was it on purpose? Did she mean to or was it unavoidable like a layover?

"Of course silly. I'm renting a car, but I won't drive it till tomorrow, you know why."

"Yeah."

"So how about meeting me somewhere. I would love to see you."

Mike thought long and hard; if he were to be in so close to her again, the pain might come back, the feelings of abandonment again, all the emotions he told himself to get rid of, to put away and get on with his life. He would meet here, but only for a while, he had to be strong. He couldn't let her get him into the situation he'd been in when he returned home all those months ago.

"I dunno Shan. You never called me back. I hurt sometimes. I was a mess."

Silence.

"You there?"

"Yes. I'm very sorry Michael."

"I thought you might've passed away."

Silence again.

"Hello?"

"Mike," He hated when she called him that, "I'll explain everything. You don't know how sorry I am, but let me have a chance to explain. Face to face."

Her words were solid and carried the full meaning of their pleas, he'd let her in for one more time. A brief time. And then he'd say his proper goodbyes and send her on her way.

"Are you taking a cab?"

"Yes."

"Tell the driver to take you to the Claimstake in Sparks. I'll see you there as soon as I can."

"I will. I'm at the airport rental car place…"

"I know where you are." He cut her off. "I'll see you at the restaurant."

And he hung up. Mike closed his eyes; it hurt to be so cold. He didn't want to be on that path again. He would see her, chat a little while and say goodbye at least he could say goodbye to her this time and finalize their relationship. *But what if she was here for something else? What if she were here to live with you?* Mike shook the unreasonable words from his head and got back into his car. It had to be Montana.

Mike sat out in front of the restaurant for ten minutes, he knew she was already there; he was just trying to harden his resolve. He couldn't have her disrupting his life again. They would be just friends, he might give her a peck on the cheek when they say goodbye-that was all. He took a deep breath and walked in the front door, telling himself a hug would be okay too.

The Claimstake was a dark place, made to look like the inside of a mine with fake rock walls and timbers. There were little tunnels connecting different parts of the place, and the waitress led him through one to the back tables, the place the cops usually sat for breaks. Mike's chest was pounding now, it was a good thing his ballistic vest covered it-the whole restaurant could see it thumping if he wasn't. His mouth went dry as they came near the end of the journey, his hands were trembling, and Mike had to laugh at himself. Just a few nights ago he arrested a biker at a bar for being too drunk and rowdy; the guy was at least six foot seven and weighed in excess of two hundred ninety pounds and Mike showed no fear. Now a petit five foot nine woman that weighed about one hundred fifteen pounds scared the hell out of him.

The waitress rounded the corner and immediately Mike's eyes began to feel moist. There she was, same as she looked the last day on the sailboat before... No, she even looked better; there was a glow about her-she smiled so brightly at him.

He opened his arms and walked as fast as he could to get to her, Shannon rose from the table and met him halfway. Their bodies collided softly, Mike could smell the familiar sweet perfume, he didn't want to let go. But then a feeling hit him. It wasn't that Shannon was pulling away-she wasn't standing as close to him as she had done before-her feet were too far away

315

from his, she was pushed back by her abdomen, her belly… she was pregnant!

Mike froze. He felt panic rushing to his head, he began tremble.

"I've missed you so much." Shannon whispered into his ear.

"Me too. Are you...?"

"Yes. Michael Greene… I'm pregnant. Seven months as a matter of fact."

Mike began counting the numbers and months backwards in his head; his eyes were darting back and forth.

"Who?"

He sat down, Shannon took her seat.

"Not you. Although I wish it were in a way. You were the most wonderful person I have ever met, but it was too late. I couldn't tell you-I didn't want to hurt you anymore. Then things started to spin out of control, I fell in love with you and things just ran a little out of repair."

"But the boat that week we… did you know?" Mike was sweating.

"Yes. I knew then. I couldn't stop myself. I wanted to so badly, I wanted to keep us just friends but like I said before I fell in love with you." Her eyes were starting to mist up.

Mike closed his eyes and took a deep breath. "Is it Matt's?"

Shannon looked at her lap and crossed her hands in it. "Yes."

"I'm sorry." He reached across the table. "I would have understood. We may have not made love, but I would have understood."

She spoke quietly like a child confronted by a parent from a major infraction; her eyes were focused on her lap, her hands that kept fidgeting.

"Michael, I had some terrible thoughts. I wanted you to think that it was your child at first, and then I was just going to tell you about the baby and who the father was on the *Stella* so we could talk about it, so you wouldn't be able to run from me. I wanted you to marry me but you said you had enough children. You weren't receptive to the hints, I became afraid, and I panicked."

"When did I say I didn't...?" Mike thought about the conversation on the sailboat. His head dropped too. "Oh." He raised it slightly. "But I would have accepted this, I loved you so much. I would have done anything..."

"Loved?"

Mike locked eyes with her. "You never called me back."

"My mother and father said it would be better if I just left you alone that you would eventually forget about me. My parents are old fashioned Michael; they thought a very well raised person like yourself would never have anything to do with a slag like me. They respect and I think they are very fond of you and your morals. They said it would take time, but you'd forget. Have you?"

"Slag?"

Shannon huffed a laugh out of her nose, "Slut."

Mike was taken aback, "They called you a slut?"

"No, but it is how I felt. When I decided to make love to you and not tell you about the baby. It's how I felt the whole time. Did you forget about me? It's important to me. Please tell me."

Mike thought about his evening on the beach in San Francisco, the night he let Shannon go.

"I haven't forgotten you. I just don't think I can love you as much as I did then."

"Because of the baby?"

Mike shook his head.

"Because you abandoned me. We never got to say goodbye and the last time we talked..."

"I was on medication, I was sick from not getting any sleep. The baby was in danger, so they gave me a light sedative. I barely remember the call."

"But you said you would call back. You never did, that hurt me more than my divorce, more than my son refusing my calls on his birthday, more than anything else I can think of." He lowered his head. "More than losing that girl in the trailer nearly a year ago."

Shannon couldn't help the tears from raining down, she realized she had shattered this man, her mother and father were wrong he loved her more than life itself. And now she had lost him, because she wanted to protect him.

"I never expected to come here. I didn't think I would ever see you again."

Mike just looked at her. He shrugged.

"My parents are so angry with me for coming to the states, uh… in my condition." She emphasized her words by rubbing her small, but growing belly. "They said you would forgive me though when I left. They said that if you loved me as much as you said, you would be here for me."

Mike didn't know what to say. He needed to know though.

"Why are you here?"

"I called Mathew after you left, a week or so after. I wanted him to know what had happened and that he was going to be a father. He flew into a rage, I could hear things smashing in his flat; he told me he couldn't have a child and he wasn't going to force me to have an abortion, but he would never see me again."

Mike just nodded.

"You know me Michael. I would never do that anyway, even though this child won't have a father, I will love it more than any other in the world. He hung up on me so I didn't know what to do. I was going to bring shame on my family in Kuranda by having a baby out of wedlock, so I decided to come here."

"To Lockwood?"

"No. To Montana. To my aunt and uncle's place on the ranch. They have staff and everything I need to have the baby and raise it. I'm going to miss my home in Australia, but someday I can go back, maybe." She took a deep breath. "But, since I was coming here to the States, I thought it would be a good idea to stop and see Mathew, just to tell him how I felt, and that I wanted no part of him in my life, or the baby's."

She took a breath and looked right into Mike's eyes, "I arrived at his flat and knocked…" A huge tear formed in Shannon's beautiful right eye. "This woman answered, it was his wife."

"Oh boy."

Mike reached over and took her hand after she wiped the tear away.

"They have been married for six years all the while the sheet trawler was with me, all the while he was visiting me he was married. They have two children…"

"I'm so very sorry Shannon."

He moved around into the booth next to her and put his arm around her shoulders, she was shivering.

"She blamed me for everything; she said it was I that lured him to me, that I was trying to trap him into marrying me." She kept crying... Mike felt so bad for her he kissed her cheek.

"It'll be okay. I know you didn't do that."

Shannon pushed him back, "I was going to trick you into believing that you were the father."

"Why?"

Shannon's tears were flowing little trickles down her cheeks now. "Before, at my place in Sydney. I wanted to make love to you, I was upset and confused. I never did it, but I thought…"

"We didn't do anything there; in fact I first told you I loved you there."

"I'm sorry. But you would have thought that the child was yours. I didn't want to trap you; I wanted you to love me without any prerequisites. If you knew I was pregnant things would have gone differently for us, you might have been so angry."

"I would never; I fell in love with you. Sure, I would've been hurt, but who wouldn't? But that was not as important as you were to me then."

"Then?"

"A lot of time has passed." Mike looked the other way, over her head towards the kitchen doors. "I wrote Mikie for the first time since the divorce and I've been writing once a month since. Even though he hasn't written back, I found it to be a distraction from you; I found a way to get you out of my mind, it was affecting my job."

Shannon wiped her nose and eyes on a napkin. She nodded while looking at her lap.

"I understand Michael."

"I hope so. I hope you know that I can't let you get to me again so easily. I loved you so much *dammit*!"

"I wanted you to love me for me. I wanted to see the real you, without any pre-conceived notions. If you'll pardon the pun." Shannon smiled and wiped her tears off on another napkin. She let a soft laugh go. "I didn't want you to love me because you felt sorry for me."

"I love you because you made me feel important still, you respected me even though you knew little about me. It is so hard to find someone who respects you for what your mind offers, for how you feel even if you disagree on something. You didn't order me around-you made it sound that way-but I always knew inside you were laughing. We had the greatest time, you…" Mike felt he could go on for hours, so he summed it up, "…taught me how to feel love again. That's why I love you."

"Thank you Michael. But it is too late for us, right now anyways. Maybe we just need time apart, time for me to have this baby."

"Why? Why can't you stay with me?"

Mike's words were already betraying him.

"You're not ready for another child, I'm not ready for one either. My life was just getting started, now it has to be stable."

The waitress had been standing away from the table; every time she came close an emotional moment would break out. The couple seemed calmer now, so she stepped forward. "Can I get you something to drink?"

Shannon looked at Mike and he looked at the waitress, "No thank you." He took Shannon by the hand and stood up. "Let's get you a place to stay."

"I don't think that would be a good idea."

"Of course not. You fly six thousand miles against your family's recommendations, and then you show up at your…"

"Former?" Shannon half smiled.

"*Former* boyfriend's house unannounced and find his wife is angry with you, then you fly to Reno to meet with a cop you haven't seen or talked to in six months…"

"I get the point."

Mike wasn't finished, "Then you have no place to stay, on a weekend no less. Everyone knows you can't drive at night. So, you either plan to sleep here in the booth or I can take you to my house and put you up for the night."

"Michael, you don't have to. I can find a place to stay."

"Someone once did the same for me, but I don't have a room with satin sheets, only flannel."

"Perfect."

"Where's your luggage?"

"In a locker at the airport, just around the corner from the rental car place. I have a change and toiletries here in my carry bag."

"Wow. Lisa usually had to carry two suitcases just for that. You are economical."

"You should see how I stuffed the locker."

"Give me a sec…"

Mike pulled out his Handi-Talkie and called Kelly, who was in the area. He said he would be there in just a few; Mike and Shannon went outside to his car.

"Well, so you're the one who almost cost me one of my best patrolmen?" A husky voice said. Kelly was walking from his car a couple of spaces away.

"Kelly Daniels, Shannon Hunter…"

Kelly put out his hand for a gentle handshake, but Shannon hugged him as was her usual manner. He wasn't anything she'd expected. A roundish pink face with large sideburns of grey and a smile that seemed so natural for him. He had grey eyes with a mirthful glitter, although he looked a little heavy he was tall and the weight seemed to fit him.

"Nice to meet you sir, I've heard so very much about you."

"Same here." Kelly's eyes bulged he stepped back and put his hands up in front of him, "Hey, you're pregnant! Is there something you want to tell me Mike?"

Kelly stepped back further to survey Shannon's belly.

"No."

"Okay. What do you want me out here for? I was on my way home."

"I'd like permission to give the young lady a ride home, she doesn't have one."

"To Australia? The city manager might complain…"

"*Kelly…*"

"Your house?" He turned to Shannon, "I wouldn't sleep there honey, the place is a disaster area. My wife and I cleaned it up while he was with you down under, but he didn't like it clean so he trashed the place again. Why don't you stay with me and my wife?"

"*Kelly…*"

"I would like that very much Mr. Daniels. Michael is a rather disorderly man. But if I am going to be a burden on somebody, I would rather it be him. He owes me for the time he *had* to stay at my flat."

Kelly's brow lifted, his eyes went wide. "Yeah, no problem. Maybe he should have gotten a hotel…" Kelly nodded at Shannon's belly.

She rubbed he stomach softly with her pretty hands; "I wish it were his, I really do. But it's not. Policeman Greene was nothing but a gentleman when he was with me. It was I that became a burden." Shannon smiled and gave Kelly a peck on the cheek. "I like you Mr. Daniels; you seem to be the best friend this poor man has, you have taken good care of him. If I don't see you again, please just keep him like he is."

"Okay? *Patrolman Greene*, no lights and sirens-no showing off. Got it? Straight home, no sight-seeing and no calls."

"Who'll finish my shift?"

"I'll have Gonzalez do it, he owes you."

"Yeah."

With that Kelly walked back to his patrol car and Mike walked around to the passenger side of his and moved his pursuit case to the backseat. Shannon surveyed the box with a half round hook for grabbing the seat. Several file folders stuffed with paperwork, three metal clipboards with paperwork, a flashlight charger that hooked into a cigarette lighter and a bag of Cheetos.

"After you."

"I've never ridden in a policeman's car before."

"We call them patrol cars; up north and in Canada they call them *prowlers*, in the south they say *cruisers*. But today, this is your limo. And I can break the law getting you home."

"Didn't your boss say straight to you place?"

"He knew I wouldn't. How about it?" He started the car.

"Not tonight Michael. I wouldn't want too much excitement; I could be forced into premature labor."

"I'm an EMT, which means I could deliver your baby, if I had to."

He smiled and backed the car out of the space and headed towards Lockwood.

Shannon smiled; not wondering if Mike would actually deliver her baby if he had to, she knew he would. She even knew he would take care of her, if she would let him, but her plans were already set. There would be no changing them.

Mike on the other hand made jokes out of nervousness, he knew that this just a little tease, Shannon was on her way to her uncle's and Mike was not going to see her again for a long while-if at all-at least it was on the table this time. She was in *his* country now. The cards were on his table for a change, and she'd said she had dual citizenship. No need to worry about immigration authorities now. He thought he'd troll the waters a bit, he wanted more in depth answers. He told her he'd take care of her and the baby. But something was up with her and she was holding something back.

"Shannon, why can't I go with you to Montana?"

"Oh Michael, I would love nothing more. Truthfully. But as was the problem with my parents, you just can't yet."

"Why not? I could look for a job, I'm sure they have cops in Montana. I don't need a visa to do that, I can look for a place to live and we can live together."

Shannon reached across the console between the seat that held all sorts of switches and buttons and little lights, and placed her hand on Mike's knee.

"I've not yet seen you in your uniform, you look brilliant. Except in the middle, is that a vest?"

Mike furrowed his brow and narrowed his eyes at her.

"What does that matter? Why won't you answer my question?"

"I am. You wear that vest because your job is dangerous, you could get shot. This whole country is dangerous with everyone carrying a gun and I can't start to think what it would be like sitting at home with my child and waiting for you."

"People carry guns because that is our heritage; it's how we became a free country. It's how we remain a free country." He blew air out of his nose sharply, "But I could find other work." He sighed sadly.

"You said to me once that this is all you have ever done. Look Michael, maybe after a month or two. I don't know... my aunt and uncle don't need the burden of me and you right now. They're not going to be receptive if I show up with one extra mouth to feed."

"I thought they had money."

"That's not the point. My father told his brother that I was arriving alone." She rubbed his leg for a moment as he navigated the last street and entered the freeway heading east to the little borough of Lockwood.

"Give me a few weeks to talk with them about it. If they are all for it, I will call you."

Mike's place wasn't nearly the disaster Sgt. Kelly had described. The drive off of the freeway was brief, just a few miles from the exit to his place. Mike's road was along a river, almost matching it for turn and length though the little town. It was a beautiful setting, the smell of fresh air and water. The greenery of willow and scrub bush along the banks. She could picture Michael sitting on a log here fishing on his days off.

Shannon giggled a little at the wooden steps and overhang that bordered the outside of the "manufactured home". It looked rather small from the outside, but when she entered Shannon noticed the double wide's rooms were placed with the walls in such a way it gave the trailer a larger feel inside.

Just inside the door to her right was the living room, spacious enough for seven or eight to sit comfortably-if Mike had another couch. One couch, one recliner, and a day bed took the four walls of the room; a woodstove fire place in one corner next to the recliner and a TV directly across from the two in the other corner suggested to Shannon this is where Michael sat often. A coffee table in the center with some magazines on it pretty much made the room complete. A few photos hung on the surrounding walls, mostly Mike and his son when Mikie was younger; a few of Mike and his father, fishing in a beautiful place. One hand written location at the bottom of the frame said: *Orofino, Idaho 1989*.

Mike swayed his hand towards the living room and nodded at Shannon; "Make yourself at home."

"It's rather dark. Do you always keep it this dark in here?" Shannon tossed her jacket on Mike's chair.

"It's just me. I don't use many lights; I rarely use the furnace above sixty-eight. Are you cold?" He asked as he was taking off his utility belt, slinging it over a kitchen chair. He walked to the wood-box and selected a few pieces of kindling.

"Are you asking because I'm pregnant? Or do you care for me again?" She smiled and watched him work.

Mike continued with stacking the small pieces of wood in the stove and then added a cupful of something out of an old coffee can. Then he stacked the larger pieces of firewood on top and reached above the stove on a shelf for an old kitchen match. He intentionally was quiet this whole time, he never looked in her direction; Mike knew this was a little dramatic, but he wanted to make a point.

"Did you…?" Shannon began.

"I never really stopped loving you Shannon. But I found a place in my heart for you, to keep my feelings safe there. So I couldn't harm myself with bad thoughts. Call it stinking thinking. I didn't want to relapse, it's been so difficult remaining sober and then have a small tragedy like that ruin everything, I just couldn't do it. I think it was a test of my sobriety, my first real test of it."

He lit the match with his thumbnail and tossed it on the black stuff out of the coffee can. He looked into the stove and watched the flame flicker; then a bright orange glow became the familiar crackling fire. Mike shut the door to the woodstove. He knelt in place for a few seconds, staring at his handy-work.

"I'm sorry Michael…"

"You said that already. You said you were on drugs, you said you needed time; you say a lot of things." He turned at looked at her saddened eyes, "I almost started drinking again. But I held out."

Shannon held her breath, she knew he hadn't, but he had a reason-she guessed. "I would suppose that your system would be cleaned enough not to end up like you were before your *vacation*."

"Doesn't work like that; you start right where you left off. Only…"

"Only?"

"Only many who start drinking again usually end up dead within a few weeks or months." He turned from the stove, still on one knee and looked away from her out the small window in front. "I won't do that, even for you."

He stood, regaining eye contact, and sat down in his chair against her coat. As soon as the air was pressed out of it, Mike could smell her perfume on it. His eyes watered.

"You should have told me, or your dad could've, I don't care. *Pregnant*?"

"Would it have made a difference? Would you have made love to me on the *Stella*? Would you have felt the same way about me if you were aware I was carrying another man's child?"

Mike pursed his lips, "I don't know."

The fire popped in the metal stove.

"What did you put on that fire to make it so hot, so fast?"

Mike sighed; he knew she was trying to change the conversation. He gave up; he should just let her stay the night, get her to the rental car place in the morning and try again to put her behind him. If it was that easy.

"It's a mixture of sawdust and old auto oil."

"Not very environmentally responsible Mr. Policeman."

He shrugged, his face emotionless.

"It keeps me warm."

Mike stood and went into the kitchen. "Do you want a drink or something to eat?"

Shannon felt a tear coming on, normally Michael would have come back with a long winded justifiable reason for his little mark on nature, or at least smile about it. She knew it was going to be just like it was at her flat, lots of tension-love was here-but they had to keep their distance. Michael was hurting, but at least he offered his place for the night; Shannon didn't want to start the simmering relationship again before she left for Montana, she had to leave. The air between them needed to remain cool-she had to resist him, he was fighting to do the same, she could see it-and feel it.

"Do you have any tea?"

"I have some canned tea."

"Thank you. I ate a sandwich on the flight in from LA. The tea will be fine."

Mike opened the tea and walked back into the living room, handed it to her, and then as he ambled back he picked her jacket up off the recliner and placed it on a hook by the door. He returned and sat back down with a canned ice tea for himself. Her scent was still there.

"So. Tell me what happened."

"When?"

"After you collapsed at the dock, after you had a bout with morning sickness. After you decided not to call me for six months. *After*… I'm sorry." Mike lowered his head.

"Its okay, Michael. It wasn't your fault at all. I love you Michael, I always will until the day I die…"

"The way things were kept from me, I thought you were."

"Again, my fault. Michael, I'm very tired, can you show me to my room, a stop at the restroom would be nice."

"Are you going to change the course of the conversation every time you don't want to answer my question?"

She shrugged and looked at her feet, as much as she could see of them over her abdomen.

"Dunny or loo?" Mike cracked a smile.

"I need a quick wash; I'm a little sweaty."

"Follow me."

Even though Shannon was barely showing more than just a little bump, she strained a little to get up. Mike strode over quickly and gave her his hand. He wondered if it was a play; he was not really in the mood, until he touched her hand. It was soft; he could almost smell her ginger scented lotion and feel her fingers tremble a little as he helped her up. When she rose, her hair had the smell of the lemon grass shampoo, the same she used on the cruiser, his heart locked up. Mike felt a pounding and he wrapped his arms around Shannon, he squeezed as hard as he thought he could without causing harm to the baby, or making her uncomfortable. She melted into his arms and kissed his neck, he followed by kissing hers and her breathing rate increased and they stayed locked together for several minutes. Mike began to shuffle his feet, slightly, Shannon began to mimic his steps. They danced without music, danced for the first time and the room was somber, quiet, the woodstove sparked occasionally. Mike thought to himself; *just like the creaking of timber on the Stella*, the wind in the mast and stays, the floor creaked with every step; that was their song…

Mike and Shannon didn't make love though; after their dance Mike showed her the bathroom and even cleaned it up a little before she went in, as she stood in the doorway smiling. They sat on the bed in the spare room after Mike made it, he did find a set of satin sheets for her, and they talked. Shannon told him about the red headed wife of Mathew and how she was so angry and upset; the terrible things she said to Shannon; how Mathew basically hid in the backroom during the confrontation.

She told Mike about her short trip up from LA, how the empty burned out buildings from the riots and completely empty beaches and piers made the city look so apocalyptic from the air. She talked about her feelings when the woman opened the door in Los Angeles. How her heart fell when she saw the two little children who looked so much like their father, the father who was now cowering in the kitchen. He was afraid of Shannon, he more afraid if his wife, who looked like she was able to kill him right at that moment.

She was broken hearted that the woman showed her no response, that Shannon was blamed for the whole thing, even though it was Mathew who came to Australia and strode into her pub and picked her up. How he'd lied to her about his life, about not being married or even thinking about being engaged ever.

Then she told Mike how she felt a little fear about coming to Lockwood and finding Mike, especially since none of Mike's friends would know about the real father and the embarrassment from everyone's notions would be for Mike. But she had to. It was burning at her more than anything. If she'd not stopped or called, she would've regretted the decision for the rest of her life. She knew she would have to call him eventually from Montana, but he might be even more upset finding out she was so close and hadn't called earlier. It had to be now. That's why when she stopped in Reno on layover, she called.

Shannon stripped down to her undies, not afraid or shy, he'd already seen her in the buff and then she lay down on the soft bed. She fell asleep in Mike's arms after telling her side of the LA story and a few tears. Mike dozed not too long afterward, Shannon in his arms and a smile on his face.

Shannon woke to the smell of bacon and coffee. She could hear a radio on in the other room, the kitchen she assumed, and the sound of pots and pans clanking. She heard the front door open and then close again. Then she heard the steel door to the woodstove open and the eventual crackling of burning wood, she could smell the light smoke of pine wafting around the room.

Climbing out of bed, Shannon found her bag at the end of the bed and dressed into sweat clothes, then went to the bathroom to clean up and straighten her hair, brushing it out and re-twisting it into a ponytail. She scowled at the mirror. Shannon ran the shower and undressed again. She found the warm water invigorating.

Mike was in the kitchen as she suspected, cooking bacon and eggs, and a can of pork and beans. The coffee was ready when she finished in the bathroom and walked down the thin hall; Mike had set her a place at the small two seat table in the kitchen.

"Good morning, did you sleep well?" Mike poured her a cup.

"Quite well, thank you. You're up early today."

"Have to get you to the rental car place." He sat down at the same time she did, he saw her eyes sparkle in the early morning light coming in through the window. "Can I ask a favor?"

"Sure."

"Can I drive you to your aunt and uncle's?"

Shannon mulled it over for a moment, she knew what the answer had to be, but still she looked for a way. She'd love him to. But she had to do this on her own. It was the first step.

"No. I'm sorry, but I have to make this journey on my own. I would hope you'd understand... things have to be worked out in my head. I promise you I will call when I get there, and then every few days after that."

"Can I call you?"

"The only number I have for my uncle is his business one, in case I have trouble, I'm afraid you can't use that. The other number is my luggage; I *will* call you this time."

Mike absorbed her intentions; he knew she was pregnant, that has an effect on the mind, he witnessed it with Lisa when she was carrying Mikie. Shannon and Mike ate in silence, and then after he poured a second cup of coffee for the both of them he tried one last time.

"Would you take a walk with me this morning?"

"Of course."

The December air was cool, although a slight breeze was blowing from the west through the small valley, Mike went out without a jacket. Winter was beginning to show in the trees, mostly cottonwoods, along the Truckee River. The bigger trees were already yellow around the tops and empty around the bottoms, the smaller willows had shed many of their thin leaves to the ground and the path they were walking on. The end of fall was a peculiar time in Nevada. Even though winter was just a few weeks away, warm air still made the days feel like it would never get below freezing.

It was if Nevada had a drunken schedule. It would be ice cold one day, warm the next and then it would snow several inches. At the end of December, the temps would fall below the zero mark, minus ten or even lower at times. In January, it could warm up to the sixties again and then fall to zero by the end of the month. Then it would be cold and drizzly for spring. Snow on Easter and the first week of June then it would be warm. Temperatures in the hundreds during the summer from July to September and cold again in October when fall actually began to show. Then it would start all over. Sometimes it would snow several feet down here on the valley floor and hundreds of inches in the Sierra Nevadas, just a few miles away. Other times it would be dry and just plain cold.

Mike and Shannon-who had looped her arm through Mike's-walked slowly from the steps of the modular towards a paved path that wound around the river bank as Mike told her of the seasons. The river water was lower than usual due to another drought year, so the bottom was easily visible; it presented itself in shades of green and brown, fingers of bright shamrock green algae grass flowed with the current. Large logs of driftwood sat along the shore, most times of the year fishermen would sit on the wood and cast their lines out into the current, but there were none today. Fish oil could be smelled still, it was warm enough for that.

The pace around the path was kept to just a few steps every few seconds; Mike was in no hurry to see Shannon leave again. Shannon was taking in the fresh air, the smell of a river in autumn, near winter and the way Mike was breathing, soft slowly; he was at peace-she assumed.

Finally she broke the silence.

"It is so calm and serene here. Such a small and quaint valley, how far does it go this way?"

"Another thirty miles-I'm sorry I don't know the metric equivalent-then the river turns north for another twenty miles and dumps into Pyramid Lake."

"Pyramid? It sounds so mysterious."

"It's a very large alkaline lake with prehistoric fish called Cui-ui, a Paiute name. I don't know what it means, but as far as I know, Pyramid is the only lake in the world that has them. They filmed that movie with Max von Sydow called *The Greatest Story Ever Told*, about Jesus there because it looks like the sea of Galilee."

"Very interesting indeed. It is truly beautiful here."

"Not as pretty as the places I saw in Australia, especially Kuranda."

"I would suppose that you don't get out enough then. To find beauty around you every day. To see the beauty around you is to see the beauty inside of you also."

Mike thought about what she meant.

"I guess. It's been a long time I had a chance to walk around here."

Shannon paused, Mike pulled her close and he leaned in closer to her. He moved slowly and placed a kiss on her ear, then in front of it for a few moments, and then he moved to her neck. The embrace lasted for a dozen minutes, and then she pulled away.

"I have to go Michael."

Mike lowered his head, "I know."

"Will you take me to the rental place at the airport?"

"Of course."

They walked slowly back to Mike's trailer and he went into the carport and warmed up his Landcruiser. After Shannon went to the bathroom she returned to his side by the car and kissed him on the cheek. He helped her in, then backed out and made for the freeway and the airport.

"This valley outside of the one you live in is rather small too. This is a beautiful place."

"I guess so."

"I can't talk you into letting me drive you?"

She shook her head.

"No. It will be difficult enough for me right now. But listen, I will call you and we will see each other again. Soon. It's a promise I will not break, ever."

Mike nodded, doubtful. Hopeful.

And the conversation ended there. For the rest of the twenty minutes to the airport Mike wanted to say things to Shannon, but they all led in the same thought, Shannon staying with him or he'd travel with her.

He turned into the rental car parking lot and walked to the office with her. Shannon handed him the key to the locker for her luggage and asked if he would be so kind to retrieve it for her, as she rubbed her belly. Mike smiled and complied, walking across the lot to the airport and the lockers, straight to the box number she described.

He retrieved her two bags and shook his head thinking how his ex would have had three or four. Smiling, Mike walked back to the lot and found Shannon standing next to a newer Buick. He loaded the bags and she stood in front of him for a long moment, a glimmer in her blue eyes that made Mike tremble on the inside a little.

"I have something for you."

She reached into her carry bag and pulled out a wrapped gift in the shape of a boomerang. He reached to get it and Shannon kissed him on the cheek, softly and then moved to his lips and they wrapped arms behind shoulders and held each other. Mike felt his heart breaking again; he knew she would try to call. He just hoped his feelings were right this time. He stepped back and surveyed the L shaped package.

"Is it a boomerang?"

"Not a very brilliant job of wrapping, is it?" Shannon blushed.

"I love it."

"It's from Akama Janna, and my mother."

Mike looked puzzled for a second; he pursed his lips a little and unwrapped it. The inscription on this one looked like it was a half of a koala. Mike noticed it wasn't painted like the others Akama was trying to hock him in Kuranda, he simulated throwing it.

"Not a very good koala, I've seen his work to be better."

"It's not a Koala."

Mike held it as if he were tempted to test it out in the parking lot.

"Not here silly. If you have some time, maybe you can figure out what the painting means."

"It has meaning?"

"Everything an aboriginal does has meaning. This is a special gift; if you can figure it out tell me when I call you tonight."

Mike looked up from the beautiful woodwork. "You'll be in Montana tonight?"

"No, but I will call you from my hotel in Idaho. I've made arrangements."

"I'll study it very hard." He smiled, but Shannon saw the pain in his eyes, the hurt in his heart.

"I love you."

"I love you so much…"

Mike felt a tear coming on, his voice cracked. He reached for her and she backed into the open car door.

"Let's not do it this way. Let us just say, see you soon."

Mike nodded.

Mike watched the car head out of the parking lot; he smiled at how adept Shannon was at driving here in the States. He wiped a tear from his eye when the Buick disappeared into the traffic and the freeway onramp. Mike cursed himself for not asking her if she knew where she was going, but deep inside he knew Shannon did. She was the smartest woman he had ever met; and she still loved him.

J Jay Ross

CHAPTER FIFTEEN

THE WAIT

Mike was barely home before he started staring at the boomerang. "Why would her mother want me to have this?" He didn't even know why Akama Janna only painted a half koala bear on it. It had meaning, but what was it? And Shannon had said it wasn't a koala.

There was two half circles, back to back. Underneath was a small circle and lower was a drawing of a stick and another half circle facing the stick. "Okay, so it really doesn't look like a koala."

He turned boomerang over and hefted it, just like he did in Australia under the tutelage of the tribesman Akama Janna. His mind flashed back to the jungle and the plantation, the smell of the grass and trees surrounding the Hunter compound. The cool breeze on the tropical air.

On his day off Mike decided to spend the day fishing along the river, something he hadn't done since before his divorce. The water was still deep enough to make a rushing noise over the granite rocks that littered the bed, geese and duck settled in pools behind the larger boulders. It was warmer in the afternoon now, the scent of algae and drying willow branches floated around in the air, a little taste of fish oil on the rolling mist generated off the rocks as it was vaporized naturally. The air was much colder today and he was dressed warmly, the water had a thin edge of ice around the edges of the bank.

He was already worried about Shannon, it was still early and he figured she would drive until it was close to dark, which put her around Idaho Falls. The relaxing sound of water put a little ease in Mike's heart, but the taste of the river air made him long for the warm deck of the *Stella*, and the embrace of its captain.

At seven thirty that night the phone rang. Mike was only a few feet away stoking the fire in his stove; he stood quickly and answered it.

"Hello?"

"G'day."

"Shannon. I suppose you made it to Idaho Falls?"

"Are you having me followed? How did you know where I am?"

"My father lives in Idaho. I've been to Montana a dozen times; I know the route you're taking, so I just put two and two together."

"Always the policeman."

"Yeah, not that you like the idea much."

"It's not that I don't like the job you do, or the responsibility you have, it's just dangerous. Besides that, I was having an emotional moment. I apologize; I shouldn't have said those things to you."

"When I said I didn't want a child right away, I thought it was because you couldn't have one or didn't want one for a while. I…"

They both realized they were beating an old path already trodden upon.

"We aren't starting his off very well. Shall we try again?"

"Okay."

"Hello Mr. Greene. I have made it to my halfway destination and I miss you."

"G'day Miss Shannon, I miss you too. I wish you were here with me."

"That's much better. So, what did you do today?"

"I went fishing. I had a lonely but somewhat bittersweet time just sitting on the log thinking of you." Mike started to relax. He knew Shannon was strong enough to make it the rest of her way on her own, on every subject. "I didn't catch anything, but still…"

"Very nice. I had a horrid drive; I had forgotten how terrible drivers are in the States. No one signals, one bloke is doing seventy, another fifty-five. Everyone passes on corners and up hills, not very safe. I wish you were here to issue them all citations."

"Me too."

A long pause that felt like hours weighed down the phone line, it wasn't that Shannon nor Mike had run out of things to say-the words they wanted to convey to one another just couldn't be done over an electronic device-it deserved face to face and eye to eye contact. Shannon heard Mike breathing and she heard strain to it, Mike heard Shannon trying to calm herself down a little. Maybe she was just a little overstimulated at the traffic, or maybe she was as lonely as he was.

"I should retire for the evening; I have an early start in the morning."

"Will you call tomorrow when you arrive at your uncle's?"

"Of course. Michael…"

"Yes?"

"Everything will work out all right. I promise."

"I believe you. Good night, Shannon. I'll dream of you…"

"I shall do the same, it will be a pleasant night."

The phones clicked dead at the same time.

And, as promised Shannon did call Mike when she arrived that afternoon in Thompson Falls. And she called every other night for two weeks, Shannon wanted to keep the conversation going over the things she had planned for the baby, how much help her aunt has been in preparing a room for the child, with colors that would match whether it was a boy or a girl. Shannon talked how much she wanted the baby to be a girl, so she could dress her up and play with her like a little doll. She'd given Mike a number to reach her; it was a private line to her little bungalow on the Hunter Ranch.

She told Mike her aunt and she were going into Missoula to see a women only male revue tomorrow and how she would pretend any one of the dancers dressed as a policeman was actually Mike when she was drooling over him. Shannon also talked about something that made her upset a little; Mathew had called her parents in Kuranda and was demanding to know where she was. Mike offered to chat with Matt, but Shannon begged him not to interfere.

Mike felt *it* was getting nearer. They would reunite and he would move there or she could move with him to Idaho and start a new life together. Or maybe back to Australia. The thoughts excited him. They both ran scenarios over one another, and there was little talk of their plans falling through. It was inevitable they would be together eventually. They both felt it, and they both were ready. Love was on their side and time was not really a factor now. It was only a small matter of it.

Shannon bade Mike goodnight, she had to get dressed for the little trip into Missoula and needed a shower. Mike was happy to hear she was in such great spirits. It made him feel better knowing she was getting along with her family as well. It would easier to introduce him in the long run to her aunt and uncle.

"Love you. Goodnight."

"I love you."

Late Friday night Shannon and her aunt had just left the small club in Missoula in her aunt's Toyota 4-Runner where the revue had taken place and just had turned off of Interstate 90 to MT 200, towards the Hunter ranch after a wonderful evening. Shannon had not imbibed, but her aunt had a few drinks and was a little giggly, but the night called for it. It had been a release for the both of them. It was dark and a little chilly with a low coat of snow on the ground; the trees around the highway had kept the wind from drifting it too much around the shoulders.

Shannon was always uncomfortable riding this time of night in any car.

Duane Turner had just left the Old Country Saloon on MT 200 after a long night holding a barstool in place with his behind. He had a bitter fight with his wife earlier that day over the chores around the house and he wasn't going to budge. He worked fifteen hours a day and he wasn't going to come home twice a week and cook dinner. If she couldn't make him dinner before she went out with her mother, then to hell with her, he would just drink his dinner each of the two nights.

Duane stumbled on the large gravel drive a little as he struggled to fish his truck keys out of his pocket, a few stabs at the lock and he was in. His first instinct was to just lie down across the bench seat and grab a nap, but his anger boiled up again; he started the pickup. He didn't want to half-freeze to death on the front seat of the truck; he wanted to be in his warm bed at home.

"Ain't no woman gonna change my life." He muttered to himself as he got the cold Chevy started after three attempts.

Shannon was trying to shade her eyes from the oncoming car, the driver had the high-beams on and one headlight was aimed directly at her, the closer the car came the less she could see. Her eyes hurt from the light, panic started to settle in. *Was this idiot aware of them coming at him?*

Duane could see headlights, at least he thought they were headlights, coming right at him. He became a little scared that the car might be a deputy and Duane didn't need another DUI; quickly he turned off on a little side road and made a few switchbacks in the moonlit shadows, his truck sliding side to side in the mucky slush. He shut his lights off so the cop couldn't see him and waited a few minutes.

After he didn't see anything moving he decided to get the hell home as fast as he could. Duane mashed the pedal to the floor; he forgot to turn on his headlights. Fifty feet from the road his all-weather tires caught the apron of the pavement and his truck lurched forward under the traction and the energy gave him a rush of momentum.

All he could hear next was the surreal sound of metal and glass tearing and shattering.

And a woman screaming.

The calls stopped Friday night. Mike waited three days to try and get a hold of Shannon but no one answered her private number which meant she wasn't in her little casita. He tried to find the number to her aunt and uncle's, but the number was unlisted. He did get the number to her uncle's business phone, but there was no answer the half dozen times he tried to call. Mike became desperate, he knew how pushy Matt was and Mike started to feel paranoid. He picked up his phone on a rainy Monday night in December and began making calls to important people.

He was scared and felt ill. Something was wrong, he knew Shannon would never go back to Mathew, but had the clown done something to her? Not knowing was the hardest part and Mike didn't know. A call to Kelly would help and in turn Kelly promised to get to the bottom of it.

"Hello?"

Mike was out in the carport changing the oil on the Toyota when the phone rang. He ran inside and was out of breath.

"Mike?"

It was Kelly Daniels. But his voice was severe sounding.

"Yeah? What's up Sarge, did you get through?"

Mike asked Kelly to contact an old friend in Bozeman Montana that Kelly went to school with.

"Mike… I called Sam Dennison in Bozeman and he put me in touch with the information officer in Sanders County where the ranch is. Mike… I have some bad news."

There were tears on the verge of Kelly's voice.

"Kel?"

Mike's heart dove to the bottom of his chest, landing on his stomach, which pushed bile to the top of his throat.

"Mike... It would be best if I just read the clipping the officer faxed me. '*The vehicle that Shannon Hunter of Thompson Falls was riding in at ten forty-five p.m. was struck in the passenger door causing the vehicle to roll over several times ejecting her out of the vehicle and then the car rolled over her- killing her instantly...'.*"

There was a long pause. "The funeral is tomorrow. I'm so sorry Mike; I don't know what to say."

The receiver was half out of Mike's hand, his eyes were flooded and his mouth was open and drying. He felt ill, his stomach was aching to turn out and he started trembling uncontrollably. He fell to his knees and leaned over the small table in the small living room and tried to cry, shock had taken his soul. Kelly couldn't stand the silence anymore, he himself had taken a liking to the young lady who stirred the life in his best officer and best friend and he hung up quietly and just sat behind his desk staring out the window towards piñion and ponderosa pine trees, towards sage covered hills that lead up to Virginia City. Kelly felt like the ghosts in the old town right now. Mike was going to take this hard.

The sun had set leaving a pinkish hue flowing along with the water in the river bed through Lockwood. The bleached out driftwood log that solemnly sat on the quiet river bank was cold and Mike shivered a little as he sat staring out over the water to the shore on the other side. A small otter was racing against the current and his wake made sharp ripples that reflected the moonlight, even though it wasn't full, the glow still gave the large hills surrounding the small valley a ghostly and dead appearance-*rightly so*-Mike thought.

He had been sitting here for over four hours, since he had the strength to pull himself from the floor of his home, where he lay from the time Kelly hung up. He had experienced nearly every stage of grief before being able to leave his home for a lonely walk to and along the river. Depression was all he felt now, helpless and alone.

First was denial: He tried to think of a way that Shannon's name was used by accident; maybe she was an eyewitness and the newspaper put her name in the column by mistake. Or it might have been she was thought to be dead, maybe the hospital forgot to list her as critical-or even they revived her at the last minute and didn't have time to report it to the paper before press time.

Second came anger: He shook his fist at the ceiling of the trailer; he had been lying on the floor pounding his hands on the carpet and demanding that God explain to him why he was punishing Mike for his life, he had tried all of his adult years to be a good person, to be the best he could, he saved lives at his job all the time, yet God has chosen him to single out, to penalize him with the recent death of Rika and the young girl at the trailer court, just a few miles from his house. He cursed the whole world for laying its burden on him.

During the anger phase Mike slipped into bargaining with the same God he had just cursed at. He asked to be taken instead of the young woman from Australia, after all she was carrying a child, he would do anything to take her place, please God, take me. Mike quietly pled to an empty room.

Two hours later, Mike finally was able to place the receiver back on the hook. He climbed into his chair, the small recliner that Shannon had laid her jacket on just a couple of weeks ago. The still lingering scent pulled him down a path of despair and depression that Mike knew he would never be able to handle alone.

For the first time in his life, he was looking to end it all-Mike looked at his utility belt hanging on the chair in the kitchen; he focused on the black and grey aluminum grip of his Smith & Wesson 5906 sticking out its holster. The gun would bring a relief to the pain he was feeling, a quick end to the horrible place the world had become, so full of misery and suffering.

Before he could find the energy to lift his heartbroken strained body off the chair, he was exhausted from crying and grieving, before he could move towards the chair and .45 caliber relief, final relief, he dozed off until a horrible dream woke Mike up with a jolt.

He was sailing the *Stella*, Shannon was lying on the deck bleeding and he was trying to get them back to the marina safely, no matter what he did he couldn't get the damnable ship to turn the right way. He pulled on the tiller till his hands bled, the sails flapped in a sound reminiscent of blood slurping from a gushing wound and lazily pouring to a linoleum floor. There was laughter in the air. A blond man stood on a small island laughing at them. A short fair haired man with round John Lennon glasses. Mike woke up as he thrashed the end table to pieces in fury. He was more tired now than before he fell asleep.

It was nearly midnight now; the water flowing by his feet was not affected by time or the passing of a man's true love. The sky was filled with chilled air, but he sat on the white log staring across the river to the bank and eventually up the side of the embankment to the freeway; where after a few hours into depression Mike could hear traffic.

It had been there all the time, people traveling to and from destinations, not one noticing a lone man sitting on a huge piece of driftwood staring out over a drought-stricken river. No one knew the pain he was feeling, the closeness the cold and cruel world had surrounded him with, he was feeling claustrophobic even in the outdoors.

At around one a.m. Mike heard a car pull up behind him a dozen yards back. The street bordered the river and since he was the only one out this late at night, he figured the car was a patrol car, either out looking for him because he didn't show for work; he didn't even bother to call, he just didn't care anymore or someone spotted him sitting there from a nearby residence and called in to the police station about a suspicious man who has sat on a log for about the last six hours. Mike heard a car door close and footfalls approaching him, he didn't even turn around. He knew the sound of the man behind him, the policeman who had stopped short of sitting next to him; he knew the breathing, the sigh, and the slight cough. The sound of Sam Brown gun leather creaking against a large girth.

"I thought I'd find you here."

"She's gone Kelly. Everything I had. Shannon, and she's gone."

Kelly Daniels sat on the natural wooden bench, his leather belt groaning louder in the nearly soundless air. "I wrote you down as a call-in, should I have put your name under no-call, no-show?"

"I don't care."

Mike continued to stare out over the river to the freeway, he was formulating a plan. One that didn't include his career any longer. At least his current one.

"Yeah. I figured as much. So I did it anyway." He put his hand on Mike's shoulder. "I'm truly sorry Mike, I really am. You don't deserve this."

"I know... I already went through that phase."

"Pardon?"

"You know the *Kübler-Ross Model for Grief*. We had that class on grief counseling a couple of years ago."

Kelly put his lips together and curled them up, he nodded in the dark.

"Oh yeah. Been through all five?"

Mike shrugged and ignored the question.

"Kelly, what do you think I should do now?"

"What do you mean?"

"I can't do my job right now, I just can't. If you need me to resign I will. I've been sitting here thinking of my life and what I intend to do with it now that I have lost everything."

"You haven't lost *ev...*"

"I have." Mike turned to his friend finally. "She was everything I wanted. She had it all and she gave me a piece of life that I could never repay. Now Shannon is gone and I have nothing to do but sit here and stare out over the river. I can't go to work, I could get somebody killed-maybe myself-I know for sure I would do stupid things because I just don't care anymore."

"How about a cushy desk job?"

"Kel, I'm quitting. I'm moving to Idaho with my dad and spend my time with him."

"I don't know what to say." Kelly pulled his hand away. "Other than you're probably right."

"Yeah."

Kelly pulled two slips of paper out of his shirt pocket and handed them to Mike.

"This is the address of her uncle in Thompson Falls. Sam got it for me; he knew I had an interest in having it. He says the funeral is today, I'm sorry but you'll miss it. The other is the fax of the newspaper article."

"Thanks. Thank you for everything. I'll have a letter on your desk tomorrow."

"Won't be necessary, I'm just putting you down on emergency leave for a couple of weeks. Take that much time to think about it; if you still want to quit, then you can. It will look better on your record this way."

"Thanks."

With that, Sergeant Daniels rose and walked back to his patrol car, his shift ended an hour ago, he was headed home with a heavy heart; he almost knew what his friend was feeling, over the years Mike and he had told so many families that their loved ones weren't coming home after horrific accidents, that you just felt the same as the people did anymore. It was too hard for Mike to go on with his job, he was right. He would do things that jeopardized his life, just to be with his Shannon, if he could. He wouldn't be able to make good decisions for the time being.

Kelly knew he was losing his friend and best patrolmen. He took one last breath of outdoor air and nodded towards Mike's back.

"Be safe."

Mike just raised a hand over his shoulder, he didn't even look back. Kelly got inot his unit and drove off.

Mike left the river at three a.m. He went to his room and packed a suitcase and tossed in his shaving kit, thinking about the time he used it in the air on the way to Australia. Then he shut the power off to everything and turned the heater down to 55, he set the key in the planter outside the door, slammed it shut and got in his Landcruiser. Mike slowly drove up his street and navigated the SUV to the freeway onramp then made the turn for the eastbound lanes. The darkness was evil, it was foreboding, it was calling him.

East to Idaho.

At ten a.m. Mike was in Boise, he stopped to get a cup of coffee since he had just a little nap in the last twenty-four hours. Returning to his Landcruiser he looked at the freeway onramp; he was set to go west on I-84 towards Orofino, but he paused. A brief flash in his mind startled him, he never had closure on Rika, he never got to say goodbye.

He didn't know the young girl in the trailer house that died of an aneurism, he then went on a drunken binge that sent him to rehab before he had a chance to find out about her, who she was, how she died. It wasn't even till he'd gotten out that he learned she was dead before she hit the floor from a vein in her head popping open like a leaky garden hose. Her name was Anne Castle. A tear formed in Mike's eye. He pulled out into traffic and jumped onto the I-84 East, ten hours away from Thompson Falls. He would not be cheated again.

CHAPTER SIXTEEN

CLOSURE

Mike approached the house, the modest structure intimidated him a little, but he cleared his throat and knocked on the door. He hoped this was the address, maybe Kelly read him the wrong one, or maybe he wrote it down wrong. Then thoughts were moving so fast through Mike's head, he barely knew what to think. After a few seconds he heard footsteps approaching the door, and then the telltale sounds of tumblers disengaging in the door's lock.

He'd made record time getting here, almost an hour shaved off normal travel time; yeah, he broke a few laws, but he didn't care. Not at all. He dared anyone who pulled him over to arrest him. They'd have a fight on their hands. Mike felt reckless and furious. God help any creature that crosses his path.

The road twisted and turned high into the mountains around Thompson Falls, into the elevations where snow could be seen. Not as much as should be seen this time of year, but Mike figured the drought was hurting everyone. It was God's country up here; the roads were a bit slippery, but not bad. Trees lined the highway, tall pines that Mike knew little about-a lodgepole here, a Douglas fir there. The scenery was calming him, the thick of trees and scrubs along the side of the road, the small rows of mailboxes lined up on a fence railing, horses in pastures. It was soothing. He longed for the country. Sure his city was small, but out here. There was nothing to get in between you and your life.

Mike approached the gate that appeared on the directions given him by Kelly, the gate was open. It split in the middle and was a tall rounded top black iron thing, operated by a control box mounted on a brick and concrete arch on both sides. White rail fencing ran off in either direction from the gate and went nearly into infinity, to where the property lines changed direction. He drove right through, along a long road of pea gravel that was meticulously maintained. Large areas of grassy knolls bordered the road along with rose bushes and tall elms.

The house itself was large. Dark blood red brick all the way around with huge dormers on the second floor. Probably about sixty feet long and maybe eighty feet back from the gravel road, the house resembled something from Constitutional times in Philadelphia. White wooden thickly framed doors and windows. A wooden covered porch that rose above the ground via six exposed aggregate steps led to the front door. There were three cars in the lot to the west of the driveway; one 4Runner, a newer pickup and a large Mercury sedan. He walked up the steps and knocked.

Mike's stomach knotted up, he felt sick to his insides; after all, he wasn't invited here, he was an intruder in a way. No one knew he and Shannon were close friends, very close, and he would be scrutinized the very minute the door opened. But he needed to close this chapter of his life, he never got to see Rika off, he never got to say goodbye to her. She just died and was buried and Mike was never invited to that funeral either-not that it mattered, he really only knew Rika a few days, although he had watched her for weeks, he didn't get to know her until the very end.

Mike didn't want to end his love story with Shannon that way, he loved her and he knew she felt the same way about him. She said it a few times that was it wasn't it-he knew that he had to say goodbye-because she loved him, he could never find that kind of love again.

The door swung inward and from behind the shadow cast by it appeared a small man, with tear stained cheeks. He was dressed in a charcoal suit; there was a lily in the buttonhole. The man was nearly fifty or a little over it.

"Yes?"

"Is this the Hunter residence?"

"Yes…" A little impatience flowed across the man's face.

"My name is Mike Greene; I was a friend of Shannon's."

"A friend?" The man's eyes brightened a little.

"Yes, you could say a close friend. "

The little man's breathing paused for a moment and then he stepped back away from the door, opening it the rest of the way. "Come in, please…" He sighed as Mike entered the house.

Mike walked slowly in; as he passed the sad looking man he noticed the house was filled from one table to the other with flowers, wreaths and vases. The room smelled wonderful, but the atmosphere was that of a funeral home, appropriately so; Mike thought. The flowers assaulted his senses; the smell burned his sinuses like acid. The meaning of the flowers was the reason, not the actual floral arrangements themselves.

The sad man moved in front of Mike and led him to a door and knocked. He opened the door without any answer and went in, turning and waving Mike forward. Mike again passed the man and turned once inside the door to find another man, not dressed in cowboy clothes like he'd expected, but in a blue semi-formal suit and tie. The man was staring out the window at a large green field with what looked to be old split rail fencing, a corral of some kind, and four horses wandering at the far end. Behind the field was a grove of tall trees and bushes; Mike thought them to be lodgepole pine, scrub juniper and ponderosas.

Between the trees there was a stream that ran from one end where the grove ended to the other side of the field which was out of view from Mike's position. The view also led from the ground up a sharp incline of hilly areas that were close to the house, maybe three or four hundred yards from the end of the field, then the hills dipped out of sight where the bottom of the mountain range began. Mike was astonished at the vision before him, the beauty was remarkable. He would have not noticed something like this before… her. The man's head was following the ridge line to the beautiful mountains in the background. The man finally realized he was being watched from behind and whirled in a startled fashion.

"Yes?"

"My name is Mike Greene. I am, uh… was a friend of Shannon."

"*Oh?*"

The blue suited man looked over Mike's shoulder to the sad man by the door and then back to Mike

"Do I know you?"

"Shannon didn't mention me?"

"She didn't." The man in the blue suit seemed irritated by Mike's presence, he had a good reason.

"I'm just a friend; I just came by to pay my respects. I just saw her about three weeks ago in Nevada."

The man grew red in the face and narrowed his eyes at Mike.

"She what? You saw her three weeks ago?"

"Yes, sir."

"I'm afraid you're mistaken *Mr.*?"

"Greene."

"Whatever, I believe you have the wrong person."

"She said she was coming back here and that's the last I heard from her, I was just trying to…"

"What the Hell do you have to do with my wife? Who the Hell are you?"

"Your wife?"

"Yes. I must ask you to leave, now."

"But…"

"Barry, see this man out. Now."

The sad man moved from the doorway and grabbed Mike by the arm; the blue suited man turned back towards the window and lowered his head in pain.

Mike turned towards the door, he had to give up.

"I guess this was too much of a shock, even if the baby wasn't mine I would have still loved it like it was."

"The baby?" The blue suited man spun around to catch Mike's gaze and tearful question. "*You're* the one?"

Finally the sad man spoke, "Mr. Hunter, I believe Mr. Greene here is *the* friend of Christine's."

Mike looked puzzled at the two men, moving his head back and forth between them.

"Who?"

The older man raised his hand and Barry let go of Mike's arm.

"Christine, it's my niece's middle name. Shannon Christine Hunter. I'm Thomas Hunter."

The man's face bore a sign of relief, small as it was, it was still happier than it was a minute ago. "You're here for Christine." The man named Hunter stepped from behind the desk and offered a hand to Mike. "My name is Thomas Charles Hunter. I'm Chris-uh… Shannon's uncle. You see, sadly it was my wife *Shannon*, who perished in the car crash." He lowered his head in sorrow.

"My God, my mistake. I am so sorry, I had no idea; I guess Shannon mentioned that she was named after her aunt, but I never put two and two together, please accept my condolences."

"Thank you. I do remember Shannon and Christine talking about her young beau."

"Is Shannon, I mean Christine here?"

Sadness gripped both of the men's faces again. The sad man named Barry spoke. "I'm afraid Miss Christine was in the car with Mrs. Hunter…"

Mike looked behind him a in a panic and fell backwards into a leather chair. "Oh God."

"She's alive-barely-but she is in critical condition." Barry exhaled sharply out of his nostrils.

"Can I see her?"

Mr. Hunter spoke; "Maybe. Barry, take Mr. Greene to the hospital, make sure he gets a chance to see her."

"I understand sir." And with that Barry offered his hand down to Mike who was still in the chair. Mike was able to grasp it and use his legs to help Barry pull him from the seat. "If you'll come with me sir, I'll take you to see Miss Christine."

"Why Christine?" Mike asked after a few somber moments during the first part of the drive.

"Pardon? Oh, it is her middle name; it keeps things from getting too confusing around here. You said you were close friends?"

"We are. I met her in Australia six months ago and we became very close. I had to return to the states and the parting was, well… shall we say, very sad. She visited me three weeks ago at my place in Lockwood and called me nearly every other night."

"Until Friday I suppose."

"Yes."

"I had a friend track down Mr. Hunter's address. I lost a… a girlfriend a little while ago and I never got to say goodbye to her. I didn't want this to happen again, I just came to say goodbye. I think it's what Shannon would have wanted me to do."

"I see. Miss Christine, I mean Shannon, is a very strong minded person."

"Sounds like her." Mike said towards the passenger window, wondering why everyone in Shannon's family talked like a lawyer. "She always had to be in control, except driving at night."

Barry let out a little laugh, breaking the tension in the car. He turned to Mike; "Yes. You do know Shannon Christine, very well." Then the mood and his voice turned morose again. "In fact, that is how this accident came into play."

Mike didn't know why he was talking so plainly to this man he didn't even know, to a man he barely met a half hour ago, and someone he knew only as Barry. But the man seemed honest and forthright about what had happened so far, so Mike thought he could push it a little farther.

"How did it happen?"

"What the police can gather is Miss Christine decided to drive because her aunt had a few too many drinks. They were coming back from Missoula Friday night and a drunk driver who was hiding from the cops came out of dirt turn-off and struck the passenger side."

"The article I heard didn't say anything about the other driver."

"He and his wrecked truck ended up in a ditch. He hit his head on the wheel and passed out. They found him there just after they found Mrs. Hunter and Miss Hunter." He swallowed even harder and a tear formed in his eye. "He didn't even have a scratch on him."

"They usually don't." Mike said, matter-of-factly.

Barry stiffened in the car seat. "You know this?"

"I'm a...was a cop. I saw this kind of thing all the time, the pain and suffering from injuries and the fatalities; yet the drunk driver walks away from the crashes eighty percent of the time. Their bodies are so relaxed they just bounce around the cab of the car and won't even get a mark, hardly." Mike looked down at the floorboards. "I am truly sorry about Mrs. Hunter."

Barry nodded.

He began to negotiate the final few turns from the ranch road they were on, then onto MT 200. He navigated the car over to the highway and began the journey south-east towards Plains. In twenty five minutes they would be at Sanders County Memorial Hospital, where Shannon was. Mike said hardly anything more to Barry; he just looked out the window and hoped that Shannon was all right. Finally, about five minutes from Plains, Mike broke the deafening silence.

"This is sure God's country."

"You're God fearing man, Mr. Greene?" Barry asked with a tinge of enthusiasm.

"I've had my moments." Mike replied, remembering *Frontiers*; The Twelve Steps and the connection with his personal *Spiritual* awareness.

The position of the rehab center was that of God's place in recovering from alcohol addiction, but Mike had neither the patience nor the interest at the time. He was raised a Catholic, but had turned away from the church at an early teen year. He barely gave God a glance, except in the common situations throughout life where someone is in dire need of divine intervention, and asks God for it. The driving point of all the lectures and groups was to ask for help from within and from your *Higher Power*, which translated to God, Mike thought. It took him almost three weeks to find his spiritual self, and just a few days after meeting Rika to understand the need for inner searching and release.

It was a full day after he had learned of Rika's death, and Mike was beside himself. He didn't attend the full group on the last day; they did give him a pass-knowing he had closeness to the young troubled addict-and he was allowed to remain in his dorm room for hours. He reflected about his life and the young girl in Lockwood that died in his hands. Not at his hands, as he had previously thought, blaming himself for her death, but the spirituality of the moment he felt her life leave her body and float away from its shell.

He thought about how many people he had saved, one way or another, and that gave him inner strength and peace. But Rika had strength about her-she broadcast it openly-and she still decided to take her life, because she was lonely.

Mike's thoughts returned to Shannon, how he had imagined her dead, laying on the ground dying, calling his name. How he felt that moment Kelly told him about the accident, how much he loved Shannon. That was it, he loved Shannon more than anything else that moment, his whole life ended that second he thought she was dead. Now his life was revived, he felt the weight of the world was lifted from his shoulders. Then it hit him square in the chest, he hadn't thought about Rika's death before without a twinge of pain in his heart; until now…

Mike had realized that he forgot about the pain of Rika, his ex-wife and son, the poor blue-green eyed girl that died in his arms at the trailer; his thought was purely for Shannon. When he thought about living and life now, he thought of her and the terrible things of his past that shrouded him in anguish and sadness and those things were gone, they were just memories now-Shannon showed him *spirituality*…

"So, you're not the father, we know that. But what was your interest in the child?" Barry asked.

"Why?"

"Back at the lodge, you said something about the baby, when you thought Miss Shannon was dead."

"I don't know. She told me about what that… *Mathew* did to her when she went to see him. I was willing to marry her and take on the responsibility, but she had made the plans to come here."

"That would have been very kind of you. I wish you were the father, in a way; you seem more interested in Miss Shannon's life than Mathew did. I don't believe we have ever met him anyways, not that I can recall."

Barry made a few more turns towards the hospital. "But from what I gather he called Miss Shannon's parents Saturday and heard the news. Ted and Lisa are on their way here they should be here tonight. As for Mathew, well Lisa seems to think that he might be coming too."

"*Wonderful.*" Resentment flared in Mike's chest.

"Yes."

"I wish I were with her Friday. She wouldn't be here today, like she is; and Mrs. Hunter would probably be alive." Mike hesitated for a moment, "Can I ask you something?"

"Sure."

"What do you do for the family?"

"Oh, yes. I live next door; and I am Mr. Hunter's personal assistant."

"Next door?"

"Yes. Well my house is the next one down the road, about twelve miles away." Barry smiled weakly. "I have been friends with the Hunters since I can remember, since before young Miss Shannon was born. Her father used to live here on the ranch, before he became a Senator and then moved on to Washington and eventually Australia. And that's where you met Miss Shannon?"

"Yes. She was a friend in need, I wasn't looking for companionship, but Shannon found me just at the right time." Mike shifted in his seat.

"I see. She was wonderful with other people, especially those in need."

"Yes."

Mike stared out the window as the car made one last turn east from the highway MT200 onto a newly paved road, about a thousand feet later Barry parked the car out front of the hospital. Mike stretched as he exited the car, his back was aching from sitting, even though it wasn't a very long ride for him; he sits in a patrol car for hours some nights.

"If you will follow me please Mr. Greene."

Barry opened his hand and extended his arm out in front of him towards the main entrance. As he approached, Mike noticed the beauty of the place. The building was constructed in accordance with the views around it; the place would almost pass for a lodge or a cabin in the woods. A giant A frame with logs for walls and river stone foundations, large windows that offered a great view of the mountains across the highway. When the doors opened, the beauty ended and the nightmare began again.

The smell was a certain giveaway this was a place for hurt and sick people; the sterile air had a taste of chlorine on it, a hint of ammonia, and of course the mediciny fragrance of hospital disinfectant. Mike's stomach immediately began doing summersaults over the atmosphere; he could hear someone moaning down one of the corridors, another man was sitting in a waiting area holding a bloody bandage-he smiled acknowledging him as Mike walked by. Barry led Mike down the far corridor to a nurse station. The halls were floored meticulous white and had tongue in groove pine slats running half way up to papered walls. Murals of granite rock escarpments and other bright outdoor features adorned the high corners and slight curves of the walkways around a courtyard behind glass windows. The nurse's station was the same as it was almost anywhere. Monitors and clipboards. Get well cards positioned across the top of the counter with just enough room for someone to talk to the attending nurse.

"May I help you?" An older woman in white scrubs asked.

"We're here to see Miss Christine Hunter." Barry looked a little livelier than he felt; he wanted a cheery face for Miss Shannon.

"I remember you Mr....?"

"Ralston."

"Ahh yes, Barry Ralston. You can go in, but I don't believe your friend here is on the list."

"He isn't, he…" Barry shot Mike a glance, "He's the father, and he just arrived an hour ago from the west coast."

The nurse's eyes brightened a bit as she looked over Mike; she stepped back and grabbed a chart behind her. "Okay, you'll have to sign for him Mr. Ralston. And the doc wants to have a few words with Mr. uh?"

"Greene." Mike said semi-enthusiastically.

"Greene. He will be right out after I page him."

The nurse returned the chart, then picked up the phone and dialed a three digit number and turned away from the pair of men at the desk.

"He'll be right out, you can sit over there." She pointed to the couches behind the station.

Mike was tapping his hand on his knee nervously; Barry was watching him closely. The twitch Mike was having started to annoy him, he tried to break Mike's anxiety.

"What do you know about the accident Mr. Greene?"

"Why?"

"Because I don't want what you are about to see be a shock to you."

Mike looked at Barry for a moment, trying to decide whether the man was actually interested or just making small talk; hard small talk. "Very little I suppose. My friend Kelly read me a newspaper clipping he was faxed. He said that the passenger-Shannon Hunter was killed when she was thrown from the vehicle. Just like an arrogant ass, I assumed it was Miss Shannon."

"Why?"

"Shannon hates driving at night. The paper said the accident took place at night."

"I see."

Barry placed his hand to his lip, curling his fingers under and using the index finger and the thumb as a support under his nose.

"I just thought that she would never try it; that is why I thought she was the one killed." Shannon would do anything for anyone, even drive at night-well maybe not any more-Mike mused to himself. He broke a half smile at his morbid thought and realized he hadn't had any real sleep in nearly a day and a half. He was tired now.

"Mr. Greene?" A tall older gentleman dressed in a white smock asked towards Barry and Mike as he leaned halfway out the door to the office. Mike rose slowly and locked eye contact with the man.

"Yes?"

"Please come in…"

The man motioned with his hand inside the room. Then stepped back inside. Mike slowly walked towards the door, stopping to look back at Barry, who nodded in the affirmative, and a reassuring smile behind him.

"Mr. Greene, my name is Doctor Tanner. I'm the attending, O B Gyn and chief pediatrician here at Memorial. I need to speak to you about Miss Hunter's physical health."

He was a small man, about five-six or seven and not very weighty. His face was calm and looked even a little empathetic. His eyes were green and thoughtful, though very tired looking. Whitening hair that was thinning and receding.

"Is she going to be all right?" Mike's face was tired looking, but talking about Shannon brightened it a little, he felt good news was coming, even though the look on the doctor's face was grim.

"Possibly, that's why I need to speak to you. You're the baby's father, right?"

Mike felt a cold shiver track up his spine moving for his head. He shook off the chill and kept looking right into the doctor's eyes. It was hard to lie, but his love for Shannon was even harder to change.

"Yes."

"Then we have to discuss the fate of the child."

"Fate?" A sharp pain hit Mike's stomach.

"The amniotic sack was damaged in the accident. It's the protective layer around the baby, keeping it suspended in fluids. The sack is leaking fluid into the mother; Miss Hunter."

"That's bad." Mike made it a statement instead of a question.

"It is. If the baby dies from the damage, the body could be partially absorbed by the mother; and more likely the womb would become infected and the infection could spread to Miss Hunter's abdomen and cause her to die." The man's expression didn't change. "In most cases since the baby is nearly full term we induce labor artificially. But in this case we can't. Miss Hunter was seriously injured in the accident and she has lost a lot of blood. She is very weak and would not be able to have a normal childbirth. A Cesarean section is also very difficult right now, for many of the same reasons, blood loss and the trauma she received from the crash. We don't think she could survive, let alone the baby."

The doc paused and wiped his face with his hands, then ran his fingers through his thinning white hair.

"What are you asking me?"

The doctor sighed heavily and looked at his folded hands on his desk. "Miss Hunter refuses to let us terminate the pregnancy."

He raised his eyes to Mike.

Mike stared directly into the doctor; not just his eyes but he tried to look into his soul. "*Why* are you asking me?" He almost whispered.

"You are the father right? You might have some influence over Miss Hunter and her decision to have the termination."

"You mean abortion."

"In other words, yes. The child is a danger to Miss Hunter's life. She could die if the pregnancy fails. She could die anyways and then the child will die too. Either way there is a great chance of fatality to the baby, and a greater chance of death to the mother. Time is of the essence here because bacteria are already surrounding the baby, lung disease and even meningitis can occur." The man settled his case by leaning back in his chair

Mike looked behind the doctor out the big window at the courtyard where a bird was nesting in a naked quaking aspen. He took a small breath and nervously asked the doc what was obvious.

"What has Miss Hunter have to say about this?"

"She refuses. We feel her…"

"If she refuses than I must also."

"But the complications, to the child mean possible brain retardation. That among several other factors…"

Mike lowered his head. He couldn't pretend any longer he was the father; he had to tell the doctor that the real father lived in LA and probably be more than happy to recommend the termination of the child's life.

"I'm afraid there has been a mistake, no. A great *misdirection* doctor…"

Mike left Dr. Tanner's office with a half-smile. The good doc told him since he wasn't the father there was going to be no way he could see Shannon till her condition was reduced from critical to stable. Doctor Tanner was a little pissed-Mike could see, but he did tell Mike that he would have done the same thing if it were him.

Barry met him halfway to the waiting room.

"What happened? I was finishing the paperwork for you and the nurse received a call and the next thing I know, she says you can't go in…"

"I told the doctor the truth. I couldn't lie about this; he wants me to have Shannon…"

"Never mind that. You're friend Mathew just arrived. He is on his way to see the same doctor."

Mike watched as a young blue eyed, blond haired man walked in the same office Mike had just left. He didn't even look directly in Mike's direction. Mike recognized the little man from the photo in Shannon's flat, and the John Lennon glasses.

An hour later Mike was sitting in the waiting room. Barry Ralston had left to get coffee. Mathew was allowed in with Shannon. Mike supposed, right now he was crying over Shannon and begging her to take him back after she had the baby put down –and they would live happily ever after. Of course Mike didn't know if that was actually happening, but Mathew did get to see her first and he seemed the sort who would want the ponytailed blue eyed girl to "do the right thing" *for him…*

Mike thought of Mathew as an egotistical bastard with trimmings of a maniacal narcissistic. But Mike was biased. Matt was in there now with *his* Shannon, he was left out here to go crazy. He wanted to meet Mathew and seconds later, Mike got his chance.

The short blond haired man walked into the waiting room with an air about him. He stood over a table for a moment pretending to look at the magazines scattered over it. Mike studied him carefully, much like he would do a suspect in a burglary or drunk driver, he wanted as much information-body language-he could gather before the confrontation. Mathew was dressed like an aging rock star in holey blue jeans, a red handkerchief poking out of the back pocket and a *Rolling Stones* T shirt. Finally the little man spoke over his shoulder.

"So you're Michael."

"Yes. Call me Mike."

He didn't stand, he waited for Matt to turn around and greet him properly, and he would have to wait.

"Did Shannon tell you she visited me at my home?"

"Yes."

"Did she tell you she met my wife?"

Mike sighed. "She did."

Finally the small man spun around and Mike finally got the full picture. Matt was a short handsome kid, he looked about twenty-five or so, the perfect age for Shannon. He wore little spectacles, but there was little prescription Mike noticed when he turned towards the light. He was wearing the *Rolling Stones* tee shirt to probably show everyone his prowess of the music industry. Mathew stepped towards Mike finally.

"Mathew Wright." He offered a small hand with manicured cuticles.

Mike stood to his six foot three height in front of the young man on purpose, he didn't like little Mr. Record Company not only from what Shannon told him, but what he could read about him. Matt conveyed an easy tell; he was a man who knew everything about everything and he would tell you so, he was worldly. Matt could save a child from a burning building and a moment later swim to save a drowning dolphin-that was the type

Mike read, all too plainly laid out before him in this little human before him.

Mike took the hand and shook it slowly, never breaking eye contact, finally Matt did. Matt turned and sat down, Mike returned to his seat.

"I don't know you from anybody, but it seems Shannon has told you a lot about me."

Mike nodded.

"My wife is leaving me and taking my children. Do you know how that feels?"

The impetuous little man said it as if he were the only one in the world with a breaking heart. They both fought off each other's gaze by looking in different directions.

"Yes. Yes I do."

"Well, I've decided to take my company's offer and open shop in Sydney. They need a good exec like me there and I have already applied for citizenship and have been granted temporary work status." He turned and looked at Mike, who had turned and looked at him. "I'm going to take Shannon and the baby back-if it survives-and put this all behind us."

Mike just stared at him like he would a drunken biker.

"You don't intimidate me Mr. Cop. All that crap in my hometown a few months ago, you bastards are a dime a dozen now. Shannon was happy to see me today. Did she say that to you? Oh, that's right; you were impersonating me and aren't allowed to see her. How *dare* you take responsibility for my child?"

Mike continued to stare. The little man broke his gaze and stood, walking towards the darkening windows.

He told Mike the end of his plans.

"We are outta here. As soon as she can fly. Understand that. You two are over; she has chosen to be with me, that's why she came by my place in LA. She wanted me to go home with her, to take care of her and the baby. Hell, she even called me right after you two got back from your little boat trip. She said she was sick in bed and was trying to dump you."

Mike closed his eyes. He heard the truth in a few of the words, the pieces fit, a tear formed in his right eye and he suppressed the urge to go and pummel the little man and toss him out the window. *It's a lie.* Mike felt it in his bones.

The verbal assault continued.

"I called her parents to ask their permission for her hand, that's how I found out about her accident. I flew here as soon as I was done with an important client, now things will return to normal." The man turned to him. "You won't be allowed to see her so you might as well leave…"

Mike could take no more. He rose to his feet slowly; to give Matt the impression he had grown another few inches in the last few minutes. He stepped slowly to the slightly shivering man and grabbed his tee shirt by the front, twisting it to make a graspable knot and hefted the man off the ground an inch.

"Look here *Matt*. From the smell of your breath all that you have been spewing here for the last few minutes could be used to green a lawn somewhere. I could care less about your plans and what your intentions are; all I care about is Shannon and the baby. If you even hurt her a little I will…"

"*Michael Greene!*"

Mike turned and saw Ted, Lisa and Thomas Hunter standing in the doorway. He lowered Matt to the ground and dusted his shoulders off, roughly.

"Thank God you came when you did Ted…"

"Shut up Mathew. Leave us alone now, go somewhere else before I let Mr. Greene finish his *lecture*." Ted's face was red, anger written all over it.

Matt turned and left the room, trying to unravel the knot in his shirt.

"Sit down Mike." Ted said as he took his over coat off. Lisa Hunter walked rapidly over to Mike and threw her arms around him.

"Mike, I am so glad you came." She said into his ear. "She would want you to be here."

"Mike, you don't know how it makes me feel to see you here. To come here without an invitation-yes I talked to my brother and Barry-what you did shows true love."

"But Mathew…"

"Is a weasel. His *wife* kicked him out of their house and now that I know about her and his kids he's lucky you got to him first." Ted grinned evilly, or at least as a man could with his daughter laying in pieces a few rooms away.

Lisa Hunter spoke like a mother to Mike.

"Love is never fearful of the consequences; it drives us to do things that seem unreasonable to others. Mathew Wright is here because he's lonely and disgraced; you are here because you love our daughter and her child-my grandchild. That is what I meant by sending you the boomerang."

Mike's eyes lit up.

"Oh yeah. Thank you and thank Akama Janna for me, I miss the old bloke." Mike pondered the gift for a moment. "Why didn't he paint the koala on it?"

"It's not a koala, Michael." She smiled at him and they sat down.

Lisa Hunter started to explain the gift and what it meant, how she came by the idea and why. How Shannon had fascinated so over him and the true love she harbored, but was afraid of how Mike would react to the child. It took nearly an hour to explain it all.

When Lisa was done, Mike sat in the chair with tears in his eyes. "So the next move is?"

"Yours." Ted answered. "Have you been in to see her yet?"

"They won't let me until she has been downgraded from critical."

Ted nodded, stood and made a hooking motion with his finger towards Mike, who rose and followed. The duo ended up at the nurses' station, the duty nurse smiled at Ted and gave a frowned nod to Mike. Mathew was standing there flirting with the nurse and this infuriated Mike, but Ted put a hand to Mike's chest to keep him from advancing. Ted cleared his throat loudly and said in a loud and clear voice so everyone on the floor could hear him.

"Mr. Wright, I have a friend at the Department of Justice who is very curious about your recent financial losses. It seems much of your cash has disappeared from sight and at the same time a new bank account has been opened up by you in Sydney. Funny thing is… I have friends there too. And," his voice rose a little more, "…it seems to be the exact amount that you forgot to report on your expenses last year, the same mount that is missing."

Mathew opened his mouth to protest but Ted cut him off sharply with a raised hand and a sly wink.

"*Yes*. When I told him you were planning to move to Sydney the DOJ became suddenly interested in you, matter of fact they're talking to your soon to be ex-wife right now and she's very curious about the money too, seems you were ready to file bankruptcy."

Ted clucked his tongue at the man who was now being reduced to pasta.

"Bankruptcy before a divorce? I thought better of you. You may remember that I have friends in Canberra. They too are curious about your recent visa and how you forgot to mention so many details about your past. My best buddy at Immigration Australia has decided that your visa will be put on hold and any attempt to enter the country will constitute an illegal one, you'll be arrested at the airport and detained until the U.S. Embassy can get you back to the States where you'll be held for Treasury the Department's agents *and* the FBI. They are so very anxious to chat with you."

Ted turned his back to the little man. Mike had to turn away also, or risk having the wannabe rock idol see the tears of joy running down his cheek. After a few seconds, Ted said over his shoulder to Mike loudly, "Is *he* gone yet?"

Mathew turned on a dime and stormed out of the hospital, looking both ways as he went, paranoid about being watched already.

Mike whispered, "Yeah, he's gone. *I'm so glad you're on my side*! Are you really serious?"

"Mess with my daughter and you get the full treatment. He's not indicted yet. But the wheels are turning as we speak. Mathew Wright will soon be in federal custody for income tax evasion and lying to a national immigration board to gain access to a foreign bank, etcetera, and etcetera."

Ted smiled again, waved his hand like it was all in a day's work and this time his face glowed with satisfaction. He turned to the desk nurse who was standing there open mouthed. Her hands were in a frozen state of holding a clip board in mid-air.

"Miss? This is Michael Greene, he is a very good friend of the family and you will allow him to see Miss Hunter."

"I can't Mr. Hunter; she's asleep now, a sedative you see, beside Doctor Tanner said…"

"Do you know the name of the geriatric ward Miss…?" Ted looked at the acetate nametag, "…Susan?"

"The *Hunter* Wing." She said coolly, appreciatively.

"Do I have to say anything else? I don't want to hurt anyone's feelings tonight. The man will be allowed to see Miss Shannon, alone."

"Yes sir." The red faced nurse gave Mike a nicer smile and pointed to the door.

Mike and Ted turned back towards the waiting room and when Mike approached Shannon's door he stopped.

"Geriatric ward?"

Ted smiled back at him, "I won't be this young forever Mr. Greene. Go see my daughter, tell her how much you love her, even if she is asleep, she will hear you, in her dreams…"

With that Ted Hunter returned and sat next to his wife; they embraced, in tears.

The door to the private room was cluttered all over the front with get-well cards from local children and businesses that were either friends or clients of the Hunter family. Mike looked at the door and felt small, he knew that Shannon had many friends; he just assumed they all were in Australia; like John and Paula. He placed his hand on an open spot, free of well-wishing thoughts on paper, and then pushed.

The smell hit Mike in the face, flowers-hundreds of them-lined the tables, counters, window sill, and even the opposite bed. The aroma was heavy; it was like walking through the Royal Botanical Gardens in Sydney again. Even though Mike knew the flowers weren't the same; he could still smell a hint of Brazilian Red-Cloak, maybe even the Floss Silk tree blooms. The senses may lie, but Mike wanted the flowers to be from the Gardens. He wanted this room to be Shannon's little flat in Sydney on Wilson Street in Woolloomooloo. He wanted this to be anywhere but here.

Mike entered the room and the smell hit him first. Mediciny, like bleach and alcohol and disinfectant all mixed together. Then the sight hit him. Shannon, in her bed with tubes and wires attached to her like a machine in some horror movie, chirps and beeps coming from a monitor that checked her heart rate, her breathing and her blood oxygen content.

A plastic bag of solution dangled above her right side at the head of the bed, clear fluid running into her right arm. Her hands were bruised and two fingers were bandaged together, probably broken. Her arms were covered in little pinpricks most likely from shattered tempered glass from the window of the car she was driving.

Mike put his hands to his face and rubbed from his forehead to his mouth and paused.

Thank God she was driving. Or she'd be dead now; he'd be attending a funeral instead of seeing her here like this. Lesser of two evils? Internal bleeding. Possible ruptured amniotic sac. Maybe even some kind of brain damage to both child and mother.

Shannon's hair was pulled into a ponytail, loosely tied by a soft looking band and turned off to one side. There was a visible blue-yellow mark on her forehead just below her hairline, above her right eye. Her left cheek was stitched with about twenty sutures, by Mike's count, and there was bruising around the cut. Mike noticed the corner of her mouth was slightly swollen and the left side of her lower lip was purple-green.

She was asleep; Mike smiled as he realized that she looked like an angel-even with her injuries-that he had the wrong vision of them in his mind. She was still beautiful as ever. He stepped forward and moved his arm towards her face, fingers outstretched, and stopped just short. Then Mike took his index and middle finger and brushed a small lock of hair from the side of her face, to the ear; just like he had seen her do it so many times before. His hand quavered a little, from the restraint he used to keep from touching her satin skin. He stepped back when he saw her eyes flutter open.

Shannon could hardly see anything, the room was blurry and there was a figure standing over her. She knew the size and the posture immediately; it was Michael. She smiled as far as she could before it hurt. A tear ran from her right eye, she could feel the moistness on her cheek. The pinch of pain from moving her facial muscles made her stop smiling, but her eyes glowed with what she felt outwardly. She tried to speak, but realized immediately there was no air to push through her voice box-she was on a respirator.

Mike saw her smile and tears immediately filled his eyes. He returned her smile and when she winced at the pain his smile turned upside down. She moved her head to look straight ahead at him and she mouthed the words *Michael*. Mike looked down and saw she had been trached, so she had no air going to her throat, she couldn't talk or hardly make a sound. He put his index finger to his lips.

"Shhh. Don't try to talk, you have a tracheotomy."
Shannon nodded.
"Hi."

She smiled again, smaller this time, but it stayed in place. "I'm sorry."

Shannon nodded again, the smile still on her face.

Then Mike saw the ring on her finger. Maybe Mathew was telling the truth, maybe they decided to get married and move to Australia-even without her parent's blessing.

Shannon smiled brighter and nodded, even though it hurt a little. She returned her gaze to Mike. Her vision was clearing a little.

Mike carefully took her hand, the one that wasn't taped to an IV board, and softly squeezed. Shannon responded by returning the grip.

He nodded at her finger, with the engagement stone and she looked down at it, Mike thought he saw puzzlement in her eyes; she frowned and nodded with a smile at him.

He took the hint. His heart sank at her nod, she didn't have to say anything now...

"I'm sorry for your aunt." He started his departure.

A tear escaped her closed eyelids and dribbled down her cheek.

"I came when I heard; I thought you were the one... never mind." Mike burst into tears; he broke his grip with Shannon's hand and sat back hard on the chair a few feet from her bed. He leaned over and placed his head in his hands and wept openly.

Shannon saw the big man weakened by her condition and the situation. She wept with him, tears streaming down her cheeks. She knew what she had said to him in Nevada was wrong. He offered to help her; to marry her if need be and raise the child as his own. She couldn't have that on her conscience. Shannon knew the odds of success, Mike already had a failed marriage and a son who doesn't like him very much, and he didn't need to worry about someone else's child.

"The doctors are concerned that you are going to lose the baby."

Mike wiped his eyes.

Shannon nodded.

"I told them I was the father so I could see you. They want me to talk you out of having the baby; to have it aborted to save your life. They really thought I was the father."

Shannon's face froze. Her biggest fear was upon her, *what did you tell them?*

As if Mike could read her thoughts he said;

"I told them, you were the strongest woman I have ever met. That you would never let me make that kind of decision for you. That you would rather die than give up on the baby." Mike stood to her side.

She nodded, and reached up for his hand. He refused to move his.

"I then told the doctor the truth. Who I was, why I was here, I told him that your decision was final."

Shannon forced a concerned look on her face; she wanted Mike to take her hand. She waved it up and down, she knew he saw it.

"I told the doctor that I wasn't the father." Mike turned and walked towards the window. He didn't want to see Shannon's next reaction. "Mathew told me what your plans are, I hated to hear it from him, but I had no choice. I love you more than anything else in this world, so I will let you go, from my mind, my heart, eventually you will fade, the pain will go away just like it did with Rika.

"But obviously Mathew has got a few problems to iron out. Your father will fill you in on the details when you're better. I'm going to live in Idaho with my dad. I quit my job and maybe I can become a logger or something like that. Maybe retire. If you still love me, you're invited to go with me. But you gotta make the call yourself. I'm committed to you, are you ready to commit to me and all my issues?"

Mike said what he wanted and he all of a sudden felt sick, he felt as if he was going to crash through the door and out of the room. He turned but a noise stopped him, a struggle behind him and a small cry stopped him in his tracks.

"*Michael.*"

He spun.

"Don't try to talk it'll…"

"*Shut up for once, will you?*"

Her voice was raspy, hissy because of the respirator.

He nodded with a smile. A very sad smile.

"Michael, I love only you. Mathew was a dreamer, but you're my dream. I love you and want you and I to… to… Michael! The baby! Call the doctor!"

Mike's face went flush and he bound out the door calling for help.

Lisa, Ted and Doctor Tanner all ran in. Tanner went directly to Shannon's side and began running his hands over her abdomen. She was white as a sheet and moving very slowly, she wasn't moaning or acting like she was in any kind of pain, she was more or less acting as if she was going to fall asleep.

"We have a rupture! We need to get her to OR, now!" Tanner shouted to Nurse Susan. He turned to Lisa and whispered loud enough for Mike to hear, "I think we have an embolism on our hands, an air bubble in the blood heading for her heart. It happens in cases like this, if that air gets to the aorta…"

He drifted off; Lisa knew what he was saying. So did Mike, Ted and Thomas who was standing by the door.

Shannon was asleep as she passed Mike on the way out the door on the gurney.

An hour later the family waited in the small hallway outside the operating room that Shannon had been wheeled into. Prayers were openly said, hugs and tears went all around. Lisa and Ted looked as if they'd aged twenty years in the last forty-five minutes. A cry rang out from the room in front of them. A child, a baby. Newborn. Lisa's heart sputtered, they all stood.

Moments later, Dr. Tanner came from the room. He was wearing surgical clothing over his scrubs, a cap and mask was gripped tightly in his hand, he was wringing it.

He sighed with a fervent smile, "We had to do a Caesarian. It's a boy."

Lisa cried.

Ted offered a hand to the doctor, but Tanner waved it away.

"But, there's a complication…"

His gaze dropped to the floor. Everyone saw the tears in the doctor's eyes.

Lisa put her hand to her mouth and sat down hard on the small bench they'd all just rose from. Mike's knees gave out and he fell against the wall. Lisa could hardly speak.

"Oh, *God*, no."

LAST
Cairns, Queesnland Australia
Two years later...

The air was moist with the rainy season on the way out in a few months. A shadow sat in a corner table of the Cairns Marina Café. He was reading from a letter in front of him with a sad smile. Next to him was another letter, one he was writing. He looked back from one to the other to check his continuity. The café had six tables outside and ten inside, many of the folks here were inside watching the TV giving the man some privacy. A view over the sailboats and fishing vessels of the large marina was in front of the table the man sat at; the rolling hills and climbing mountains across the harbor were green and full of life after a fairly good wet season here.

The sky was clear and blue; a small breeze wafted the odor of sea to his nostrils, the burning desire of his for two years now. He was a man of the sea, he was fully licensed to operate a sailboat in open blue water and sail the world, but there was no destination on his mind. Oh yeah, he was going sailing, but his trip would take him where he could not say, nor would he want to know where he was traveling to. It was fate. The same fate that brought him here.

Anger and hate filled his heart for so long. Then booze and rehabilitation. Confusion and respite. Followed by compassion and friendship, ending in tragedy yet again. He was strong. Stronger than he was two or three years ago. He was of iron now, nothing could stop him and what lie ahead in his journey.

A young boy dressed in tan kid khakis and a mini blue polo shirt with a boomerang emblazoned on the right pocket of the chest. The boomerang had a familiar look, it was the symbol created for the man and his love. The man adopted it as his family crest of sorts, just as the Hunter clan from America assumed the banyan tree as theirs and the symbol of their sugar cane plantation. The child wore a sailor's hat.

The man smiled at the young blond boy with electric blue eyes as the toddler played with the birds that came in to grab snacks of crumbs at the nearly empty tables. It was afternoon and most of the locals were pubbing it, watching football-Australian Rules. The man had other things to do.

He read the hand written letter once again and drew the paper to a spot in front of him and picked up the pen. He began to write with a satisfied smile on his face.

Dear Mikie,

I'm glad that one of my letters finally got through to you. I guess your mother must be getting soft. Maybe she read my letters I've been sending and decided it was time to let you decide your future, who knows. Anyways, I'm happy that you are graduating this June and I wish I could be there, but I also am so excited that you've decided to visit here later that month.

I'm officially a citizen now of Australia. Maybe I'll learn the language next? Ha Ha. Ted Hunter hired me as a consultant to security for his place in Montana and here. Although he had to advertise the job in the papers, Akama Janna did the interviews and for some reason he said he must do them in full aboriginal war dress. No one took the job. I love Akama, he's my best friend here and you'll love him too. He has a way of looking at the world and seeing all the good.

Ted and Lisa also helped me adopt Mathew Shannon Greene. My second son. I hope and pray that I can do a better job this time than I could with you and I hope someday you can forgive me for the person I was then. I hope that you can see it in your heart that you forgive me a little. He's a handful this little guy, but he's smart as a whip report and he'll never climb a gum tree. Whatever. So much for learning the language. You'll love your little brother. He's excited to see you too!

Mike rose from his seat and picked Matt up from the ground as the waiter came out and handed him the check. Mike sat Matt on the table to get his wallet and drew a credit card out of it. Before he closed the worn leather billfold he noticed a picture of Mikie and he smiled at it as any proud father would. As he was stuffing the picture back into the little slot he saw another picture.

Shannon at the beach with a smile on her face, her eyes like tunnels of blue laser light. She was wearing a pink bikini and not much else. Mike caught his breath. A tear formed in his right eye and his left burned with painful salt water building behind it. He sighed and pushed the picture back into place. He thought about that day, so long ago.

The waiter returned with the check and Mike signed for the bill and returned the card to his wallet. He nodded at the waiter and re-sat Matt on his shoulders. They walked out onto the boardwalk of the marina.

...it took nearly two years to get the Stella *ready to sail again after the Hunters purchased it from the previous owners; John and Paula. You'll like John. Hell, you're a teenager, you'll like Paula too, if you know what I mean. Don't say anything huh? Two years of blood and sweat to get her ready to sail for this adventure that Shannon had told me about so long ago.*

Mike ran his hand along the soft and sleek side then stopped at the stern of the *Stella Taurus* and gave it a solemn smile as he hefted Matt onto the fantail. He climbed aboard himself and shook hands with Kurran, the Hunter's harbor man. An aboriginal too, Kurran was much younger than Akama, but he looked like the man in many ways. Mike was only now beginning to be able identify all of the people who worked for the Hunters by name. Mike fired the engine after casting off and maneuvered the cruiser out of the slip and into the harbor towards the open sea.

It was Shannon's dream to let the Stella go in the tide under the stars, to follow the Southern Cross, to drift on the calm breeze at dusk. It's great dream. And that's just what the Stella is going to do tonight. I guess it was then that I fell in love with Shannon Hunter, that night she told me her secret dream to sail the southern seas only on a breath of air in the night.

Mike checked the sails and let the sailboat gather speed as the sun waned in the distance, Matt kept wandering around the deck playing with the ropes and capstans. After a while he calls to Matt and they head down the gangway towards the cabin. Inside, Matt grabbed a teddy bear and sat at the table. Mike walked deeper in to the bowels of the *Stella*, to a shelf in the clean compartment, on the starboard side, and his face dark with sadness. In front of him is an urn, bright gold and shaped like a sailing trophy. A small tea candle sits in a cut glass dish and a box of wooden kitchen matches. Mike sighs and looks over to Matt who has found a new toy in the plates on the table. The smile that Mike lets escape is one of pain, anguish and solemnness. Looking back to the urn, Mike reached up and moved the candle to the side a little and pulled a boomerang out. The same one that Lisa had commissioned for him from Akama Janna, the one that showed family from a single entity of father and mother and child.

Brushing the boomerang off, Mike placed back on the shelf so it was leaning against the side of the small cupboard space where the urn and candle rest. He looks at a photo of Shannon's family with her the prominent one on her knees in front holding a puppy; she couldn't have been more than twelve or fifteen then. Mike looked the entire picture over, freezing his eyes on various family members.

I'll end this letter now, and get it mailed off to you before I sail. Tonight is the night that I've been waiting for, for two years. To sail at the mercy of the wind and surge, to drift on nighttime breezes and search for the meaning inside. Because for the next three months, that's where I'll be. Wherever the silk and flow goes.

But first, let me say: There is a young woman coming here that would like to do some work on the Stella *while sailing over the summer. Her name is Jessa, and she's a good deck hand and we'll be picking her up from the airport a day after you arrive. She lives in the Bay Area. I'm no matchmaker, but I bet she'd like you. She's nineteen. (And real cute too!)*

Taking a match out of the box, Mike lit up the candle. He pursed his lips and sighed at the same time, his eyes obviously still watering. He lowers his head and wipes his eyes.

I just want to say I miss you but I'm glad we finally can see each other eye to eye after all these years. My life has been full of downs lately; it's time for some ups. You coming here will make it nearly complete; I want to show you all Shannon showed me. I want you to meet her family, I want you to sit and learn from Akama Janna about the Murri, the aborigines and the land that once belonged to them. I want you to sail on the Stella *and feel the wind over the sea on your face. I dare you not to fall in love with it as I have. But, sadly one more task has to be completed before twilight and it's an important one...*

A woman's hand reached up to Mike's left shoulder, and then another hand to the other side from behind. The hands began to flex over the aching muscles of a man who looks exhausted but feels inside, exhilarated. The woman walked around to the front of Mike and they embraced, both in tears.

"It's time, honey."

The woman beckoned to Matt with an outstretched hand, who promptly jumped down from the dining table seat and joins them at the base of the urn. Picking up the urn, Mike began a procession up the stairs of him in the lead, holding the hand of the woman and she is in turn towing young Matt.

Mike looked to the woman who nodded. It was time. She wiped a tear as the slight breeze made a whistling sound in the stays, the silk flapped crazily as if it knew what lay ahead. She nodded to Mike who carefully took the lid off and handed the urn to her.

...Thomas Hunter asked if we could scatter half of Shannon's ashes out to sea, the Coral Sea to be exact. He knew that his wife loved the ocean as much as her niece Shannon Christine, my wife. She agreed and here we've come to that point. The docs in America say that Shannon lost her chances of becoming a mother again, due to complications from her injuries and Matt being born.

Shannon kissed Mike on the lips and then she gave Matt a peck on the cheek. The boy promptly wiped the kiss off and ran for the bow, to watch the dolphins chase the wake coming from the bow. His giggles made Mike and Shannon snigger too.

I guess Carlton Mitchell *was right, he said:*

'To desire nothing beyond what you
have is surely happiness... that is
why sailing is a way of life, one
of the finest of lives...'

I have one of the finest lives and I hope to share it with you.

I love you Mikie, and we can't wait to see you in June. Dad

Shannon and Matt walk down to the cockpit and she shows him how to steer the *Stella* with the shiny steel big tiller wheel. Mike's thoughts are on the family that took him in, the Hunters, both here and in America. Looking at Shannon he realizes that he would never had made it this far in life without her. Her dream became his dream, and they are sailing on it now.

The sky began to turn pink, the sound of seagulls fade as the further they flow from the coast, the quieter it becomes. The sound of water splashing over the hull, the light whistle of wind through the wires, the snap and flap of the silk just before it's pulled taught. The wisp of sea air mixed with briny salt as the spray vaporized over the bow caught their palettes and stirred the desire of the adventure that lay ahead of them even more.

Mike took a deep breath and let it out slow with eyes closed. He smiled, sadly for his wife's aunt Shannon, who passed away tragically, but the smile was half happy-for the journey that lay ahead of them. Himself, his beautiful wife Shannon Christine Greene, their handsome son Matt…

…And…

P.S. Mikie, we'll have a little surprise for you when you get here in June.

Shannon leaned back into Mike's embrace as they let Matt sail the boat, of course Mike had one hand on the top of the wheel and Shannon had one in the middle, but to a little one like Matt, he was in full control of the *Stella*. Mike let his other hand rest on Shannon's belly and she moved her hand and drifted down to his. Together they massaged her pregnant belly.

END

J Jay Ross

Acknowledgements

First of all I would like to thank my family-for understanding the late nights and early morning sessions of writing and research. The library-for not complaining about the times it *looked* like I was sleeping when I was researching on the comfortable couches. To the folks who purchased *Circle the Moon*, so I could afford to have this work published, a few fans are better than none, the best work is always done for the smallest audience. And Hazelden, Joe G., the staff and friends; for believing in me.

To many of my first readers that gave me advice to ease my writing instead of forcing the words, to many others who inspired characters and to Australia-the greatest inspiration of all for this novel.

To Jeanette, Cindy, Char, Angela, Angel, and Grandma Valda-my first real fans. To the crew at Radio Free Jericho. Charlene, Jessica, John, Debbie, and others. If I missed you, I'm sorry.

And of course thanks to you Dad…

As always, if you find an error or have a suggestion, email me @ circlethemoon@sbcglobal.net

J Jay

Also available by J Jay Ross

Circle the Moon Author's Edition
Glance Over My Shoulder
Glance Across the Bay (Josh Kennedy Book II)
Darkness in the Shadow
Asyla Series (Kindle only)

You can e-mail J Jay @
www.circlethemoon.net

J Jay Ross

www.ingramcontent.com/pod-product-compliance
Lightning Source LLC
Chambersburg PA
CBHW060346260626
47160CB00006B/2220